Books by Alina

The Holbrook Cousins
- The Successor
- The Screw-up
- The Scion

The Frost Brothers
- Eating Her Christmas Cookies
- Tasting Her Christmas Cookies

The Svensson Brothers
- After His Peonies
- In Her Candy Jar
- On His Paintbrush
- In Her Pumpkin Patch
- Between Her Biscuits
- After Her Fake Fiancé
- In Her Jam Jar

Weddings in the City
- Bridezillas & Billionaires
- Wedding Bells & Wall Street Bros

Check my website for the latest news:
http://alinajacobs.com/books.html

FROSTING HER
Christmas Cookies

FROSTING HER Christmas Cookies

A HOLIDAY ROMANTIC COMEDY

ALINA JACOBS

Summary: Baking artist extraordinaire and die-hard Christmas hater Morticia has to survive The Great Christmas Bake-Off while dodging bake-off sabotaging cousins, applying for a long-shot prestigious museum internship, and trying to survive being broke in Manhattan. Handsome, Christmas-loving billionaire Jonathan Frost isn't making it any easier!

This book is a work of fiction. Names, characters, places, and incidents either are products of the author's imagination or are used fictitiously. Any resemblance to actual events or locales or persons, living or dead, is entirely coincidental.

Copyright ©2020 by Adair Lakes, LLC.
All rights reserved, including the right to reproduce this book or portions thereof in any form whatsoever.

*To my adoptive grandmother...
you made a mean lasagna*

*On the third day of Christmas,
my true love gave to me...*

CHAPTER 1

Morticia

Christmas. The absolute worst time of year. It was Black Friday—not so named because it was a day of pagan rituals but rather because it kicked off the season of shallow consumerism and obnoxious Christmas music that burrowed into your ear. I walked down the avenue near the harbor. Workers were putting up an excessive amount of street decorations, including wreaths, lights, and huge bows that would make Mrs. Claus salivate. One of the men waved to me.

"Merry Christmas!" he shouted.

I ignored him.

"How about a little Christmas cheer, sweetheart?" he called out.

I pulled my Taser out of my black bag and brandished it.

"Merry Christmas this!" I yelled at him.

He flinched and almost fell off his ladder.

I smirked.

When people saw me with my gothic outfits, long black hair, and dark makeup, they assumed that I was weird and off-putting. Once they got to know me, they found that their assumptions were, in fact, correct.

I adjusted my grasp on my cat Salem's carrier and on my Victorian steamer trunk. I had to finish up the final decorating touches on the set for *The Great Christmas Bake-Off*. Cue the elf barf.

The Great Christmas Bake-Off was another character in the nativity scene of things I hated about Christmas. Baking, sparkles, ornaments, and festive Christmas outfits. Blech.

Salem howled as I took a shortcut and picked my way through the defunct industrial warehouse complex from the 1850s that had not yet been renovated to another soulless Manhattan condo tower development. Though with all the COMING SOON! signs on neighboring properties, the guillotine would soon fall on these old buildings too, I was sure.

"One more hour," I assured Salem, "then we will be on a train back to Harrogate and the old Victorian house, where we will watch Penny and her walking sack of money, Garrett, be all lovey and couple-y."

It was almost enough to make me not want to go home. But staying in Manhattan was out of the question. Christmas was encroaching. I needed to isolate myself in my crypt and count down the days until Halloween—and count the days until I *hopefully* started my internship at the Getty Museum in Los Angeles. I sent up another prayer to the spirits. I needed that internship. Working at the Getty was every artist's dream. It would earn me bragging rights and my work a spot in some of the nicer galleries around Manhattan. The art world would finally start taking me seriously.

I threw open the door of an eight-story brick building in which Romance Creative had set up production for the show.

"Thank goodness you're here," Dana Holbrook said when she saw me. She and her business partner, Belle Frost, hurried over. "The bake-off bachelorettes will be here soon. It's a disaster."

I scowled at Dana. "I did the best I could with what I was given," I said, gesturing around the historic heavy-timber building. Though I hated Christmas with a passion, I had nevertheless managed to turn the studio space into a fairyland of merriment and cheer. I had made it as tasteful as possible, with loops of garland—real pine and juniper boughs, thank you very much—large glass ornaments, and, of course, Christmas trees.

"Aside from the voodoo doll you hid in the elf-on-the-shelf scene," Dana said, handing me the creepy doll with two fingers, "it all looks great. No, the issue is that one of our bachelorettes fell pregnant, and the doctor put her on bed rest."

I raised an eyebrow. "Fell pregnant? Like pregnancy just plummeted down from the heavens?"

"That's what she's telling her ultrareligious boyfriend," Belle said dryly. "Swears up and down that it must be an immaculate conception, because she and her boyfriend were saving themselves until marriage."

"Uh-huh," I said, setting down Salem's carrier. "So penises are just falling out of the sky now."

"Yup," Dana said. "Better watch out."

"But now you're here," Belle said, "and you can help!"

I looked at her suspiciously. "Wait, this is a bake-off, right? So why are you calling the contestants bachelorettes?"

"We're upping the ante," Dana explained breezily. "The bake-off just isn't drawing the numbers we need. Now it's a bake-off slash date-off. *The Bachelorette* meets baking plus Christmas. It's a gold mine!"

"Sounds like you all have your hands full," I said, leveling my gaze at Dana then at Belle. I wasn't stupid; I knew where this was going. Now to see if they had the balls to ask me. Of course, my answer would be no.

"There's our lady and savior, bachelorette number thirteen!" boomed Gunnar Svensson, one of the producers of Romance Creative, as he came out of a side hallway, lugging the decapitated head of a reindeer…mascot that is.

"No," I said, giving them my best witchy glare.

Belle, who might as well have been the Witch of the North herself, was unaffected. But Gunner stopped short.

"Uh…" he said, gray eyes flicking between us. "Now, Morticia…"

"No," I said. "I will not debase myself and sacrifice my values to parade around as some simpering girl in nothing but tights and a holiday sweater and tell some douchebag billionaire that he's so handsome, and I want him to make my Christmas Eve!"

"See, you're a natural!" Gunnar wheedled.

"The beauty of it," Belle added, taking the head from Gunnar, "is that you barely have to do anything. That's what the mascot costume is for. Just show up dressed as a reindeer. In this iteration of the show, the fans have a say in who stays and who goes. You're abrasive and odd. No one will like you, the fans will vote you out of the kitchen and the bedroom, and then you can collect a check and be back in Harrogate by tomorrow evening."

"We just need a sacrificial Christmas goose," Gunnar begged. He took out a check and waved it at me.

"I cannot be bought." I crossed my arms. "I spent a whole summer on an art retreat in Mississippi wearing clothes I made out of animals I hunted myself."

Gunnar shuddered.

Dana tossed her dark, shiny hair. "I can arrange for one of your sculptures to be installed in the Holbrook Enterprises tower lobby," Dana negotiated. "It will have a big plaque displaying your name as the artist. There would be a press release."

"Oh!" Well, maybe I could be bought a little bit. The Holbrook Enterprises tower lobby was three stories tall.

No! Stay strong!

"Unlimited budget," Dana bribed.

I caved as visions of the homage to Hecate that I would create sparkled in my vision. "Only if I get to choose what it is," I countered.

"Only if we approve the design first," Dana corrected.

"Fine, but I'm naming my price."

Dana extended her hand, and we shook.

So sue me. It was Christmas, after all: the season of commercial sellouts.

Gunnar handed me the head and the skin of the reindeer. "Looks like it's going to be a Merry Christmas after all!"

Thirty-six hours, I told myself as I headed to the bathroom to change into the reindeer suit.

"You may want to take off as many layers as you can," Belle suggested, following me as she tapped on her tablet. "All that fake fur makes the costume hot."

I nodded then texted my sister, Lilith, to come pick up Salem. Then I inspected the costume. It was itchy and smelled like peppermint.

"Thirty-six hours," I chanted as I removed my layers of clothing.

There was a certain type of women all men fantasized about. She was usually tall and thin but somehow inexplicably had hips and a big butt and large, round boobs. I was tall and thin but with a boyish figure, small boobs, and big hands and feet. The billionaire bachelor was not going to find me attractive.

"What the hell do I even care? He can shove a candy cane up where the sun don't shine," I grumbled as I stepped into the furry suit. "It's not like I need some billionaire's wandering eye to pump up my self-esteem. I don't even want a boyfriend, let alone one with more money than sense."

I adjusted the large red bow at the neck of the suit then twisted my hair up into a bun.

Belle was waiting impatiently when I stepped out of the bathroom. "It's showtime in five," she said, grabbing me by the shoulder. I was a respectable five feet eight, but Belle was six feet tall barefoot. Now there was someone who would have been a Celtic priestess in the early third century and had no problem sending the Romans back where they came from and probably sacrificing them during some sort of winter solstice ritual killing.

I smirked slightly.

"Don't murder anyone," Belle warned me. "You're going to be baking, too, so no slashing. Don't burn down my brother's studio, and don't poison anyone."

"When have I ever?" I demanded.

"Oh yeah? Then what was the voodoo doll for?"

"That deliveryman was rude, and the metal light-up reindeer he brought had absolutely been damaged in transit. There is no way I would have accidentally busted half the lights on that thing and bent all the antlers," I told her stubbornly.

We went out a side entrance and walked a few yards away. The film crew, the huge lights, and the producers milling around signified another reality TV show production in progress. New York was lousy with them.

Gunnar gave me a dildo-sized plastic candy cane.

"This better not be what I think it is."

"It's your Christmas greeting gift," he said. Then he shouted into his headset, "Zane? Yeah, get camera two on her...ten-four." To me, he added, "Every girl is supposed to bring something meaningful to how she celebrates Christmas...yadda, yadda. This was all they had at the shop down the street."

Belle stuffed me into a limo that was idling out of the shot. It drove me a few paces to make it seem like I was arriving in style. In front of the building, a tall man waited—a winter prince with platinum hair, icy blue eyes, and a general demeanor that screamed fuckable but not in a serious-relationship way.

His eyes pierced the glass of the limo, and I froze then forced myself to relax. "He can't see through the tinted glass," I assured myself as I twisted the reindeer head on.

The lights sparkled in the cold air as I stepped out of the car and then jerked as the antlers caught on the door.

"Fuck!" I cursed.

The billionaire smirked as he watched me struggle.

"Thanks for the help, asshole!" I shouted as I finally forced the antlers through the car door.

The smirk turned into a sneer. "Play stupid games, win stupid prizes. You're supposed to be here to impress me."

"I'll show you stupid prizes!" I yelled. I hefted the giant candy cane and threw it at him.

CHAPTER 2

Jonathan

I work out—like, a lot. I hit the gym every day, alternating weights and cardio. I do MMA fighting three nights a week. How the fuck did I not dodge that candy cane?

It must have been the shock of being cussed out by a giant reindeer.

"What the hell?" I yelled at bachelorette number thirteen, though I was going to start calling her the bachelorette from hell, because no one treated me like that!

"My face is insured for twenty million dollars," I snapped at her as I gestured to my assistants. They looked at me dumbly as they tried to figure out what I wanted.

"I'm going to go out on a limb here and assume you hired them for their good looks and not for their organizational prowess," the reindeer drawled.

I sputtered.

"He needs ice for that nasty bruise that's already forming on his porcelain skin," bachelorette number thirteen said to my assistants.

"A bruise?" I snarled as my assistants hurried off to find ice. "I'm pressing charges."

The bachelorette gave me the finger, or at least what might have looked like the finger if she hadn't been sporting giant furry hooves. Then she shuffled past me into the building.

"Hey!" I yelled at her. "We're supposed to exchange pleasantries, and you're supposed to fawn over me and tell me how you want me to make your Christmas Eve."

She turned. "Christmas is already the worst holiday in the world," she said, her raspy voice slightly muffled by the large reindeer head. "There's no way I'd make it worse by spending it with you!"

I drew back.

"You hate Christmas? What kind of monster hates Christmas?" I demanded, hurrying after her, taking the ice pack from one of my simpering assistants and pressing it to my cheek. I ducked around the cameras as the cameramen hurried to keep up with us. "Christmas is about family and friends, children opening presents, and baking cookies. Everyone else here wants to create the perfect family Christmas card with me." I grabbed her shoulder.

She whirled around to accost me and hit me on the other side of the face with one of the antlers.

"Ow!" I yelped.

"Christmas," she spat as I switched the ice to the other cheek, "is just an excuse for people with sad little lives to pretend like everything is just peachy. It's the candy cane–colored fondant veneer over dry, stale fruitcake. You know, I might have actually…not, like, fucked you but maybe gotten myself off one night thinking about you while I was drunk and horny, if only you had even shown a *hint* of derision toward the holiday season. Unfortunately, it seems as if you seriously believe in the magic of Christmas."

"Of course I do," I said stubbornly. "Christmas brought my family back together. It's a holiday about friends and neighbors and finding the beauty in the moment. Also the snow—I love snow."

She tossed the giant reindeer head, sending the plastic googly eyes spinning. "I'm going to go bake now," bachelorette thirteen said. "Because unlike the rest of the people here, I am not chasing after your Christmas package."

She walked into the studio as if she owned it—which she definitely did not. I owned this building. But I felt off-kilter.

One of the producers motioned the bachelorette to her baking station. The nameplate read Morticia DiRizzo. "Of course some crazy Christmas-hating woman is going to have that name," I muttered under my breath. It was a bad omen on a day when I needed a good one.

A few years earlier, my hedge fund had bet big on alcohol by buying up a number of craft distilleries. Now was my big moment. My net worth was a measly two billion. But if I could make my alcohol into the must-have-item of the holidays, I could triple my net worth. I knew the product was worth it. The craft liquor was high quality, and I had a lot of product to sell. My team had been working on branding each item. My participation in this bake-off was native advertising to create buzz for the various liquors.

All the bakers would make desserts that had to feature one of my alcohol items. The recipe and videos would be posted online; I had a whole social media integration strategy. But that hinged on having, one, good bakers, and, two, women who were bubbly, pretty, and worked well on camera.

Morticia was not one of those women.

"Welcome to *The Great Christmas Bake-Off*, season three," Anastasia, the host, announced when Gunnar gave her the signal. "If you love Christmas and baking, you're in the right place. Same as last year, our esteemed judges, Anu and Nick, are back! Anu Pillai is a chocolatier and baker from L'il Masa bakery in NoLiTa. Then we have Nick Mazur, a pastry chef and restaurant owner with businesses all over the New York area."

The judges smiled for the cameras.

"In addition to baking, we have a bit of a twist. In each of the last two seasons, one of our contestants has gone on to fall in love with one of the Frost brothers, who were judging. This year, we wanted to make it an equal opportunity! What's better than dessert with a side of true love?"

The bachelorettes cheered.

"In addition to being able to showcase your baking prowess, you must also show how well you can create a dessert that features alcohol. Hillrock West Distillery, Jonathan Frost's company, is our sponsor this season. And it looks like one of our contestants is already sampling their wares!"

Morticia had tipped the reindeer head back and was taking a swig of craft whiskey made by a small distillery outside of Knoxville, Tennessee. She toasted Anastasia with the bottle. I caught a flash of dark-red lipstick, wisps of black hair, and creamy skin before the reindeer head came back down.

"As usual, we take our baking seriously, so don't be fooled by the dating shenanigans. We won't mess with your desserts or your stations, because those are sacred!" Anastasia assured the women. "You have ample amount of time to bake tasty, photogenic desserts. While you're baking, Jonathan is going to be doing a little speed dating to get to know everyone."

The cameras centered on me. I smiled, hoping my face wasn't too bruised. I decided Morticia had better be going home for that little stunt.

"Keep in mind that while the judges, Anu and Nick, are here to give you a ranking based on your baking, their score is going to be combined with the fan score. The viewers will be deciding which contestants they want to see with Jonathan the most. So be your charming, holiday-loving selves!"

There was another eye roll from the reindeer and more drinking.

"For this speed-date baking challenge, please make a fun, flirty dessert! The timer starts now."

The other girls, in short-skirted Santa outfits, tall boots, and cute elf hats, giggled as they raced around, gathering ingredients. Morticia took another swig from the whiskey bottle.

I headed over to her. I knew I should just leave her alone, but I always did have issues—probably stemming from my childhood, not that we were going to go there—about not being able to just let go of people who clearly didn't like me.

"Are you just going to serve alcohol as your dessert?" I drawled, hand in my pocket. The ice had seemed to do the trick; my face didn't feel that sore as I grinned at her.

Morticia removed the reindeer head and set it on the table. "What's wrong with a whiskey?" she remarked in that slightly raspy voice that sent shivers down my back.

She's evil and crazy. Do not start fantasizing about her.

Morticia rummaged in the drawers and took out a knife, setting it next to the reindeer head with a *thunk*.

CHAPTER 3

Morticia

Jonathan flinched at the knife. Good.

"It seems you're not as much of a Christmas purist as you want people to believe," I said as I grabbed the basket that I had festooned with ribbons and mini ornaments a week ago as part of my decorating contract with Romance Creative.

Jonathan stepped up to walk with me to the pantry.

"Move," I ordered him as he cut in front of me.

"Not until you tell me why you hate Christmas so much," he said stubbornly.

"You're lucky I left my Taser with the rest of my clothes," I snapped at him.

He stopped suddenly, making me almost run into him. A slow smile spread over his stupid, perfect face. "You mean you're not wearing anything under that costume?"

I gave him my best death glare, but it was like trying to throw pillows at a block of ice. Jonathan Frost was unmoved.

"You know, if you need to scratch an itch under that suit, I'm happy to assist," he purred, leaning over me.

Crap, he was tall. I could stand toe-to-toe with most men, but Jonathan made me feel short—and I didn't like it.

"Don't you have some more potential wives to impress?" I retorted, trying to squeeze past him.

"Mr. Frost," one of the production assistants said, "we're ready for your first speed date."

He headed over to another table. I watched in spite of myself as Jonathan turned on the charm for another contestant while she giggled and made flirty faces at him. Morons.

I already knew what I was going to bake—a gingerbread amaretto chocolate tart. My grandmother, who had gone to the great cannoli club in the sky, had loved to bake. After Halloween, Christmas had been her favorite holiday, and she found any excuse to make a dessert.

"Thirty-five hours," I chanted to myself as I walked into the pantry then froze.

"Hey, cousin."

That voice.

"*Keeley*."

"Morticia. Taxidermy any mice lately?"

"Sleep with anyone's husband lately?" I shot back.

Keeley's nostrils flared. She raised her hand as if she was going to slap me then thought better of it.

"You're just jealous," she said haughtily. "I'm going to snag that billionaire."

"I would hope so," I said, turning my back to her to gather my ingredients. "Otherwise, all that money you spent on boob and butt implants would go to waste."

"Stop pretending you don't want him." She huffed.

"As if I want to chain myself to some Christmas-loving simpleton with more money than brain cells," I scoffed.

Jonathan was on a date with another contestant when I went back out onto the studio floor. Like the rest of the bachelorettes, she was wearing a skimpy Christmas outfit. This one was a sexy nutcracker, her skirt short enough that everyone could see her matching panties every time she crossed her legs as she perched like a model on the edge of the large wooden baking table.

"I hope you aren't serving a dessert to anyone with your bodily fluid on it," I said a bit too loudly as I walked past them. The camera guy stifled a laugh. "You're going to make people sick."

The contestant pouted at me.

"Don't worry, sweetheart," Jonathan told her. "I'll eat whatever you're making."

I pretended to barf.

"Don't act like you don't want a little frosting on your Christmas cookies," Jonathan said to me.

Fortunately, the producers led him away before I could do something drastic.

My phone went off. I fished it out of the reindeer head.

Belle: *Don't kill my brother please.*
Morticia: *You have five of them. Surely you won't miss this one.*

I tried to center myself. I could just blow off the contest and make something dumb like a Jell-O mold, but I was competitive—hence my ill-advised attempt to go after the Getty internship.

Tarts were on the dessert menu. I took a deep breath then gritted my teeth against Jonathan's flirty comments and the other bachelorettes' giggles.

When I cooked at home in Harrogate, I had dead quiet, just Salem for company, and a soundtrack of Tibetan singing bowls. Here, though, I was surrounded by a torturous cacophony of Christmas carols, high-pitched giggling, and that bubbly fake bonding that women who are clearly going to be at each other's throats in a few hours do when they first meet each other.

The first step of the tart was the crust. One could use store-bought graham crackers, as Becky, another contestant, was doing while Jonathan watched and made horrible Christmas-themed jokes. Or you could hand-make a crust. Clearly, I chose the more difficult method.

My crust was going to be a flakey gingerbread shortbread recipe. I melted butter on the stove then sifted flour, ginger, cinnamon, allspice, cloves, nutmeg, salt, and baking soda into a bowl. In another bowl, I mixed the butter, a little olive oil (that was my secret! Besides, I'm Italian), and sugar to cream it. Then I added grade A maple syrup and the amaretto and stirred it into a thick mixture. Then I carefully folded in the dry ingredients a cupful at a time. I couldn't knead the dough because that would destroy the flakey texture. At the end, I had a pungent, spicy, rich, caramel-colored dough.

An arm clad in a fancy bespoke suit reached over my shoulder and took a pinch of the dough. "Yum," Jonathan said in my ear. "Tastes like Christmas."

I groped around for the knife.

"Looking for this?" Jonathan teased, waving the knife around.

"That is not a toy," I snapped at him. "And you better not cut yourself and bleed all over my station."

"Oh, so she does want to win the contest," he said.

"And he does want his arm broken or worse," I retorted, grabbing the next-sharpest thing, a metal spatula, and brandishing it at his crotch region. But Jonathan just chuckled.

"I knew as soon as I offered to frost your Christmas cookies that you were going to be all over me," he said in his stupid deep voice. He set down the knife carefully then quickly pinched off another piece of dough before gliding away.

"Thirty more hours, then I'm out of here," I chanted as I wrapped the dough in cling wrap and stuck it in the fridge to chill.

While it cooled, I moved on to the tart filling. A rich chocolate ganache spiked to boozy perfection with amaretto, it would be the perfect counterpoint to the spicy gingerbread crust.

I shaved the rich dark chocolate while the heavy cream warmed in a double broiler on the stove. The kitchen was heating up. I fanned myself. Why had I not insisted I be allowed a change of clothes? I wanted to tear the heavy costume off. I had no qualms about walking around in my bra and panties, but all the other bachelorettes were nipped and tucked and plumped to TV body perfection, whereas I was probably going to look like a deathly specter in my black underwear. Plus, I didn't want to give Jonathan any ammunition to insult me.

The other girls had wised up that if they wanted that billionaire for Christmas, they'd better step up to the stove. They were working furiously at their stations. But my ganache was glossy and perfect and would be hard to beat.

I scooped the shavings into the pot, creating a thick, rich chocolate sauce. I whisked it to make sure they were incorporated then added the amaretto and a pinch of cinnamon. I set it aside to cook slowly while I started the garnish.

Candied cranberries would provide a pop of red color and a bit of sourness as a counterpoint to all that chocolate. They burbled away in their syrup while I started the most technically difficult portion of the dish. I was going to make pine-scented sprigs of holly out of sugar.

Sugar leaves and flowers, normally used on wedding cakes, added a bit of flair. I mixed up the powdered sugar, a bit of gum paste, and amaretto for flavor then carefully rolled out the paste and cut out each individual pine needle and shaped it with a small, pointed wooden stick. It was tedious work, but slow and careful was the best way to make art. One couldn't rush perfection.

While I worked, my mind wandered. Jonathan's deep voice boomed around the studio. He was still working his way through all the contestants.

Guy like him is probably going to try and come down all their chimneys, I decided meanly.

I wasn't going to let him come down mine—not that I wanted to. I knew guys like him didn't go for girls like me. There was no way in hell he would be interested. Not that I cared—I didn't like him anyway.

"You're hot," that deep voice said in my ear.

It took all of my practice in meditation not to flinch. "And you must have a death wish," I hissed at him.

"What? I was just asking after your well-being," he said, still too close to me as I looked over my shoulder. "It looks like you're hot in that costume. Why don't you take it off?" He grinned.

I ignored him. Or tried to.

Jonathan started whistling "Have Yourself a Merry Little Christmas."

"I'm trying to bake."

"And I'm trying to date!" he said.

"Not interested."

"We have to," he said, coming around to the other side of the bench. "Besides," he whispered, "I think you secretly think I'm hot."

"I secretly think a lot of things about you," I said, turning my attention back to my sugar pine sprigs. "None of them use the words 'Jonathan is hot' in any form or combination."

"Can you pretend to be interested?" Gunnar begged from behind one of the cameras. "Zane, why don't you try and get a shot of her trying to teach Jonathan how to make the sugar leaves?"

"Don't touch my stuff," I warned.

"All the other girls let me touch their stuff," Jonathan said, leaning against the table in a casual, sexy way that made the overheated and slightly tipsy part of me think maybe a Christmas package wouldn't be all that bad.

No!

Gunnar mimed signing a check. I rolled my eyes, prayed to the goddess for strength, then grabbed a swig of whiskey just to cover all my bases.

I stared at Jonathan. He made bedroom eyes at me.

"Wow, what a fine specimen of a man," I said robotically. "I think I want him under my Christmas tree. There," I said to Gunnar, "that all you need?"

Jonathan's grin was predatory. "If you take off that reindeer suit, I'll give you a Christmas miracle."

CHAPTER 4

Jonathan

'll give you a Christmas miracle. Geez, what had I been thinking?

Morticia was not impressed. She didn't even deign to respond with a cutting comment, just returned to her sugar plants. I had been dismissed.

"Almost wrapped up for today," Gunnar said, waving me back to the judges' table.

I watched Morticia as she deftly formed the leaves then took the tart dough out of the fridge and quickly rolled out a crust, draped it, then pressed it into the tart pan and put it in the oven.

She was exactly the opposite of everything I desired in a woman—abrasive, mean, all sharp angles, and dark makeup. Morticia wasn't like any of the bubbly young women at the other stations with their colorful Christmas outfits, rosy cheeks, and soft tits. They were the kinds of women I usually went after. I would say I took them into my bed, but I didn't let people into my personal space. I had made that mistake one time and would never repeat it. I liked to maintain boundaries. If a woman was coming into my home, then I wanted her to be the one I married. The girls I met at bars were just for fun; I fucked them in hotels if we could wait that long, but usually we did it in a car, in my office, or in the VIP section of a swanky club.

When I had signed up for the bake-off and Dana had floated the idea of the date-off component, part of me had wondered if maybe this would be my opportunity to find the love of my life. As soon as I met the contestants, though, that dream had been squashed. Though the girls were soft, sexy, and fuckable (Morticia aside), they had that predatory edge that let me know they wanted to be Mrs. Frost for the lifestyle and not for me.

However, just because I wasn't planning on putting a ring on it didn't mean I couldn't fuck one of them or even most of them. I'd just have to be careful and take the condom with me...

"No!" Dana slapped the back of my head.

"Ouch!" I glared at Dana.

"I told you, Jonathan, you cannot sleep with any woman during the contest or for three months after. You must wait until after we stage the breakup," Dana said. "No sex."

"I wasn't doing anything," I complained. "I was sitting here fully clothed."

"I can see lecherous thoughts leaking out of your eyeballs," Dana said. "*The Great Christmas Bake-Off* is a family-friendly show. People watch this with their tween and teen daughters. They want to believe in Christmas cookies and true love. Keep it in your pants."

"I have been!"

In fact, I had been so busy over the last two months with the big Hillrock West Distillery launch that I hadn't had any relief. Usually, I was at the office all night while I went over all the specifics with my team. I only went home to shower and work out. I needed the launch to be record blowing. That industrial property across the street? I needed to buy it. The Svensson brothers had said I could partner with Svensson Investment on the Hamilton Yards development, but I had to bring an influx of cash to the table and show that my hedge fund was the real deal and not some vanity project.

Between the launch and trying to convince the crazy old property owner to sign the sale papers, I hadn't even so much as jacked off in the last six weeks, let alone been laid. My balls weren't just blue, they were frozen. I was so horny that even Morticia was starting to look like a good prospect. I wondered what she looked like under that shapeless reindeer mascot costume. Honestly, I wouldn't even need to find out. I could just push her over the table, rip a hole in the seam...all that profanity coming out of her mouth while I parted her and—

Crack!

"Ow!" I rubbed the back of my head.

"Didn't Dana just tell you to cool it?" Belle said, a rolled-up edition of the *Vanity Rag* in her hand. My older sister's voice was icy.

I gulped. Belle was not to be trifled with. When we were kids, she had ruled the house with an iron fist. My parents were too busy to raise us, and my mom did not believe in nannies, so the child-rearing had fallen upon my sister. She wielded her power effectively.

"My investment firm has money riding on this bake-off venture," she said, tone frosty. "I will not have you screw it up because you never outgrew being a horny fourteen-year-old boy."

I smirked. "All the women I've been with have told me I'm *definitely* a man."

Crack!

"Shit!"

"No swearing," Belle ordered. "The judging is about to start. Try to say something insightful."

The girl in the holiday nutcracker outfit was first to present her dessert. "I made for you this evening," she said with a giggle, "red velvet baked Alaska with peppermint schnapps."

She set what appeared to be a decayed jellyfish in front of me.

"Is that the entrails of the Christmas goose?" Nick asked, poking it with his fork.

"Nick!" Anu exclaimed.

"She tried," I said. The girl simpered at me. What was her name? Hannah? Haley?

Anu took a knife and cut open one of the jellyfish meringues. Bright-red ice cream oozed out like blood.

Only the fact that I knew my older sister would literally kill me if I couldn't even keep it together for one show kept me from cursing.

"I wanted to make it festive!" the girl said in excitement. "You know, like my underwear." She winked at me.

Keep it the fuck together.

"A baked Alaska is deceptively difficult," Anu said more diplomatically than I would have been able to. "You have to form the merengue around the ice cream quickly then put it in the oven to crisp the outside before the ice cream melts. It looks like you didn't time anything right."

Underwear Girl batted her long eyelashes.

"When Jonathan and I are married, it won't matter, because I'm going to hire people to cook for us."

"That's news for Jonathan, I'm sure," Nick said dryly, pushing the dessert to the side.

"You didn't even try it!" Underwear Girl whined to me.

"Oh, uh." I took the smallest forkful of the red-and-white goop I could and gingerly tasted it.

"It's raw still, isn't it?" Nick asked me grimly as I sort of mashed it around in my mouth.

"*Water...*"

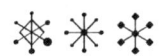

❄ ❅ ❆

The rest of the contestants were marginally better. At least their food was edible.

Keeley had made a Bananas Foster crêpe that was pretty good. "It's great for a corporate event," she said brightly. "You know, like the kind the wives of powerful businessmen host to help them seal a deal."

"At least she had a good attitude," I said after she had left.

"Keeley made a pancake, not a crêpe," Nick said, picking apart the dessert. "It's too thick. And it's a bit lumpy."

"Sounds like it needs a doctor's visit!" I joked then blanched when Belle shot a death glare across the room.

Morticia was the final contestant. She was still wearing the reindeer suit, though it looked as if she had had it off earlier and hadn't been able to zip it back up. A black, satiny stripe of bra strap was exposed as the reindeer suit slid partially off one shoulder.

"I made a chocolate gingerbread amaretto tart. Eat it or don't."

"Look at that presentation," Anu said, admiring it. Morticia hadn't just made a chocolate tart. She had decorated it with the green sprigs of sugar pine needles, glittering candied cranberries, and ornate gingerbread shapes frosted with white icing.

"That is so photogenic," I remarked. "We have pictures of that with the bottle of alcohol, right?" I asked one of the producers, who nodded.

Morticia cut out neat, even, perfect slices of the tart.

"Damn," I joked, "I think you're the only woman in the world who could make being dressed as a shapeless mascot sexy."

"Hm," Morticia said as she carefully slid a piece of the tart onto the plate. "Yes, or maybe you're some sort of goddamn perverted furry."

CHAPTER 5

Morticia

The bar across the street was empty. It was at the bottom of the Hillrock West Distillery offices. The only reason I was there was because I was still wearing the stupid reindeer suit. Otherwise there was no way I would have patronized any establishment run by that arrogant billionaire.

Jonathan had not appreciated my furry comment.

I chuckled as I remembered how Belle had chastised him, descending on him like a winter storm when he started raging at me.

I refreshed my text message app, hoping that a text from my twin, Lilith, would magically appear. She had all my clothes and our cat. And my Taser.

I sipped my drink at the bar, my reindeer skin unzipped as much as possible while still maintaining some modesty. The bar was empty. The bored bartender polished glasses. If this bar was any indication of Jonathan's big, expensive alcohol brand's popularity, I had low hopes for its survival. The decor was extremely pretentious, with a polished concrete bar top, thousand-dollar barstools, and lights that were imported from Japan.

I swiped through my phone.

Belle, Dana, and their team would be editing the footage to put out tonight for the premier. They were already posting photos from the filming. I grimaced at the video of me lobbing the rubber candy cane at Jonathan. It had not been one of my finer moments. I preferred to set a sneaky trap, not go for out-and-out violence. But the shock on his face had been worth it. The post already had millions of likes; the video was going viral. Even Jonathan's alcohol company had jumped on the bandwagon. I idly flipped through its feed.

"Gross. Basic. Seen it."

Hillrock West Distillery's feed sucked, to put it nicely. Not that I cared. After tomorrow, I was going to collect my check from Gunnar, then I was out of Manhattan. If Jonathan was determined to blow a ton of money on some marketing firm with no design sense, that was his massively overpriced funeral.

I felt as if I had done a decent job of convincing everyone I had no business being a bachelorette. Once I was voted off, I could concentrate on winning that internship.

My phone beeped with an incoming email.

"Finally," I muttered, but it wasn't from Lilith. It was from the Getty Museum! I took a steadying sip of my drink then opened the email. I read it, stifling an uncharacteristic cheer.

Morticia: *I made it to the next round!*
Morticia: *Where are youuuu?*

Morticia: *Currently dying in the world's most pretentious bar.*

"Drinking alone?"

I stiffened. "I need it after dealing with you," I said to Jonathan.

"I can't have you in here ruining the atmosphere," he said, spinning the barstool around to have me face him. "You're like roadkill that dragged herself in here."

"Ah yes, because a billionaire with delusions of adequacy is someone whose opinion I care about," I shot back.

"I am way more than adequate," he said, striking a pose. The glow from the expensive fixtures highlighted the slight bruise on his perfect face.

I smirked slightly.

"Like something you see?" Jonathan asked.

"Just that dildo-shaped bruise on your face," I replied, sipping my drink. "Your company has our first meeting all over its feed. Better than the basic images you have up there now. At least people can laugh at the spit flying out of your mouth when you ran into my candy cane instead of dying from boredom at those images you're posting."

"You're just jealous," Jonathan retorted, eyes narrowing as he leaned over me. "I have one of the best marketing firms in the city working on my social media push."

"Guess you can't buy good taste," I said, draining my drink.

"Says the woman wearing a reindeer costume," Jonathan shot back. He reached out and hooked two fingers right at the neckline of the costume, pulling me forward slightly. "At first I thought you were wearing it under duress, but you're still parading around in it. Like you said, you can't buy taste."

"Oh my god! Don't touch my sister, creep!"

Now Lilith shows up.

Our friend Emma was hovering behind her.

Jonathan jerked his hand back then looked between Lilith and me wildly.

"Holy shit. Of course you're creepy identical twins."

Lilith and I glared in unison—or tried to. Lilith was dressed in her standard gothic garb, while I was bedecked for Christmas.

Jonathan turned on his heel to leave then looked over his shoulder at me. "I'd tell you good luck on the competition, but after your little stunt, everyone is going to put you in last place."

"Was he trying to have his way with you?" Emma asked breathlessly. She was a member of the private equity group that Dana and Belle had started. The two women were demanding and exacting. It was a stressful job, and Emma stress ate, not that I was judging. I liked pizza and brownies as much as the next girl.

"I still have some dried hemlock from the garden. I can put it in his bulletproof coffee," my twin offered, narrowing her eyes at Jonathan's retreating form.

"I can't afford to go to jail. I'm this close to winning that Getty internship," I said, showing her the email. "I'm one of thirty in the running now. I have a video interview scheduled and everything."

"Maybe Penny will let you set up in one of the *Vanity Rag* offices," Lilith said as Salem butted his head against my leg. "Then you can have a swanky background."

"Do you think that's too bougie?" I chewed my bottom lip.

"It's the Getty," Lilith countered. "You can't do the interview in front of Mimi's antique doll collection. You're competing against all those trust fund girls who studied art as a pastime while waiting for a rich man to marry. You need to up your game. Also, I'm not sure that throwing a candy cane at Jonathan Frost was the best move."

"It will blow over," I said.

"Girl, you are a full-on meme." Lilith pulled out her phone. "People have been swapping the candy cane out for all sorts of things. Here's one of you throwing a cat. Here's one of you throwing a bucket of fried chicken. Here's one of you throwing a bottle of tequila. Actually"—she frowned—"I think Jonathan's firm made that one."

"Hail corporate." I grabbed my purse from Lilith so I could pay.

Emma watched me thoughtfully.

"You know," she said finally, "I may have to start dressing as a Christmas furry if it's going to make hot guys stick their hands down my shirt."

CHAPTER 6

Jonathan

"Did that girl have a cat on a leash?" Carl Svensson asked when I walked out of the bar.

I was still reeling from my interactions with Morticia. What had possessed me to put my hand down her…well, not exactly down her shirt; more down the front of her costume. The heat of her skin against the cooler back of my hand had been a jolt.

I needed to know what she looked like without the costume on.

As we walked across the street to the neighboring industrial property I was hoping to buy and turn into an award-winning development, Carl commented, "You know, Greg is not pleased that there's a video floating around the internet of you getting hit in the face with a dildo."

"Please tell your brother that it was not a dildo," I snarled. "It was a giant rubber candy cane."

"Same difference to Greg," Carl retorted. "He's not sure he wants to go into business with someone who gets dildos thrown at him on a regular basis."

"Did Greg not try and fail to secure the buying rights to this property from Dorothy?" I asked as we picked our way around what looked like a scrap heap but was actually an in-progress sculpture Dorothy was working on. "I'm her neighbor. She likes me. I bring her enough alcohol to kill an elephant. Greg has to work with me if he wants this development in his portfolio."

"He's skeptical of whether you can actually pull it off. A number of my brothers are betting that you can't," Carl said.

"I can," I said stubbornly as we approached a large, round, stained glass door. I pulled the rope beside the bell. It let out a metallic clang.

"World's sexiest alcohol delivery!" I called out.

"*Hisss!*"

A huge bird came careening around the corner, racing straight at me.

"Holy shit!" Carl cursed as we scrambled onto a nearby bench to escape the rabid goose.

It snapped and hissed at us, flapping its wings, the red-and-gold bow around its neck sparkling evilly in the early-evening light.

"Come, Prancer!" Dorothy called, opening the stained glass front door. "Leave those nice boys alone. Jonathan's already had one altercation today with something long and thick."

"It was a candy cane."

"Oh, I'm sure all the girls love your candy cane!" Dorothy cooed, striding out into the cold. She was wearing a red-and-green velour tracksuit. Her usual shock of short white hair had been colored in what might generously be described as Christmas tie-dye.

"Back to your post," she ordered the goose. It waddled off but not before hissing menacingly at me and Carl.

"I was going to serve him for Christmas dinner. Still on the fence about it, but he has spirit, and I like that. I also like attractive men that bring me alcohol," she prompted.

I held out the bottle. "This is one of our new limited-edition winter vodka lines," I told her. "With just a hint of juniper and cranberry."

She opened the bottle and took an appreciative sniff. "I hope it tastes as good as it smells. Something I might say about a few other people here," she said and took a swig. "Goes down smooth."

"Smooth enough to sell me this complex?" I asked in what I hoped was a joking, easy manner.

"So you're just trying to get me all liquored up then take advantage of me?" Dorothy laughed. "I *have* been told I'm the best-looking eighty-year-old north of New Jersey."

"Really? You don't look a day over fifty-five," I assured her.

"You're such a charmer."

Give me the property. Give me the property.

Dorothy patted me on the cheek. "I ought to put some sort of crazy condition on selling you the land," she joked.

"Like make me get married to a good woman first so I can prove that I am a wholesome family man?" I prompted. I could totally scrounge up a fake fiancée.

"No, I meant like doing a striptease in the snow and covering yourself with edible body paint," Dorothy said, wrinkling her nose. "This place is far from wholesome. I'm working on a vagina sculpture that is big enough to walk into right now! I'm thinking about decorating it for Christmas and selling tickets."

CHAPTER 7

Morticia

The night before, I had hung out with Lilith and Emma at Emma's microscopic studio apartment, eating pizza I was going to expense to Gunnar and Dana. I had ignored their calls and text messages stating that I needed to be in the apartment with the other baking bachelorettes. I would surely be leaving today, and I didn't see the point. Especially since my cousin was there.

Keeley was three workstations over from me, wearing a sexy gingerbread girl costume that exposed her midriff and pushed her boobs up to her chin. She had always been boy crazy, not to mention just plain ol' crazy. The months Lilith and I had been forced to live with our aunt and uncle after our mom split had been the worst of my life. High school had been torture enough without having to come home to the same person who had tormented us in the hallways.

I almost wished she and Jonathan would end up together. *Almost*. Jonathan was a prick, but I couldn't in good conscience wish Keeley on anyone—not even that Jonathan.

He was leaning casually against the butcher block judges' table, one arm gripping the edge behind him, his body twisted like a perfect David statue.

Except I bet his dick is like five times as big.

Stop thinking about his package!

Jonathan's blue eyes met mine from across the room, and I lowered my head, letting my bangs fall into my eyes.

Five minutes, then you're out of here.

I already had an Uber ordered. Lilith was outside with Salem. As soon as I returned to Harrogate, I would make a big pot of tea and bake an eggnog pound cake.

Wait, Christmas baking? No freaking way!

"Welcome to day two of *The Great Christmas Bake-Off*!" Anastasia announced. "I know we're all anxious to move on to the next challenge and take another step closer to Jonathan finding his true Christmas love. Based on the judges' rankings, there was a clear favorite and a clear weak dessert. Morticia and Heather, could you please step up? Heather, the judges said that your baked Alaska was essentially inedible."

"But I made it with love!" Heather started sobbing.

If I were a normal reality contestant, I would have pretended to comfort her. Instead, I crossed my arms. I had seen that baked Alaska. It was tragic.

"You can't serve people raw eggs," I chided her.

"Gosh, you're such a bitch!" she cried. "Jonathan, I love you! We're meant to be together."

"Keeley, would you please step forward," Anastasia said over the sobs.

My cousin pranced into line.

"Keeley," Anastasia said, "you were voted the fan favorite."

"Of course I was," she preened. "Jonathan and I are going to have a picture-perfect Christmas wedding."

I smirked to myself as the billionaire's eyes widened slightly in horror.

"You were the fan favorite," Anastasia repeated, "tied with Morticia, that is."

"What? There has to be some mistake," my cousin insisted. "No one likes her."

"I assure you that we have Quantum Cyber providing top-notch security on our online voting system," Anastasia informed her. "Morticia, since you also were the judges' top pick for yesterday's baking competition, this means you have won the first episode. Congratulations! You may return to your stations."

No. No, no, no.

I'm not supposed to be here!

"Heather, you are, unfortunately, going home. Please pack up your baking tools."

"No!" she wailed, collapsing in a heap on the floor and throwing a literal tantrum. "She's supposed to be going home. I'm supposed to marry Jonathan!"

❄ ✳ ❈

I was still in shock as I gathered my ingredients for the next bake-off contest.

I wanted to corner Belle and demand to go home, but there were cameras on me. As much as I wanted to make a scene, Lilith was right. I didn't want the Getty internship committee to see a crazy video of me online and decide they didn't want me anywhere near their museum.

Jonathan was waiting at my station when I returned with my basket of ingredients.

"Guess you like Christmas and me more than you care to admit," he prodded, looking me up and down.

His gaze was intense. I suddenly wished I still had my reindeer costume on. I was wearing a form-fitting mock corset top with long sleeves over black skinny jeans. I was fully covered except for my face and hands, but standing in front of him, I felt like I wasn't wearing anything at all.

"Apparently there is an inverse correlation between your skills as a baker and how much filler you have injected into your lips," I said as I started shaving a large brick of glossy dark chocolate.

Jonathan laughed, the sound reverberating deep in his chest. It made my teeth vibrate.

"Aren't you supposed to be harassing everyone in the room?" I asked crossly.

"Nope," he said. "Today, the dating activity is you all decorating the window of my store."

"You mean free work."

"And a snack!" he said, stealing a piece of the chocolate. "But right now, I am free to flirt with whomever I choose."

I shoved him out of the way with my shoulder—or tried to. His chest was solid muscle. He didn't even budge.

I was already furious that I was here for another episode. Now I had to deal with Jonathan! It was too much. I gritted my teeth against his running commentary.

"Why are you putting pumpkin in those brownies? That's not Christmas," he remarked as I mixed up the pumpkin with brown sugar, cinnamon, and nutmeg. "That's a Halloween ingredient."

"I wish it were Halloween," I said. "But we have three hundred thirty days left."

And my Halloween dessert was my ticket out. No one was going to vote for a person who made pumpkin cream cheese bourbon brownies at a Christmas bake-off, even if they were gooey and amazing and delicious. I liked a rich brownie with big chunks of dark chocolate. To the cream cheese, I added a bit of lemon and sugar and egg to give it a richer taste. I folded it and the pumpkin-bourbon mixture carefully into the brownie batter to make pretty white-and-orange chocolate swirls.

"Happy Halloween," I said under my breath as I put the pan in the oven for ten minutes and cleaned off my table while I waited for it to bake.

After taking the pan out of the oven, I stuck it in the blast freezer to cool and to stop the cooking process. It wasn't a brownie if it was crumbly and overdone. After a few minutes, it was solid enough that I could cut it into perfect squares and set them on a plate for the producers to take photos and B-roll of them with the alcohol I had used. When they were done, I put a few squares on a plate with me to take outside. They were the middle pieces, of course; only heathens liked edges and corners.

Because I had made a simple dessert, I was done before the rest of the bachelorettes. After being cowed by my winning the first round of baking, they all seemed to be trying to up their game. Good. I refused to stay here another week.

The cameras followed me as I made my way to the showroom of the Hillrock West Distillery, where Jonathan was talking with one of his employees.

"Aw, did you come out early to spend more time with me?" he mocked when he saw me.

"Nope. I came out here to fix your disaster of a store."

"No Halloween themes," he warned, stealing a brownie. He took a bite, and his eyes lit up. "Holy shit. That's fantastic!"

"That's for the decoration!" I scolded, trying to swipe the brownie out of his hand.

But he held the dessert aloft. "Guess you'll have to jump for it!" he teased.

"If there weren't cameras on me, I'd throw these in your face," I hissed at him.

"So you want me covered in chocolate. Good to know. I'll keep that in mind for when Dana wants everyone to do a very intimate date with me."

I froze. There was no way in Christmas hell I was participating in any intimate activities with Jonathan. I had to make sure I was out of the contest by then.

CHAPTER 8

Jonathan

I was miffed that Morticia didn't want to go on an intimate date with me. I mean, come on! It was me! Every woman in Manhattan wanted me—except Morticia, it seemed.

She was already inspecting her assigned window of the showroom adjacent to the bar at the base of the Hillrock West Distillery offices. She was sketching something intently. The other bachelorettes had finished their desserts and were streaming into the showroom and bar to stand at their assigned windows.

"You have the rest of the day to decorate," Anastasia told them. "When it's dark, time's up, and we will be reviewing everyone's dessert-and-window combo. Remember, part of being Mrs. Frost is being able to support Jonathan in his professional endeavors."

"I think you mispronounced 'unpaid labor,'" Morticia said loudly.

"I'm the payment," I reminded her.

"Some payment," she scoffed. "I can't even sell you at a consignment shop."

I ignored her and walked around to watch the rest of the contestants decorate. I needed to just leave Morticia alone. She wasn't worth the hassle.

The rest of the girls were giving the challenge their best shot. Many of them did have some design skills, though their windows were a bit too scrapbookish and feminine for my taste. Morticia's window, though, looked very professional and on-brand for Hillrock West Distillery. The bottles of bourbon were placed next to the artfully arranged brownies on small, round reclaimed-wood tables. Gold foil and warm wood accents covered the inside of the narrow shop window. The arrangement was flanked by gold ribbons and glass ornaments. Strands of twinkling lights reflected off of the glass ornaments and the bottles of bourbon.

I snuck another brownie while I watched Morticia work. As I chewed, I counted down as she first realized I was standing behind her, then as she struggled to try and ignore me, then when she finally turned around and threw a Christmas ornament at me. I caught it easily as I regarded the window.

"I bet you wish you hadn't made orange brownies."

"They're not that orange," she said defensively. "They're more caramel colored. Anyway, it doesn't even matter. You're getting free photos out of this. If you don't like it, pay someone to do it."

"Hey, I like it," I assured her before stealing another brownie before she could stop me.

❋ ❋ ❋

The judges didn't seem to care for Morticia's window or her brownies.

"These are good brownies," Anu said later that evening, when the sun had set.

The windows were lit up, sparkling lights onto the sidewalk. Morticia's window looked even better in the dark. Along with the brownies, she also had made actual craft cocktails with the bourbon. I had snapped pictures with my phone and posted them online, immediately earning thousands of likes.

"They just feel like fall, not winter," Anu continued. "Also, a brownie is not that impressive a dessert."

"Your window is pretty," Nick said. "But yeah, not getting holiday vibes. If you wanted to do the gold-caramel-colored theme, you should have done a *croquembouche*. With its tower of puff pastry drizzled in wisps of caramel, the dessert would have gone great with your window."

"Yes, but this is *America*, and in *America*, pumpkins are absolutely a Christmas food," Morticia interjected.

"They are?" I asked, frowning.

"In the 1600s, when the Puritans came to America, along with burning witches, they also introduced the concept of pumpkins for Christmas. The leaders wanted to ban Christmas completely, because in England, Christmas was celebrated with brawls in the street and drunken fornication, which included priests in some instances. The Puritans turned Christmas into a religious holiday, and what goes better with self-deprivation than the humble pumpkin? Christmas wouldn't be Christmas in America without pumpkins," Morticia said fervently.

"I don't eat pumpkins at Christmas," Nick told her flatly.

Morticia didn't even blink. "Maybe you should branch out."

"Hope this doesn't get you sent home," Anu said, cutting the tension.

"Hope it does," I thought I heard her mutter, but then we were on to the next contestant.

Keeley had made an impressively tall layer cake. When she cut it open, sprinkles and edible glitter spilled out.

"The cake is very good," Anu praised, "with a nice crumb. The color gradient on these layers definitely says Christmas."

"The window display is a bit too sparkly for my taste," I said. "I'm not sure that it's as on brand as what Morticia installed."

Keeley scowled for a moment, and Morticia smirked, though her face returned to its mask when she noticed my gaze.

"But," I said, showing Keeley the Instagram post of the video of her cake I'd made, "it seems like a number of people do like your cake."

"Oh, Jonathan," Keeley said with a sharp grin, "*everyone* likes my cake."

"And she does mean that," Morticia said.

✷ ✷ ✷

"I need a break," I said later when I was back at my condo. I owned a penthouse in one of the developments the Svenssons had done across the street. Now that we were fully in the swing of our Christmas marketing push for Hillrock West Distillery, I actually had time to spend at home. "When did it become so lonely?" I mused aloud to the empty living room.

I wanted more of Morticia's brownies. Actually, I wanted some of Morticia.

I flipped to my Instagram feed. There were a ton of likes on the pictures of her window. There were also calls for the recipe for the brownies and a heated argument about whether pumpkin was an appropriate Christmas food. On the post of Keeley's cake, however, there was more drama, including someone claiming she had stolen the idea from Chloe Barnard, my brother Jack's girlfriend and owner of the Grey Dove Bistro franchise.

I flopped down on the couch in the open living-kitchen area in the renovated historic loft. I desperately wanted a family. I couldn't believe my older brother, Jack, was taking it so slow with Chloe. He wasn't even engaged. If I'd had a great girlfriend like Chloe, who was fun and bubbly and loved Christmas and family and entertaining, I would have married her already and had a box of babies.

"Do babies come in boxes?" I wondered aloud.

I needed to get it together. My condo wasn't even decorated for Christmas. It felt cold and bleak. Normally, when I felt like this, I would go out to a club or a high-end bar and find a pretty actress or model to bang. But my sister would kill me if I messed up her show. Also, I wanted to keep any controversy centered around baking, not my personal life. It was Christmas after all.

I threw open the window, hoping to cool off, as I tallied up the days until I would be able to have casual sex—hell, any sex—without messing up the show.

"Months," I said, leaning out over the balcony railing. "It's going to be four months."

I was not going to make it.

"You need to figure out how to convince Dorothy to sell you that property."

In the distance, the abandoned smokestacks and towers of the industrial warehouses and factories were silhouetted against the skyline. My redevelopment plan was to keep the existing buildings and restore them to pristine condition. Between them, I would have new buildings—modern glass boxes that wouldn't compete with the highly crafted brick detailing of the historic structures.

I would expand the Hillrock West Distillery restaurant and tasting room. We'd host big events, there would be expensive condos, and Archer Svensson had said that he and Greyson Hotel Group would put in a boutique hotel. At Christmas, the whole place would be decorated, with an ice-skating rink and horse-drawn carriage rides through the complex so people could look at the lights.

But it didn't matter how much alcohol I gave Dorothy or how much I flirted with her. She wouldn't budge.

"Fuck," I growled, staring down the street and trying to will the project into existence.

I might have willed too hard, though, because instead of a phone call from Dorothy stating that yes, she was willing to sell me the property for nothing more than a kiss on the cheek, a black-clad specter materialized from the shadows. And she was walking a cat.

CHAPTER 9

Morticia

"You want me to do what?" I growled to Gunnar.

He took a nervous step backward. "Look, you have to live in the apartment."

"I'm not even supposed to be here!" I complained.

"You signed a contract," Dana interjected, waving a sheaf of papers in my face.

"Besides, the judges hated my brownies, and I'm sure that I'll be gone by the next bake-off day."

"I wouldn't be so sure," Dana said, swiping through her phone. "You have quite the following. There's a fan page dedicated to you. People are shipping you and Jonathan so hard. You can't buy this kind of publicity."

"Which is shocking, really, because I'm hardly being paid anything," I griped.

"Aren't you pimping yourself out on Instagram?" Dana asked.

"No. I refuse to debase myself to get followers. I am an artist with integrity." I crossed my arms.

"Really? Because your follower count increased to twenty thousand over the last couple days," Dana said.

My eyes twitched ever so slightly. I had followers?

We will be strong. Consumerism is a curse. Followers are not friends.

"You could get sponsorships," Dana singsonged.

Well, hell, that Getty internship clearly wasn't paying for itself.

I grabbed the phone from her. "With my newfound power, I will educate the unwashed masses on the genius of Martha Edelson, feminist artist extraordinaire!"

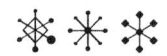

※ ※ ※

Unfortunately, my new crop of Insta fans did not care about art. However, I had received an excessive number of requests for the pumpkin brownie recipe, and the episode hadn't even aired yet.

"Oh!" I said, scrolling through my DMs. "I have a sponsorship offer." I peered at the message. "What the hell? They want me to post about their Christmas-themed sex toy in exchange for a free one? No thanks. I only take cold, hard cash."

"Broaden your horizons," my friend Emma said as she helped me carry my stuff up the stairs, because of course there was no elevator, because of course Jonathan owned a building that did not include an elevator.

"A Christmas-themed sex toy might be fun. You know, bring a little holiday cheer to the act."

"Isn't it jolly enough without a singing dildo that lights up?" I asked.

Emma made a face. "You didn't say that it lights up. That sounds dangerous."

I showed her and Lilith the picture.

"I'm not sure I want to shove anything shaped like a Christmas tree up there. Seems like a disaster waiting to happen," my twin remarked.

"I don't know," Emma said. "Seems like you're going to need something to take the edge off if you're going to survive *The Great Christmas Bake-Off*."

"The plan is not to survive," I reminded them as we lugged my trunk up the stairs to the door of the shared apartment. Last year, *The Great Christmas Bake-Off* had been in the Quantum Cyber tower. They'd had a whole penthouse.

This year?

"Guess a billion doesn't go as far as it used to," Lilith said as we peered into the small apartment.

The space was in a renovated loft above the main studio where we filmed. There was a great room with an open kitchen and two doors off of the large common area to what I assumed were bedrooms.

"This place is in need of some sage."

"I think you're going to need a lot more than incense to make this place habitable," Emma said.

The place had been trashed. Whoever said girls were neater than boys was lying. There was dried nail polish on the rug. An empty mug of tea with the tea bag fused to the bottom sat atop a stack of Christmas plates shaped like reindeer. My blood pressure was rising.

Through the large windows, Jonathan's company headquarters gleamed across the street.

"Isn't it wonderful?" Keeley gushed. "I love that we can watch him come in to work in the morning. You can see right across to the conference room where he works sometimes." She sighed longingly. "I'm learning all his habits for when I become Mrs. Frost."

"Because that's not creepy."

"Maybe you should try getting a job," Lilith added, "instead of stalking any man that crosses your path."

"And maybe you two should stop acting like weird teenagers, fix your wardrobe, and start behaving like someone a man would want, and you wouldn't be unemployed and homeless."

"We aren't homeless," Lilith insisted. She had had it just as bad as I had from our cousin.

"Really?" Keeley scoffed. "Then why are you bringing your cat here?"

"Emma can't have cats on her lease. Salem is staying with Morticia."

"Be careful," I told my cousin. "He likes to talk to ghosts."

"You were always strange and off-putting. No wonder all the boys hated you. And I don't know why you're even bothering being in this competition. I knew you couldn't bake. Those brownies were such a stupid idea. I'm going to easily beat you."

That was the point, I tried to assure myself, but my competitive nature was rising. *I should have made them with pomegranate. Then they would have been red.*

My twin and my friend shoved me into my new bedroom before I could lose it.

Lilith took a bundle of sage out of her purse and lit it, waving it in front of my face.

"And we're inhaling and we're exhaling. We are calm like the ocean," Lilith intoned.

The room was more like a prison cell. Oh, the exposed brick walls, tall windows, and heavy timber beams did make a nice space. However, it would have been nicer without six bunks crowded into the bedroom.

"At least you aren't bunking with Keeley," Lilith reminded me as I gingerly set my purse on the empty bunk bed then opened Salem's carrier. He hissed, yellow eyes wide as he took in the surroundings.

"Hopefully you'll be out of this purgatory soon," Lilith said. "Use this trauma to fuel your art."

"Or you could just use Jonathan!" Emma said, bouncing on the balls of her feet.

"Gross! I don't want him anywhere near me."

"Really?" Emma wheedled. "Not even a little bit? Because you two seemed hot and heavy in the bar."

"He's got some sort of fascination with women in furry suits."

"Could be fun," Emma mused. "You could branch out a bit."

Salem extended one black paw out of the carrier.

Out in the common area, the other bachelorettes were shrieking and laughing.

"I will be eliminated tomorrow. I am sending positive thoughts to the universe, and I will be eliminated tomorrow," I chanted.

"If not," Emma said, "you should totally make maple-glazed bacon donuts. I bet that would have Jonathan after you. You know, give him some meat for his meat."

"I do not want to think about Jonathan's meat," I said flatly.

"Don't you mean his candy cane?" Lilith joked.

"His Christmas package!" Emma shrieked.

"Now they decide to be creative!" I rolled my eyes.

Emma gave me a hug. "Lilith and I need to go. It's going to take hours on the subway back to my apartment."

"You'd think being an investment banker would pay more," I said.

"Not when you're the sole person in charge of a private equity firm run by women with a lot of grit but not that much liquid capital. But if *The Great Christmas Bake-Off* does well," Emma said hopefully, "then Belle and Dana will have a big cash influx."

"So you're saying that all your hopes and dreams rest on Morticia," Lilith deadpanned. She snorted. "You might need to find a day job."

I threw up my hands after I walked them out through the cacophony of drunk gold diggers singing Christmas carols.

"I'm an introvert. How am I going to survive the rest of this competition? No." I stopped myself as I went back to the shared bedroom. "We will not be here longer than tomorrow. Maybe two episodes tops. The thing to do," I decided as Salem bounced around the room, "is to make a terrible dessert so I'll have to leave."

Except…except I couldn't. I couldn't *not* be competitive. Also, I *needed* to at least beat my cousin. There was no way I wanted Keeley to have bragging rights over me.

My mind was already spinning on what dessert I would cook next and how I would win the competition.

Not win, just beat Keeley.

Salem howled and jumped onto the top bunk to leap like a trapeze artist between it and the neighboring bunk. The only thing worse than being stuck in a cell of a bedroom with a bunch of bachelorettes was going to be being stuck with bachelorettes and a cat with cabin fever. Back in Harrogate, he had the run of the house.

"You know," I told him, "if you had just been a better-behaved cat, Emma's landlord wouldn't have found out about you, and you could be at her apartment right now."

He swung upside down off the top bunk to bat at my hair. I fished out his harness and clipped it onto him. Time to walk the cat.

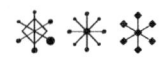

❄. ❄ ❄

A lot of people think you can't walk a cat. However, with the right motivation, anything is possible.

Since we were in New York City, I didn't get any strange glances from passersby. Actually, that was probably because there weren't any. A lesser woman would have found it creepy to be out so late in the cold and the dark with no one around. However, I lived for the shadows and the spooky night. Also, I needed the peace and quiet. I was developing a migraine from all the high-pitched squealing and the incessant chattering about *Oh, isn't Jonathan hot?* and *Oooh, I wonder how big his dick is* and OMG, *my friend's hairdresser's cousin slept with him once and said it was life changing!*

"He's such a manwhore, Salem," I said to the cat as we walked to a nearby park.

Actually, calling it a park was being generous. The little patch of grass with one lone tree was not even big enough to allow two people to throw a Frisbee. But it was enough for

Salem. He pranced around on his lead, hissing at shadows as I scrolled through my phone.

"I'm just doing research," I told myself. "I'm not stalking Jonathan. I don't even like him."

There was a trove of information on Jonathan on the internet. It confirmed every stereotype and snap judgment I'd made about him.

"Manwhore, check," I said, scrolling through photos of him slightly sweaty and dancing with scantily clad models. "Terrible business sense, check," I said at a headline about how investors were skeptical that he could turn his alcohol company into a billion-dollar juggernaut. "And terrible taste, check," I said as an ad for his alcohol popped up on my feed.

"Honestly," I told my cat. "You would think that for the amount of money those Manhattan marketing firms charge, they could come up with something that was at least attractive." The ad showed several bottles of alcohol against a concrete wall. I guessed it was supposed to be masculine, but it just looked like they didn't try hard enough.

Salem yowled.

"Yes, I suppose we should head back," I said to the cat and pulled at his leash…only to come up with a leash attached to an empty harness and no cat.

"Salem!" I yelled.

He meowed, but it was pitch dark, and a black cat was impossible to find at night.

"Fuck this competition!" I fumed. "Screw Jonathan. Screw them all. First I have to be subjected to Christmas merriment, and now they've made me lose my cat! *Salem!*" I turned on my phone flashlight, swinging it around wildly. I saw motion as I swung the beam of light toward the tree.

From above me in the bare branches, two yellow eyes slowly blinked.

"Salem, come down this instant."

The cat ignored me. I jumped up and down. It was freezing, but Salem seemed perfectly happy in the tree. He coiled then sprang to an even higher branch.

"Salem! I'm calling the fire department if you don't come down right now!"

"Salem? Shouldn't you be yelling for Rudolph?"

CHAPTER 10

Jonathan

Morticia turned around and swore when she saw me.

"Are you stalking me?" she screeched. She reached for her purse.

Mindful of her threats about her Taser, I grabbed her wrist.

"Don't touch me," Morticia hissed, batting at me with her free hand.

I grabbed her other wrist, holding her in place. "Then don't tase me."

She kicked me in the shin with her heavy boot.

"Ow!" I yelled, letting her go. "Just for that, I'm not helping you rescue your cat from the tree. Good luck trying to get the fire department out here. I called them one too many times after Dorothy lit the roof on fire doing one of her art projects. Now they basically refuse to come out here for anything less than a nuclear bomb."

"Salem!" Morticia called. "Please come down. I'll buy you all the fish."

The cat ignored her and started grooming himself.

"Stupid cat," Morticia grumbled.

"Yep," I said casually, putting my hands in my pants pockets. "It's a bitch when someone just sits there and ignores you."

"I do not owe you my attention."

"No one said anything about owing," I told her. "But how about a wager?"

She looked at me suspiciously.

"If I rescue your cat from the tree, do you promise to fawn over me and be super excited when you see me?" I offered.

"I'd rather get a new cat," she retorted.

Salem made an offended noise.

I clasped a hand over my heart.

"Cruel mistress of the night. She would rather leave you up there, Salem," I told the cat, who had settled in to watch our interactions. "You will always have a place to live with me, young Salem."

"You are not taking my cat."

"Are you going to stand here all night babysitting him?" I asked her. "Baby, it's cold outside…" I started to sing.

"I'm not cold," Morticia lied. She was wearing a thin jacket and sweater. She was dressed for fall, not winter. She didn't even have a hat.

"Where's your coat if you're so concerned about the weather?" she asked.

"I never get cold," I bragged. "One time, my mom locked me outside because she said I was annoying and loud, and I stayed outside in the freezing cold all night with no shoes. Didn't even get frostbite."

Morticia gave me a slightly pitying look. But I didn't want her pity. I wanted…well, I wasn't sure. I wanted her to like me.

"So do we have a deal?" I held out my hand, rushing on before she could ask me about my horrible childhood.

The corners of her mouth were downturned. Salem made angry cat noises from up in the tree.

"Salem says it's cold outside!" I singsonged.

"I will say one nice thing to you the next time I see you," she finally grumbled. "Take it or leave it."

"Because I am a gentleman and a friend to all animals, I accept."

Morticia tapped at her phone.

"What are you doing?"

"I need a video of you trying to climb that tree," she said with a slight smirk.

"Oh," I said, advancing on her, "I'm not climbing that tree." Then I grabbed her, pinning her hands behind her back, holding her against me.

Morticia screamed and flailed in my arms, trying to kick at me, but I tightened my grasp.

"Let me go, you fucking creep! Help!"

"You're mine now!" I threatened in my best ax murderer voice. I even threw in a creepy laugh for good measure.

"Let me go!" Morticia screamed, but I clapped a hand over her mouth and started to slowly drag her away.

In the tree, Salem was furious! The cat howled then launched himself at me in a ball of fur and claws.

"Gotcha!" I said happily. "Ow!" I yelled as one of Salem's murder mittens swiped across my hand. I held the wriggling cat.

"Let him go! Let him go!" Morticia yelled, attacking me with a purse that must have contained rocks.

"Oof! No! We just convinced him to come down from the tree. Nice acting, by the way. I can see why you're such a natural on TV."

"You...!" Morticia sputtered.

"Have your cat..." I prompted. "I'm waiting for the thank-you."

Morticia didn't look at me as she took Salem from my arms and slipped his harness onto him. The black cat was still furious, hissing and spitting at me.

"Hey, little guy, it was just an act," I said soothingly. I reached out to pet him then jerked my hand back when he swiped and spat. His yellow eyes were demon slits, and I was sure if I could speak cat, I would have heard Salem cursing my ancestors.

Morticia still wouldn't look at me.

"I'm sorry," I said gently, suddenly feeling bad. "I didn't think you would actually be scared. You always act so tough." Had I screwed up? I shifted my weight.

"I wasn't scared," Morticia said brusquely, finally looking at me. "You just surprised me. Now we need to go clean your hand off."

I looked at the scratch. "It's not that bad."

"Cats have bacteria that grows on their claws; you could get cat scratch fever. The infection starts spreading, hits your heart, and bam, you're dead in three days."

"That sounds histrionic," I said.

"Don't call me a liar," Morticia scolded. "Now where is your apartment? You better have a first aid kit."

"Not gonna take me back to your place?" I teased, waggling my eyebrows.

She grabbed me by the arm. "I live in a baking flophouse with over a dozen horny gold diggers who want nothing more than to string you up on a Christmas tree and milk you for all your net worth."

"Sounds pretty kinky, to be honest. I might dig it."

"Yeah, until you're on divorce number three, paying for a pack of kids who aren't even yours."

"Dang," I said as we headed in the direction of my building. "I wasn't thinking that far ahead."

"Of course you weren't," Morticia said with a sigh.

The doorman at the building gave me an odd look when I approached with Morticia.

"This isn't what it looks like," Morticia explained in a clipped tone when the doorman opened the door. "We're coworkers."

"Oh, I gotcha." He looked relieved. "Jonathan never brings women here."

"Geez, way to blab my business!" I complained when we were in the elevator.

Morticia had a slight smirk on her lips. "So either you aren't the sexual Casanova you want everyone to think you are, or you're just having sex in public places and other people's apartments."

"That's how you know you aren't with a serial killer," I explained as we rode up to the top floor of the renovated factory building. "People are less likely to kill you in their own space, because then they have to clean up the mess."

She raised an eyebrow.

"I'm just making you more comfortable," I said breezily, "since you are coming up to my condo." I swiped my keycard at my front door. "Welcome!"

"This is such bullshit!" she said derisively, peering inside.

"Honestly, this is the first time I've brought a nonfamily female up here, and I'm a little disappointed by your reaction. This was a very expensive penthouse, I assure you."

"Penthouse?" She snorted. "This is what, the eighth floor?"

"It's at the top of the building, Morticia. That makes it a penthouse."

"Penthouses are supposed to be on top of a tower," she said as we went in. "Like the slit on the tip of a cock."

That made me perk up.

Clang! went my brain. There's a woman here.

Clang!

You haven't had sex in six weeks.

Clang!

She said "dick." That means she wants you.

Clang!

"How about some Christmas music," I said in a rush, tapping the home automation tablet and filling the living room with Bing Crosby's crooning.

Morticia scowled. "Where's your bathroom?"

"Back here." I gestured.

You can't take her to the master suite!

But what if this was all a ruse for her to sleep with you?

Or maybe it's a test, and she'll sleep with you if you don't act like a dick. You should not have told her to go to the master. Tell her to use the half bath.

But Morticia was already walking down the hall.

"Wait!" I said, grabbing her shoulder and dodging another swipe from the cat, which was now perched on top of her head. "I'll get it."

"My cat clawed you," she pointed out.

"It's my house; I'm the host," I said more forcefully than I meant to.

She gave me a strange look then returned to the living room.

In the master bath, I leaned against the counter. "Why is it so hot in here?" I wheezed, ripping off my suit jacket, undoing my tie, then throwing open a window. As the cold winter air streamed in, I fished in a drawer for the first aid kit.

I shouldn't have let Morticia come back here. I was clearly on the verge of losing my self-control.

"You look flushed," Morticia said from the doorway.

I jumped.

"Why is the window open?" she asked.

"It's hot," I croaked.

She reached up and felt my forehead. "Maybe the infection has set in."

I grabbed her hand then thought better of it and released her. Man, I was in bad shape.

She took the first aid kit and grabbed a disinfectant wipe and took my hand. Her fingers were long and her motions sure as she cleaned the cat scratch with the alcoholic wipe then rubbed Neosporin on it and stuck on a Band-Aid.

"We'll see if he makes it through the night," she told Salem, who was sitting on the bathroom counter, tail curled around him.

"Does that mean you're going to stay here and play nursemaid all night?"

"No," Morticia said tartly, washing her hands, "that means I'm calling your sister and letting her know to put you on plague watch."

CHAPTER 11

Morticia

I am a night person. I think best at night. I do my most creative work at night. I usually am not awake until noon at least, and I don't go to sleep until five a.m. This was fortunate, because when I returned from Jonathan's, the bachelorettes were still up, and it looked as if they had set off a cake bomb in the kitchen.

"We made cake penis pops!" one of them shouted at me over the din of the movie *Elf* blaring on the large flat-screen TV.

Of course Jonathan kept the nice apartment for himself and stuck us all in here like cows.

I sighed loudly as they continued to chatter then went into my shared room and slammed the door.

Salem purred as I stroked him under the chin and took out my sketchbook to plan what I was going to say during my internship interview the next morning.

❄ ❄ ❄

Salem was nibbling on my hair, tugging it, the next morning. I yawned. It was ten a.m. Too early for me. I dragged myself through showering and pulling on clothes. The studio was empty, as we weren't doing a bake-off competition that day.

"I wish I had a better background," I told Salem as I clicked on the video link I had been sent by the Getty internship program. The Christmas decorations I'd put up in the studio the week before twinkled under the lights. The whole place smelled like gingerbread and sugar.

"What a festive scene!" one of the interviewers, an older woman in a Chanel suit, remarked when the video chat screen opened.

"Yes, quite," a short, balding man with a rosy complexion added.

"This was just some paid decorating work I was asked to do," I explained. "Nothing special."

"If I'm not mistaken, is that ornament arrangement that I see to the left of your screen an homage to Fang Fei's art biennial pavilion?" the woman asked.

I smiled. "So glad you noticed!"

The interview went smoothly after that. They asked me about various pieces in my portfolio and my philosophies on various restoration processes. They were impressed with my involvement in the Art Zurich Biennial Expo in Harrogate that summer.

"We were all there," the male interviewer gushed. "What an event! And what was done with that small town was miraculous."

"I'm sure it had nothing to do with all those good-looking billionaire Svensson brothers roaming around," the woman said slyly.

"They are easy on the eyes and handy when checks need to be signed," I said.

"And you have your own billionaire," the woman continued, eyes sparkling. "A Mr. Frost?"

I grimaced. So they'd heard about *The Great Christmas Bake-Off*.

"I wasn't actually going to be in the production," I said in a rush. "Of course, a reality TV show is not my cup of tea…"

"But it must be so inspirational," the woman said. "You could do a whole exposé on art, femininity, consumerism, and domestic ideals. It would be a great piece to submit for the scholarship for the internship."

Forget cake. Nothing perked me up like free money.

"Yes!" the man said excitedly. "We very recently had a generous endowment finalized, and a portion of the money is to be set aside for young interns. We ask that everyone submit an original art piece that speaks to what it means to be a young person in the twenty-first century. We'd love to have your vision included."

"I will absolutely send in a piece," I assured them.

After signing off the call, I carefully made sure I wasn't being watched then jumped up and down like a cheerleader.

> **Morticia:** *You are looking at the person who just aced her interview!*
> **Morticia:** *And there is a scholarship just waiting for me to pluck off of the tree!*
> **Lilith:** *Praise the goddess!*
> **Lilith:** *We're going to make an offering.*

Emma: *And we should order some celebratory pizza and cake. You can't eat offerings to the spirits.*

Lilith: *I mean you could but that's probably bad luck.*

Morticia: *I need an award-winning idea for an original art piece.*

Emma: *Do something food related since you're doing all that baking anyway.*

Lilith: *We'll do tea leaves and tarot after you get kicked off the competition.*

Lilith: *That will help you know what direction to go in with the judges.*

In just a few more hours, I would be back in Harrogate. Sure, I would have to suffer through living with Penny and Garrett for a few weeks, as I'd told them to go ahead and renovate the carriage house, because I was absolutely winning that internship. If they became too much, I would find somewhere else to live. Shoot, I'd sleep in the park if it meant I didn't have to suffer through another night of nonstop baking and Christmas music.

The contestants were supposed to assemble in Jonathan's bar across the street to send the next bachelorette off on the Christmas float to freedom. I was a little early, but since I was sure I was about to leave, I decided to celebrate prematurely with a cocktail.

"You can't bring that cat in here," the bartender told me.

"He's my emotional support animal," I said, leveling my gaze at him.

He sighed.

"Come on, it's not like anyone else is in here."

"Yeah, because its eleven a.m.," Jonathan said, sauntering up to the bar. "Normal people are at work and not drinking." He made some sort of cryptic signal to the bartender. "Though it's not like anyone would insult you by calling you normal."

The bartender set about making a drink. I watched him.

"So..." Jonathan drawled, leaning against the bar counter.

I petted Salem.

Jonathan made a hurry-up motion. "You owe me a nice compliment. I saved your cat and was severely injured in the process."

I grabbed his hand and undid his watch.

"We're in a public place, Morticia!"

"Cool it. I'm checking for an infection," I said, trailing my fingers around the cut on his wrist. I ignored how large his hand was and the way the tendons jumped under my fingertips, and the muscle rippled on his forearm when I unbuttoned the cuff links and pushed up his sleeve.

This is the closest to a man you've been in a long time...
Not true. Last night, we were much closer.

I swallowed then cleared my throat. "I don't feel any heat or inflammation."

"I'm flattered you care about me!" Jonathan grinned. "I feel like I'm slowly moving into your sphere of important people."

"Don't get your hopes up. The last thing I needed was for Belle to come after me because my cat put her little brother in the hospital."

The bartender slid my drink over. I reached for it.

Jonathan cocktail-blocked me. "I want my nice comment," he purred.

I blew out a breath. "You look very rich today."

Jonathan frowned then leaned forward. "Do I look like I'm worth ten figures or a measly nine?"

"How is two billion dollars not good enough for you?" I asked him.

"I need at least sixteen so they'll put my picture in the *TechBiz* magazine in February."

"I hope you're not banking on the alcohol sales and *The Great Christmas Bake-Off* to raise your net worth," I said with a snort.

"No," he said, rocking back on his heels, "I have a bigger reindeer in the stable for that!"

"I see that we're at the point of the day where we're doing Christmas puns. I'll take my drink now."

"And I'll take my compliment now," Jonathan said, picking up the drink.

"You don't need any more ego stroking."

Jonathan inspected the drink. He did cut a fine figure. The bar must have been designed with him in mind. With his platinum hair, charcoal suit, and blue eyes, he looked electric against the masculine lines of the bar.

"A black old fashioned with cane sugar from Colombia, a splash of spring water, a booze-soaked black Luxardo maraschino cherry, and of course a dark blood orange and General George whiskey aged five years."

"Actually, it's the ten, sir," the bartender said, setting a bottle on the counter.

My fingers itched for my phone. The way Jonathan was holding the glass, the dark, almost black flesh of the blood orange, the way he studied the bottle…it was art. Well, arty enough to go on a magazine page and sell two-hundred-dollar bottles of whiskey. I snapped the photos.

Jonathan turned his head to me and grinned. "Like what you see?"

"You make an attractive pairing," I grumbled.

"I suppose that's the best I'm going to get from you," he stated with a dramatic sigh and passed me the drink.

I took a long sip. "Perfect."

Jonathan and the bartender gaped at me.

"What?"

"Usually, women want…" Jonathan gestured helplessly.

I raised an eyebrow.

"Just—" Jonathan said, tripping over his words, "they want, you know, fruity, fun drinks."

"They want juice with a little alcohol. That's not a cocktail," I said bluntly. "A cocktail is alcohol, alcohol, more alcohol, and a citrus peel. Honestly, the cherry is a little much, but," I said, plucking it neatly out of the glass tumbler, "there's something about booze-soaked fruit that melts my black little heart."

"Oh, Jonathan!" Keeley cooed in the fake sexy baby voice that made me want to suffocate myself with a gingerbread house. "Are you making drinks for everyone?"

"Yes," I said, leveling my gaze at him, "he was just telling me how much he enjoys a woman who likes a sweet, fruity drink."

"I love craft cocktails," Keeley said, punctuating the words with her high-pitched, braying laugh.

I took Salem and my cocktail to enjoy it by the window in peace. In the daylight, my window still looked clutch. The brownies were still there, artfully arranged. I snagged one.

"Still good," I told Salem. "That's why you need the cream cheese and the pumpkin—it keeps it gooey."

Though I was glad I was about to be kicked off the show, a part of me was…well, not sad to be going, but I would miss having a bar right across the street.

The rest of the contestants filed into the establishment.

"Before we start shopping for our next big Christmas bake-off challenge," Anastasia announced, "one of you, unfortunately, is going home. Morticia, please step up."

Salem, my drink, the rest of my brownies, and I went to stand in front of Anastasia and the cameras.

"Morticia, the judges were not impressed with your fall-themed brownies. Pumpkin is a Halloween item, and the judges also felt your dessert wasn't impressive enough."

I took a big bite of the brownie and chewed it noisily then slurped my cocktail for good measure. Damn, I was going to miss this.

"Keeley, please step up. You were the winner of this round. The judges loved your cake. It felt fun and surprising," Anastasia said.

Keeley preened.

"You are the winner of the baking challenge. However, Keeley, you lost the fan favorite challenge by a large margin," the hostess continued.

I snorted a laugh. "Guess Chloe stans didn't like that you stole her idea," I said.

"I didn't steal it!" Keeley insisted, nostrils flaring.

I was going home, and Keeley got owned? I guessed this was going to be a good day after all.

"That means you both tied for a middle-of-the-pack placement, and neither one of you is going home," Anastasia said.

Keeley's eye twitched. Mine wasn't much better.

"Someone has to be sent home," Keeley said shrilly after a tense moment. "Those are the rules. And it needs to be Morticia."

Anastasia ignored her and surveyed the rest of the bachelorette bakers.

"Fatimah," Anastasia called. A girl wearing a colorful headscarf came up. "While you made a passable dessert, the judges thought your deconstructed Turkish delight was a bit rubbery. Though you did not have the worst fan score, but because your baking score from the judges was so low, unfortunately, we have to send you home. I hope you and your family have a lovely holiday."

Fatimah was teary eyed as she hugged the new friends she had made. Meanwhile, I didn't know whether to gloat at Keeley or fall into a sobbing, drunken mess on the floor. How was I here for another week?

"For our remaining baking bachelorettes…Jonathan is still the prize. While we all love an attractive man with money, I'm sure we all want to take a peek under the hood. Therefore, the next date is going to be a hot tub party! So suit up. We're going shopping, ladies, but not for bathing suits—for baking ingredients!"

❄ ❄ ❄

"I can't do a hot tub party!" I groaned to Lilith. She and Emma had met me at the fancy imported food store, because I now needed to have them babysit Salem for me. Again. Because I was in *The Great Christmas Bake-Off* for another round. Again.

"Do you even own a bathing suit?" Emma asked me. "I don't think I've ever seen you go swimming."

"I don't go outside. I burn in the sun," I said flatly. "In summer, I stay hidden indoors."

"I don't even know if you can find a swimsuit to purchase right now," Lilith mused.

"Surely there are rich women in Manhattan who just jet off to their private islands and need an emergency swimsuit," Emma said. "We'll find one for you. Don't worry!"

"I can't believe you all think it's a given I'm getting in a hot tub."

"That's part of the competition," Emma said as she tossed packets of bacon into my cart. "Besides, I figured you would be all in on besting your cousin. You're always a stickler for revenge. I figured that maybe this was part of your long-range plan to get back at Keeley and ruin her life for ruining yours."

I looked over at my cousin. There was no question she was going to look great at the hot tub party. She had the perfect narrow waist, big boobs, and curvy hips that somehow coexisted with her thigh gap. Meanwhile, I had no boobs and was rail thin but had narrow hips like a tween boy, yet I still had chafing issues with my thighs.

"It's not fair."

"I know!" Emma said as she took a sample cheese cube from one of the smiling grocery store workers. "I can't believe she spread rumors around the school about the love potion you made for that kid. What was his name?"

"Justin," Lilith said.

"She pretended to be my friend," I snarled. "It was like three weeks after my mother dumped me and Lilith at our aunt and uncle's house. Keeley pretended to be friendly, saying that she was glad to have a few more sisters. She was the one who told me I should make the love potion for Justin. Then she offered to slip it into his food at lunch. Except instead, she shouted to the whole school that I had a crush on him and was trying to poison him so that he and I would be together in the afterlife."

I was breathing hard, and my jaw hurt from clenching my teeth. My aunt and uncle had been horrified. I had been immediately sent to a psych ward, while Lilith had been sent to a foster home. Fortunately, Mimi had stepped in and taken us. I still had been forced to go through years of therapy with dimwitted women who couldn't hack it in med school and kept showing me pictures of ink blots and asking me, "How does that make you feel?"

"I've been waiting for your epic revenge scheme," Emma said, taking an offered salami cube. "There needs to be some justice in the world. You're like a black widow weaving your web."

"The best revenge is a life well lived," I quoted.

"No, the best revenge," Lilith said, tossing blocks of dark chocolate into my cart, "is Nair in her shampoo bottle."

"That's not subtle enough for my tastes."

"You should steal Jonathan from her!" Emma said, clapping her hands in excitement.

"I'm not stealing him. I don't even want him," I scoffed, refusing to think about trailing my fingers over his hand.

"You have a small but dedicated fan base online," Emma said, pulling out her phone. "There's a Tumblr fan page and everything. Everyone loves that you're channeling early-2000s emo style. It's basically retro at this point."

Lilith said, "Just post a picture of Jonathan with a pithy caption, something like, 'Guess I'll have to keep seeing this guy around for another few days!'"

"Gross!"

"Do you have any good pictures of him?" Lilith asked, grabbing my phone out of my purse as I loaded a bag of icing sugar into my cart.

I had a pretty good idea of what I was going to make for my hot tub dish. I didn't want to think too hard about the challenge, because then I would have to think about Jonathan, and then I would have to think about how I was going to see him in no shirt, just swim trunks. He would be all wet and...

"So. Freakin'. Hot!" Lilith said giddily.

"I'm sorry, what happened to being a staunch feminist?" I complained to my sister as she salivated over the pictures of Jonathan I had taken in the bar earlier.

"There were totally sex rituals in the pagan religions. The Celtics were all about that sex life. They had orgies all over the place."

"That was all Roman propaganda," I retorted, trying to take the phone back.

"No. We are posting this picture," she said. "Then Emma and I are going to make caramel popcorn and laugh at the carnage when Keeley notices. You, of course, will be too busy being a hot tub nymph to partake with us, but we will screenshot the best comments for you."

CHAPTER 12

Jonathan

I wasn't sure if my libido could handle a hot tub party. I had barely been able to keep it together when Morticia had been doing nothing more than trailing her fingertips across my hand.

"You have to be the luckiest guy in New York right now!" Carl boomed. He had been waiting for me outside my office. "All those hot women in skimpy bikinis, a hot tub, and all the desserts, specially made for you, that you can eat." He nudged me. "You better watch your diet."

"Please. I already have it covered," I said. "I went for a ten-mile run instead of my usual five this morning."

"Greg will be pleased about that," Carl said. "He was worried you were going to lose your girlish figure. Oh shit!"

I turned to see my sister, in four-inch heels and a black skirt suit, striding over to us. "Come on, boys. We don't want to be late for Greg's meeting."

"Dude, no!" Carl whispered to me in horror. "She can't come to the meeting."

"Why?" Belle countered. In her heels, she was almost as tall as Carl, though I knew from experience that when my sister turned that cold gaze on a man, he and his balls shriveled up to the size of a peanut.

"I just—er—there are trade secrets!"

"*The Great Christmas Bake-Off* is my show, which my company is producing," Belle reminded him. "Jonathan is attending the meeting to discuss the performance of his…" She blew out a breath. "Alcohol company. It interfaces with *The Great Christmas Bake-Off*, which means it is in my purview."

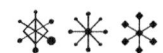

❋ ❋ ❋

"Did you tell Greg?" I whispered to Carl as we shuffled behind my older sister into the lobby of the Svensson Investment tower.

"I decided it would be better to surprise him. If I'd told him earlier, it might have given him a chance to stew in his anger and resentment and then explode all over everything when we showed up."

"I don't know. It could have given him a chance to cool off," I said uncertainly.

Carl looked concerned for a moment. "Ah, shit. Maybe I should have…"

"Carl!" Greg barked as he stepped off one of the elevators that let out onto the polished marble floors. "You better not have brought her here." He turned to Belle, who was completely unfazed. "This is a proprietary meeting," Greg spat at my sister. He seemed very angry.

I was concerned for a moment that he might actually hit her. I wasn't sure what had gone on between them. My older brother, Owen, had said that they'd had a, quote, "thing," but the tension in the lobby didn't seem remotely like even the most toxic aftereffect of any bad hookup I'd ever experienced.

"And that's my little brother, and we're pimping his alcohol on our show. If you're not talking about the alcohol sales, then I don't need to be here, of course," Belle said simply. "Maybe, instead, you're talking about a big potential land deal. Far be it from me to speculate, of course. I don't know what you do. You're so disorganized over here."

I had sworn up and down that I wouldn't talk to anyone about the land deal. The Svensons had sworn me to secrecy under pain of…not death, but they had threatened that they would tie me up and make me spend a weekend subjected to the whims of two dozen of their half-feral little brothers.

Unfortunately, it seemed Belle already knew or at least had an inkling about the pending Hamilton Yards deal. I looked up at the ceiling then at the floor—anywhere but at her. Because if she wanted to, she could make me spit it out. The woman should have been a CIA agent.

"There's no land deal," Greg and Carl's half brother, Hunter, called from across the lobby, putting his phone in his pocket. "Belle. Nice to see you again. Hope your business is going well."

"Likewise." She shook his hand.

"Hope Meg is well," Greg spat at Hunter.

Oof! *Shot off starboard, Captain.* Meg was Hunter's unrequited love. Carl had told me Hunter was in the middle of some sort of elaborate scheme to win her back. Personally,

I would have just groveled apologies, but hey, what did I know?

Hunter's nostrils flared slightly.

Belle looked between them. She was almost at eye level with the brothers, and the two gray-eyed men seemed slightly off-kilter at having my ice queen sister taking their measure. "Since there is no land deal, and we're all here to talk about Jonathan's alcohol vanity project, I look forward to the meeting," she said, striding into the elevator.

The elevator ride up was awkward. Carl looked between Hunter and Greg. "How the tables turn."

"Shut up!" they both barked at him.

"You know how I like my coffee," Belle stated to Greg when we stepped off the elevator.

"Get her coffee," Greg barked at Carl.

"What the—I don't know how she likes her coffee," he whispered frantically to me. "How does she like her coffee?"

"Black," I told him. "Double espresso."

"Dayum, your sister is a lot to handle."

"Yeah, she'll flay you alive."

"No kidding!" he said as he made the drink for Belle.

My sister and Greg were arguing when we returned to the conference room. Greg was losing.

Two more of Carl's half brothers, Weston and Blade, who owned the ThinkX consulting firm, were watching the volley.

"You can't honestly tell me that these are successful numbers," Belle was saying. "I don't know why you let him use that marketing firm. Those Instagram posts are terrible."

"It is Jonathan's company," Greg said through gritted teeth.

"That you are investing in and sit on the board of," Belle said sharply. "You share some of the blame. And now you expect me to devalue my brand so you can try and recoup some of your losses?"

"What's wrong with my company?" I growled.

"Your marketing is terrible," my sister said. "We're not posting these pictures your marketing consultants sent over on our social media."

"It is part of your contract," Greg insisted.

"You all are acting in bad faith!" Belle snapped.

Greg sighed. "It feels like you're here just to be petty."

"Really? Because it seems like you're still sore I stole a big development contract out from under you."

"Just because you won one contract doesn't make your investment firm hot shit. You barely have an office. In fact, if I'm not mistaken, your accountant works out of her apartment," Greg sneered. "You will never build up your company to be any real competition to mine."

Even though the Svenssons were investing heavily in my business and, hopefully, in the Hamilton Yards development, I wasn't going to let any of them speak to my family members that way, let alone my sister.

"Watch your tone," I snarled at Greg.

He and Belle both swiveled their gazes back to me. Next to me, Carl was silently freaking out.

"I don't need my little brother to defend me," Belle told me smoothly. "Greg is acting like any mediocre middle-management male when faced by a start-up that has the runway to grind him into the dirt. He's scared. And instead of innovating and cutting off some of the bloat in his company, he's stooping to personal attacks."

"Are you talking about me?" Carl piped up.

"Of course she's talking about you," Greg hissed at him.

"Gentlemen, I'm here to talk business, not run your therapy session," Belle said sharply.

"Agreed," Hunter said.

Greg opened his mouth.

"You aren't being rational," Hunter drawled to his brother, who shot him a death glare but kept his mouth shut.

"It's the holiday season," Hunter said to Belle. "Makes him emotional. Look, Jonathan's sales numbers are not good. We all understand that."

"It's only the first few days; give the product placement time to work!" I protested.

"It's December first," Hunter told me. "You're not hitting the benchmark now, and there's no reason to think you're going to hit it later."

"The problem," Weston explained, "is that Romance Creative is targeted toward women in a certain demographic. And these ads"—he pulled them up on the screen—"are not targeted to women. Really, I'm not sure who they're targeted to."

"They're for men who want to buy alcohol," I insisted.

"Uh-huh. So I ran numbers," Weston said, tapping his tablet to pull up an image on the large screen at the front of the room. "And actually, the numbers show that while yes, men do buy alcohol, it's not during Christmas. Instead, their wives, girlfriends, and mothers actually buy it as a gift for their men, or tell their men to purchase it for their fathers, brothers, or friends as gifts."

"All the men who are really into craft liquor had likely already made their purchases when you first launched earlier in the year," Blade added. "They aren't going to be who you're targeting during the Christmas blitz. You should be targeting women who love to shop. And you are targeting the opposite of that."

"Fuck!" I said, leaning back in my chair.

"We are seeing a bit of an uptick," Weston said, "but it looks like it's traced directly to the bake-off images. Let's pull up your online sales chart."

I felt sick as he called up the chart on the screen. The growth line was anemic. We could see that all my advertising since Black Friday had hardly done anything.

"What's that uptick there from today?" Belle asked, pointing.

"Running a sale maybe?" Blade said. "With this software we designed, you can get granular data. It looks like ninety percent of this traffic is coming from one Instagram post. From this morning by... who is this? The handle says Witches vs. Patriarchy."

"That's Morticia," I said, studying the profile picture.

Blade pulled up the post.

"That's me!" I said happily. It was the picture Morticia had taken at the bar. I preened as I added, "I look hot!"

"And yet somehow, we are all shocked that he doesn't have a handle on his company," Belle said.

Greg smiled slightly. He and Belle caught each other's eyes then immediately looked away, like two cats who didn't mean to be on the same shelf.

"Okay, so I'll just tell the marketing company to make more pictures and posts that will appeal to women," I said confidently. "Easy."

"Actually," Weston suggested, "you need to pay Morticia to do it, since she has the proven track record now. Also, you need someone nimble. Christmas is over in twenty-five days, so you need to move on this right now."

"Shit."

"Don't tell me you can't manage that," Hunter growled. "We've invested a lot of money in your company."

"Er...yeah," I said. "It will be fine. Morticia..."

Likes me? Hates me? She took that picture of me and posted it, so she must not hate me all that much...Maybe she was still mad I grabbed her in the park?

"I'll work it out with Morticia."

"I bet money that you don't," Weston said with a snort. "That meme of her throwing the candy cane dildo at you is all over the internet. She hates your guts!"

CHAPTER 13

Morticia

"Why are you posting pictures of him?" Keeley demanded, cornering me in the pantry and ruining my concentration.

I needed to find inspiration for a scholarship-winning art piece. But all I could think about was Christmas. The poppy holiday music that had been piped into the store on a loop was stuck in my head. I needed to listen to a Baroque funeral requiem and clear all the fake snow out of my mind.

I gave my cousin a flat look. "I don't know who you mean."

"Yes you do!" she insisted. "You're posting pictures of my future husband."

"So we've come to this part of the evening," I said, pinching the bridge of my nose.

"What part?" Keeley was confused.

"The part where you have completely given in to your delusions and think someone like Jonathan is going to willingly shackle himself to someone like you."

"Oh yeah? It's not like he's going to be with someone like you," Keeley shot back.

"I don't want him," I said slowly. "I am happiest alone with my cat."

"Because you're a weirdo," Keeley hissed. "You're going to die old and alone, eaten by that animal."

"Better than being bitch-slapped to death after you sleep with the wrong woman's husband."

Keeley huffed. "They weren't married then."

"Sarah is your own sister, and that was her fiancé. They were about to be married," I reminded her.

"You're jealous that I'm going to be Mrs. Frost. I have a plan. I'm going to get pregnant. Then he'll have to marry me or at least pay child support."

I rolled my eyes. "Jonathan's dumb, but he's not that dumb."

Keeley took a little pillbox out of her purse. "I have Santa's little helper," she said, shaking the box at me. "It's guaranteed to knock a grown man out for eight hours but still keep everything down there working."

"You can't drug someone and sleep with him!"

"I can if I'm his fiancée, which I will be when I win the contest."

❋ ❋ ❋

You cannot leave Jonathan to Keeley's mercy, I told myself. Though I dressed like a devil worshiper, I didn't consider myself a bad person. I could be malicious, but Jonathan didn't deserve to be tied to Keeley his whole life. However, if

I went to him and told him her plans, Keeley would just spin it like I was the crazy one, just like she had done freshman year, which had ended with me locked up in a psych ward.

"They're never going to be alone," I assured myself.

But how can you know?

"Morticia." Jonathan, hiding in a doorway, grabbed me as I walked back from the studio after dropping off my ingredients from the shopping trip.

"Stop grabbing people!" I demanded.

"Sorry!" he said, trying to dust me off and fix my clothes. I batted his hands away.

"Look," he said, "I need your help."

"No."

"You don't even know what I'm going to ask!"

"I don't want to help you with anything," I said, crossing my arms.

Jonathan grabbed my arm and shoved his phone into my face. "Can you take more pictures like that?"

"Of you?"

"Of me and the alcohol. A ton of people bought this bourbon when you posted the image," he explained.

"I'm not doing free work for you," I told him.

"I'm going to pay you," he scoffed.

"I cannot be bought."

Jonathan narrowed his eyes. "Name your price."

"No price."

I needed to concentrate on the scholarship and keeping Keeley from drugging Jonathan and getting pregnant. I could not also be responsible for propping up his dopey company.

"What happened to that expensive marketing firm?"

"Fired them," he said flatly. "So I'm desperate. I need you to work for me!"

I pointed to his phone. "You have a camera."

"Yes, but I don't know what women want!" he pleaded.

"So all those women you were sleeping with were faking it," I remarked, raising an eyebrow and inspecting my black nail polish. "You don't say."

"Wouldn't you like to find out?" He grinned.

"Like I said, I'm very busy trying not to lose my mind with all the Christmas in the air. Maybe try someone on Fiverr."

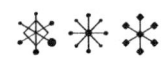

❋ ❋ ❋

After ditching Jonathan, I went outside to the neighboring property. I sat on a bench, surrounded by nothing but large sculptures, half-finished murals, and blessed quiet.

Unfortunately, though it was an inspirational space, I had no idea what I was going to do for the scholarship piece. If my entire life trajectory and livelihood hadn't been riding on this project, I wouldn't have been so anxious. I forced myself to just close my eyes and sketch. That usually started the creative juices flowing.

My pen scratched across the paper as the cold winter wind chilled my nose. After a few minutes, I opened my eyes. I had drawn an entire Christmas gingerbread house, complete with frolicking snowmen and happy reindeer.

"This is garbage."

I tore the page out, balled it up, then tried again. When I opened my eyes the next time, on my pad was a sketch of Jonathan, naked, wearing nothing but a Santa hat. And I do mean nothing.

"I bet his dick isn't even that big," I grumbled, ripping the page out and wadding it up.

"There you are!" Lilith and Emma called as they picked their way through tufts of weeds to my concrete bench.

"Guess what!" Lilith said happily. She and Emma were practically jumping up and down. Salem, riding on Lilith's shoulder, was looking a little pukey. "We got a job!"

"Doing what?"

"We—or, well, you and Lilith—are going to be making marketing material. I told Jonathan that I had to be the manager though," Emma gushed. "We get per diem and all the alcohol we can drink!"

"I'm sorry, did you say Jonathan?"

"Yeah, he practically got on his knees and begged us," Lilith said.

"It was very hot!" Emma said, flapping her sweater to fan herself.

"I already told him no," I said frowning.

"Come on," Lilith begged. "We need the money."

"I'm working on my internship scholarship submission," I said primly.

"Oh yeah?" Emma asked. "What have you got?" Before I could stop her, she snatched the balled-up pieces of sketch paper.

"Oh my god!" she squealed. "You saw him naked?"

"No! Give that back! That's private," I demanded.

"Oh," Lilith drawled, "private. How interesting."

"You're going to see him shirtless tonight at the hot tub," Emma said breathlessly. "Everyone online is talking about it. There are requests for thirst pictures of him. I have this great idea that the more Hillrock West alcohol people buy, the more revealing the photo we're going to post. What do you think?"

"I'm not doing a nude photo shoot of Jonathan," I told them, gathering up my drawing supplies.

"It would be more about the strategic placement of poinsettias and liquor bottles," Lilith said.

"But still tasteful," Emma insisted.

"Sounds complicated, which is why I already told Jonathan no," I told them. "But you two have fun."

My twin gave me an odd look. "You have to be in charge of the creative. That's why Jonathan hired us."

"Nope," I said, heading back to the studio building.

"Do it!" Lilith begged. "We're broke! Salem will starve! I bought him special cat food from the high-end grocery store, and now he won't touch the store-brand cat food. He only wants this super-expensive, all-natural stuff. We can expense it with Jonathan and pretend it's part of our dinner!"

"Not to mention," Emma said craftily, waving one of my sketches around, "he would be the perfect inspiration for your art."

"I'm not submitting pictures of Jonathan for my scholarship."

"You don't have any better ideas."

She was right. I didn't have any better ideas, and the clock was ticking. But I was not stooping to making art centered around Jonathan Frost.

"This is a win-win-win all around," Emma coaxed.

"Plus free alcohol," Lilith reminded me. "We just give the bartender our account number!"

"A drink would be nice right about now, and I do need backup cash if I don't win that scholarship," I said slowly. "Which is looking more likely, because I have no art direction."

"That's the spirit," Lilith said in excitement. "Emma and I will start working on a posting schedule and ideas, because we know you're about to be getting busy in the hot tub."

"Take lots of photos!" Emma said.

A text from Jonathan popped up as I followed my friends into the studio building.

Jonathan: *I am now your boss.*
Morticia: *Correction, you're my customer.*
Jonathan: **Wink emoji* and it sounds like customer service comes with a bikini and baked goods.*

If Jonathan thought he was going to see me in a bikini, he had another thing coming.

CHAPTER 14

Jonathan

I was probably more excited than necessary about the hot tub date. The Romance Creative production company had set up a whole patio and hot tub off of the studio. The bachelorettes made their various hot tub–friendly desserts while the production company took B-roll of me walking around and flirting with the contestants.

Morticia studiously ignored me, but I was going to have her soon enough. I wondered what type of swimsuit she would wear. I wished it would be just us in the hot tub, alone, at night, with candles and snow falling. The chill air would make her nipples hard, and I'd suck them through the skimpy swimsuit I was sure she would be wearing…

"You need to change," Dana told me. She ushered me into another room, where cameras were set up and a selection of swim trunks decorated in various Christmas characters was waiting. I chose the red pair covered with dancing Santas and started to strip off my jacket.

Dana raised an eyebrow as the cameras flocked around me.

I grinned at her. "Come on, you know I'm sexy!"

"You're my friend's little brother."

"I'm not that little," I said.

"Just give us some nice shots," she said, rolling her eyes. "We're using these as part of the promo."

After changing and adding a Santa hat to complete my look, I settled down in the hot tub as the first of the bachelorettes came out, bearing a tray of baked goods and cocktails.

"I made peppermint ice cream floats with whiskey," she said proudly. "And to snack on, holiday sugar cookie bars with cream cheese frosting."

She was curvy, and her boobs bobbed when she slipped into the steamy pool. Her hands ran over my chest, but even though we were wearing far fewer clothes and were in a much more intimate position, I didn't get an electric spark like I had when Morticia had simply touched my hand.

"These are good," I said after taking a polite bite. Actually, the cookie bar was dry. I took a sip of the cocktail to wash it down. It was more like a milkshake. I loved sugar as much as the next person, but this was a lot, and the evening was just getting started.

Another bachelorette paraded out with her offering. Keeley gave me a sultry look. "I made adorable Christmas tree mousse cups with a spiked chocolate malt cocktail."

I took a bite of the mousse.

"It's made with white chocolate so that I could dye it green," Keeley said, giggling as she stepped into the steaming hot tub.

The mousse coated my tongue, and I took a sip of the chocolate malt to try and find some relief. With the heat from the hot tub, all I wanted was a tall glass of ice water and to jump into a snowbank to cool off.

"You know," Keeley purred while I tried to think of waterfalls and blizzards, "I have another sweet treat you can eat if you want to try." She drew snowflakes in the water droplets on my chest then reached up to cup a hand along my jaw.

"Next contestant!" a producer said. He waved to the glass garage door that opened between the porch and the back patio. "Morticia, just make sure that you walk toward camera C, please."

I perked up. Morticia!

I had run through a few scenarios regarding what she might be wearing. Would she go on-brand with a skimpy spiderweb string bikini or ironic with a retro Christmas-themed two-piece?

"What the fuck are you wearing?" Keeley asked loudly as Morticia paraded out with her tray.

"That's not a bathing suit," I said, frowning.

"Actually," Morticia clarified, "this is a bathing suit. In fact, it is a pattern modeled on one of the first instances of such an item."

"You're wearing a dress and pants!" Keeley complained.

"Pantaloons," Morticia corrected, handing me a tall, frosty glass of ice water.

I took it gratefully, gulping it down.

"You can't bring water for your cocktail," Keeley insisted.

"Just a palette cleanser to wash the trash out of his mouth," Morticia said.

I still couldn't believe what she was wearing. Morticia had on stockings, thin leather shoes, and a dark charcoal-gray dress with a collar and short puffed sleeves.

"Are you actually swimming with all that on?" I asked in shock.

"Of course," Morticia replied. She handed me a donut then carefully stepped into the hot tub and waded right to the middle, her bathing suit floating around her like a bloom of ink. "Now eat your donut. It has bacon on it."

I took a bite. It did have bacon. The icing had bourbon in it and had a light burnt-caramel flavor that contrasted nicely against the salty, crispy bacon.

"Shit," I mumbled, taking another bite. "This is the best thing I've ever eaten. Do you have any more?"

"They didn't want you to ruin your appetite," she told me with a slight smug smile that I imagined she might wear after she got me off. "But I'm sure someone might save you some."

She handed me the other cold glass on the tray. "Drink up before the ice melts. I made a mistletoe martini with the elderflower liqueur," she said.

The cocktail was bright, fresh, and ever so slightly tart. The cranberry garnishes burst in my mouth when I bit down on them, complementing the elderflower liqueur.

"Thoughts?" Morticia asked. "Comments?" She lay back in the water, buoyed by all her skirts.

The Victorians might have actually been onto something, because when she sat back up, the fabric clung around her curves enticingly.

"I need another donut."

❄ ❄ ❄

I was not going to get another donut, however. Instead, I was subjected to hypersweet dessert after hypersweet cocktail. When the bake-off was finally done, I felt nauseous and too hot. I was also pretty drunk.

Morticia glared at my hand when I held it out to her to help her out of the hot tub.

"You can't possibly hate me so much that you'd rather drown in the hot tub than let me help you," I slurred.

She took the offered hand. "I was more concerned that you were going to fall in and drown."

Fuck. I wanted to peel her out of those layers of clothes and fuck her in the pool.

"Or," I murmured in her ear, "were you worried that you might have given me the wrong idea by letting me see your bare ankles? Trying to tempt me with something else sweet to eat?"

"I would have thought you would be all sugared out, but I suppose I underestimated you," she replied, shoving me away.

"Oh, I'm definitely about to barf up a lot of different colors, but I think I can manage it if you're feeling up to it," I said with a crooked grin.

"Uh, no. I work for you now, remember?" she said, wringing out her dress.

"You're a consultant, and I'm your customer," I corrected.

"Yes, and I don't need to give you a reason to sue when your harebrained plan goes down the drain."

"It won't," I said confidently. "I have complete faith in you, and I expect to see great things at the meeting tomorrow."

Now that I was out of the hot tub and the winter wind was freezing the droplets of water on my skin, I was feeling much better. But Morticia seemed cold. All that sopping-wet fabric was starting to freeze, and her already pale complexion was getting even paler.

I wrapped an arm around her shoulders and led her inside. "Need any help undressing?"

"No thanks. I've spent as much time in close proximity with you as I want to. Besides, after all the sugar you've eaten, I have no desire to play nursemaid to you," she added.

After grabbing a towel from one of the producers and dripping off to a bathroom, I went in search of another donut. Though, yes, I had eaten a lot of sugar, I had a high tolerance. The producers had just finished taking pictures of the baked goods, so I snagged several of the donuts and went back outside. I let the freezing air chill my skin, to the shocked looks of the production staff.

"Hey there, hot stuff—or should I say cold stuff?" Dorothy shouted. Her headlamp glared in my face, and I squinted. The older woman was riding a unicycle and was dressed in a sparkly red catsuit and a red Santa hat. Two geese raced after her.

I still had my own Santa hat on, and I tipped it at her. "You ready to sell me that property yet?" I joked.

"Maybe if you keep posting all those thirst pictures on Instagram," she replied, jumping off the unicycle with more spryness than someone half her age. She came over with her phone. "This picture of you in this hot tub is criminal! I can see how you have all these women hanging off of you the way you ate that donut."

On the company Instagram feed was a frankly lecherous video of me eating the bacon donut Morticia had made.

"Seriously, was someone sucking your dick under there or what?" Dorothy asked.

I silently handed her one of my remaining donuts. She took a bite.

"Holy moly, that's good!"

"Life changing."

❄ ❋ ❅

"Boss man!" Carl said later when I walked into my condo building. "These numbers are killer! The bourbon is sold out. There's a waiting list. Weston told us to up the prices, so I increased them by ten percent. We could be profitable in a few days. Everyone is talking about it! Also, where the fuck are your clothes, man?"

I was still wearing my swim trunks. They were almost frozen, but I loved the cold. Plus it kept the sugar nausea down.

"Think I'm going to eat dry toast for dinner," I told him.

He followed me into my condo then handed me a parchment-colored envelope bearing fancy calligraphy script. "That witch girl dropped that off for you."

I opened it as I walked into the kitchen. There was a note on an envelope of pungent herbs.

FOR YOUR HEADACHE.

Now that I was out of the cold, I did feel a headache coming on.

"You're not going to drink that, are you?" Carl asked in horror. "It might be poison!"

"No way!" I said, grinning broadly as I turned on the kettle. "This means she likes me."

CHAPTER 15

Morticia

"You poisoned me!" Jonathan exclaimed when Lilith and Emma and I walked into the conference room of the offices of Hillrock West Distillery the next morning.

Lilith and Emma, excited to have an expense account and unlimited alcohol, had spent the rest of the previous evening in the bar, talking to fans online, swapping recipes, and posting thirst pics of Jonathan with food, of Jonathan with alcohol, and of food and cocktails by themselves. Because I did not want to be trapped in the apartment of Christmas hell, I'd stayed down at the bar with them. Now it was eight in the morning, my usual bedtime, and here I was in a meeting, already being yelled at.

I would not stand for it. "It's not poison!" I yelled back at him. "I'm drinking it myself."

"It did vile things to me," he bellowed.

"It cleaned you out. Those were fresh herbs. I picked them myself a couple days ago."

Jonathan gave me a horrified look. "You picked those where?"

"Off the vacant property down the street," I said, sipping my tea and wishing I was in a dark bedroom with blackout curtains, a candle, and my cat. Instead I was here with not just one but several morning people.

"You can't eat all that sugar and drink all that alcohol and not have ill effects," I lectured Jonathan. "Do you feel dehydrated? Foggy headed?"

"No," he said shortly then looked thoughtful. "Actually, I feel great! You're a miracle worker! Too bad we didn't have that tea in college, right Carl?"

They fist-bumped. I gagged.

Jonathan clapped his hands. "What's cracking, ladies?"

"You if you ever use that word again," I said, my eyes slits.

The sun was glaring through the curtains, bouncing off the tinsel on the tree in the conference room, and blinding me. I slipped on my round, dark glasses. It was slightly better, but I still had a headache. I also still did not have a clear direction for my art project, and the clock was ticking.

"We have a schedule all made up for posting pictures to the site," Emma said. She had coffee in one hand and a color-coded and tabbed three-ring binder in the other. "You are the biggest draw to get people on the page in the first place. Once they're in our sphere of marketing and see all the yummy desserts and cocktails you can create with the alcohol, it's super easy to convince people to buy. Plus," she added, "we have this great idea to set up a special chat room for people who have bought the alcohol. We'll post extra-special content there."

"I'll have my software engineers set that up for you," Jonathan promised.

Outside in the office, his employees were having an impromptu breakfast party and watching the sales report chart climb.

"That's all from the stuff we posted last night," Lilith explained. "Carl gave me access to your special software from ThinkX."

"Between the company Instagram posts and *The Great Christmas Bake-Off*, women are ripping off their panties and whipping out their credit cards," I said blandly, causing Jonathan to choke on his coffee.

❋ ❋ ❋

A few hours later, after yet another bachelorette had been chucked off Christmas Island, we were back out shopping for the next round of the bake-off.

Even though I was wearing my favorite shirt that said ...AND THAT'S WHY MY HOUSE IS FULL OF SPIDERS, I still felt like a zombie.

"You look like shit," Keeley hissed to me. "Where were you last night?"

"Working."

"On one of your ridiculous art projects, I bet," she said snidely. "You should be working on how not to scare off men."

"She has plenty of interest from men," Emma said, jumping to my defense.

Keeley pursed her lips. "So now you have your legbeard, forever-alone squad following you around? I guess the walking would be good for her." Keeley tipped her head toward Emma.

Emma shrank slightly.

Cold fury flowed through me. Emma had always struggled with her weight and was sensitive about it. I would be damned if I was going to let Keeley get away with making mean comments.

"If you must know," I drawled, "I was working on my grand plan to steal Jonathan out from under you and utterly humiliate you in the process."

My cousin's nostrils flared. "As if you're going to be in this competition much longer."

"I was just saved for yet another round this morning," I reminded her. "The judges thought my cocktail and donuts were fantastic."

"They said it wasn't restaurant quality," she countered.

"And they thought your mousse wasn't fit for selling at a gas station," I scoffed.

"Jonathan loved it!" she cried.

"Jonathan didn't like it," I sneered, "but he did like what I was serving. In fact, he asked me to come back to his condo and make him another round."

Keeley was shaking with anger. "You're going to regret this! I'm going to take you down!" she said shrilly. Then she stomped off down the aisle of the store.

"Oh my god, that was epic!" Emma exclaimed. "Did Jonathan really want you to go up to his condo?"

"He didn't blatantly ask. It's not like I actually want to go up there. It's bigger than the one I'm living in, but it's not anything, you know, super fancy."

Lilith and Emma clutched each other, shocked. "Wait, you've been up in his apartment?" my twin demanded.

"Why are you two acting like this is a big deal? He's just some douche with too much money."

"And you went into his condo at night alone," Emma said.

"Not alone."

"So it was a gang-bang orgy situation? I mean, I'm not here to judge," Lilith said.

"Salem was with me," I told my twin.

"You have to sleep with him," Emma said, grabbing my arm, "and take pictures and post them online."

"No way!"

"At least send them to Keeley; she'll flip her shit!" Lilith said.

I grabbed bags of candy sugar to throw into my cart. I'd made art out of sugar before. "I'm not sleeping with a guy just to make some girl jealous; I won't stoop to that level. I will, however," I said, "win the competition, smear the floor with her, and cackle loudly as she's voted off."

CHAPTER 16

Jonathan

"You have to do a photo shoot," Morticia announced. I jumped slightly; it was as if she had appeared out of thin air. However, I was glad she was there. I had been wandering down a thought path that I usually tried to stay away from: the constant worry that everyone I loved was going to leave me. Sarah had. Belle had. She hadn't seemed happy at the meeting with Greg and the Svensson brothers. I needed to do a good job; I needed Hillrock West Distillery to be a success. If I wasn't good enough, she might leave again.

As it was, this was the most I had seen her since she had returned after having disappeared a few years ago without a word. I was almost drunk on the attention, even though most of her comments to me were some flavor of big-sister bossy. I still loved it. It felt like back when we were kids and it was Christmas, and my mom would put Belle in charge of making the house perfect for the marathon of parties my parents hosted.

"How did you even get in here?" I asked Morticia.

She held out a lanyard. "Carl gave me a keycard."

I smiled at her. "So you can come up and see me at all hours of the night?"

Her face remained a perfect mask. "No."

"So you're not spreading a little Christmas cheer?" I leaned forward in my seat.

"Don't let the nails confuse you," she replied, displaying a set of freshly painted fingernails that had tiny Christmas scenes meticulously drawn on them. A few nails even sported the Hillrock West Distillery logo.

She set a bottle of alcohol on my desk then pushed me back into my chair and swung me around.

"I like a woman who's forceful," I half joked. Really, I wanted her to straddle me and ride my cock.

"Bake-off starts in two hours. I don't want to lose the good light before your face gets too puffy with all the sugar you're about to consume," she said tartly as she grabbed my tie then deftly undid it. She snaked the fabric from my neck and draped it around her own then studied me with a practiced eye, her mouth ever so slightly open.

I could just lean up and kiss her.

Except my multibillion-dollar net worth and my company were on the line. I couldn't afford to alienate Morticia. I needed her.

I'm a great kisser; nothing would be alienating about it.

Morticia unbuttoned my white dress shirt, popping up the collar. She stood back and examined me.

I gave her my best bedroom eyes.

She reached over and ran her fingers through my hair, and the touch alone was enough to end me. My dick was half hard, and there were dancing elves in my vision, reminding me that it had now been seven weeks since I'd been laid.

I shifted in the chair to ease some of the pressure on my balls.

"Yeah, that's good," Morticia said in her raspy voice as she held up her phone to take pictures. "Spread your legs like that a little bit."

"Isn't that my line?" I said before I could stop myself. I froze slightly.

Was she going to tase me? Hit me? Fuck me?

The artist extended her hand, her nails sharp as talons. I flinched slightly as they grazed my cheek then reached for the bottle of brandy and handed it to me.

"No," she purred, "that's my line."

Hot fucking damn. My dick jumped.

There was more smirking from Morticia. "Yeah," she said, "lick your lips a little bit, and think sexy thoughts."

I pulled at my shirt collar. It was boiling hot in here. "Am I giving you sexy thoughts?" I asked in a deep voice.

"You're giving me all the sexy thoughts," she said. She leaned over me and grabbed my jaw in one hand, her nails lightly pressing into the skin, then ran her thumb over my mouth before snapping a few more shots.

The elves that had been dancing in my vision were now taking turns pummeling me with toy hammers. Morticia was so close to me, not even a foot away, inspecting the pictures, I could just reach out and—

"I think I have what I need," she said.

"I don't have what I need," I said, reaching out and resting a hand on her waist. Her eyes met mine and flicked down to my crotch then back up.

"I have the bake-off." She abruptly turned and left.

Fuck.

"Make me proud," I called after her, trying to salvage the moment.

Double fuck.

※ ※ ※

Morticia was waiting outside the studio an hour later. I had needed that much time to calm down. I was fighting a nasty battle with myself not to jerk off in my office. It was all glass, for fuck's sake. I had barely started to salvage my sale; I couldn't be plastered all over the news for acting like a pervert.

But all I could think about was Morticia—the curve of her waist under the heavy fabric, the smoky sage smell of her.

"I'm sorry," I said to her. "I'm just losing my mind a bit. That was totally inappropriate. Also, you still have my tie. Wait." I peered at the girl. "You're not Morticia."

"I am her twin, and I will be here to take candid thirst shots. The photo shoot she did of you is doing awesome, by the way." Lilith showed me the post.

"That's graphic," I said, reading the comments.

"There are a number of women who wrote that they got off to the video of Morticia running her nails all over your face," Lilith stated.

There was only one woman I wanted to get off all over my face though.

Morticia's twin and her friend—and for some reason, her cat—all busied themselves with prepping for their social media image creations while I answered emails on my phone and waited for *The Great Christmas Bake-Off* to start.

I wondered what Morticia would wear. The bake-off was holiday party themed. Everyone was supposed to dress in a Christmas costume.

"Here's your outfit," Belle said, handing me a garment bag.

"I'm not wearing a costume," I said, looking up from my phone.

My older sister didn't say a word.

I sighed loudly. "Are you serious? I'm in a suit! I'm dressed up as a CEO."

"It's not a Halloween party," my older sister said, rolling her eyes. "You're supposed to dress up in a nice outfit."

"Oh," I said, taking the bag and unzipping it. It contained a blue velvet tuxedo jacket with black pants and a black silk bow tie. "This is not my usual style."

Belle made a threatening noise.

"But I guess I can wear this," I said grudgingly.

"You better," she warned.

When I walked into the bake-off studio, all the other bachelorettes were also dressed up, most of them in fifties-style dresses with lots of petticoats and pearls. Except for Morticia.

I burst out laughing, the cameras catching me doubling over. "What are you wearing?"

CHAPTER 17

Morticia

The producers had said that we were supposed to dress up for this next bake-off challenge. That meant a costume. I hadn't been to a Christmas party before, preferring to wait out the season from the comforts of my bedroom surrounded by candles, tea, and baked goods. However, I did love an occasion to dress up.

Clearly, if this was a Christmas costume party, I was going as Krampus, the half goat, half demon that followed Saint Nicholas around Europe, punishing the bad children.

"What are you doing?" Emma exclaimed when she saw me.

"I'm late," I said, hurrying past her, the chains of the costume clanging as I jogged. The fur goat suit was already making me sweat. Fortunately, I had forgone a mask and instead had meticulously applied my makeup then attached the horns on a headband.

"Forget being late," Emma said. "You're going to scare everyone! This is Christmas not Halloween."

"Oof," I said when I opened the door to the studio to take my place at my station and saw all the other girls' outfits. "I think I may have misread what this bake-off challenge was supposed to be about. Took it too far…"

"I'll say!" Lilith giggled. "Never change, Morticia!"

All the production staff were muffling their laughter as I walked in. A part of me felt the icy hand of embarrassment. It was just like high school.

"What are you wearing?" Jonathan burst out then doubled over laughing.

Anastasia, a smile playing around her face, remarked, "And what are you supposed to be?"

"A freak!" Keeley spat. She was wearing one of those retro dresses from the fifties with a corset, petticoats, and heels.

I drew myself up to my full height, which was an extra foot with the horns. "I am Krampus," I announced theatrically.

"While this is supposed to be a dress-up-for-the-holidays challenge, I suppose Krampus isn't totally out of place for Christmas," Anastasia said. "Of course, before we start the challenge, one of you is going home."

The bachelorettes all held hands and hugged each other, their sparkly makeup glittering. I rattled my chains and tried to ignore the bit of metal that was poking into my lower back.

Across the soundstage, Jonathan was struggling to keep it together. He caught my eye and mouthed, *You look hot.*

After Anastasia announced that the girl who had made Christmas Jell-O shots yesterday was leaving, Jonathan headed in my direction. He looked—not hot. I refused to think of him as hot, but I did appreciate the creativity he had put into the outfit he was wearing. Yeah. That.

The velvet tux was like a second skin on him. The blue brought out the color of his eyes, making them bright as starlight.

"I can't tell," Jonathan said, taking me by the hand and spinning me around, "if you really want to be here or hate being here. This is a lot of effort to put in for a Christmas show."

"Someone has to uphold artistic integrity," I sniffed as I began the tedious process of melting down sugar.

Jonathan looked alarmed. "You're not going to make Jell-O shots, are you?"

I smirked at him. "You mean you don't want your Christmas desserts à la fraternity party? I would have thought that was your jam: staying up all night drinking and fornicating with undiscerning abandon."

"I'll have you know I'm very particular about who I sleep with," he retorted.

I raised an eyebrow as I checked the temperature of the sugar. "Uh-huh. Is that why all those pictures are up online with you stumbling into town cars with various girls whose names I bet you don't even know but yet you bring them back to your condo?"

"Hell no, I don't sleep with women in my house. We do it at theirs or in the club or in a hotel. I never, ever bring them to my condo. Never. It's a terrible idea," he said, shaking his head.

"With an attitude like that, I'm shocked you still have a fan base," I remarked as I stirred the sugar. "But then, some people are so easily impressed and would do anything to sleep with a billionaire."

"Or maybe you're just jealous," he joked, leaning in too close to me. "I can get you drunk and fuck you in a town car if you'd like."

I was glad I was wearing all that makeup, because I went red. "I'm sure I'm not missing much."

"Don't you want to find out?" he asked in a low voice.

I swallowed. The way he was looking at me—like he wanted me more than any other woman—let's just say that if no one else had been around, I might have just let the sugar burn and taken him up on his offer. No man had ever looked at me like I was desirable before.

"I need to finish my dessert," I croaked.

Jonathan grinned, winked, and then went over to another contestant.

I glanced over at him in between adding in a bit of cream of tartar and corn syrup then set about stirring slowly. He was flirting with the bachelorette two tables down from mine. The way the contestant was giggling and batting her eyes at him, he was clearly turning on the charm.

I stirred my sugar mixture furiously.

Did you seriously think he actually wanted anything to do with you? I scolded myself. *Jonathan clearly doesn't want someone who dresses up as a nightmare creature. He wants someone soft with big boobs and a sexy outfit who will stroke his ego and tell him how awesome he is.*

Just forget him. Win this contest then win the scholarship.

I paused in mid-stir.

Win the contest? I needed to be *out* of the contest. But a part of me desperately wanted to show up Keeley. She was so sure she was better than me, that she was going to beat me again.

I wanted to trounce her, and I was sure my cake was going to do it. I was planning on serving cognac three ways. The first was in a royal Manhattan with an alcohol-infused cranberry. The second was in a cake that looked like the bottle of alcohol, for which I had brought in a whole set of edible paints to make the cake look as lifelike as possible. The third was in a layered mousse dessert in a glass made out of sugar that was going to look identical to the cocktail but be a completely different experience.

Too bad I couldn't just submit this dessert as my scholarship, I thought as I started heating another saucepan with a generous slosh of cognac and a handful of cranberries to start soaking.

I was concerned about the scholarship. I was still floundering around, trying to come up with a winning idea. This was while also anxiously waiting for information from the Getty museum to see if I had made it to the in-person interview round. I needed to assemble a portfolio that would be enough to impress my interviewer.

In between stirring and checking the temperature, I measured out the ingredients for my cake. I could have just made a standard yellow cake, but instead, I was going to make a layer cake with cognac-infused cream, chocolate ganache, and a cranberry reduction.

It took the sugar mixture about an hour to reach the boiling point. By that time, my cake was in the oven. I carefully poured the boiling candy into the silicon martini glass molds and then set them aside and began to make the filling.

I happened to glance over to the other side of the room. Jonathan was staring at me. I quickly turned back to my stove.

"It's hot in here, isn't it?" Lilith said, coming up to me.

I made a noncommittal noise.

"Jonathan certainly seems obsessed by you," Emma added.

"Doubtful. He's been flirting with every girl in here. He's just a player."

"I've been following him around for the last few hours, and every chance he gets, he's looking at you," Lilith said, showing me her camera.

"It's because you're playing hard to get," Emma said breathlessly. "There was a really good article in *Vanity Rag* about how to make a guy obsessed with you in time to bring him to Christmas dinner at your parents' house. Rule number one was don't give it up too early. You have to time the sex right so that it happens ten days before Christmas. It has to be good and addicting. Then he'll agree to come home to impress your parents."

I pinched the bridge of my nose. "I am not looking for a man to bring to my nonexistent parents."

"Maybe he would take you to visit his parents," Emma said.

"I do not want a boyfriend, and even if I did, being asked to meet the guy's parents is not on the list anywhere," I said. I poured heavy cream into the double boiler along with the egg yolks and whisked the mixture.

Crap, it was warm in here! The Krampus costume was basically a fur coat. Fortunately, I had worn more than a bra underneath, not wanting to repeat my reindeer-costume experience. I unzipped the suit to take off the fur top and set it aside.

"I knew I stayed around for a good reason," Jonathan said, sauntering over to me.

"You're such a creep."

"Please," he scoffed, casually picking up the whisk and stirring the custard. "You so wanted me to watch you take your clothes off."

There he was, flirting with me again.

He doesn't mean it.

But what if he did?

I stewed over Jonathan's intentions as I carefully cut out each layer of the cake in the shape of the curved bottle of cognac with its tall stem. Next, I layered the cognac-spiked cream, the cranberry preserves, and the chocolate ganache. It was closer to sculpture than baking, and I used a level and several metal triangles to ensure that the cake was perfectly straight.

Once it was finished, I put it in the blast fridge to cool while I painstakingly painted the ornate gold design of the cognac logo onto the oval sugar glass medallion I had made. Then I mixed the fondant and frosting while the paint dried.

After I double-checked that the alcohol bottle cake was good and stiff—

Bet Jonathan's good and stiff!

Shut up, brain!

—the cake was ready to frost. Normally, I would have placed the cake on a turntable to evenly frost it, but I would have to do this one by hand because the bottle was not round. I had appropriated one of my small painting spatulas for the job, carefully applying the frosting until the whole cake was coated. Then I very carefully draped the whole thing in a paper-thin layer of fondant, using pointed bamboo skewers to add the ribbing that would be seen in the glass bottle.

When I had the shape sculpted, I set about using the paint to give the illusion that the cake was actually a bottle of expensive liquor, which meant it had to look like a hollow container with liquid inside. Fortunately, yours truly was an artist and could paint much more difficult subjects hungover.

Wonder if Jonathan would pose nude for you.

No cake for you, brain, if you can't keep it together.

Against my better judgment, I glanced over at him.

Maybe he is interested in me.

He could also have been interested in the cake. He was doing his signature pose at the judges' table, casually leaning on it, his body in that perfect David pose, the tuxedo accenting the triangular shape of his torso, the abs that I knew from seeing them in the hot tub leading down to his hips and—

I took a breath, trying to steady myself. I could not let Jonathan distract me. And he was a distraction. He was there just in the periphery of my vision as I finished painting and set the cake aside to dry.

I had less than an hour left to go, and I hurried to make the mousse for the fake drink in the sugar martini glass.

The actual cocktail was an amber color. To mimic that, I made a caramel cognac mousse. So as not to melt the sugar, the filling needed to be cool but not cold when I put it in the glass. If it was too cold, the glass would shatter. After making the filling, I set it aside in the blast freezer then carefully removed the sugar martini glasses from their molds. The first one broke.

The judges made a noise, and I glared at them. Jonathan flashed me a thumbs-up.

I took a few deep breaths. The next two came out of the mold easily. Using a hot piece of wire, I trimmed off excess sugar and placed the glass next to an actual martini glass. They matched perfectly.

For the garnish on the real martini, I had a booze-soaked cranberry. I could use the same for the mousse, but I was an artist.

I made a cranberry glaze then dropped balls of the raspberry cognac mixture into a molecular gastronomy chemical that turned them into jelly balls. When I had a large enough one, I carefully placed it on top of the mousse in the sugar martini glass.

I checked the clock. Ten minutes! Crap! I still had to make the actual cocktail.

CHAPTER 18

Jonathan

Morticia was working furiously. I was dying to see what she was making, but the cameras were hovering around her.

"Don't even think about distracting her," Belle said to me, coming over to talk to the judges before the judging started. "She's one of the few people actually making artistic desserts."

"I'm not looking forward to having to eat any more fried ice cream balls covered in frosting and colored coconut," I quipped.

Belle laughed.

"Hey, Belle?" I said tentatively.

We hadn't had any time to really sit down and have a serious talk since she'd returned. My other brothers monopolized all of her free time. Classic middle child—I was always overlooked. Plus, even if I had been able to have one-on-one time with my older sister, I wouldn't know what to say.

Sorry for being a terrible brother? Sorry for letting our parents treat you like shit?

We had all been so reliant on her for basically the entire thirty years of her life that I always felt guilty trying to take any more of her time.

"What?" she asked, half paying attention while she was on her phone, watching the schedule.

"Nothing," I said in a rush.

The clock counted down. Morticia placed the final garnish in her cocktails right as Anastasia called time. I was itching to see her dessert. But first…

"I made for you," one of the contestants announced, placing her dessert on the judges' table, "snowpup cream puffs!"

They were little pastries filled with cream, though you couldn't see that because they were covered in frosting and toasted coconut.

"Do you see?" she said, giggling. "They're little snowpup Pomeranians wearing tiny sweaters!"

Nick sighed loudly, and Anu carefully excavated the puff pastry from all the frosting.

"This is actually a good puff pastry," she said, "but remember what Coco Chanel always said—take one thing off before you leave the house. I think in this case, you could take three things off of this dessert."

"And all of them are frosting," Nick added.

The rest of the contestants were more of the same.

One girl made pigs in a blanket, except that the pigs were candy canes. "It's fun party food!" she said happily as I almost broke a tooth on one of the confections.

"Really scraping the bottom of the barrel here," Nick remarked after the contestant had left for the green room. He tossed the rest of her dessert in the trash can.

"We were trying to spice it up," Dana said, ushering a makeup artist over to powder Anu's nose. "It's working; the ratings are sky-high!"

"Probably with people hate-watching," I said.

"The contestants aren't that bad," Dana said.

The next few desserts were pretty good. Keeley had made miniature pie bites, including a mini pecan pie, a mini gingerbread spice pie, a mini chess pie, and a mini eggnog pie.

"I'm very impressed with the crust on these," Anu told her, "and that you didn't overcook these. Very good attention to detail."

Another contestant had made mini apple and cranberry dumplings with a caramel dipping sauce.

"These are great," Nick praised. "Perfectly balanced, not too sweet, awesome crust. Jonathan would be lucky to have you on his arm at a Christmas party!"

Finally, there was Morticia. "Ah!" Anu said. "The artist."

Morticia's dessert was miraculous. It looked exactly like a bottle of cognac with several cocktails. The cake that was the bottle of alcohol actually looked like the bottle. I stood up to inspect it more closely.

"I feel like I'm tripping balls," Nick joked.

"I almost don't want to cut it," Anu said as she joined me in marveling at the dessert.

Morticia smiled slightly, clearly pleased. "You have to see how it tastes!"

"I'm just surprised you were able to do all this in a furry suit," Nick said to Morticia and clapped her on her bare shoulder.

I clamped down a snarl.

What the fuck is he touching her for?

Nick must have read my expression, because he held up two hands. "Whoa there, you're supposed to only pick one of these fine bakers."

Morticia glanced at me then away.

What was she thinking? And why was I acting so possessive? I didn't like her. I just wanted to sleep with her, right?

"Can we see the original bottle?" Anu asked. She thanked the production assistant that brought out the bottle of cognac.

"Uncanny."

"Enough admiring. It's artistic, but it's not art," Nick said. "It's dessert; it's meant to be eaten." He carefully cut a slice out of the cake as the cameras hovered around him.

"Don't forget the drink," Morticia said.

Nick picked up a cocktail while Anu took one of the custards. "Astounding."

"Don't get me wrong," Nick said, sipping the drink. "Of course, this all tastes amazing. But it is a little corporate. You could not serve this at a restaurant and be taken seriously. However, the goal was a corporate holiday party. You can't get any better than this."

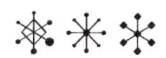

❄ ❄ ❄

"Holy shit, dude!" Carl said the next day at our daily meeting. "That cake Morticia made—insane! You have to ask her to make another. It's unreal, man, unreal. The morning shows are all over it. Kelly Ripa did a bit at the beginning of her show. Even Oprah's talking about it. The cognac is sold out of that particular brand, and the rest of them are almost sold out too."

"One down and how many hundreds of bottles more to go?" I asked, staring out the window.

"Cheer up, man," Carl said. "You're surrounded by hot women, your company's on the up-and-up, everyone is talking about us, and we're making all the 'what to buy your special someone for Christmas' lists. People are loving it! There's a rumor a well-known rapper wants to feature some of the scotch in his new video."

"Awesome," I said, still staring out the window. I wasn't sure what I was looking for. Morticia? Belle? My mother?

"Perk up! We need you to be your fun, happy, thirst-trap self. We have that meeting with Dorothy in a bit," Carl reminded me.

I followed Carl downstairs as he continued to chatter away about the company.

Greg was waiting impatiently in the lobby. "I have a very strict schedule," he said by way of greeting. "I hope you've been buttering the old woman up."

"Jonathan's been taking her free bottles of alcohol," Carl assured his older brother. "I told him he should start sunbathing nude on her property."

"Do not sunbathe nude," Greg warned. "I will not do business with someone on the sex offender registry."

"He could just do it in a thong," Carl joked.

We walked through the outdoor art installations. "All of this needs to go when we purchase this property," Greg said to Carl, who made notes. "It's a public health hazard. I want to put a hotel here…Holy shit!"

Several geese came charging at us. Carl swore and hid behind Greg, who snarled at the geese. They honked and rushed him.

"Is this group of good-looking men here to see me?" Dorothy exclaimed. "Prancer, Blitzen, Dasher, get back here!"

"There are more of them?" I asked weakly. "I brought you a very special bottle of cognac," I said, turning on the charm. "It's now officially sold out."

"I saw the clips online!" Dorothy exclaimed as she took the bottle. "That gal, Morticia—wow! So talented. You should pick her."

"Actually, the fans decide."

Dorothy nodded. "That's why I've been voting like crazy! She has vision."

"Speaking of vision," Greg said smoothly, "I'd like to discuss our vision for this industrial property."

Carl took out the prints of the renderings Svensson Investment had commissioned. Dorothy studied them while she petted one of the geese. It hissed menacingly at me when it saw me watching.

"Looks like every other development that people try and peddle," she said after a moment.

"We can have these done by an actual painter if you'd prefer," Greg offered.

"No," Dorothy said, "it's not that. I'd rather you kept some of the flavor. You even removed my sculpture."

"This is a very preliminary design," I assured her. "Obviously all of this is in flux."

"Uh-huh," she said. "Well, why don't you all think on that vision some more and get back to me."

❋ ❋ ❋

"I thought you said you buttered her up," Greg groused when we were back in front of my office. "Or are you just giving her free alcohol? How much have you given her? I know that bottle of cognac was worth, what, three hundred dollars?"

"It's going to pay off," I insisted. "She likes me."

"Likes you? Of course! She has you wrapped around her finger. She doesn't have to sign a thing, because you show up and keep her entertained and liquored up. Honestly," Greg said, shaking his head in disgust. "Every time I deal with one of you Frost brothers, I tell myself never again. Yet here we are."

"I'll get her on board," I promised.

"I doubt it," Greg sneered. "You acted like you were hungry to make the top-one-hundred-richest list, yet you're acting like an amateur."

"I will convince her to sell," I told him.

"Hm."

Except I didn't know how.

CHAPTER 19

Morticia

"Why won't he leave?"

Jonathan was across the street, arguing with two tall blond men in dark suits and overcoats.

I was in the bar at the base of his office building. Lilith, Emma, and I had set up shop there and spent every free moment in the place when Romance Creative wasn't filming. At night, I would sometimes catch myself staring up at Jonathan's condo in the residential building across the street. I would wonder what he was doing. Was he cooking, showering, lying on the couch? Did he sleep nude? Did he walk around his apartment barefoot and shirtless in gray sweatpants?

"Where is his coat?" Lilith asked, sliding into the seat next to me with Salem in her arms.

I stroked the black cat's head.

"Maybe he's a winter spirit," Emma said, "or the god of snow."

"She's been rereading *Twilight*," Lilith told me, rolling her eyes.

"You totally need to sleep with him," Emma said with a giggle.

"Wow, where did that come from?"

"It might help your creative juices flow!" Lilith said, poking me in the side.

"And other juices!" Emma snickered.

"You still don't have an idea for the scholarship, since you refuse to use my naked pictures of Jonathan idea," Lilith reminded me.

"I need a better idea than that," I said, standing up. "I'm going across the street to that property with all the art to work." But I needed Jonathan to move first. Why was I so worried about running into him?

You're acting like a high school freshman, I scolded myself.

I grabbed my cape and my bag and frog-marched myself outside. I ran mental scenarios of what I was going to say or not say to him. It was just like high school, when I'd had a crush on Justin…until it all blew up in my face.

Which is exactly what's going to happen with Jonathan if you aren't careful.

I needed to just walk right past him, maybe deliver a cool but casual nod.

But when I walked outside, he wasn't there. Instead, Keeley was. "What are you doing in Jonathan's building?" she demanded.

"None of your business." I pushed past her, but she followed me.

"You think he likes you?" she spat at me. "Jonathan doesn't. He's just tolerating you and stringing you along."

"Kind of like how your parents tolerate you?" I cut in.

"You bitch!" Keeley screeched.

"Like we're all supposed to pretend like you didn't fuck your own sister's fiancé the night before their wedding? Don't try to intimidate me or my friends," I told my cousin, jabbing my finger at her. "I will put a curse on you then post all over the internet about how you're a cheater. All the fans of the show will vote you off next episode."

"Oh yeah?" Keeley snarled. "Well, I'll tell people how you stalked a boy in school then tried to kill him."

"That's not what happened! You set me up. You're such a liar!"

"I guess we're at a stalemate," Keeley said nastily. "Stay out of my way. You have more to lose than me."

Furious, I went to my favorite spot on the bench in the old industrial property, but I couldn't concentrate. It was as if I had been transported back to that fateful day in high school. The cops had been called. I had tried to explain that it was a love potion, but the principal took one look at my dark hair, makeup, and goth clothes and gave me a one-way ticket to the psych ward. Fortunately, a nurse there had taken pity on me and given me paper and pencils. Still, it had been the worst five months of my entire life.

Use your trauma and let it fuel your creativity, I told myself.

Sometimes I didn't want to have my creativity fueled by anger and trauma. Maybe I wanted to draw pictures of a hot guy eating a cupcake and wearing nothing but a Santa hat.

"Drink?" offered an older woman flanked by several geese wearing Christmas outfits as she came over to me with a familiar bottle of amber liquid and two glasses. "You look like someone who needs some lubrication, though not the sex jelly kind," she continued.

I took a glass from her.

"The famous Morticia—baker and artist extraordinaire," the old woman said, pouring me a generous amount. "Contemplating the beginnings of the universe?"

"Are you Dorothy, the sculptor?" I asked, pointing to the plaque. "It's a brilliant piece." I toasted her, and we drank.

"Damn, that man makes a mean liquor!" she said appreciatively.

"When you made this piece," I asked, looking for inspiration, "how did you come up with it? How did you capture the beginning of the universe?"

"Actually, the label is completely bullshit," she said cheerfully.

I barked out a laugh.

"That's the funny thing about art. At a certain point, it's about creating something aesthetically pleasing then coming up with a good story to sell it to people!" Dorothy winked. "The explanation has to make you sound wise and insightful, even though what really happened was that you were super horny and in between rounds of being fucked by the biggest cock east of the Mississippi, and you decided that orgasms that good needed a sculpture in their honor."

※ ※ ※

Unfortunately, I did not have any orgasms or cocks for inspiration. The clock was ticking. I spent the next two days trying to draw various ideas, failing, drawing Jonathan, kicking myself, then drawing various baked goods, and researching then trying recipes I found online.

As I baked, I told myself that all those cupcakes, trifles, and cake pops were Instagram props to fulfill the marketing contract. Pop a sexy cocktail next to the dessert, post it on the Hillrock West Distillery Instagram, and bam! Viral content.

Because I had so many sketches of Jonathan, Lilith started co-opting them before I could ball them up and give them to Salem to play with. She created little scrapbook pages from them and posted them on the Instagram account along with my sketches of various alcoholic beverages and desserts.

And yet I still had no idea what I was going to do for my scholarship piece. If I even landed that internship, I was going to be living out of my car in Los Angeles. Oh wait, no I wasn't, because I didn't even have a car. I was just going to sleep in a ditch.

At least I had managed to avoid Jonathan for the past few days. Unfortunately, we had another bake-off challenge. I couldn't tell if I was dreading or excited to see him.

You need to just see him and get it over with.

But when I saw him, my heart started fluttering.

It's all the sugar you've been eating.

"For your challenge today," Anastasia announced, "we're having a decorating party! You should make creative desserts that are great to share with family and friends. Then head over to the Hillrock West Distillery showroom to trim the tree and decorate!"

More free labor. Whoo.

Though I was mostly annoyed, a part of me welcomed the task of baking and then decorating—anything to keep me from spinning my wheels about the scholarship and about Jonathan.

As soon as Anastasia started the timer and all the other contestants had rushed to the pantry and fridge to grab their ingredients, Jonathan sauntered over to me. He was wearing a dark-navy suit similar to the one he'd had on a few days ago—not that I was noticing because I liked him! I noticed because I was an artist, and I noticed color and form.

Jonathan's form...

"I love to see you in the Christmas spirit!" he quipped, taking a Santa hat out of his pocket and placing it on my head.

"I am not wearing that."

"But you look adorable in it!" he exclaimed.

"You're not going to feel so warm and fuzzy about Christmas when the bachelorettes are force-feeding you dessert in a few hours," I reminded him, jerking my head toward the other contestants with their armloads full of sugar, candy canes, and chocolate.

Jonathan grimaced. It wrinkled his forehead and the lines around his mouth. I wanted to reach out and smooth them away.

Get it together.

"Just do me a favor," he said, a hint of desperation in his voice. "Don't make something too sweet."

"No can do. I have a Jell-O-shot cupcake tower covered in an inch of fondant planned. Guess you're gonna have to suck it up."

Jonathan grabbed me around the waist and growled, "Don't play with me like that."

Crap, his body was hard where it pressed against mine. It was like that night in the park—he was all bulging muscles and sinew under that suit.

It took a second, but he realized what he had done and released me. "I uh—"

"I need to start baking."

I looked around at my competition. The low performers were mostly gone, and the other contestants were upping their baking quality.

Meanwhile, I wasn't feeling all that confident about my dessert. I was making peppermint schnapps cannoli. I could make tasty cannoli in my sleep and had adapted a special Halloween version for Christmas. My old-school Italian grandmother had loved to cook, and the cannoli was her recipe.

But Keeley had a whole array of Platinum Provisions molecular gastronomy equipment set up at her station and was making an elaborate, complicated dessert. I didn't need to read the tea leaves to tell that I probably wasn't going to win this round. But I could at least win Jonathan and score some fan-favorite points.

It always seemed to tick Keeley off when Anastasia announced me as either the first or second fan favorite. And I had to admit that it was nice to actually be liked. Plus, a not-insignificant part of me wanted Jonathan to like me too.

My grandmother had always said that the way to a man's heart was through his stomach. She also advocated overfeeding your man so that he would literally be dependent on you for his shortened life. However, I wasn't going to take it that far.

I'm just doing this to make Keeley mad, not because I like Jonathan. I am a badass queen of the night.

I was also a queen of the night who knew how to make a mean lasagna.

※ ※ ※

The decorating party was in full swing when I walked in to present my cannoli to the judges.

"They taste like you just dug up my grandmother to make them," Nick said after biting into one.

Mimi, a Halloween fiend, would have been proud.

Anu also insisted on tasting the lasagna.

"It's not a dessert," I demurred.

"I don't care," she said flatly. "If there's lasagna, I want it."

Nick took a large bite then came around the table and gave me a hug.

"I need you to come make this at one of my restaurants," he said.

At the other end of the room, Jonathan was sitting on a chair next to a Christmas tree, surrounded by platters of desserts and half-consumed cocktails. Keeley was straddling him in some misguided attempt to give him a lap dance.

Christmas music blared, and the whole place reeked of sugar and alcohol. Keeley let out an exaggerated moan when she saw me standing there. At first, I wanted to just turn around and leave, but the expression on Jonathan's face looked like it belonged in Dante's inferno and not on a sexy Christmas card.

At that moment, as I took in the scene, I had it: my inspiration for my scholarship art piece. The theme would be all about sex and consumerism and trying to be the perfect wife, all wrapped around Christmas. It would be a three-part piece using a mix of collages, oil painting, and line drawings. And it would give me an excuse to take sexy pictures of Jonathan and bake.

That scholarship is mine!

The producer motioned to Jonathan. He shoved Keeley off of him. She rolled onto the floor with a squeal.

"Are those cookies?" Jonathan asked, wincing.

CHAPTER 20

Jonathan

"You can't eat your dessert until after you have your Christmas lasagna," Morticia said, whipping the small metal dome off of the plate she was carrying. The smell of crispy cheese, red sauce, and meat hit the air.

It smelled delicious—like home and family. "I need that lasagna," I said, salivating. I stood up and ripped the Santa hat off my head.

I did not cook. I did not know how to cook. If the world was going to be destroyed and the only way to save it was if I cooked dinner, we would be alien toast.

Morticia stepped up to me and pushed me back down onto the chair. "I believe," she said in that raspy voice, "that we're supposed to be feeding you."

"Don't do it, Jonathan," Keeley complained.

I opened my mouth.

"Fair is fair," Morticia said, shoving a bite in.

"Shit," I mumbled around the pasta. "I need this in my life every day. How did you know how to make this?"

"My Italian grandmother," she said with a small smile as I shoved another forkful into my mouth.

"I'm Italian!" Keeley insisted, butting in and grabbing the plate from me. "Mimi was my grandmother too."

"You never visited her." Morticia bared her teeth.

"Can I—" I reached for the plate. There were a few more bites of lasagna left. I needed them.

"Don't eat that, Jonathan," Keeley said, jerking the plate away. "I'm going to make you something better than this lasagna, just you wait."

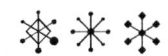

※ ※ ※

I didn't want anything other than the lasagna. It was amazing. Of course, there was none left when I went browsing in the studio after the filming was over.

> **Jonathan:** *I will trade you anything you want for more of that lasagna.*
> **Jonathan:** *A private jet to the Bahamas, a life-size doll that looks exactly like me, someone to serenade you at all hours of the night.*
> **Morticia:** *No. I'm working.*

Fuck. I felt slightly bereft.

I didn't just want the lasagna because I was hungry; it had felt like home. Sure, my family had had its ups and downs: my two older brothers didn't talk to my parents, and my sister had cut and run and gone with no contact for three years. But that was family, right? The Frosts needed someone to keep everyone together. I longed for a Christmas like those of my childhood, when all eight of us had been together in my immaculately decorated childhood home with candles and dinner.

> **Jonathan:** *Hey, how are you all doing? Just wondering how you were. Would love to see you.*

I waited a beat. I had been texting my parents over the last few weeks but hadn't received a response yet. I reread the message. Did it sound too whiny? My mother had always complained when my brothers or I acted too needy. Then she would tell my father, and he would give us a lecture about being a man.

> **Diane Frost:** *The ballet just let out. We have twenty minutes. You can come meet us at the Olive and Twist. Otherwise we aren't free for another few weeks.*
> **David Frost:** *Do not be late. You're always late to everything.*

Yes!

I had friends who hated their parents. Carl's mom was constantly badgering him and his brothers for money. And the Svenssons' dad lived on a compound with a handful of sister wives and was holding a number of their younger siblings hostage. I felt lucky by comparison. I loved my parents. My dad was a neurosurgeon, and my mother had two PhDs in science. My parents were always busy, but they were doing important work. Sure, that had meant they hadn't had time for me or my siblings when we were younger, but I was sure that now that we were all adults, things were going to change. I just had to work at our relationship.

My parents were waiting impatiently at the bar when I walked in.

"What is it?" my mother asked. She was a tall brunette. I had my father's coloring. With his platinum hair, ice-blue eyes, and broad shoulders, people loved to put him on medical magazine covers and have him headline conferences.

I stopped short. "I just wanted to see you guys."

My mother sighed. "You made it seem like such an emergency. We do have other things on our schedule tonight."

"Oh, sorry," I said. "Just thought, you know, we haven't caught up in a while. I thought maybe you'd want to hear about what I'm doing."

"I know about what you're doing," my father said, signaling the bartender for another drink. He did not offer me anything.

"They're using the alcohol from my company here." I pointed to the top-shelf liquor. "Belle is working with Romance Creative and Dana Holbrook now. She's helping me on my advertising," I said in a rush.

My mother made a face when I mentioned my sister's name.

"I don't know why you had to start an alcohol company," my father complained. "Of course Belle is encouraging you. Why couldn't you be like Jack or Owen? He has a cybersecurity company. He's working with the Svenssons."

"I am too!"

"Not Svensson PharmaTech," my mother countered.

"You like them?" I asked. "I could organize a meeting between Mace and you. He's the CEO."

"I know who he is. I spoke with him at the medical technology conference last year. He is very interested in my research."

There was silence. The bartender brought my dad his drink; he sipped it.

"Did you see *The Nutcracker?*" I asked them.

"Yes," she replied. "Your father was given tickets. We met friends there. We were supposed to meet them at a restaurant after, but we delayed because of you."

"We really should be going," my father said, finishing his drink. "Don't want to keep them waiting."

"I can pick up the tab," I offered as my father helped my mother into her coat.

"Fine," my father said, blowing out a breath as if I had annoyed him. Which I probably had.

"Okay," I called to their retreating backs, "it was great to see you!"

※ ※ ※

I took the train home. I wanted the anonymity, and I didn't want to make chitchat with the town car driver.

They were just busy, I told myself as the train rushed through the tunnel. *You sprang a meeting on them, and they were busy, and they didn't expect it. At least they agreed to meet with you.*

But the usual lies that I told myself about why my parents couldn't be there for the lacrosse game or the school play or high school graduation or my big capstone college presentation weren't working as well as they usually did. I was tired of making excuses for them.

But I had to, because the alternative was not acceptable.

You just need to make a bunch of money, I assured myself as I took the stairs up to the street two at a time at my stop. *They just don't understand the alcohol business. Once you land the Hamilton Yards development, then they'll be impressed. Owen and Jack have big real estate projects, and this would be a million times bigger than theirs. You just need to convince Dorothy to sell.*

Instead of heading into my condo, I walked across the street and pushed through the opening in the chain-link fence to Dorothy's property. It had started to snow, and backlit against the light of the skyline, the sculptures gave the property an otherworldly feel.

Greg wanted to tear all the art pieces out. He had said that we needed the land. But I felt they added a unique sense of place. It made it seem like the portal to another realm, one of those mythical dark fairy courts. I rounded a corner.

There, like an escaped fae princess, was Morticia. At first, I thought she was performing some sort of pagan ritual, but as I advanced, the snow softening my footfalls, I realized she was photographing something.

"Is that a gingerbread house?"

She turned to me then grinned.

CHAPTER 21

Morticia

I knew I shouldn't be so happy that he liked my food, that I should aspire to higher things in life than feeding an overprivileged billionaire, but dammit if I didn't get a rush of joy at seeing Jonathan happily eat my lasagna. I now knew why my grandmother had loved parties and entertaining so much. There was no better high than seeing someone you loved enjoying something that you'd made just for them.

Wait, uh, love? That's…no. Nope. Freudian slip. I didn't love him. We hadn't even kissed or had a date. Jonathan had blithely ate the lasagna while I had had a mini existential crisis.

Why was I planning first dates and kisses? That was never going to happen. Ever. Never. I was going to keep a very professional distance from him.

It must be the holidays, I told myself after the bake-off challenge. *It's making you crazy.*

I should be safely wrapped in my bedroom with heavy black curtains and candles, yet here I was baking a gingerbread house. Now that I had my inspiration for my art piece for the scholarship, I had to start working. It was ten p.m., and this was prime creative time for me. Because the theme of the piece was Christmas consumerism and the female gaze, I needed more pictures of baked goods. The ones I had from the bake-off were not going to be enough.

"You also need some pictures of Jonathan," Emma said around the bite of lasagna. She and Lilith had stolen several little round tins of it after photographing them for the marketing photos.

"Give your man sex, lasagna, and whiskey for Christmas," Lilith said as she typed out the Instagram post. "Hashtag don't fuck with his food, hashtag Italian Christmas, hashtag keep it simple. Ooh, look at all those likes coming in!"

"You should have him pose nude with a strategically placed gingerbread cookie as the main focal point of your art piece," Emma told me.

"No, that's not bombastic enough," Lilith said. "You need to make one of those *Cake Boss*–type confections of a giant pile of presents and then a picture of you in a fifties getup frosting him or something kitschy like that."

"I'm not including a nude picture of Jonathan," I said flatly. Fortunately, the other baking bachelorettes were out for a night on the town, and we were alone in the shared kitchen.

"Um, I'm sorry, I thought we were friends," Emma retorted. "Maybe your friend needs a picture of him nude."

"Are you that hard up?"

"It's been a three-year dry spell," Emma admitted. "Can I have some gingerbread?"

I sighed. "The kit only has the exact number of pieces you need for a house."

"I can't believe you didn't bake your own gingerbread," Lilith said, wrinkling her nose.

"I'm just photographing it, and I wanted the super plastic-looking one. This isn't for eating, it's for art."

"I'm disappointed," my twin stated, stealing one of the gumdrop decorations. "What kind of baker are you?"

"Oh, for the love of—Emma!" I shrieked. My friend was eating part of the chimney.

"What?" she protested. "I have a problem, okay? Just use some extra icing."

❄ ❄ ❄

I had had to fill in the chimney with candy. Then it turned out I didn't like the way the gingerbread house looked anyway, so I ended up baking my own gingerbread, much to Emma's delight.

Now I was out in the cold, the sleet, and the snow, taking pictures of my new and improved super-duper-fancy gingerbread house. The photos were missing a little something though.

"You need a man!" Dorothy shouted over the wind. She was bundled in a huge, sparkly green-and-white parka. A number of geese in their Christmas best strained against the cold.

"I don't need a man; I just need to finish my art piece."

"No," Dorothy said, "take it from a fellow artist. You look like you're making a piece that you're trying to get money for in some form or fashion, no?"

"Yes," I said grudgingly. I didn't like to air my private business, but even though I had a direction for my art piece, the vision still wasn't coming together.

"It's a funny thing about art," Dorothy continued. "There's this idea among younger artists today that no one wants to pay for art and that back in the good old days, art was appreciated. The reality is no one has ever wanted to pay for art." She made air quotes. "They always wanted it for free. Churches would pay for it to market their message, and wealthy people had portraits made, yes, but you want to know how most artists made a living?"

I shrugged.

"Porn," Dorothy stated. "Sex sells. Sex has always sold." She pointed to the "beginning of the universe" sculpture. "I've been trying to sell that thing for decades. It won awards and all that, but no museum wanted to buy. Guess what? It had a companion piece I made the same month. The sculpture didn't have a fancy title; it was basically just a woman with big tits getting her freak on with a centaur. Dontcha know, I sold that thing for a million dollars to a Saudi oil prince."

She tapped her forehead. "Sex sells. Whoever you're trying to sell that piece to, slap a picture of a good-looking man on it, and everyone's going to want to buy it." She saluted me. "It's colder than a witch's tit out here. You better go in before you freeze your clit off."

"I have a few more photos to take."

But as I tried to get a better angle, I could see that Dorothy was right. I needed something electrifying. Maybe not at the level of centaur sex, but I definitely needed more than some pictures of baked goods and the occasional photo of Jonathan.

I bet this picture would spice up a lot better if it was of Jonathan, shirtless, taking a bite of the gingerbread with those bedroom eyes looking over the top of it.

"Nice gingerbread house!"

As if he had materialized like magic from my thoughts, there was Jonathan.

"You know," he said, ambling over to me and standing close but not touching, "I was here looking for some inspiration, and I found you."

"Funny," I said, "because I actually need a little inspiration from you."

"What are you making? Is that for the Instagram account?" he asked.

"Er..."

I couldn't tell him about my art project. How would I even explain it? *Hey, I'm just going to take indecent photos of you as a commentary on Christmas consumerism because I'm broke and don't want to live in a tent during my internship. That cool? Cool.* That would be...well, it would be weird. It would be love-potion-level weird. It would be restraining order–level weird.

"Yes," I lied, "for the Instagram."

"Where's the alcohol?" he asked, studying the gingerbread house scene.

"The alcohol?"

The alcohol, Morticia, because for an Instagram account for the alcohol company, you need alcohol.

"Dorothy has it," I said.

Jonathan laughed. "Of course you're friends with the old broad!" he said affectionately.

"I'll be right back."

Crap! I hoped she was awake. I knocked tentatively on the door. Her pet geese honked in irritation.

"I have condoms and a dental damn," she said when the door opened.

"I need alcohol," I said in a rush.

"Not the best lubricant, but it will do in a pinch."

"To photograph," I said. "We're not, uh, you know."

She raised an eyebrow. "I've been around the art community for decades. Let me tell you, if you're making the kind of art I think you are, a few shirtless pics are not going to cut it. People can see that shit on Instagram any day of the week. You need to get on the wild stallion and ride. Or should I say reindeer. It is Christmas," she mused. "Would you like vodka? Schnapps? What about this nice dark rum? Who doesn't like a little rum in their eggnog?"

Me, I would!

I needed to calm down. It was my crush on Justin all over again, when I would spend hours making scrapbooks using the pieces of paper with his handwriting I had stolen and the clandestine photos of him I had taken.

Oh god, I'm recreating my childhood nightmare!

But Jonathan didn't look like anything out of a nightmare when I returned with the rum and a few glasses. He was already half-undressed and was peeling his white undershirt over his head when I walked up.

I paused, holding up my phone to capture the movement in slow motion. With the snow falling, he was hot enough to turn winter in New York into a tropical paradise.

And now we've come to the part of the evening when Morticia makes clichéd comparisons.

"Found the rum?" he asked, sauntering over, his muscles flexing, seeming not to mind the cold at all even though I was shivering. He wrapped his arms around me. "Are you sure you need this shot right now?" he asked, lines of concern forming around his eyes.

"Yep, Christmas is coming. Can't dillydally."

Get it together.

This was why I tried to put men, especially hot ones, in the "stupid and useless" box, because if I didn't have them tightly contained, my mind would latch onto them like an internet stalker.

Jonathan hugged me tighter. The warmth from his bare skin flowed through me. Then he stepped back, grabbed his suit jacket, and draped it around my shoulders. "Take pictures quick," he said. "I don't want you to freeze."

"You're going to freeze first," I retorted, ignoring the way his jacket smelled like him, like mountain spring water, winter air, and fresh pine.

"Nah. I was made for the cold," he said. "So what do you want me to do?"

Ride him like a reindeer!

He ran a hand through his hair, and it fell over his forehead in loose waves. The billionaire casually picked up the bottle of rum and twisted the top off, his forearms and the muscles in his torso flexing. Then he poured out a glass and took a sip. I reveled in the lines of his body. I'd done nude figure drawing classes but none with anyone like him modeling.

"Do you want a sexy perfume shot?" he asked me after I had enough pictures of him staring off moodily into the falling snow.

"A what?"

"You know how on all those celebrity perfume commercials," he explained, taking my hand, "they have his and hers perfume. Then there are two people practically having sex on camera."

"It's Instagram not Only Fans," I said. "Besides, I don't have a female model."

He pulled me to him. "I have one right here." He took my camera and held it up. "Look at the camera," he whispered. "Sexy eyes."

His arm was strong around me. All I could think about was that I was this close to his mouth. He had said look at the camera, but all I could look at were his eyes; they were mesmerizing.

Was he going to kiss me? Did I want him to? Who the fuck was I kidding? Of course I wanted him to.

He's your employer and, more importantly, the subject of your artwork. There's probably some sort of ethical rule that you'd be breaking, my mind chattered.

Before I could decide if I wanted him to kiss me or not, he released me. I had missed the moment.

Or maybe there was no moment, and it's all in your head like with Justin.

I scuttled away from Jonathan, letting my hair fall over my face. "Let's finish the shoot."

He picked up the gingerbread house and took a bite right out of the roof as I snapped pictures. "Dang!" he said. "This is great."

"Baked just a few hours ago," I said, glad that I hadn't used the store-bought stuff after all.

He took another bite, chewed thoughtfully, and smirked. "I knew I would like eating your gingerbread."

CHAPTER 22

Jonathan

While sipping my coffee the next morning, I smiled as I scrolled through the pictures Morticia had posted on the Hillrock West distillery Instagram feed. Between the snow fall, the gingerbread house, and yours truly, the pictures screamed Christmas. People were going crazy in the comments, and we'd added another ten thousand followers since the previous night.

> **Jonathan:** *I knew you were a secret Christmas lover.*
> **Morticia:** *Never. I just like money. Some of us don't have trust fund IVs.*
> **Jonathan:** *Correction. The marketing firm I hired and subsequently fired liked money. You have an obsession.*
> **Morticia:** *I do not have a closet Christmas obsession.*

Jonathan: *Then the only other option is that you are completely obsessed with me.*

Morticia: *Screw you.*

Jonathan: *Don't worry, when you kidnap me for Christmas to show me off to your family I'll totally play along.*

Morticia: *If I kidnap you, I'm not taking you to Christmas dinner.*

Jonathan: *So you want me to come be a sex slave in your dungeon. Got it.*

I was composing another response when my phone rang, sending the cheery lilt of "Jingle Bell Rock" around the loft.

"Merry Christmas!" I said.

"Where the fuck are you?" my oldest brother, Owen, demanded.

"Shit. I forgot the kids!"

"Yes," Owen said. "You promised you were going to go pick up Oliver and Matt from the train station. They're outside. Fortunately, they aren't freezing. If it's warm enough for snow, then it's not actually that cold out."

❄ ❄ ❄

Because I was supposed to pick them up, my younger brothers had not taken the train all the way to Penn Station and instead had gotten off at a stop closer to my company headquarters. They were slumped on a bench when I pulled up.

"Why didn't you take a nicer car?" Oliver complained when he saw me.

"And a Merry Christmas to you too."

"Did you bring any food?" Matt asked.

"It's no wonder Belle left if you two are going to act like spoiled brats," I snapped.

My younger brothers reacted as if I had slapped them.

"Sorry," I said, giving them each a hug.

"Is she still mad?" Oliver asked apprehensively.

"She's not exactly a bright, shining beacon of Christmas cheer."

"It's probably because you aren't being a good bake-off judge," Matt said accusingly as I dragged their bags to my SUV.

"I'm a great judge!"

"You haven't made any insightful comments," Matt replied.

"What, are you watching and taking notes?" I scoffed.

He and Oliver looked at each other. "The Svenssons say that one of us has to be on the show next year to slingshot our company. I want to be a billionaire by next Christmas," Matt said grandiosely.

I shoved him and Oliver into the car. "There's more to being a billionaire than fast cars, women, and booze," I said.

"There's also the money, fame, and magazine covers," Matt said happily.

"It's a lot of work," I warned as I drove back to my condo.

"You don't work. You just eat desserts all day and get your picture taken," Oliver scoffed.

"Just for that, I'm not cooking for you," I said. I parked the car and dragged their bags into the lobby.

"I don't want you to cook anyway!"

"But can you convince your girlfriend to make lasagna?" Oliver begged as we rode the elevator up.

"Morticia's not my girlfriend," I said sharply.

"Why? Falling down on the job?" Matt said as he texted on his phone. "I would have expected better from you."

"If you're going to act like dicks, maybe you need to stop spending so much time around the Svenssons," I retorted as we headed into my condo.

"What? No! Tristan is my boy!"

I shook my head as I perused the fridge. I could make eggs, since that seemed to be all I had. I had a service that delivered prepared meals every few days. But I hadn't received the next shipment yet.

I haphazardly cracked the eggs into a bowl while my younger brothers chattered on about Harvard and their brilliant business ideas. I had some cookie cutters, and I cooked the eggs in little patties shaped like Christmas trees, ornaments, and reindeer.

My brothers were not impressed when I slid the dishes in front of them. Oliver made a face and poked at the eggs. "Is this supposed to be John Cena?"

"No, that's Santa Claus," I said, sprinkling some parmesan on his eggs.

Matt took a bite. "Why is it crunchy?"

"Er—"

"Because there's shells in it!" Oliver said, holding out a piece accusingly.

"I'm going to Jack's," Matt said, grabbing his coat. "Chloe always has good food."

"Jack's busy and said you had to stay here!" I shouted to them as they traipsed out. I followed them out to the elevator. "You'll be back."

"I should send all my little brothers over here if you're hosting," Carl announced when the elevator doors opened. He stepped off, and my brothers stepped inside.

"I don't need all your younger brothers over here."

"Were we that obnoxious in college?" Carl complained. "Honestly, all Tristan and Eli can talk about is how they're going to create the next billion-dollar company. I've heard the gamut of stupid ideas, including Uber for dog babysitting, some sort of sex toy delivery company, and then one of them wants to start a SpaceX rival. Like Greg's going to let one of them strap into a rocket and go to the moon."

I barked out a laugh. "Is he still in a bad mood?"

"Dude," Carl complained, sprawling on my couch. "He went on an hour-long rant last night after our younger brothers got back from college. One of them suggested starting a porn network—as a joke, mind you—and that just set Greg off. Then Adrian had the balls to tell Greg he needed to get laid."

"I'm surprised you don't have a concussion from the nuclear bomb that kid set off," I commented, handing him a drink.

"It was pretty epic. Then I had to work all night. Greg is furious you haven't sealed the development deal yet."

"I'm working on it," I promised, not wanting to admit that I had stalled out.

"Maybe you can convince your sister to get back together with him, just for a little bit, to give us all a reprieve. You know, for Christmas," Carl wheedled.

The front door swung open, and we cursed as Belle walked in, high heels clicking on the wood floors. "As if I'm going to sleep with Greg just because you're too spineless to stand up to him."

"He's terrifying!" Carl cried as my older sister gestured behind her.

"Morticia?" I said in confusion as she dragged a cart filled with Christmas decorations into my condo. "Did you come to see me?"

"No," she said grimly, "I came to decorate."

CHAPTER 23

Morticia

I needed a break from Jonathan. Being with him the previous night had put me in a tailspin. The way he smelled, the way he looked at the camera with those piercing blue eyes, the deep, rumbling laugh whenever I made an acerbic comment. My obsession with him was growing despite my best intentions. I had spent the previous night carefully editing the photos to make sure they showed off all his muscles and the planes of his handsome face to maximum effect.

One might even say I was developing an intimate familiarity with his naked torso.

Stop making this more awkward.

Even if I did want to see what was wrapped up in that Christmas package.

It's the sugar. You shouldn't eat so much sugar.

I was being weird and obsessive. I needed to spend the day working on my art piece. In the future, I would have to keep some professional distance from the billionaire. That meant no more late-night photo shoots.

"There you are!" Belle said as I walked past the studio. "Come. We're going up to Jonathan's condo."

"What? Why?"

"Pajama party."

✳ ✳ ✳

Jonathan didn't seem all that excited to see me when Belle and I showed up at his front door.

Told you so.

In fact, he was visibly aggravated when Belle ushered me into his condo. Behind me, I pulled the large, overstuffed wagon filled with Christmas decorations.

"We're filming the pajama party here tomorrow tonight," Belle told him.

"Not in my penthouse." Jonathan scowled.

"Excuse me," Belle said, "this is my show. Now, Morticia, I think we should keep the filming to the open kitchen and living area. Let's concentrate our efforts there."

"I don't want any of them here," Jonathan growled.

"We'll have it deep cleaned afterward," Belle promised.

"That's not good enough."

I didn't know what was going on between them, and I didn't care. The temperature in the condo had dropped about twenty degrees.

"I'm not arguing with you," Belle said sharply. "Considering that you seem perfectly fine to go talk to Mom and Dad and spill everyone's business, I don't see why filming a bake-off episode should be that much more of an invasion."

"Fine," Jonathan spat.

"Good."

Jonathan stormed out, the blond Svensson rushing after him.

Belle walked around the space. "Make it festive. Can you do something nice with the balcony? Get a few Christmas trees in here. Have it done by tomorrow when we film."

I looked around the space after she left for yet another meeting. The place was bigger than I remembered from when I had come over to clean Jonathan's cut. Then, I had been focused on not being sued and on making sure my cat hadn't killed him. Now, I was confronted with the fact that I was in his space alone, and he did not want me there.

Keeley is right. He doesn't want someone like you.

I wanted to leave, run away before it turned ugly, but I was still under contract with Romance Creative for emergency decorating.

I needed a drink. And reinforcements.

❄ ❄ ❄

"I brought cupcakes!" Emma said happily. "And pizza!" She handed me a stack of boxes. The smell of cheese and garlic was fortifying. "Oh my god, I can't believe you're just hanging out in Jonathan's condo," she gushed.

"It smells like male in here," my twin commented as she swept in, decked out in a black Victorian morning dress complete with sunglasses and a top hat.

"She's really feeling her creative energy," Emma said with a giggle as she unwrapped one of the cupcakes.

"Needs more black," Lilith remarked as she walked around the living room, Salem prowling behind her.

"No black. We're going for Christmas and sparkles and glitter."

"Like an elf murder scene!" Lilith said gleefully.

"Wrong. Like a snow globe," I told my twin.

We sorted through the decorations in the wagon. A lot of it was left over from the previous year's bake-off and wasn't in the best shape.

"Where's the man of the house?" Emma asked, eating a slice of pepperoni pizza.

"Stormed out," I said. "He is not pleased I am here."

"His loss," Lilith said, selecting her own slice of pizza.

"You know what you should do?" Emma exclaimed. "Sleep with his business rival and make him jealous!"

"I'm not—" I sputtered. "That is not what is happening here."

"I thought you were luring him away to stick it to Keeley," Lilith said.

"No! I just wanted to annoy Keeley. Jonathan is inept and likes Christmas. He's a walking sack of testosterone and bad decisions. He thinks girls like Keeley are not only a good idea to sleep with but also to marry. He's such a waste of time," I ranted. "He coasts by on his good looks and his—"

Someone cleared their throat.

Jonathan stood in the entrance to the open kitchen. Salem meowed and pranced over to him. Jonathan walked into the room, and I was struck suddenly by how very tall he was.

Emma gaped, her open mouth full of cupcake. Jonathan ignored her, advancing on me. It took all my self-control not to scurry backward.

"Though you seem to think I'm useless and a waste of time, I would suspect that you're not above using my credit card to decorate for this event," he said in a clipped tone, reaching into his suit coat pocket and pulling out a black credit card.

I didn't move. I felt bad for saying those things. I hadn't even meant them. I was just trying to convince myself that Jonathan wasn't worth another Justin repeat.

Jonathan grabbed my hand and slapped the credit card into it. "It has no limit, so go crazy," he spat then turned on his heel.

"It's a good thing you totally don't like him, because he definitely hates you now," my twin said after the front door had slammed shut.

"Shut up," I told my sister.

"Morticia, be nice," Emma chided. "She's the only family you have left that's not a hoebag skank." She picked up another of the cupcakes. "Eat this. It will make you feel better."

I took a bite of the chocolate cupcake. It was black like my soul. Jonathan had looked so heartbroken when he'd walked in. That couldn't be right, could it? I was imagining things.

"Cheer up!" Emma insisted, feeding me another cupcake. "We're going shopping!"

CHAPTER 24

Jonathan

What the hell had I been thinking? Of course Morticia didn't like me. I wasn't her type; she probably wanted one of those rail-thin TV production guys with the guyliner and the tattoos and the combat boots. They were crawling all over the studio when I went to find my sister.

"Did you remember to catch Morticia and give her the credit card before she left?" Belle asked me, not looking up from her laptop.

"Yep." Yeah, did I ever catch her. "Do you want to ride together?" I asked Belle.

"I'll meet up with you all. Save me a seat."

"You're coming, right?" I asked her.

"Of course," my sister said absently.

It was snowing again. The town car drove me down a wide avenue decorated with lights and wreaths and bows for Christmas. I wasn't feeling the spirit. It was the holiday season, a time for family and coming together, but it felt like my family was falling apart.

My brothers were waiting at the Salt House restaurant when I arrived. My oldest brother, Owen, was texting on his phone while the next oldest, Jack, was arguing with Oliver and Matt about one of their business venture ideas. Owen put his phone away when I walked up to the bar.

"Why were you talking to Mom and Dad?" my older brother demanded.

"I haven't had enough to drink yet if we are having some sort of family therapy session about our parents," Jack said, signaling to the bartender.

"At least Oliver's old enough to drink now," Owen said, leaning against the bar top.

"Is Belle coming?" my youngest brother asked as he happily took the drink the bartender slid across the counter. Owen glared at him as he started to drain it.

"This isn't a frat party," my older brother growled. "That's expensive liquor."

"Just order him water next time," Jack drawled. "He doesn't even know how to drink like an adult."

"How were Mom and Dad?" Matt asked as he sipped his scotch under Owen's watchful eye.

"Let me guess," Jack said, "they were self-absorbed and image obsessed as always."

"They weren't that bad," I said, feeling as if I had to defend our parents.

"Uh-huh. Did they even ask about Matt and Oliver?"

"Er—"

"Of course not," Owen scoffed and downed his drink.

"Hey!" Oliver complained. "You didn't savor that."

Owen shoved him slightly with his shoulder and ordered another drink.

"They don't care about anyone other than themselves," Jack told me flatly. "You need to cut them off."

"But it's Christmas!" I said.

"Eventually, you're going to have to pick a side, because you're not going to feed them information about me and my life," my older brother warned.

"I didn't tell them anything," I insisted. "Besides, it's not like we had a long conversation. They squeezed me in between the ballet and dinner with their friends."

Owen snorted.

"Hm," Jack said, staring into his glass. "I would have thought that they would have been all over you with your hedge fund."

"You clearly don't know them all that well," Owen stated. "They don't think their friends will be impressed enough with Jonathan selling alcohol and running"—Owen made air quotes—"a hedge fund. Mom and Dad are math and science people. They only like what they care about. Anything else is unimportant. They even complained that Belle had gone traveling and didn't have a real job the last time I was unfortunate enough to talk to them."

"That's rich," Matt scoffed, "considering that Belle is turning into them."

"Hey," Owen growled at him.

"You can't act like it's not true!" Oliver complained. "She got mean."

We all looked at each other. None of us had wanted to say it, but there it was.

"You can't just expect women to be nice all the time. That's sexist," I told Matt.

"She's not *not* nice. She seems really unhappy," Jack reflected.

"Maybe it's because she came back," I said. "She left for a reason, remember? She was tired of being forced to be a mother to a bunch of kids she didn't choose to have."

"Or maybe it's Jonathan," Jack said. "She's had to see him for hours every day for the past few months. That's enough to put anyone over the edge. She was nicer earlier this year."

"That was because of Greg," Owen said. "Of course, none of the Svenssons will give me a straight answer on what happened."

"Maybe she'll get back together with him over Christmas," I said as the bartender handed me my drink.

"Or maybe she'll peace out after the bake-off," Jack said.

"She wouldn't leave, would she?" I asked in concern.

"She's not here now, is she," Jack pointed out.

I checked my watch. We'd been waiting on her for almost half an hour. I took a deep breath.

Before I could make some excuse, the restaurant hostess came over. "The rest of your party is here, and we can seat you now," she said cheerfully.

"Belle!" Matt and Oliver said happily. "You came!"

"Apologies. I had a late meeting."

"A late-night meeting with Greg?" Oliver asked drunkenly.

The look Belle gave him could have flayed him. Oliver sobered up very quickly.

"Can we sit on the roof deck?" Belle asked the hostess as she led us to a large table.

The hostess took in Belle's boots, thin black jeans, and short-sleeved top. "Outside?"

I nodded. "It is boiling hot in here."

The hostess gave us odd looks as she led us outside and had another of her coworkers sweep the snow off the table.

Owen took off his suit jacket. The waiter's eyes bugged out of his head.

"So Mom and Dad didn't even ask about your girlfriend?" Jack prompted after we had ordered appetizers.

"You have a girlfriend?" Owen asked as he continued to study the menu.

"No," I muttered, the anger and hurt when I had walked in on Morticia's rant about me coming back in full force.

"The internet says you do," Oliver told me, holding out his phone. There was more than one fan page dedicated to me and Morticia.

"Good lord," Owen said.

"She's not like Jack's or Owen's girlfriend," Matt told me. "She looks scary."

"Maybe she's tired of dealing with two-faced imbeciles with too much money and a serious empathy deficit," Belle said.

I looked around. "You're not talking about me, are you?" I asked, offended.

"She's probably talking about Greg," Owen said. "I can go beat him up for you."

Belle screwed up her mouth.

I became very interested in my appetizer, which had just arrived.

The steam from our sister's breath curled around her like smoke as she laid into Owen. "I don't need my little brother to jump to my defense," she snapped.

"I'm just saying," Owen said, digging in his heels, "you were there for us when we probably didn't deserve it. Mom and Dad did you wrong, and they never had to pay for it. But I can definitely make Greg pay for it."

"It. What?" Belle's voice was dangerously cold. Even I started shivering.

"I don't know," Owen said stubbornly. "But you're my sister, and no one messes with my sister, not even the Svensson. Not even if there are dozens of them and they're crazy as hell."

Belle's face softened. "While I appreciate the sentiment, I'm fine. Just trying to keep my investment firm afloat and somehow keep Jonathan's company from hemorrhaging money."

"My company is doing great," I bragged. "The bake-off is a huge success. We're selling out like candy in an elf village."

"I'm glad to see the attitude change," she said, "because you can't go back to your condo tonight; it's being decorated. You need to stay with Jack."

"No!" my brother and I both said at once.

CHAPTER 25

Morticia

"Is there anything better than midnight shopping?" Lilith exclaimed when we arrived at the mall. Christmas hours were in full swing, and the mall boasted a closing time of two a.m.

"Midnight pretzels!" Emma said. "There's an Auntie Anne's on level two. Come on."

"I have a whole list of things we need," I reminded my friend as we rode the escalator up to look for the pretzel shop.

"I know, but I can't shop on an empty stomach," Emma said. "And you're still in a bad mood and need carbs. Look! They have special sugarplum pretzel bites with cream cheese frosting dipping sauce!" Emma pulled out her credit card.

"I want a pretzel with spicy cheese dipping sauce," Lilith said after reading the menu posted on the wall. "And Morticia wants the pretzel dog, because she couldn't get the sausage from Jonathan."

"I never wanted it."

"You totally wanted to get laid," Lilith said as she held out her hand. "Where is his credit card? Gimmie!"

"We're supposed to be buying Christmas decorations, not pretzels, with Jonathan's credit card," I told my twin as she tried to wrestle my purse away from me. "We're not going to be pretzel gold diggers. We're not like Keeley."

"I thought that was you all," a dry voice said.

Lilith used the distraction to snatch my purse.

"Sarah?"

My cousin Keeley's younger sister stood there, along with Karen and Larry, my aunt and uncle. We stared at each other. I hadn't seen them since my grandmother's funeral a little over a year ago. They had disappeared off the face of the earth, just like they had when Keeley had had me sentenced to a stint in the psych ward.

"Fancy seeing you here in the big, scary city," Lilith drawled. "Come down to enjoy the holiday lights? You didn't get mugged, did you?"

Our aunt and uncle had a serious aversion to any sort of urban area. Even downtown Harrogate was too big for them, and it was a small town.

"We are here to support Sarah in her journey," my aunt said, blinking nervously.

"Did you finally dump your cheating husband?" I asked Sarah. "Good for you."

"Oy, Matilda!"

"Morticia," I seethed as Sarah's husband, Trevor, sauntered over.

"Did you order my pretzel, babe?" he asked Sarah.

"I believe in forgiveness," Sarah said, voice quivering. "I have forgiven Trevor for his transgressions against me."

"You mean cheating on you with your own sister and maid of honor the night before your wedding?" Lilith asked, dipping her pretzel bite into cheese sauce. "I hope that forgiveness came with a vacay to Hawaii and a shopping spree."

"We're working on our relationship. We are going to have a baby to fix things," Sarah said earnestly. "But first, we have to heal old wounds and move on from the past."

Trevor was shifting his weight on his feet. "She won't let me exercise my husbandly rights until we work this out," Trevor stated. "Hey, can I have one of your pretzel bites?" He reached toward Lilith's paper tray. One of Salem's paws snuck out of her purse and swiped at Trevor, who jumped back with a curse.

"Good cat," Lilith said smugly.

I looked between Trevor and Sarah.

"You haven't consummated your marriage from eight months ago?" Lilith asked.

"Hey," Trevor said, wagging his finger in Lilith's face. I grabbed my twin before she could bite it off. "After my transgression, I have repented and become a spiritual leader. Sarah is purifying her thoughts before we truly become man and wife."

"Or maybe she was so turned off by you that she is putting it off," Lilith retorted.

"Babe," Trevor whined to Sarah, "tell them it isn't true. You and me are going to have our own little spiritual retreat out in the woods together and have twenty-five babies and have our own reality TV show, right?"

My womb shriveled up.

"That's right," Sarah said earnestly. "But we have to move past this hurdle before we can become one spiritual and carnal being."

"Guess we better order you a sausage pretzel dog, too, Sarah," Lilith said.

"She's still a virgin," Aunt Karen said. "She's a good girl, keeping herself tidy for marriage."

"There's tidy and then there are mental hang-ups," I drawled.

Emma stood by and scarfed down her pretzel while watching the drama unfold.

I felt sorry for Sarah. She had always been the mousy one compared to Keeley and her partying ways. All Sarah had wanted was the fairy-tale ending—the husband, the family, the kids—and now she was saddled with Trevor.

"Dump him and find someone new," I urged her. "There are a lot of elves in the toy shop."

"The sex toy shop, that is," Lilith cackled.

Sarah shuddered. "I would never use something like that."

"Of course my daughter wouldn't," my uncle blustered. "She's a good girl. You two were always horrible influences. You're the ones who turned Keeley to a life of denigration."

"Because it wasn't her own sociopathic nature," Lilith said, rolling her eyes.

"I can feel the devil wafting off of you," my uncle continued, fanny pack quivering with indignation. "Begone!" he thundered, pointing a finger at us.

I took a bite of my pretzel as my uncle panted. I didn't want Larry to think I was leaving because of him.

"Babe," Trevor whined. "I want a pretzel. Why haven't you ordered it for me yet?"

❈ ❈ ❈

"And that's why cats are better than men," Lilith said, petting Salem as we walked into a high-end department store with towering Christmas displays.

"Cats won't cheat on you on your wedding day."

"But they will be super demanding for expensive food," I said as Salem made soft meows. I gave him a treat to keep him quiet.

"You're not supposed to bring animals in here," one of the well-dressed saleswomen said, hurrying over. She was wearing a black Chanel suit with snowflake earrings and several large, sparkly Christmas brooches.

"He's my emotional support animal," Lilith deadpanned. Salem stuck his tongue out.

The saleswoman made a face. "Outside," she ordered.

"Guess we'll go somewhere else," Emma said.

"Yeah," Lilith added with a predatory grin. "Too bad you're going to lose out on the commission."

"I highly doubt…"

Lilith pulled out Jonathan's credit card and fanned herself.

"We better hurry, Morticia. We don't want to show up empty-handed and disappoint Mr. Frost."

"Frost?" the saleswoman was intrigued. "We have some lovely decorations to choose from."

She led us through the store. Lilith and I pulled yards of gauzy fabric, boxes and boxes of glass and metallic ornaments, ribbons, and lights. We did not buy fake Christmas trees. I had a feeling Jonathan would only like real ones.

"I sure hope Jonathan loves Christmas as much as he says he does," Emma remarked as the saleswoman checked us out. "Because this seems excessive."

The shocked, hurt look on his face flitted before my eyes. I felt guilty. "He'll like it," I said firmly. *I hope he does.*

There was a Christmas tree sales lot in the parking lot outside the mall.

"Sorry," the owner said in a thick Long Island accent. "We only have the huge trees left. We'll get some smaller ones in tomorrow." He pointed to three tall, bushy trees in the back of the lot.

"Actually, those are perfect," I said. Jonathan's condo had fifteen-foot ceilings. We needed a large tree.

"These are blue spruces," the owner bragged, "from upstate. Not gonna get a better tree than this, let me tell ya! Should I bag it up?"

"Yes, please," I said. I wanted to see Jonathan's face when he saw the tree.

Not because I like him. It's an apology.

"Do you deliver?" Emma asked the salesman.

"I certainly do not," he said as he ran Jonathan's credit card. "You ladies have a good evening."

The Uber driver we ordered laughed at us when we asked him if we could stash the twelve-foot tree on his car roof. He was still laughing as he drove off.

"It's freezing!" Lilith chattered, jumping up and down. "How are we going to transport the tree back?"

"Train," I said grimly. "That's the New York way. I saw a guy moving his whole saltwater aquarium on the subway one day." I checked my phone. "The nearest stop is half a mile away."

"Crap."

"Don't worry!" Emma said cheerfully. "I'm from the Midwest. Midwestern women are made for handling cattle, birthing babies, and carrying heavy loads."

She picked up one of the plastic straps holding the tree together. "Ladies, let's march!"

* * *

"I'm covered in pine sap," I huffed as we hauled the tree down the sidewalk. Fortunately, the high-end department store did deliver, or we would have been in bad shape.

"Are we almost there?" I wheezed. I was not made for exercise. I was made for reclining in a moody salon.

"We've only walked a block," Emma said. "Buck up! You ate a sausage pretzel roll earlier!"

"Yes, but then I had to shop for Christmas decorations. All the scented candles made me light-headed," I complained.

"We should sing while we walk," Emma said cheerfully. "Jingle bells! Jingle bells…"

Salem yodeled along to her off-key singing.

"Hello!" a woman in an oversized wool coat called, hustling up to us. "Is that a cat? I love cats. Would you like another one?"

"Uh, what?"

"Another cat," the woman repeated, holding up a cat carrier.

"We just had a Christmas pet adoption at the cat rescue. But no one wanted to adopt this beautiful baby. Her name is Cindy Lou Who. Her former owner was a very rich high-society lady who, unfortunately, passed away, and her kids wouldn't keep Cindy Lou, poor thing. She's grown accustomed to a certain level of luxury, and I've been trying to find the perfect owner."

"Ma'am," I said firmly, "we are walking our Christmas tree to the train station. I don't think Cindy Lou will be very happy with us."

"Nonsense. That's a twelve-foot-tall blue spruce, a very fancy tree! I'd bet even if you don't have money, you are very close to someone who does."

"We cannot take that cat. I am very sorry."

"Merry Christmas," she said, placing the strap of the cat carrier around my neck. I had my hands full of sticky Christmas tree and couldn't disentangle the cat carrier before the woman danced away, singing, "We wish you a merry Christmas!"

Cindy Lou Who hissed at me from the cat carrier.

"Maybe Jonathan wants a cat?" Lilith asked after a stunned moment of silence.

CHAPTER 26

Jonathan

There were not any breakfast leftovers. Chloe, Jack's girlfriend, had cooked for Jack, Matt, Oliver, and me. However, my brothers had vacuumed up all the food.

"This isn't a hotel," Jack told me when I pointed this fact out.

"I wasn't complaining," I retorted, "I was just making a comment that I did not get enough to eat."

"Oh no!" Chloe cried. "I don't want people to starve!"

"He's fine," my brother insisted, trying to block Chloe from the stove. "Jonathan has ten thousand bake-off dessert calories to eat later today. He shouldn't have a big breakfast."

❄ ❄ ❄

My stomach rumbled as I hiked to the studio.

"Where are your pajamas?" Belle asked when she saw me.

"I'm not walking around in pajamas," I informed my sister.

"It's a PJ party. It's going to look weird if you're wearing a suit and the contestants are all in pajamas."

I surveyed the women at the baking stations. To call what they were wearing pajamas was a gross inaccuracy. They were wearing lingerie—sheer teddies with skimpy, lacy underwear festooned with lots of feathers, sequins, and fur.

"Maybe I need to put on my silk bodysuit with the strategically placed holes," I joked.

"Do not," Belle warned.

I settled at the judges' table while Anastasia sent one girl home then explained the day's challenge.

"This is the Christmas morning challenge, bakers! Create a fun, festive breakfast dessert that would be a perfect way to kick off a morning of opening presents. And don't forget that Christmas is not just for kids! Do make liberal use of the Hillrock West Distillery liquors to give your baked goods a punch."

My eyes swung to Morticia's station. She was studiously avoiding me.

Now that I had had some time to reflect, I couldn't fault her for her rant. After all, I hadn't acted in the most gentlemanly manner. I had, at times, been pretty downright insulting.

It's your own fault she doesn't like you.

I wondered if it would be too late to fix things.

After the contestants had started cooking, Belle gestured to me.

"You need to go home and change."

"Seriously?" I complained.

"One of the production assistants went and bought you some pajamas. They're waiting in your condo. Go try them on and pick one." Belle surveyed the contestants. "I foresee a lot of loaded pancakes in your future, so you may want to choose some pajamas with a bit of give."

❉ ❉ ❉

I wasn't sure what I had been expecting when I walked into my condo, but a space decorated similarly to my parents' house during Christmas hadn't been it. It was like walking into a snow globe. A huge *real* Christmas tree stood in the corner with impeccably wrapped presents underneath it. The tree was trimmed with glass and gold ornaments with big red bows and glittering lights. A number of the ornaments were ones we sold in the distillery's online store.

Garlands and lights hung from the heavy timber beams on the high ceiling. On the mantel over the gas fireplace (unfortunately, I couldn't have a wood-burning one) was a miniature Christmas village. Stockings with the various contestants' names on them hung over the fireplace in a neat row. My whole condo smelled like Christmas, all fresh pine and spices. The table was set for a feast with Christmas china, more garland, candles, and miniature metal Christmas trees, reindeer, and sleigh.

I opened the french doors that led out to the balcony. Outside, Morticia had draped the railings with more garlands and lights. There was a small metal café table set with poinsettia, a few Christmas figurines, and an antique oil lamp, one of the tall ones with the glass chimney.

It was the nicest thing anyone had ever done for me—except Morticia hadn't done it for me. "She did it because she was paid to," I reminded myself.

But she hadn't had to go to this much effort. I mean, a real Christmas tree, real garlands—the place smelled amazing! I could just lie on my living room floor with the doors open and breathe everything in.

What if Morticia had gone the extra mile for me because she had known I would love it?

All the contestants and crew were going to be over in my condo filming soon. I had to get dressed.

I grimaced when I went into my bedroom. The production assistant had left a stack of pajama sets in my bedroom. They were not my style. I loved Christmas, but the pajamas looked like those designed for toddlers, just scaled up. There were happy dancing elves making toys on one set, Santa riding on his sleigh on another, and snowmen on the third.

I put that one on first; it seemed like the least offensive. The bottoms were snug. I looked down.

"Maybe I should wear two pair of underwear."

At least the pants almost fit though. The shirt didn't fit at all. The seam split right down the side when I tried to tug it over my head. So did the next and the next.

Belle: *Are you ready??*
Jonathan: *Everything is the wrong size.*
Belle: *Just make do. It's a twenty-minute segment.*

Fuck. I looked around at the shreds of ruined pajama tops. I didn't want to run around shirtless. With all those girls in their skimpy outfits, it might give a few of them the wrong idea. I didn't even want them in my condo. Now instead of it smelling like fresh snow and Christmas, it was going to smell like cheap perfume and flammable lingerie.

I pawed through my drawers and pulled out a black shirt.

Belle: *First contestants are coming!*
Jonathan: *Five minutes.*

I inspected my reflection. In the mirror, the pants were actually a few inches too short. I looked like Tarzan.

I had a robe somewhere that someone had given me way back when. I rummaged in the back corners of my walk-in closet, trying to find it, as my phone buzzed with texts from my sister telling me to hurry up.

"I think this is it," I grunted. I fished around and grabbed something soft and fluffy and moist. I jerked my hand back.

"*What the fuck?*"

I shined my phone's flashlight into the back section of my closet. Two blue orbs stared back at me.

"It's the Krampus!" I yelled.

"Jonathan?" my sister called. Her footsteps came down the hall. "How long does it take you to get dressed?"

"There's a demon back there!" I yelled, running out of my closet.

My sister stifled a laugh when she saw me.

"Hey," I protested, "you wanted me to wear this."

"Do you just have a normal set of pajamas?" she asked me.

"No, I don't wear pajamas," I said mulishly.

"Then put on some sweatpants. I swear to god, I'm not doing Christmas next year; I'm going to the Bahamas."

I sagged a bit.

"You can come too," she assured me.

"Can we go to Iceland instead?" I pleaded.

"Sure, whatever. Just change. I'll get your 'demon.'" She made air quotes. "It's probably a band T-shirt or something you bought during a drunk shopping session."

I heard her rummaging around in the closet while I tugged on a pair of sweatpants. "Holy shit!" my sister exclaimed. "When did you adopt a cat?"

CHAPTER 27

Morticia

Jonathan looked pissed during the bake-off challenge introduction. I didn't know what to do.

Why do you care what he thinks of you? You two are completely different. There was no hope anything was going to work out. *He doesn't like people like you. You're abrasive and odd.*

Around me, the other contestants in their lingerie baked their desserts, their perky boobs bouncing as they worked. I was wearing pajamas, yes, but I had a whole layer of clothes on under them including tights, a bra, and a chemise.

Concentrate on the food, I told myself. I was making apple-caramel cinnamon rolls, one of my favorite recipes.

As I made the dough (using buttermilk to make the cinnamon rolls as fluffy as possible), I fretted. When we had finally finished our trek back to Jonathan's condo with the cat and the tree last night, we still had to decorate. Unfortunately, somehow, we had lost the cat.

> **Morticia:** *Did you find Cindy Lou Who?*
> **Lilith:** *We looked all morning. Now they are getting ready to start filming.*
> **Emma:** *I hope the poor baby didn't escape outside somehow.*
> **Morticia:** *We should have kept a better eye on her after we gave her a bath.*

The British shorthair had tolerated about thirty seconds of us drying her off then had jumped out of Lilith's arms and disappeared into the depths of Jonathan's excessively large condo.

We had had too much decorating to do to try and hunt down the cat. We had figured she would come out of hiding once we had finished the decorating and there wasn't as much commotion.

Except she hadn't reappeared.

It was one more rubber band on my ball of anxiety. My art piece wasn't done, and I had just two weeks left before I needed to submit it. Somehow, I was still in *The Great Christmas Bake-Off* despite my best—or worst—efforts, I had to create all the marketing materials for the distillery, and now I had a mountain of cinnamon rolls to bake.

After placing my finished dough in a greased bowl and sliding it into the warm oven to rise, I started heating the sugar on the stove while I chopped up the Granny Smith apples.

Even though I despised Christmas, I loved cinnamon rolls. These apple-caramel cinnamon rolls were actually one of my fall recipes, but I was going to add some green and red sprinkles to the cream cheese icing to make them seem Christmassy. I tossed the apples with heaps of cinnamon, nutmeg, and a generous splash of bourbon.

As the sugar heated, I stirred it until it formed clumps then finally started to melt into a golden syrup. I carefully added the salted butter, whisking vigorously. Once it was combined, I slowly drizzled in the heavy cream. The salty-sweet smell wafted to my nose, and I started to relax. Caramel was my go-to treat. Some days, I liked it even more than dark chocolate!

I bet Jonathan will love these.

Wait. I was just upset because I felt bad about hurting his feelings; I could not start obsessing over him. That was what it was—just an obsession, an unhealthy obsession. Jonathan was a bit like these cinnamon rolls. Sure, maybe one was okay, but if I wasn't careful, the next thing I knew, I would have eaten the whole pan and would have to spend the rest of the day sleeping off a sugar headache.

The caramel was done; I added a dash of sea salt to bring out the flavor then set it aside to cool. Then I cooked the apples a bit on the stove, enough to soften them but not to stew them. While they cooked, I rolled out the dough into a large rectangle that covered a good portion of my table.

Once they saw I was finally assembling the cinnamon rolls, the camera guys hustled over, directing me to rearrange my station so they could get the best shot.

Lilith hovered next to them. "Sharing is caring," she told me. "You know, sisterly love and all that."

"Not until after I get my B-roll," Zane said from behind his camera.

"Just put Lilith's and mine in a separate special dish," Emma wheedled. "You know how I feel about cinnamon rolls!"

"These are for Jonathan," I reminded her as I spread a thick layer of European butter on the dough.

"Oh, for *Jonathan*!" Emma giggled.

"You can't be obsessing over him if it's going to start to impact me," Lilith said. "Remember that song at the beginning of *White Christmas*: 'Lord help the mister who comes between me and my sister...'"

Emma snorted. "And I believe it ends with, 'And Lord help the sister that comes between me and my man!'"

"Jonathan is not my man," I said through gritted teeth as I sprinkled spoonfuls of cinnamon, nutmeg, and a little sea salt on the buttered dough.

"You're making him apple cinnamon rolls," Lilith insisted. She tried to swipe a spoonful of the caramel sauce, but I rapped her hand with a spoon.

"I need that," I said, drizzling it on the dough.

"You're surely not going to use all of it."

I sighed and handed my twin the container after I had used what I needed. "Don't come complaining to me when all your teeth fall out."

"And now the apples," Emma whispered as I spooned heaps of the apples onto the dough.

"You totally have the hots for him," Lilith said around a spoonful of caramel. "I pleaded on my deathbed for you to make these for me when I was sick, and you turned up your nose. Now Jonathan—who, I may add, you have known for all of what, two weeks?—warrants his very own pan of cinnamon rolls."

"Yesss," Emma said, "roll it up into a big, thick roll! *Oh yes!* This is so much better than any porno."

"We all live such sad little lives," Lilith said, stuffing a spoonful of caramel into Emma's mouth.

After the dough was rolled up, I cut it into two-inch slices then carefully arranged them into several pans.

"All the extras are mine," Lilith insisted when I slid the pans into the oven.

"Nooo," Emma begged, "I need my own pan."

"I can't believe I made so many," I complained as I set the timer.

"It's sacrilegious to make less than enough cinnamon rolls to feed everyone on the block," Lilith reminded me. "You're channeling Mimi's spirit."

"You need to channel some caffeine," Emma said. "You're the last one left."

"You can't rush perfection."

"Jonathan's going to be too full from all the other desserts to eat yours," Emma cried.

"Too bad," Lilith said happily. "Guess I'll have to eat all these myself."

I chewed on my lip and started making the cream cheese frosting. I was the last contestant. Would Jonathan even bother? Maybe I should have made something less labor intensive, but apple cinnamon rolls seemed like exactly the type of breakfast goodies he would enjoy. Of course, if I were actually cooking him breakfast, I would make him a full English breakfast with sausage, fried eggs, and heirloom tomatoes. The cinnamon rolls would only be a part of the spread.

"Uh-oh," Lilith said. The tone of her voice let me know some sort of wild accusation was incoming.

I turned on the electric mixer. "Can't hear you!" I yelled as it whirred. I hoped my twin would forget all about what she was going to say.

She raised a black eyebrow when I was done. "You like—"

I turned the mixer back on.

My twin tapped her foot then pulled the plug out.

"Hey, I'm cooking here!"

"You don't just like Jonathan, you have a full-on crush on him. Yes, you do! Admit it!" she cried.

"Shh," I said. "That's not true."

"You're doing nice things for him, and you were just daydreaming about him," she said, accusingly.

"You couldn't possibly know that," I scoffed.

"I'm your twin," Lilith said. "I know what you're thinking."

"I don't have a crush on him. I may be, admittedly, a little *intrigued* by him, but he is a fine male specimen."

"Besides," Emma said, "she can't like him or be in a relationship. She's going to be literally on the other side of the country in Los Angeles come New Year. A man like Jonathan is not going to want to do long distance."

"We have to exorcise your obsession with him then. You won't be able to concentrate on the internship if you can only think about him," Lilith said as I took the cinnamon buns out of the oven.

"I'm not obsessed," I countered. I spread the cream cheese frosting on while the rolls were still warm.

"Just sleep with him," Emma suggested, snapping pictures of the cinnamon rolls. "It's probably not going to be that good, because guys like that only care about themselves. He'll do a few crappy porno moves, ejaculate, and not get you off. You'll be so mad that he'll be exorcised right out of your head."

"I was thinking candles, incense, and holy water," Lilith said, "but yeah, I suppose hate sex could work."

"I'm not sleeping with him," I told my friend as I pried a few rolls out and arranged them on a plate.

"I better take these over there. Keeley probably has her claws in him."

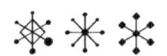

※ ※ ※

I raced across the street to Jonathan's condo building. My mind was spinning. I should have been asleep; I had been up all night. Instead, I tried to mentally prep myself for what I was going to say. I didn't want to look stupid on camera. Should I go for resting bitch face or a death glare? Maybe Jonathan wouldn't acknowledge me at all.

The elevator doors opened. There, in the foyer, was Jonathan. He was shirtless, barefoot, and wearing gray sweatpants. He was also snuggling a familiar gray-and-white British shorthair to his chest.

He looked up, a bright smile on his face. It quickly fell when he saw me.

Told you not to get obsessed. So much for sleeping with him.

"I brought apple-caramel cinnamon rolls," I said lamely. "Guess we should go and get this over with."

CHAPTER 28

Jonathan

I wasn't sure what I had been expecting when I saw Morticia. After she had so lovingly decorated my condo, I had thought maybe there was something there. But now she was looming in the elevator doorway, scowling at me.

She said she didn't like you. Just let it go.

"Where did you find Cindy Lou Who?" Morticia asked.

My mouth quirked. "Cindy Lou Who?" I looked at the cat. Her wide blue eyes blinked back at me. "Yes, I think you are a Cindy Lou Who!"

"Sorry," Morticia said in a rush. "I'll text my sister to come pick her up. It was a disaster last night with the tree. We couldn't get it in the Uber, and we had to take a train. Then there was a crazy woman who said we had to take the cat because she was a poor little rich girl, and her rich owner had died, leaving her penniless."

She reached for the cat.

I cradled Cindy Lou to my chest. "No, this is my cat."

"You can't have that cat," Morticia said flatly.

"What are you going to do with the cat?" I teased lightly, "Aren't you homeless?"

"I'm not homeless," she said through gritted teeth. "I am currently consciously uncoupled from my former residence."

"She's homeless," I said to Cindy Lou, nuzzling the cat's nose. "But she brought cinnamon rolls, so I guess she can stay." I set the cat down then stole a cinnamon bun off the plate before Morticia could stop me and took a bite. "Holy shit!" I sank down to the floor.

"Are you all right?" Morticia asked in concern, hovering over me. "I didn't actually taste them yet, which I should have; it's a cardinal sin."

I took another big bite then held out the rest of the fluffy cinnamon bun and grabbed her chin.

"Eat it," I ordered.

Morticia took a bite.

"Fucking amazing." I sighed and polished the rest off. "Life changing." I grabbed another cinnamon bun.

"You're supposed to eat that in front of the camera!" Morticia reminded me.

"These should be in the same category as sex," I said, shaking my head. "You should only eat one of these cinnamon buns in bed with a special someone and not in front of an audience."

"If you're going to get cream cheese frosting all over your face, then yes." Morticia huffed.

Cindy Lou leaned in to delicately lick my chin.

"Stop that," Morticia ordered the cat. She swiped my face with the kitchen towel that had been covering the buns. "Belle is going to kill me," she said.

The condo door opened.

"I'm not going to kill you," Belle assured her. "Honestly, Jonathan, you said you were coming out here because your cat was having anxiety issues."

"Cindy Lou is a delicate flower," I said, standing up.

"I thought you said her name was Princess Muffy."

"I changed it," I said, taking another bite of the cinnamon bun.

"What are you eating? Oh my god, I cannot believe you!" Belle exclaimed. "I'm trying to put on a show."

I silently fed my sister a bite of the cinnamon roll. "You're welcome," I said sagely then took the plate with the last remaining one on it and stood in front of the nearest camera.

"Dear America," I said as Cindy Lou struggled up to perch on my shoulder. "Today I have eaten the greatest dessert in the history of Christmas. This caramel-apple cinnamon bun is life changing. I am a new man!" I held up the last one. "Behold, Christmas perfection!"

I grabbed Morticia and pulled her in next to me. "Now that I am three rolls deep, Morticia, would you like to tell the fans about your cinnamon buns?"

"Secret family recipe," she said brusquely.

"You sound unhinged," Belle hissed at me.

I looked down at the plate. "Hey! Who ate all the cinnamon rolls?"

"For f—" my sister began.

"Party games!" Keeley all but shrieked.

I winced. Cindy Lou made an irritated noise. I handed her to a production assistant to put her in my bedroom. Unfortunately, I could not be so lucky as to escape the PJ party myself.

"I think I smashed those cinnamon rolls a little quickly," I whispered to Morticia.

"Each one is so large that it's about four serving sizes, so you probably ate two weeks' work of your daily cinnamon bun allotment in about five minutes." A small smile played around her mouth.

Maybe she didn't despise me completely.

"Drink?" Keeley offered, shoving a mug of bourbon hot chocolate in my face.

"Can I just have the bourbon?" I asked weakly.

"But it's Christmas!" she insisted. "Look! There are peppermint marshmallows in it!"

I handed the mug to Morticia. She took a sip and winced. "There's peppermint schnapps in it too."

"And essential oils!" Keeley chirped.

I took the mug back and tasted it. "That's like a Christmas Long Island iced tea."

"There's nothing wrong with it," Keeley insisted. "Besides, you have to drink while we play spin the bottle."

I almost spat out the drink. "No," I said flatly.

"Come on," Keeley whined.

I looked helplessly at Belle.

"Just one spin. It's good TV."

Fuck.

"What happened to being a protective big sister?" I demanded.

"You ate all the cinnamon rolls," Belle retorted, "then went on an unhinged rant. I doubt we'll be able to use the footage."

"I—yes, I did."

"I thought this was supposed to be a wholesome PJ party," Morticia whispered to me.

"Not when they're all dressed like that," I retorted under my breath.

"You should talk," she said in a low voice. "You're not wearing a shirt."

We settled on the floor as Keeley handed me an empty bourbon bottle. "Whoever it lands on, you have to go kiss."

"Yes," Morticia said, "because apparently none of us here has matured past the age of fourteen."

"I'm sure some of us haven't," Keeley growled at Morticia.

Morticia's mouth was a hard line of blood-red lipstick.

"Go on, Jonathan, spin the bottle."

I looked around at the scantily clad women who had invaded my space. I didn't want to kiss any of them. There was a reason I kept very firm boundaries between my personal life, my business, and my social life. The last time I had brought a woman back to my place and had a relationship, it had been like throwing a nuclear bomb into a dumpster fire.

I didn't want any of these women to think they had some sort of a chance with me. I would never settle down. Even if I did wish I could have a family and the traditional Christmas with the kids and presents and cinnamon buns in the morning, that was all it was—a dream. But all these women waited breathlessly, like I was about to make their dreams come true.

All except for Morticia, who glared at the bottle as if she wanted it to explode into a million pieces.

Unable to put it off, I drained my spiked hot chocolate, the warm alcohol burning my throat. Then I reached out and spun the bottle, the light glinting off the gold foil label as it rotated. I held my breath as it slowed, did one more rotation, then stopped, pointing straight at Morticia.

CHAPTER 29

Morticia

When Jonathan had spun the bottle, I had willed it to land on me. When I was younger, I liked to pretend I was Matilda and that I could move things with my mind. It was what had helped me survive through my mom fighting with her boyfriend du jour.

I never could make a deck of cards fly around the room or even a door swing shut. But now I willed the bottle to land on me, though it was more of a wish. I didn't know what I would do if the bottle actually landed on me. It had been years since I had kissed a guy, and he hadn't been even ten percent as hot as Jonathan.

But now I was staring down the end of the empty bourbon bottle.

"You can't kiss her," Keeley said, reaching for the bottle to spin it again. "She'll give you a disease."

I waited for the humiliation to descend, for Jonathan to sneer and say of course not. He stood up and reached for the bottle.

Of course this is happening.

But instead of spinning it, he picked it up then extended a hand to me.

"Rules are rules," he said, face serious as he set the bottle on the coffee table. Large hand on my waist, he guided me to a room off of the hallway and softly closed the door.

I was reeling and barely registered that he had taken me into his study.

Jonathan left me frozen by the door as he went to a small bar off to the side to pour a drink. "Bourbon?" he offered.

I shook my head.

Jonathan sauntered over to me, the gray sweatpants slung low on his hips.

My mouth was dry. "Actually." I swallowed. "Actually, I think maybe I will have one."

He extended the glass to me, and I downed it.

"You don't have to..."

Jonathan tilted his head slightly.

"You know..." I made a motion in the direction of the living room.

But Jonathan stepped closer, circling one arm around my waist. "Rules are rules," he whispered, leaning forward, his mouth inches from mine. "But you have to tell me you want it."

I want it! my body screamed.

I hesitated. I wanted him to kiss me. But my thoughts were spinning.

"You know," he said, smile crooked, "you don't have to actually like someone to fuck them."

"I thought we were just talking about kissing," I croaked. I couldn't take my eyes off of his mouth.

"Were we?" he said mildly. "Oh, that's right." Then he pressed his mouth to mine.

His lips were soft, and I moaned against his mouth as his other hand came up to cup the back of my head. His hand tangled in my hair as he kissed me harder, his tongue insistent as it danced with mine. My hands groped wildly then landed on his bare, muscular back.

It was suddenly too much. The sensation of his bare skin, soft and warm, shook me out of my stupor. "Holy shit!" I gasped, pushing Jonathan away.

He leveled his gaze at me. He wasn't smiling.

"Guess we should rejoin the party."

❋ ❋ ❋

"And you just left?" Emma shrieked.

We were down at the bar at the bottom of the Hillrock West Distillery office.

"You just left him after he said he wanted to hate fuck you?"

"Girl," Lilith said, shoving a drink in front of me, "what happened to exorcising your sex demons? You had the perfect opportunity."

"Not to mention we still have to work with this guy," Emma reminded me.

"So I should have slept with him to keep him from firing us?"

"No!" Emma said. "You should have slept with him because he was hot and half naked."

"There were other people in the apartment," I hissed.

"Then take a rain check, don't just push him off then duck out. Finish your drink, then go up there and salvage the situation," Lilith ordered.

"Salvage? I'm not sleeping with him," I hissed.

"No one said you have to sleep with him," Lilith told me. "Just smooth things over—maybe take him a dessert."

"I could take him some more cinnamon rolls. He really liked those," I mused.

"Well, not those. There are none left," Lilith said.

"Where did they all go?"

"That is not important," Lilith said primly. "What is important is your own growth and self-care and our paycheck that is supposed to fund your internship."

"Come," Emma said. "I will ask for to-go drinks, then we will go bake him something and smooth things over. It's not like you have to become best buddies. After all, he didn't want to make love to you, he wanted to hate fuck you."

But that was the problem, wasn't it? I wanted him to like me, not hate me. But there it was. He had as much as said that he despised me.

CHAPTER 30

Jonathan

"I guess I blew that," I said to Cindy Lou, toasting her with my umpteenth drink after the production team had finished filming.

I shouldn't have just kissed Morticia. I should have waited for her go-ahead.

It seemed like she was into it.

Then why had she pushed me away?

The problem was that I had mixed not just personal and social life but also business life. The lines were blurred. Morticia worked for me. She was a contestant. I had kissed her. In my condo. I did not bring girls back to my condo, especially not ones who I offered a hate fuck to.

I paced around, then I poured another drink.

I should have just left her alone, but the reality was that I wanted her. I wanted her in my home, baking and decorating and making cutting remarks. There was a softness there toward me. I was certain of it.

My new cat meowed.

"Okay, maybe not a hundred percent for sure, but like eighty percent certain."

"*Meow*."

"Fifty? Thirty? Ten?" I gestured with the glass.

The cat curled up on the fancy pillow I had had couriered over. She stretched out in front of the fire.

"So I blew it!" I told Cindy Lou. "Just let me have it." I flopped down next to her on the carpet and sneezed. "Ugh, the whole place smells like perfume."

I threw open the french doors to the balcony. It was evening, because for some godforsaken reason, it had taken the entire day to film.

"This better be worth it," I told the cat, who had fallen asleep.

I prowled around the condo, replaying over and over how it had felt to hold Morticia in my arms, the way she had moaned when I kissed her. It had now been almost eight weeks since I'd had sex. It had taken all my self-control not to push Morticia up against the wall and take her pussy until she screamed.

I was half-hard, and standing out on the balcony in the cold didn't help any.

I was toying with whether it would be a good idea to dye my hair and sneak off to a club and pretend to be Irish just so I could get laid and get Morticia out of my mind when the doorbell rang.

As if she had just jumped out of my fantasies, there was Morticia, carrying a steaming container, her large black bag slung over her shoulder.

"You shouldn't have come here," I growled.

"Oh." She tipped her head down, her long black hair falling over her face. "Sorry, I just wanted to—"

I grabbed her, pulling her inside. I didn't give her a chance to say anything else before I shoved her against the wall.

"What is wrong with y—"

Her complaints turned into moans when I crushed our mouths together. I kept my hands clamped to her hips. I didn't trust them to roam, because I knew I would start taking off her clothes if they did. She made enticing little whimpers as I took my time, kissing her slowly, enjoying the way her mouth felt, the way her body pressed against mine. It took all my self-restraint to peel myself away from her.

I leaned over her, one hand on the wall above her head. "Not going to run away?" I asked her.

She shook her head.

I tipped her chin up and kissed her again, harder this time. "Then did you come here to get fucked?"

Her pupils were dilated, two pools of black.

"Say yes," I whispered to her, punctuating the words with kisses. "Say the word, and I will ram my thick cock into that tight, hot little pussy of yours."

She made a sort of strangled noise and reached out to stroke my chest but stopped the motion short. I wanted her to run her hands all over me, rake her nails over my skin, run them over my cock.

Morticia clenched her hand into a fist, and her eyes darted up to my face, down to my dick, then up to the ceiling. "I brought spaghetti carbonara to help soak up that sugar and liquor," she said in a choked voice.

I leaned down to nuzzle her neck. "Sex could also work," I suggested. "You know, it's high-intensity exercise."

"You're extremely drunk," she told me. "The bourbon is leaking out of your pores." She slipped under my arm.

"It's the holiday season. A time of excess."

"You're thinking of Mardi Gras."

I prowled behind her as she went into the kitchen. Cindy Lou was waiting on the counter.

"I brought something for you too," she told the cat.

Morticia walked around my kitchen as if she owned it, grabbing a plate out of the cabinet then placing some bits of raw pancetta on it for Cindy Lou.

"You're extremely sexy," I said, taking another sip of my drink.

Going over to the long table set for a Christmas feast, Morticia picked up one of the Christmas china bowls. I supposed she had bought it, because I hadn't.

"And you are completely inebriated." She opened the container of pasta, scooping a generous amount into the bowl.

The smell hit me like a blizzard, and I started salivating. I had eaten two huge forkfuls before I remembered my manners. "You want some?" I asked Morticia.

She took the fork from me and took a bite. The slight sound of pleasure she made was a hammer to the back of the head.

"At least the smell will chase away all the perfume," I said. A breeze from the open window wafted around another hit of the perfume that seemed to permeate my condo. I sneezed.

Morticia opened her large black bag and emptied it onto the counter. Out tumbled bundles of dried leaves, a spray bottle, a ceramic bowl, little vials of crystals, and a giant feather.

"I'm going to do a ritual cleansing," she said, arranging all her instruments on the counter. She sprinkled some of the little crystals into the bowl and lit them on fire. Then she set the bundle of dried leaves on fire.

Cindy Lou meowed as the leaves started smoking.

As I ate, I followed Morticia as she went around the living room and kitchen, slowly passing the burning sage all over the space and tracing some sort of shape in the air. Then she put the sage in the bowl with the little crystals, which were letting off a scent that mixed citrus and rosemary. She picked up the metal bowl and banged it, the sound ringing through the living room. Then she fanned everything with the feather.

"That should do it," Morticia said and took out a large candle. "Just leave your window open to keep the rest of the evil spirits out."

"Or you could stay and guard me."

"Or I could go work." She lit the candle. "Just let that burn for the next hour."

I kissed her one more time before she left. I felt as if I was going to be burning from both ends until I saw her again.

How can I convince her to sleep with me?

Did she actually want to though?

CHAPTER 31

Morticia

We had the next two days off from the bake-off. Jonathan spent them furiously texting me. His messages included pictures of him playing golf with his new cat and a video of him enthusing about how nice his condo smelled now.

"He's really got the hots for you," Emma commented. "Did you put a love potion in his food? Kidding, kidding! Too soon?"

"It was Justin's loss," Lilith assured me.

I spent the days alternating between working on the marketing content for Hillrock West Distillery and working on my scholarship art project. I did have to admit that Jonathan and his sexy kisses and promises of something more were very inspirational. The piece was coming together.

Lilith peered at it over my shoulder. "You know what you need?" she suggested. "You need some super-sexy pictures of Jonathan. Like this one where he's eating the gingerbread—you need an X-rated version of that. The piece should be an exploration of female sexuality bursting from the confines of the kitchen and reclaiming her place in the world!"

"You just want naughty pictures of Jonathan," I told her flatly.

"I mean, that too."

※ ※ ※

Another day, another bake-off challenge. Unfortunately, Keeley still had not been sent home. Instead, it was one of my bunkmates. I actually liked her. She cleaned up after herself and had showed me how to make a mean cheese-and-herb soufflé. Unfortunately, the judges had said that her stuffed French toast wasn't cooked all the way through, and that had earned her poor marks.

Keeley was triumphant when the girl walked out.

I had always thought it was odd that she had made such a rookie mistake. Soufflés were hard, much harder than French toast. All you had to do was stick a thermometer in the middle of it for a reading…

"It's always great when it's time to bake!" Anastasia told us brightly. "However, sometimes baking can be stressful, especially if there's a big business contract on the line."

I yawned. Why did they have to start so early?

"The next Mrs. Frost will be the wife of a corporate leader. She will be expected to host parties, business dinners, and luncheons. Today, we are doing an expanded bake-off. This evening, you're going to be hosting a cocktail hour for Jonathan's clients. Create a menu of foods that will showcase the distillery's alcohol along with, of course, desserts. This is, after all, a bake-off."

Easy, I thought. *I can make a boozy appetizer with one hand tied behind my back.*

"We understand that this is a lot to do in an afternoon. Therefore, you will be working in pairs to produce the savory snacks. Each bachelorette will make her own dessert to be judged. Keeley and Morticia, you will be working together. Jasmine and Selena, you will be pairing up…"

I didn't hear anything after that. *No. I refuse to work with my cousin.* This was a disaster!

Keeley sauntered over to my workstation, smirking. "Fabulous! I'm going to have a front-row seat to watch you fail."

"I don't see how," I snapped. "I'm going to make my own snacks, and you can simmer in your own incompetence."

Keeley gave a mocking laugh. "Funny, your bunkmate said the same thing. Except now she's gone, and I'm here. So I guess I had the last laugh."

"You did something to her food!" I said accusingly.

"There's no evidence," Keeley said snidely.

I fumed as I started cooking. Why did they even pair us up?

"I can cook for a crowd, no problem," I complained to myself. I prepped oysters Rockefeller, mixing up spinach, Romano cheese, some good olive oil, salt, and whiskey and putting a dab on each oyster. "You didn't even want to be in this competition," I reminded myself. "Just let them send you home." But I refused to lose to Keeley. She was singing Christmas carols at the top of her lungs while she assembled some sort of god-awful snack of avocados and grapefruit.

"We are not serving that," I told her. "You're going to get us both low scores."

"You're just jealous," she insisted. "Jonathan's going to love my snack. A man like him is on the keto diet."

I thought back to the pasta I had fed him the previous night. "I have it on good authority that he is not."

"You *wish* you knew all about him," Keeley said haughtily as she approached my station. "You always wanted to be like me—the popular girl, the cheerleader. But you're just the weird girl who hides in the bathroom and eats lunch."

She slammed the platter of avocado and grapefruit onto the table. It caught the corner of my oyster pan, sending the pan seesawing and several of the oysters flying. They skittered over the counter and onto the floor.

"You did that on purpose!" I shouted at her.

"Oops!" Keeley said, twirling a lock of her dyed-blond hair on her finger. "Clumsy me."

The oysters weren't salvageable, and I was furious as I threw them away. As I made my Swedish meatballs and Caesar salad, I constantly checked to ensure Keeley wasn't anywhere near me. But she kept finding any excuse to come over to my station.

My nerves were frayed, and I came up with new inventive and evil ways to make her disappear as I made the mousse, custard, and cake for the chocolate Bavarian torte shot glasses I was creating. There wasn't enough chocolate in the world.

"Ten minutes!" Anastasia announced. I assembled my food and put the remaining three oysters in the oven to broil. They filled the station with the smell of sizzling cheese.

I paced around my station, making sure Keeley didn't come over. If she was in sabotage mode, I needed to go on the offensive.

To finish off the party offerings, I mixed up the mistletoe kiss cocktail I'd made with cranberry muddle, smoked rosemary sprigs, simple syrup, and two kinds of rum. I wasn't sure if Jonathan was going to like it, but I knew I was going to like it, which was important, because I needed that drink.

I watched Keeley as she brought her food over to my station.

"You should just throw that away," I told Keeley as she arranged her now-warmed-up slices of grapefruit and avocado.

The other contestants had actually collaborated, and their snacks were of much higher quality than Keeley's and mine. I hated presenting anything that was less than perfect. It reflected badly on me.

Jonathan was waiting in the other room when we wheeled out our cart of snacks. He sauntered over, one hand in his pocket.

"Where's your costume?" he asked me, a lazy smile on his face. It was clear he was thinking of only one thing.

"Some of us were busy baking."

"I'm not too busy to dress up for you, Jonathan," Keeley said, desperately throwing herself on him.

Jonathan inadvertently reached out to support her.

"Oops!" Keeley said with an obnoxious laugh. "It's these heels! I don't know how the women in the 1950s did it. Between the corset, all the petticoats, and the pumps, it's like I've lost my head."

"Uh-huh," Jonathan said. He turned to me.

"Don't pay any attention to her. Morticia refused to play along."

I was still in my combat boots, black jeans, and a T-shirt that read "Witches vs. Patriarchy."

"You didn't want to dress up as a good little corporate wife," Jonathan teased, his eyes heavy lidded. "I'd bet you'd look pretty hot in all the underwear."

"No, she wouldn't," Keeley said, lips pursed. "Morticia doesn't have any junk in the back or the front. She's just a string bean."

"I will not debase myself for the male gaze," I told him.

"Really?" Jonathan said, his eyes flicking to my shirt. "Because I'd be willing to debase myself for the female gaze."

"Yes, please do," Keeley begged.

Jonathan ignored her and reached for one of the oysters. "I was reading up on all that Wiccan stuff after you came and smoked out my living room. Turns out there are all sorts of rituals that center around sex."

I tried to avoid looking at Keeley, whose eyes were boring into my head.

Jonathan tossed back the oyster. "Usually the female is on top."

CHAPTER 32

Jonathan

Morticia seemed intrigued, as I had known she would be. Unfortunately, the lust I was hoping to ignite did not lead to us fucking like reindeer in a storage closet somewhere.

I wonder what she sounds like when she comes.

I wanted to find out. I needed to find out. But I still had a ways to go to reel her in. It would be worth the wait, assuming I survived that long.

"I knew you were a man who knew how to eat oysters!" Dorothy remarked, sidling up to me. "Get a load of that tongue action. Nothing like a man in his prime before he loses all his teeth."

"Really?" I said casually, reaching for another before Dorothy beat me to it. "Seems like the lack of teeth could be a bonus."

I had invited Dorothy because I was hoping to score bonus points and convince her to sell me the property by the end of the year. Wouldn't that be a merry Christmas! Between the booze, the snacks, and the desserts, she seemed to be softening. She took a look at Morticia's shirt and flashed her a thumbs-up.

"I like a gal who doesn't take shit from men," she told Morticia.

"That's exactly what I was saying," I said conversationally as I picked up the tall glass pitcher, holding the pink cocktail Morticia had made—

Bet it's the color of her pussy.

—and topped off Dorothy's drink.

"Did you know that there are all these pagan sex rituals? I've been very much into female positivity," I told the property owner.

"How about that! I didn't know you kids were into all that. In the seventies, we were at it like rabbits. Literally. In the woods, in a stream—there was the one time we had an orgy in a desert. This guy was bit by a rattlesnake right as I was riding that anaconda, as the kids say nowadays. Anyways, he let out a scream when that snake bit him, then his dick swelled up to the size of an eggplant. He was literally stuck inside me, and it took five hours to make it to the nearest hospital."

"Sounds like our kind of pagan ritual!" I nudged Morticia.

"If your dick gets stuck inside me," she said, "I'm cutting it off."

"That's fair. But—" I leaned down to whisper her ear. "I'm glad you're thinking about when I'm finally going to make you come begging for my cock."

She went red, and Dorothy laughed.

"You have to lighten up, Morticia. This is art! There's nothing more inspiring than a sexy-looking man," Dorothy told her. Then she launched into another raunchy story.

Carl waved to me from across the room. I pressed a kiss to Morticia's neck before I left her.

"Great party," Carl said. "Did you make any headway on Dorothy? She seems to really like you."

"You tell Greg," I bragged, "she'll sign the paperwork by Christmas Eve. I have a good feeling about this. Shit, we might as well start celebrating."

"Too bad Dana said she'd duct-tape you to a Christmas tree if you slept with the contestants," Carl joked.

"If she doesn't find out," I said, tapping the side of my head, "it doesn't count."

"You certainly have your pick," Carl remarked. "Any of them would bend over and let you fuck them right here. Well, not all of them," he amended, angling his chin toward Morticia. "She looks like she'd gut you first. Not that it matters—I bet she's sucks in bed. Too angry and man hating."

I grabbed Carl by the collar.

"Whoa, whoa! Shit, man," he said.

"Don't ever talk about her like that," I snarled at him.

"All right, all right!" he said, throwing me off. "Holy smokes." He adjusted his clothes. "My bad, Morticia just doesn't seem like someone you'd want in your life, especially if you're being this possessive about her. You remember what happened last time with Sarah. Just seems like you should take a step back."

✳ ✳ ✳

I didn't want to take a step back. I needed Morticia.

Unfortunately, she was too busy giving the interview that the producers were going to splice into the bake-off episode.

Jonathan: *Come see me.*
Jonathan: *I mean, I'd come see you, but I didn't think you'd want me to eat you out in the bedroom you share with four other people.*

Now I was inviting her to my condo? I remembered Carl's warning.

The last time I had felt this way about a girl had been right after college. Belle had just left with no warning, and my family had imploded. I had been reeling. Sarah had made me feel like I was on top of the world. She catered to me, was great in bed, and left her imprint on my space and my life.

Then one day I came home, and she had all her bags packed. She said that I wasn't the type of person she wanted to spend the rest of her life with. Me! I was a billionaire, I ran a successful-ish business and hedge fund, and I was handsome and had a fantastic body that I put a lot of effort into. I did nice things for her and bought her fun little presents I had thought she would like. Then she had just thrown it all away.

I had begged her to stay, promising that I would forgive whatever had happened, that we could move past it, but she just…left. I begged her to tell me why, but she just said that she had had an epiphany and realized that she was better off without me.

Cindy Lou came over to me and rubbed her furry head against my bare ankle.

"You're never going to leave me, are you, my precious Cindy Lou Who?" I cooed to the cat, kissing her perfect little toes.

I sighed. My house smelled like snow and Christmas. Too bad I didn't have anyone to share it with. Or more pasta.

"I can't believe Morticia only made three oysters," I said to the cat, carrying her into the kitchen and staring at the empty fridge, willing food to appear in it.

I was in the middle of scrolling mindlessly through the Door Dash app, trying to decide what food would taste best after it had been driven for thirty or forty-five minutes, when the doorbell rang.

Morticia gave me a small smile when I opened the door.

I grinned. "The sex fairy is here! You know oysters are an aphrodisiac, right?"

"You only ate one." Morticia rolled her eyes.

"Yes, because there were hardly any left. You made me starve to death, then you got me all hot and bothered with the talk about sex and paganism."

"That sounds like a personal problem," Morticia retorted.

I set Cindy Lou on the ground then wrapped Morticia in my arms. "You know, I was starving, but I can think of something else to sate my appetite."

The T-shirt fabric was soft as I pushed it up, revealing the smooth, creamy skin underneath. Morticia gasped and then moaned as my hand moved up to caress her tits under the thin, lacy bralette she wore.

My hands roamed around her back, down her waist, then to the buttons on her jeans. I undid them one-handed—yes, ladies, I am that good!—and slipped my hand in, grazing the soft lace of her panties. They were wet. And I was hard.

"I need you," I whispered hoarsely. Her jeans were tight, and it was hard to get any leverage.

Her mind seemed to catch up to what her body wanted, and Morticia grabbed my hand, yanking it away. She turned around to fix her clothes.

I wrapped my arms around her, pressing against her, wanting her to feel how hard I was through the fabric.

"You sure you don't want to do a bit of historical reenactment of the Celts ushering in the winter solstice?" I growled, kissing her neck then nipping her ear. "I felt how wet you are. You can't lie and say you don't want me."

She turned around in my arms but didn't throw me off. "I'm here to work," she said.

I kissed her. "That's fine. I can work it."

"No," she said, rapping me on the nose. "You hired me to do your marketing, not get you off."

"You could do both."

Morticia glared at me.

"Er…Crap, that was the wrong thing to say."

"Yes, it was," she said.

I stepped back. "Usually I'm smoother than this," I explained as I followed Morticia into the kitchen.

She set an even bigger black bag than last time on the counter and started pulling out cameras and props.

"Are those cupcakes?" I asked her.

"These are for the photo shoot." She pulled out several more Tupperware containers and put them in the fridge. "It's a sexy photo shoot, but I'm making you chicken parmesan if you cooperate and keep your hands to yourself."

CHAPTER 33

Morticia

I had had to sit through the judges giving a list of all the ways our dishes were wrong and Keeley gloating beside me because she had sabotaged my score. I was furious and in need of some serious self-care after the bake-off ended. I was all set to hang out with *The Chilling Adventures of Sabrina* and work on my art project. The next episode of *Sabrina* in the queue was the Christmas special.

"I wouldn't mind Christmas so much if there were more witches," I told Salem.

All the other girls had gone out for a night on the town, and the apartment was blessedly quiet. I was making Italian food, lighting candles, and drinking wine. I hadn't heard back from the Getty yet. Maybe they weren't going to take me. All this bake-off work would be for nothing if I didn't even need the money to pay for the internship.

The phone rang, breaking the silence.

"This is the Getty museum!" a cheerful older woman said. "I called to let you know that you made it to the next round. We've sent your interview information to the email address you provided. Don't forget about the scholarship deadline."

"Absolutely," I said after thanking her profusely.

"Yes! I'm going to California!" When I scanned the email, I knew I had it in the bag. Dorothy was going to be my interviewer.

I flopped back on the couch, feeling relaxed and happy… until I realized I was not all that far along on my art project. I ran into my bedroom and, after looking around to make doubly sure no one else was there, I pulled it out from under the bed.

The last thing I needed was for Keeley to get her hands on the project. I had been working on it in the middle of the night out in the hallway. Fortunately, it was mainly collage and found objects. The piece itself was a triptych that could fold up like an advent calendar so that it could be propped up. I had about a third of it done. I was calling the first third "The Awakening," and it contained the shots I had been taking of Jonathan interwoven with baked goods and images of fifties housewives bearing various holiday Jell-O molds.

The biggest panel was the middle one. I couldn't just have a repeat of what had been in the first third. I needed more content; more importantly, I needed spicier, steamier content.

My phone beeped with messages from Jonathan. He was at home. My heart raced.

What if he found out about the art piece? With the types of pictures I needed, at some point, he was going to realize that I wasn't using them for marketing purposes. Giving up was not the answer. I needed to win this scholarship. I couldn't spend another year suffering for my art. The Getty internship was my ticket to the high-society art world.

But damn, did Jonathan look good when he opened the door. And he felt even better.

Thou shalt not sleep with thine art subject, I chanted to myself as I set up for the photo shoot.

"So what am I doing this time?" Jonathan asked. "Fabio? Magic Mike? Borat? I have a lime-green swimsuit I could cut up."

I wanted him spread out on a white fur rug, the firelight playing all over his muscles.

Make art not sex! Eyes on the scholarship prize!

"Use your imagination," I said. "Look sexy, like you want people to bust down the door to come get a piece of you."

"You mean like you did?" he joked. He lounged in front of the Christmas tree, legs splayed slightly, his six-foot-five form draped over the white chair, a Santa hat drooping over his eyes.

To maintain the charade, I had him do a few poses with bottles of alcohol, setting the camera to automatic shutter to take scores of pictures as Jonathan posed and tilted his head this way and that. It still wasn't exactly what I needed for my art piece, though the photos were hot.

"You sure Instagram is going to let you post these pictures?" he asked with a grin.

"They're not that sexy," I told him crossly.

His smile widened. "I bet they're pretty sexy." His voice lowered an octave. "But yeah, it's way sexier when there are two people." He grabbed my waist, pulling me toward him. I stumbled and half fell into his lap.

One large hand came up to tangle in my hair. The other slowly trailed down my torso. He rubbed a thumb over my pebble-hard nipple. Then his hand slid down to my jeans and slowly unfastened them.

"It's way sexier," he said in that deep voice that had me mesmerized, "if one person is completely obsessed with the other, and you see it in the picture."

He pulled the zipper down; his mouth was inches from mine, his breath cool on my lips.

"When you can see the promise of pleasure on their face," he continued as he pulled down the jeans to give him enough access, "and then that first crush of pleasure." He rubbed my clit through the panties.

I whimpered.

"Don't you want this?" he whispered. "I told you, it doesn't matter if we don't like each other. Nothing better than a hate fuck."

I wanted it. And I was all ready to peel off my pants and press his face to my clit.

However, this time he was the one to pull away.

"But…" Jonathan drawled.

He was too casual compared to me; I felt like I was about to combust.

"As you said, you are working."

I let out a breath.

He smirked up at me. I didn't know if I wanted to slap his face or kiss him.

"If you're not begging for it, then I don't want it," he said.

"Smug much?"

"Someone has to be the best," he said with a laugh. "Did you get all the pictures you need? I'm starving. Since pussy is off the menu, I'll take that chicken parmesan."

※ ※ ※

Morticia: *Are all billionaires cocky sociopathic assholes?*
Emma: *Pretty much. But I hear that makes them really good in bed.*
Lilith: *Did you see his candy cane?*
Morticia: *No. I was taking pictures for my art project. Got some for the Insta account too. Sending them over.*

I scrolled through the pictures, choosing the ones to send my friends for review. They were spicy for Instagram but too bland for the scholarship submission.

A part of me had wanted to just say fuck it and fuck Jonathan, but he had basically flipped a switch and was refusing to touch me, even though my pussy was throbbing and aching.

"It's stress," I growled, gripping the computer mouse.

Before I had left, he had kissed me almost chastely on the neck right where my jaw met my neck.

"Beg me for it," he had said, "and I'll give you a magic sleigh ride."

I should have done it just to get pictures of him sweaty and sated. I bet that would appeal to the judges.

"Oh, fuck!" I said when I reached the last of the pictures. There were a number of them of Jonathan and me with Jonathan's hand in my panties. I made a move to delete them…except I couldn't, because they were exactly what I needed for the next part of my art project.

Heart pounding, hoping no one returned, I printed the best one out, carefully cut it, and positioned it on the canvas. It was perfect! Unfortunately, it also showed my face and my body. I quickly used pictures of Christmas desserts to cover my face.

I stood back and regarded the piece. It had a sort of dystopian sexy retro vibe. It was also daring and sent a clear message.

"Scholarship, here I come!"

And maybe Jonathan would make me come.

CHAPTER 34

Jonathan

I bet I could have had Morticia whimpering and moaning as I made her come on my hand. But I still wasn't sure where we stood.

It's just sex. You're overthinking it.

But it felt like more. Morticia had cooked for me, after all. The chicken parmesan had been crunchy and tomatoey, and she had made garlic bread with parmesan cheese on it. Yet none of it had felt as good as stroking her through the lacy black panties. The slick wetness, the way her hips had moved slightly…I had wanted to strip her down and ram her pussy onto my cock.

But that was for later; the first time, I was going to go slow and savor it. I wanted her to like me, *needed* her to like me or at least want me. I was craving that connection with someone.

"Don't," I warned myself. "You're horny, and it's making you crazy. You should have just fucked her last night and gotten it out of your system."

My assistant stuck her head into the office. "Carl Svensson is here to see you."

While I waited for my friend, I looked out through the large window that took up a good portion of the masonry wall of the renovated factory.

The door opened a few minutes later.

"Hey, Carl," I said, not looking up from my phone, "you want to grab a drink then complain about your brother?"

"Is that what you all do all day?"

I whirled around in my chair then jumped up when I saw Greg standing there next to Carl, who was making frantic cut-it-out gestures.

"Why am I not surprised? And to think I wondered why on earth you still hadn't managed to secure this property deal."

"I'm close," I promised him.

"That's what you always say," Greg retorted, walking slowly around my office. "And yet you have failed to deliver. It's nothing but empty promises from you while you waste my time and my money."

"I told Carl to tell you I'll have it by Christmas Eve."

"Carl did say that." Greg turned to face me, gray eyes flat. "You know what else Carl told me? He said you had an in."

"A what?"

"You have a secret weapon to make Dorothy give you what I want."

I was confused.

"Jesus Christ," Greg said. "You're worse than your brothers."

"Morticia!" Carl said excitedly. "Dorothy likes Morticia. You can convince Morticia to put in a good word for you. You know, make it seem like we're going to make the development all artsy-fartsy."

"I thought we were keeping some of the character," I said, frowning.

"No," Greg said. "The historic buildings, yes, but not those nests of sculptures."

"Morticia won't go for that," I said slowly. "She'll want to make it as art centric as possible."

"That's why you don't tell her," Greg said impatiently. "Tell her what you want her to think so that she will convince Dorothy to sell. I can sense the old woman's close. She just needs a little push."

"Morticia's not going to just do that for me; we aren't friends," I said bitterly. "She doesn't even like me."

"Then make her like you," Greg ordered. "Make her get obsessed with you and fall in love with you so that she'll do anything for you, up to and including convincing Dorothy to sell."

I ran a hand through my hair. "That sounds…"

"Brilliant," Greg replied. "Are you committed or not?"

I needed that property. My parents would finally love me if I had that property. Hell, if I had all the money and clout from being a member of the Hamilton Yards development team, I could start to repay Belle for all the sacrifices she had made. Maybe Sarah would even come back!

"I don't want to hurt Morticia."

"I'm sorry, do you actually want to run with the big dogs, or do you want to sit at the bottom of the pile, wondering if today is the day that the market swings and turns your 1.2 billion dollars into millions and makes you a has-been?" Greg spat. "Who cares about Morticia?"

I do.

It's just horniness. You just want to sleep with her, not marry her.

"You can be charming when you want to be," Carl cajoled. "Just convince her that you're in love with her and want to build a life with her."

I nodded mutely.

"By Christmas Eve," Greg said.

"By Christmas Eve," I repeated.

The problem?

I sort of did want to build a life with her.

CHAPTER 35

Morticia

"Dayum, that art piece is steaming hot!" Lilith exclaimed when I showed her the progress on my scholarship collage. "I'm impressed! Your art is reaching a higher level."

"She has to get up that high because Jonathan's dick is so long!" Emma said, cackling.

"Shhh," I hissed at them. "Keep it down."

We were about to go down for yet another bake-off, and the apartment was emptying out, but I didn't want to take any chances.

"You know," Emma said as I hid my project. "A part of me is thinking you might actually have a shot at winning this bake-off. There's a big pot of prize money. Between that, your scholarship, and the money from doing Jonathan's marketing, you'd be living large in Los Angeles."

"You might even be able to afford to rent a whole bedroom instead of a doghouse," Lilith said.

"For today's bake-off challenge," Anastasia said when we were all assembled, "we have the pamper-your-man challenge. Tell him you love him with personalized desserts, and follow it up with a massage. There's nothing like spending an intimate winter evening with your partner. Create the perfect couple's retreat with your dessert."

"I'm going to let him eat the desserts off of me," Keeley said.

At the judges' table, Jonathan's eyes widened slightly. Was he excited at the prospect?

Probably, I told myself. *He probably is tired of the game you two are playing. He just wants something low effort. Like ordering dinner or a car, he just wants his women to come to him easily.*

I bet he could make you come easily.

Less sex! More baking!

But Jonathan was just sitting there at the judges' table, leaning back in his chair. He wasn't watching the action. He was watching me.

I prided myself on being a woman who was not easily flustered. Haunted houses, abandoned properties, snakes—I didn't even flinch. But now I was making mistakes and forgetting ingredients, all because Jonathan was staring at me. Not doing anything else. Just watching.

I cursed under my breath as I accidentally dropped a chunk of eggshell into my batter. For the pamper-your-man challenge, I was making my own special towering chocolate lava cake torte. It consisted of two layers of rich chocolate cake with a light, creamy whipped custard mixed with fresh berries. On top, I would pour a thick, fudgy frosting and top it with another heap of berries and a dusting of powdered sugar. To drink, I was serving a refreshing juniper champagne cocktail.

To keep the cake moist and fudgy, I used less flour than I normally would for a cake. This recipe would not work if the cake was crumbly and dry; it wouldn't hold up to the berries, the custard, and the fudge frosting.

I poured the dark, chocolaty batter into two greased, floured, and lined baking tins and slid them into the hot oven. Then I started on my custard. In a double boiler, I stirred the egg yolks, heavy cream, sugar, and amaretto liqueur over low heat. Cooking was meditative, and I was meditating on Jonathan.

I don't want to sleep with him, I assured my inner rationalist. *I just want to use him to get pictures for my scholarship.* It was about money, not sex.

And even if it is about sex, who cares?

I cared. I didn't know what Jonathan's deal was. Was he being nice to me because he wanted to sleep with me? What if, after that happened, he decided he had had enough and bounced to the next girl? That was his mode of operation after all. All the tabloid articles I had read during my stalking—*ahem*, research sessions—were always quick to point out how Jonathan had never been seen with the same woman twice.

I looked down at my scuffed boots. What made me think I was the one person special enough to break his habit?

All that introspection still didn't fix my problem of needing more pictures for the scholarship art project. Regardless of how he felt about me or I felt about him, I'd have to keep him interested long enough to take all the photos I needed.

I chanced a glance back over my shoulder toward him. I definitely wanted him. Just from looking at him, my panties had magically caught fire and were burning away cheerfully like a Yule log.

I sniffed. "Wait, that's…" I opened my oven. "Smoke!" Thick black smoke billowed out. "What the fuck?" I coughed.

Keeley looked over from her station. "You should have used a bigger pan."

"These cakes don't rise; they don't need a bigger pan." I bared my teeth at her. "You fucked with my recipe."

"I did not!" Keeley said haughtily.

"You did something to my cakes," I accused as I turned off the oven.

I hastily tried to scrape all the burned batter from the bottom of the oven without burning myself. I chipped at the pieces of smoldering chocolate, spattering myself and the floor with it.

I swore one more time for good measure then took stock. I had some time left but not a lot. Fuming, cursing Keeley's ancestors, then backtracking because those were also my ancestors, I found more chocolate and remade the cake, also remembering to check on my custard as it cooled.

"Needs more booze," I decided when I tasted it. I added another splash along with fresh vanilla bean and nutmeg.

This time, as I made the cake, I checked the ingredients carefully. That small tablespoon of flour I was about to add? I sniffed it. It smelled acrid. I tasted it, and it was bitter and salty.

"What the—" I glared at Keeley.

She had a smug look on her face. "Are you sure you didn't mistakenly bring baking powder?" she asked, voice syrupy sweet.

"You're going down," I hissed at her, stomping back to the pantry to grab a new bag of flour, this time tasting it before I put it in my batter.

While the new cake baked, I mixed up my frosting. Then I cored cherries, washed the bright-red currants, raspberries, and blueberries, and stemmed the blackberries. I also whipped the cream, making sure it had stiff peaks so that the custard would be light but not runny when I mixed the two.

I had wanted to have my chocolate cake layers cool before I assembled the whole dessert. Now I was worried I wouldn't have the time. As soon as they were out of the oven, I impatiently waited five minutes then flipped the cakes over onto a cooling rack and stuck them in the blast freezer.

I was sweating as I hurriedly made the base for my cocktail. I would add the champagne at the last minute, but I had to first boil the juniper berries in sugar water to create a flavored simple syrup. After I strained it, the syrup went into the glasses along with Grand Marnier liqueur and blood orange juice. I put a sprig of juniper in each glass and got my champagne ready to pop.

I was covered in chocolate, orange zest, flour, and whipped cream when I ran to grab my cakes out of the blast freezer. They weren't as cool as I wanted them to be, but that was what I had.

The assembly of the cake was, thankfully, easy. It was supposed to feel rustic and bountiful. I heaped the custard on top of the first layer along with a generous handful of berries then more custard. I placed the second layer on top, mindful of the clock, and poured the fudgy chocolate frosting over it slowly, allowing it to run like lava down the sides of the cake. More berries went on top. Then I arranged the clusters of red currants around the rim of the platter. A fine dusting of powdered sugar and the cake was done.

Thirty seconds were left on the clock when I popped open the champagne and poured it into the glasses.

CHAPTER 36

Jonathan

"Time!" Anastasia called.

Morticia took a long drink of the champagne. I was still unsure how to convince her to fall in love with me. I was also unsure if I even should.

She doesn't like you.

I had spent all afternoon with my eyes glued to her, searching for some sign that there was something there. But did it really matter? I needed that property. *Besides*, I told myself, *even if she likes you now, that's no guarantee that she would stick around.*

I needed to hedge my bets.

It's part of being a good businessman. You have to make the hard decisions.

"Ready to be pampered?" Belle asked me.

"Bring it!"

❋ ❋ ❋

Five contestants in, however, and I would rather have been anywhere else. I had not known that a back rub could be bad, but somehow, the last contestant had managed it. All of the bachelorettes had insisted on touching me somehow while I ate the desserts they had made.

"You know," Nick said to me as I rubbed my neck and winced, "at first, I was jealous you were getting back rubs, but now, I'm like, keep that away from my spine."

"I have ibuprofen in my bag," Anu offered. "Not sure how that's going to react with all the alcohol you've been drinking."

"I swear," I told the judges, "New Year's Day, I'm starting a whole-food diet with water and pressed kale juice. No alcohol, no desserts, no fatty foods. Clean eating."

"Really?" Anu asked. "Because I don't know if I could give up a cake like that."

"That doesn't count," I said as Morticia approached with her dessert. "That has berries on it, so it's pretty healthy."

"And it's low carb-ish," Morticia added. "The recipe contains very little flour, at any rate."

"Sounds healthy enough for me," I said. I grimaced as that pulled something in my neck. "I'm never having another massage again."

"I would have assumed you would be in hog heaven," Morticia said as she slid her dessert on the table.

I grimaced then winced as the expression pulled another muscle in my neck that one of the previous contestants had manage to cramp up.

"It's the most American thing ever," Morticia said with a small smile, setting down the tray with the cocktails. "You strained a muscle while gorging yourself on dessert."

"I proudly represent my country," I said, rubbing my neck then reaching for a cocktail.

"Lean back," Morticia ordered, brushing my hand away.

I sighed. "I just need a foam roller, maybe a sauna."

She pushed me to sit back in my chair.

"This is stupid," I complained.

Morticia put one hand at the base of my neck and the other on my shoulder, rubbing it. Then she tugged. My neck popped.

"Don't stand up too fast," she warned.

"You fixed me!"

"My neck is tense too," Anu said.

Morticia worked her magic on the other two judges then served the dessert. It was amazing. The chocolate and the berries and the custardy filling were everything I wanted in a cake.

"This is such an aesthetically pleasing dessert," Anu marveled.

"It reminds me of one of those paintings from the eighteenth century," Nick added, "where they have heaps of fruit and bread and meat."

❄ ❄ ❄

After the day's judging was over, I hung around to try and catch Morticia.

I didn't just need her to like me; I needed to make her fall in love with me. I needed her one hundred percent on my side so that she could help convince Dorothy to sell me the land.

What if she saw through my lie, though? I couldn't just say, "Let's go up to my apartment and bang. Oh, by the way, can you put in a good word for me with Dorothy?" No, I needed to really sell it. I needed to take her out on a date.

The thing was that I did not date and had not dated since Sarah. I slept with women. I did not have relationships with them. I had sworn I never would again. I barely knew where to take a typical woman, let alone someone like Morticia. I paced around the lobby.

The studio door opened as Morticia exited. She held a container of cake and a thermos.

"Wait, I didn't know that we could take dessert home!" I complained, all my carefully crafted pickup lines going out the window.

"You can if you grab it fast enough. I basically had to get in a knife fight with your sister for this last piece," she said. "Now I plan on going home and enjoying it."

No, she can't go home. Stick to the plan.

"You want to grab a drink first?"

She raised the thermos. "Already have it covered."

"Come have a drink with me."

"Don't you mean come up to your condo and sleep with you?" she replied.

"Do you think I'm really that much of a manwhore?" I asked.

"Is this the part where you give me a rundown of all the ways you're going to make me come?"

"When you put it that way…"

She snorted.

I took her hands. "I like you, Morticia. Go out with me. Let me wine and dine you."

Shit, that sounded too strong. I should have studied up on strategies for fake dating.

Morticia looked at me with suspicion. "What are you playing at?"

"I, uh, nothing! I just want to take you out to dinner," I insisted.

She blew out a breath. "Honestly, I would have respected you more if you had just come right out and said that you wanted to fuck and were willing to play hardball for it."

CHAPTER 37

Morticia

"**B**ut I don't want to just do that with you," Jonathan crooned, one hand encircling my waist. "I want to get to know you and spend time with you. I have to admit I'm a bit infatuated with you."

Those were the words I had secretly longed for a man to say to me, even though I had long ago resigned myself to the fact that no man would ever want someone as weird and strange as me.

Something's not right here, the rational part of me said. It was warring with the teenage girl who had always wanted to be wanted by the most popular boy in school.

You can't trust him.

I tried to disentangle myself. "What are you playing at?" I asked Jonathan.

He jerked back as if I had slapped him.

"I'm not playing at anything," he said, sounding convincingly offended. "Geez, you're so angry all the time. I said I liked you. Stop pushing me away."

The rational part wouldn't let it go. "It's strange, though, you have to admit," I countered.

"Okay, you got me," Jonathan said, holding up his hands. "I did have an ulterior motive."

I blanched. Was the public humiliation incoming?

He looked away slightly then back at me, his teeth catching his lip. "What I really want is for you to come to a pop-up Christmas restaurant with me!"

Relief flooded through me. Maybe he did like me for real after all.

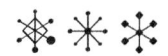

❋ ❋ ❋

You're supposed to sleep with Jonathan and take secret sexy pictures, not date him, I reminded myself as we followed the hostess into the Christmas-themed bar.

Actually, "Christmas themed" didn't do it justice. In place of tables were giant wrapped presents with seats made out of plastic that was formed to look like giant bows. The bar, which stretched almost the whole length of the room, was decorated to look like an elf's workbench. The bartenders were dressed like elves and were handing a steady stream of Christmas-themed drinks to patrons.

Jonathan and I were led to an out-of-the way table that gave us a view of the space. Presents, lights, and ornaments hung from the ceiling. In the opposite corner was a Christmas tree strung with tinsel and the fat, retro colored lights that I'd secretly always loved, though I would never admit it.

Jonathan helped me out of my coat, his hand brushing the back of my neck.

What ever happened to millennial men just wanting to hook up and not wanting to put in all the work to date? Why was Jonathan suddenly now deciding to be a romantic? It struck me that this was the first actual, factual date that I had ever been on in my life. The drunken hookups with the wannabe hipster artists who thought showing me their great American novel, which a publisher was for sure going to pick up any day, counted as foreplay.

I stared around awkwardly. I was not the type of girl men took out on dates. Yet here I was. Between the Christmas wrapping paper on the walls and the attractive billionaire across from me, I was very much out of my element. I had changed my clothes before we left, and now I was wearing a black Wednesday Addams dress. It was a little short on me, but I didn't think Jonathan would mind.

Jonathan ordered us two Mrs. Claus cocktails then leaned back in his chair, regarding me intently.

It doesn't matter what his motivations are. You need to finish the art piece. That's priority number one. You can't blow this date. Maybe this is some strange mating ritual. Maybe he's been moved by the Christmas spirit. Just be normal.

If Jonathan ghosted me, I wouldn't have any way of finishing my art project. I would have no money, and I'd have to live under a bridge in Los Angeles.

Jonathan likes women like Keeley, right? Just channel your inner Keeley.

Barf.

The things I do for my art.

"So," I said, twirling a strand of my hair and crossing my legs. My knee bumped the table, sloshing the water glasses. "Shit!" I cursed and tried to wipe up the liquid.

"After you drank all that champagne, I'm not surprised you're sloppy," he teased, helping me dab up the water.

The server brought our cocktails. I twisted my glass around on the coaster. What did people talk about on first dates? The weather? Crazy exes?

The servers brought out our Christmas-themed drinks.

Say something to make him like you.

"What are your plans for Christmas?" I asked. I sipped my drink then winced and took a big swig of water.

"How is it?" Jonathan asked.

"I need something strong to wash this down." The drink tasted like imitation vanilla and had a greasy texture.

Jonathan took a sip. "This is nasty. I didn't know these would be this bad. I should have just taken you to my bar, but that seems trite."

"Compared to this?" I gestured.

"You need some Christmas cheer and some Christmas food."

I couldn't tell what any of the dishes on the menu were. They were all named after Christmas items.

"They should give you dice so you can just guess," he said after a moment. "I really want a steak."

"They have elf steak," I told him.

"That sounds cannibalistic."

❄ ❄ ❄

"Do you still hate me?" Jonathan asked. His hand rested on my waist right where it curved to my ass as he guided me into his condo.

"After you took me to a Christmas restaurant, and I had to eat something called reindeer in a blanket?"

"Hey, I had to eat elf steak, which was basically just a piece of marzipan!"

"You ate that thing like a champ!" I rubbed his bicep.

Jonathan laughed then kissed me. "Remember when I told you hate sex can be the best sex?"

"Was that your whole motive in all of this?"

"Maybe," he murmured.

He was bearing down on me, too close for my comfort, looking at me like he was a predator waiting to strike.

Did I want him to? I didn't know the answer to that. Or maybe I was just afraid of the answer to that.

He didn't wait much longer before he was on me. His lips were heavy on mine, his kiss so intense and powerful. Jonathan was a domineering man, one who knew what he wanted.

And that was me.

He sensed my anxiety. Maybe he savored it. Maybe I could be more generous and say that he wanted to calm me down. Getting me all hot and bothered like this, though, felt like the damn antithesis of calming me down.

"I need to show you what awaits you if you open yourself up to me, Morticia."

He slid his hands down my body, making my skin tingle. His fingers trailed down my dress, nudging my bra, making my tits perk up even through layers of fabric. He wrapped his arms around me and hoisted me onto the kitchen island, leaving my feet dangling.

I should have been pushing him off. He was supposed to be in the compromising position, not me.

But he was reading my mind. Or maybe he knew me better than I knew myself.

Whatever it was, he flashed me a smile and slid down my body, making me lean against the wall. He went lower still, spreading my legs.

"Mind telling me what you're doing?" I asked, incredibly curious as to what was in that twisted mind of his.

"You'll see. It's a surprise."

He hiked my dress up. I could feel the cold marble of the counter below me against my flesh, but it was quickly warming. Jonathan's hand finally reached between my legs, and I gasped as he pressed it to my pussy.

"Already hot. Already wet. Tell me, Morticia, have you been having sinful thoughts about me?"

I didn't dignify his question with a response. But my silence didn't stop him. He rubbed me through the thin, lacy fabric, making me gasp. The electricity of his touch felt undeniably good. It had been so long since I had felt something like this.

He kept on the pressure, forcing a moan out of me, making me shudder for him. His touch was experienced, knowledgeable. But that was hardly enough. He wanted to do more than just give me a dry rub. Oh no, there was so much more than that.

His fist balled around the waistband of my panties, and he yanked them down, ripping them.

Jonathan grinned and stopped what he was doing just to gaze at my panties. "Black lace. I shouldn't have expected anything different, though I was hoping you'd choose a little Christmas number—you know, in the spirit of the season and since I'm about to come down your chimney."

"I can't believe you ripped those," I gasped. "Those are expensive."

He silenced me with a hard kiss. "I'll buy you new ones, sexier ones, with dancing snowmen." He threw the ripped panties into a nearby trash can. Then he smiled as he dropped to his knees and made his intentions suddenly oh so very clear.

"I thought you said you were coming down my chimney."

"Mmhm," he said, voice slightly muffled. "Think of this as the one present you open on Christmas Eve. It's a preview. Besides, I told you I wanted you begging for my cock. You can't open the biggest package under the tree first, you know."

Under my skirt, he went straight for another kiss, this one far more obscene than the one before it.

I gasped as he suckled my clit ever so briefly, causing me to cry out. His licks came in with force, pushing at my folds, making my pussy wet and achy for him.

He began to lap at me voraciously, his tongue pressing in, all while his finger rubbed my clit to put an exclamation point on everything that he did. Every little thing he did down there he did with purpose, and that purpose was making me cry out in bliss.

I gripped the edge of the counter as my back arched. He built the orgasm inside me higher, hotter, stronger. I was moaning for him, calling out for him. I was at his mercy, and when he demanded that I come for him, I wasn't really able to refuse.

The intensity of it all—it had been much too long since I had come this hard. Jonathan just instinctively knew what made me tick, how to press my literal button in just the right way.

When the tidal wave of bliss finished washing over me, I was left panting and sweaty on top of the kitchen counter, and he was just standing there with the most infuriating shit-eating grin on his face.

Sugarplums, snowflakes, and candy canes danced in my vision, all eclipsed by the winter prince in front of me. Jonathan scooped me up in his arms, nuzzling me as he carried me to his bedroom. He laid me down on the bed and proceeded to unbutton his shirt.

As he took it off, I thought in a panic that it wouldn't be enough to stave off the oncoming sleepiness now that Jonathan had made me good and relaxed. *Where is my camera? I need to capture this for my art!*

CHAPTER 38

Jonathan

When I turned back to Morticia, she was sound asleep. My dick was hard, and I had wanted her to ride the sleigh, so to speak. But now she was sprawled on my bed, fast asleep.

My phone beeped, and Morticia stirred. I ran to the hallway and closed the door softly behind me.

Carl: *Greg wants to know how the date was.*
Jonathan: *Made it to third base!*

My phone rang.

"You aren't supposed to be sleeping with her. You're supposed to make her fall in love with you." Greg was irritated on the other end of the line.

"I did. I am."

"I'm doubtful."

"These things take time," I told him.

"Exactly," Greg said. "You're not supposed to sleep with her on the first date. That's just a hookup."

"What do you know about how to make a woman fall in love with you? You hurt my sister," I snapped at Greg.

"That's none of your business!" Greg shouted into the phone. I pulled it away from my ear. "Don't argue with me about this," Greg said, voice rough. "If you blow this, I'll make sure you never do business in the city again."

I paced around the living room after he hung up. Cindy Lou pranced after me. I hadn't brought up the Hamilton Yards development that evening. Morticia was already suspicious. But I would have to find some way of broaching the subject eventually.

I went back to the bedroom, opened the door, and peeked back in. Morticia's black hair was spread all around her, and she was breathing slowly. I wanted to curl up next to her, forget the development, and have a happily ever after.

None of this is real, I reminded myself. *She doesn't even like you. And if—scratch that, when—she finds out what kind of scam you're running, she's going to be furious.*

But the noises she had made, the way she had clung to me, and how she had said my name when she came were addictive. I was obsessed. I was already planning our life together, the Christmases we would have, baking cookies and decorating with our kids.

Aaand this is why we don't mix business with pleasure, I reminded myself.

※ ※ ※

I didn't sleep at all that night. I didn't trust myself to be that close to Morticia. I had tried sleeping in one of the various guest rooms, then the couch in my study, and finally in the living room.

When four a.m. rolled around, I gave up trying to sleep on the couch and went into my home gym to work out. That didn't help at all. All I wanted was Morticia. It warred with my tenuous self-control and Greg's instructions to make her fall in love me.

I checked on the baker. I had covered her with a blanket, and the fluffy gray cat had taken advantage of the opportunity to curl up neatly by Morticia's head.

Make her love you.

Who didn't like breakfast in bed?

I opened the fridge. Just like the last few times, no food had miraculously appeared. It contained the usual chicken breasts and steamed vegetables that I ate, but I didn't think that was going to work for Morticia. I needed her to be infatuated with me. Poached chicken breast wasn't going to cut it.

There was no grocery store near me—not that I would know what to do if I went to one. I hadn't stepped foot in a grocery store since the last time Belle had dragged me when I was a teenager.

In the end, I bribed the doorman to go buy me stuff for breakfast.

"What kind of stuff?" he asked, confused.

I shrugged.

"Do you have a list?" he prompted.

"No. Just what you think a woman might want for breakfast."

I wished I could wave a magic wand and have cinnamon buns appear. I still had dreams about them...and dreams about Morticia feeding them to me and dreams about her wearing absolutely nothing.

Nothing in my dreams resembled the basket of raw ingredients the doorman brought over an hour later. The sun was just starting to peek up over the buildings in the distance and stream in through the French doors that led out to the balcony.

"What am I supposed to do with this?" I asked the doorman when I looked into the bag.

"It's all the fixings for a full English breakfast," he replied.

"I don't know how to cook any of this!"

"You just put it in a hot pan," he insisted. "You'll impress your lady friend." He patted me on the shoulder. "Morticia's good people. She helped me figure out my tattoo design." He took out his phone and showed me a scan of a drawing.

"Wow," I said, staring at it. I wasn't sure what I had expected, but of course the tattoo design Morticia had drawn was beautiful and stark and unique, just like her. It was a partial line drawing of a cat stretching, a subtle pattern on the ears and paws, all working together to evoke the essence of a cat.

"It's cool, right?" the doorman said with a grin.

It was cool. Morticia was cool, and I knew she was not going to be cool with what Greg was planning for the development of Dorothy's property.

She doesn't have to find out, and once it gets going, I'll steer Greg to a better path, I assured myself.

I tried to put it out of my mind. I had a pound of raw sausages that I had no idea what to do with.

"Okay, English breakfast," I said, reading the first recipe that came up on Google. "First, make the beans." I had figured I would just have to open the can and heat the beans in a pan, but this recipe called for onions and bay leaves and celery.

"Fuck," I cursed. I set the can aside and picked up one of the packages wrapped in white butcher paper. "Bacon. I can cook bacon!"

When the smoke alarm went off ten minutes later, it turned out that I could not, in fact, cook bacon. I had tested a small piece, and it was a good thing I did, because sometime between it sizzling away happily and my trying to crack an egg without shattering shells in the bowl, the pan caught fire.

"Shit!" I yelled, running around looking for the fire extinguisher.

"Oh my god!" Morticia exclaimed behind me.

"Evacuate!" I told her. "Where's the cat?" I picked up a dish towel to try and fan the flames.

"No!" she shouted, snatching it from me and grabbing another pan, stacking it on top of the frying pan. She held it there while I found Cindy Lou, who was spitting and hissing, fur on end.

Morticia peeked under the lid. "Fire's out."

"Cindy Lou, we almost didn't make it!"

The cat meowed at me.

"That was a lot of excitement," I said, flopping down on the couch. "I say we call it a day and go get McDonald's."

Morticia poked around at my haphazard stack of ingredients.

"I was trying to make you breakfast," I explained as she took stock of the excessive variety of meats. "I swear, as soon as my development is signed off across the street, the first thing I'm doing is putting in a restaurant. It's going to serve breakfast, lunch, and dinner twenty-four seven!"

"What development are you building in Hamilton Yards?" Morticia demanded.

"Er…" I coughed dramatically. "Smoke inhalation. I need a doctor."

"You're trying to bulldoze the art retreat that Dorothy runs," Morticia said accusingly.

"Of course not!" I said. Morticia was still holding the hot frying pan. "I'm obviously going to keep all the art, just spruce it up a bit, you know."

Her eyes narrowed.

I smiled.

"You know how much I appreciate art," I said, mind racing to try and convince her that I was totally not going to build a tacky, generic development. "I'm absolutely going to keep the character of the place. In fact, next year during Christmas, I'm going to have the whole place decorated, with a Christmas market featuring local artists and vendors."

Her face softened slightly. "Good," she said. "I'm so sick of all these hedge funds coming in, buying up property, then completely erasing the historic character."

"Not my hedge fund," I assured her. I stood up and carefully removed the frying pan from her grasp.

She didn't seem completely convinced.

"Look, don't even worry about it. Dorothy doesn't even seem to want to sell to me." I sighed and set the pan on the stove.

"Why not?" Morticia asked.

"Who knows?" I threw up my hands. "She probably doesn't trust a billionaire hedge fund manager."

"Hm," Morticia said. "Probably smart of her."

I tried not to feel hurt.

It's probably for the best that she sees through you. This could have ended badly.

Morticia grinned at me. "I mean, if you can't even manage to cook bacon, how are you going to create a development?"

"I wasn't just trying to cook bacon," I said. "I was trying to make a full English breakfast."

Morticia wrapped an arm around my neck and reached up to kiss me.

I held her close, deepening the kiss. "I am, of course, open to other suggestions for breakfast," I purred.

CHAPTER 39

Morticia

I snuggled down into the big, comfortable bed. I hadn't been sleeping much because I was up all night working then doing the bake-off during the day. Being in Jonathan's bed had been the best sleep I'd had in ages. And of course the happy ending to yesterday's evening had also helped me fully relax.

Pulling the covers over my head, I tried to go back to sleep. But I was wide-awake and horny. I wanted Jonathan. The taste he had given me the previous night had only awakened my sexual appetite.

However, I needed my camera. What if the first time we had sex ended up being the last time? I couldn't waste my chance; I needed those pictures. I had my interview with Dorothy today. I was going to ace it. I knew it. I needed that scholarship, though. I was so close!

"Actually..." I said. I pushed Jonathan away, even though everything in me wanted to strip his clothes off, straddle him, and ride his cock into the sunset. "I'm starving. You gave me a bit of a workout."

"I can give you a better one," he purred, kissing my neck.

I needed to hold him off a little longer. "Breakfast!" I said loudly, grabbing a can of tomatoes out of the bag. Jonathan blew out a breath.

"Do you need help?"

"That depends…can you slice the blood sausage without cutting yourself?"

Jonathan laughed. "Wait, that wasn't a joke, was it?"

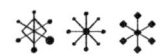

❈ ❋ ❅

"Are you a five-year-old?" I asked as Jonathan stared at the blood sausage on his plate. It was good quality. The little card that had come with it said it was from one of the heritage pig farms outside of Harrogate.

"It just doesn't feel like Christmas to me," he said. "That feels like something you might eat on Halloween on a dare."

"It's good and contains a lot of iron," I told him. "I would have expected you to be a bit more of an adventurous eater. You have all the money in the world; you can get exotic food delivered."

He looked at me balefully. "I don't want people to fuck with my food. I just want to eat it. I'm a meat-and-potatoes guy."

"And dessert."

"Yes," he said. "Speaking of." He rubbed his hands together. "After my performance last night, will that entitle me to more cinnamon rolls?"

"That is a special-occasion food."

"Please? They're haunting my dreams," he said, shaking me slightly.

I narrowed my eyes. "Eat all the blood sausage without making weird faces, and I'll think about it."

He scowled slightly.

"Your face is going to stick like that," I teased.

He grinned at me.

"How badly do you want those cinnamon rolls?" I teased back. I cut off a small piece of the blood sausage along with a scoop of beans, tomatoes, and fried mushroom. "Open up!" I said, slipping the fork into his mouth.

He chewed. "That was actually pretty good."

"It's earthy and strong," I said, taking another bite. "It goes well with whiskey. If you survive *The Great Christmas Bake-Off*, you should do a cooking series with pairings of cured meats and liquor."

"Only if you're around to help me," Jonathan said.

My heart raced. *He wants me around!*

❄ ❄ ❄

Lilith: *Deets deets, we need deets!*
Emma: *Did you survive?*
Emma: *Did you see his cock?*
Emma: *Was it the best sex of your entire life?*
Morticia: *Still no cock. But it was a nice date.*
Lilith: *You're turning into quite the high-society girl.*
Morticia: *Don't get too excited. He took me to a pop-up Christmas bar then ate me out, and I fell asleep.*
Emma: *…That's not good.*
Morticia: *What do you mean not good!?*

Emma: *You're supposed to make a good impression on the first date. You fell asleep. You basically told him he was bad at sex.*
Lilith: *If he doesn't completely ghost you, you need to up your sex game.*

I couldn't be ghosted by Jonathan! I had to finish my project. But first, I needed to survive the Getty internship in-person interview.

"Leaving already?" Jonathan asked as I stuffed my phone into my bag.

"Yeah, I have some things to take care of," I said, hoping he didn't press the issue. I didn't need him to know about the project or the scholarship. That would all lead to questions, and the questions would lead him to the inevitable conclusion that I was a weirdo loser who stalked men and built bizarre shrines to them.

"I'll call you," I said, slipping out of his arms to the door.

He reached out to stop me and turn me toward him. "I had a nice time, Morticia," he said, then leaned down to kiss me.

※ ※ ※

It was freezing as I crossed the road and headed for Dorothy's studio. It was like going to see the witch that lived in the woods, except Dorothy lived in a converted shipping container in the middle of an abandoned industrial property. Her tiny house and studio had been festooned with Christmas lights, and there was a Christmas scene sculpted in metal out front.

I paused to peer at it. It didn't look like the usually kitschy holiday yard art.

"It's my own interpretation," Dorothy said happily as she opened the door. "It's Mrs. Claus welcoming Santa back home."

"That's graphic."

"It's art," she said sagely. "You should see the offers I have on that piece."

I followed her into the shipping container. Inside was a minimalist Scandinavian décor with white walls and blond Baltic birch accents. On the walls and hanging in the windows were minimalist holiday decorations in a similar vein. A fire burned cheerfully in a small ship's stove in one corner.

"You know," I said, looking around, "I wouldn't mind Christmas if it all looked like this."

"I love Christmas!" Dorothy exclaimed. "The parties, the booze." She pulled out a bottle and started to make us drinks. "I even have a soft spot for the music and the movies."

"It's all so commercial though," I commented.

"Of course it's commercial; everyone knows it. But there is still something magical about Christmas for me. I see old friends and make new ones, drink and eat and reminisce. Christmas is what you make of it. You want to have minimalist decorations and eat nothing but donuts, then you can go ahead and call it Christmas!" She handed me my drink. "Speaking of which, it looks like you've been making a new friend."

"I don't know what you mean."

Dorothy cackled. "I know a gal who got some last night! How is he?" she asked, lowering her voice conspiratorially. "I usually don't go for younger men—can't handle all the drama. Give me a seasoned penis that's not afraid to stand outside and do yoga naked in the snow. Still. That body though." She whistled.

"It's a very nice body," I admitted, then drained my glass to try and keep from thinking about said body.

"Is it inspirational?" she asked gleefully.

"That too."

"Did you take my advice on the art project?"

I blushed, thinking about the pictures of him and me.

"You have to let me see!" Dorothy demanded.

"It's not done yet," I warned as I pulled out my phone to show her the in-progress art piece. "Is it too avant garde?" I asked her.

Dorothy inspected the photo on my phone. "Damn, girl. If you go the direction I think you are, you're going to have a unanimous vote from the women on the scholarship board. The artist, Zarah, is heading up this scholarship. She loves the type of art where women turn the tables." Dorothy fist-bumped me. "And way to commit. I'm always trying to convince young female artists to go all out, throw caution to the wind! You have to bare your soul, and sometimes other things, but the end product is always fantastic. You have the gift."

I beamed at her.

She motioned for me to sit and made me another drink. Then she pulled out a piece of paper. "The Getty Museum gave me this list of questions I'm supposed to ask you." She trailed her finger down the page. "Blah blah tell me your history: you're a go-getter who's been hustling her whole life, check. Blah blah what's your inspiration? Men and sex, check. Blah blah, more questions about your influences."

"You, honestly," I said bluntly.

She beamed. "Like I said." She tapped her head. "Sex always sells. Commit and follow through! Make sure to seal the deal with the big finish. Sex positivity! Multiple orgasms! Be in touch with yourself and experiment in art in life and with your partner. Hell!" she said, balling up the papers. "Who knows? You might get a two-for-one deal out of this. Jonathan could turn out to be your boyfriend!"

I choked on my drink. "I don't think that's going to happen," I said, coughing. Eventually, Jonathan was going to find out about the project. Then he would see what a complete weirdo I was and want nothing to do with me.

"Men love sex," Dorothy assured me. "They're used to women who don't, and when they find a woman in touch with her sexuality, it's like catnip for them. Trust me."

"I don't know if I'm that in touch," I admitted.

Dorothy peered at me. "That's no good. We need you to win that scholarship. Get up," she commanded. "Now strip. We're doing some sensual yoga."

CHAPTER 40

Jonathan

"You seal the deal yet?" Carl's voice asked on the phone.

"Dude, you just talked to me last night."

"Man, Greg is on my case," he said. "He went on a major rant last night. He's obsessed with winning this project. Apparently the Harringtons are ramping up their development portfolio, and he wants to land this property before they do."

"I'll be in the office a little later," I told him.

"Good. ThinkX wants to have that meeting about your logistics just to check in. You're moving a mad amount of product. We might even sell out by Christmas!"

After the call with Carl, I played with Cindy Lou. Even though I had a variety of expensive toys, the cat was obsessed with going out onto the balcony. I was afraid she was going to jump off.

"You know what," I finally said to her, pulling out the leash I had bought. "Apparently, I am going to stoop to a new low point in my life and be that weirdo who walks a cat."

Cindy Lou, however, did not want to be walked. She made it across the street before she flattened herself to the ground. I picked her up. "We will get there eventually," I told her, perching her on my shoulder. "The important thing is that I have an excuse to casually check in on Dorothy."

Upbeat Christmas music played as I approached the converted shipping container the old artist lived in.

"Keep your pelvic floor muscles clenched!" Dorothy yelled over the music as I rounded a corner past a partially caved-in brick wall. "And gyrate!"

"Getting your morning workout—" I began then froze. "Holy shit!" I clapped my hands over my face.

"Now don't go acting like you haven't seen a naked woman before," Dorothy boomed. "You were with Morticia here just last night."

I peeked through my fingers and saw Morticia, shivering in the cold, wearing a lacy bra and panties, cheeks flushed. Dorothy, however, was proudly wearing nothing but holding a glass filled with amber liquid.

"We're doing sensual yoga," Dorothy informed me, prodding Morticia with a long stick. "Get your legs spread farther! Let your hips breathe!"

"This is insane," Morticia muttered.

"You need to put this on your Instagram channel," Dorothy insisted.

"I don't think they'd allow it," Morticia said faintly.

"Oh, come on. It's just like I was telling you earlier, Morticia, about the best type of art—"

"Right!" Morticia said loudly, running to grab her phone. "Yes, we are so going to put you on Instagram!"

"We are?" I asked her, carefully looking up at the sky, the brick walls, anywhere other than at the naked older woman—and also anywhere other than at the almost-naked Morticia, because I had doubts that I was going to be able to control myself.

"Yep," she said, shoving me out of her shot. "We can't pass up an opportunity to create new content for the Instagram marketing!"

I carefully disentangled Cindy Lou from my jacket then took it off and handed it to Morticia.

"Thanks," she murmured. She set a bottle of whiskey next to the multicolored rug Dorothy was posing on. "Can you give us a very quick master class?"

"Can I ever!" Dorothy said then commenced a series of poses. "You need to watch these, Jonathan," she declared.

"No, ma'am," I replied, a hand firmly over my eyes.

Dorothy cackled. "You're too prudish for your own good. But don't worry. I'm sure Morticia will give you a personal display later."

I grinned up at the sky. "I'm looking forward to it."

"I think we have what we need," Morticia said after a moment. "You can look now, Jonathan. Dorothy's decent."

The older woman was wrapped in a colorful gauzy fabric. She sipped her drink then said, "Another good-looking guy was over here the other day. Can't remember his name."

"*Harrington*," I said through gritted teeth. Fuck, they were going to steal my development!

"That's right!" she said, snapping her fingers. "He was tall, dark, and handsome but didn't bring alcohol, and I know he wouldn't have spread the word on the cleansing powers of cold yoga." Dorothy slapped Morticia on the lower back. "Also, his girlfriend looked like he bought her at the girlfriend factory. Not like yours."

I wrapped my arms around Morticia. "I like them weird!"

CHAPTER 41

Morticia

Crap, that had been close!

I couldn't believe Jonathan had just shown up like that. I tried to think back to when exactly he had appeared. Dorothy had been espousing ideas about what I should put on the collage for the scholarship application. Had Jonathan heard any of what I'd discussed with Dorothy?

"So meeting up with Dorothy was the big, important thing you had to do this morning?" he asked, mouth quirked.

My mind raced. Jonathan could not find out about the piece. Sure, a lot of guys liked to say they wanted the unique, quirky girl, but really, they wanted the manic pixie dream girl who dyed her hair pink on a whim and cried at swans and loved to dance at festivals. They didn't actually want someone who was weird and different.

Taking photos of someone in intimate positions without their knowledge is probably out of the weird-and-different territory and into the illegal stalker, go-directly-to-jail territory.

And that was why I should not have a boyfriend and instead needed to retire to the mountains and live in a hut with a feral cat colony.

"Why were you over there?" Jonathan prompted, "I can't believe you wanted to do cold yoga."

"I—" God, why couldn't he just drop it? "I thought about what you said," I lied. "About wanting the Hamilton Yards property. I think it sounds like a great idea."

"You do?" He paused suddenly. "You told Dorothy about it?"

"Uh, yeah."

"What did she say?"

He was so excited and happy. I felt like a complete bitch for lying to him.

"Oh, she said she would think about it," I said, "but it sounds promising, right? I mean, she didn't like those other guys, the Harringtons."

He impulsively swept me up in his arms and kissed me. "You're the best," he told me. "Hamilton Yards is going to be amazing. Just keep bringing it up to her, okay? Make it seem like a no-brainer."

"Of course," I said weakly.

Just make it through Christmas, and then you can ghost everyone.

Jonathan wrapped one arm casually around my waist as if he was my boyfriend. I didn't know how to feel about that. I didn't do boyfriends; I barely did relationships generally. The last guy who might have counted as a boyfriend—though he had been more of a casual hookup—had flooded the apartment when he passed out drunk in the bathtub in my college dorm.

Jonathan tugged me into the building then up to his office. "I want to show you something," he said in excitement, pulling up a chart on his screen. "These are our sales numbers."

I read the chart. "Impressive," I said. The chart was a bunch of lines going upward, so I supposed that was the thing to say.

"No." He pointed to a spot where the chart turned dramatically upward. "This is you and your amazing marketing. You saved me."

"I just took some pictures," I demurred. "You're paying me; you don't have to thank me."

"Maybe I want to," he whispered.

My eyes darted around his office, flicking to the glass dividing wall that was the only thing between us and his staff as I realized just what his devious mind was up to. He pressed his kiss deeper, his fingers going lower, brushing against my flesh, my breasts, my abdomen.

He wouldn't. Not here, of all places. Would he?

The situation seemed innocent enough at first, at least from the outside looking in. Then his hand went between my legs and up my skirt.

He looked around to make sure no one was coming then kissed me hard.

"We can't do this here!" I protested softly.

Jonathan ignored me, continuing to kiss me.

I knew I should push him off, but my body ached for a repeat of the Jonathan Frost experience. "This is a bad idea," I finally gasped out.

Jonathan frowned. "We're just having a professional conversation. Nothing wrong with that."

He pressed his hand against my clit through the fabric, causing me to gasp. His touch was always so potent, and he was so very quickly learning how to turn my lustfulness against me.

I tipped my head back.

"Eyes forward," he murmured.

I moaned, worried about someone looking my way and seeing my face for what was really happening. As much as I tried to stay stoic and unchanging, there was only so much I could resist. Jonathan was just that good.

He even casually stopped kissing me to take a drink, all while his finger continued to weasel in beneath my panties, rubbing against my flesh. I shuddered as he pressed on my clit and then started to fuck me with his fingers good and properly. Merely seconds later, he escalated his campaign to make me come on the desk, his fingers sliding in and out of me, faster and faster, never truly letting up on my clit.

The pressure building inside me was intense, coming at me so damn fast. I nibbled on my lip to endure it, hoping to ride it out just a little longer. I braced myself against the desktop, the little vibrations inside of me trying to make me collapse into a pile of orgasmic goo.

His two fingers pistoning in and out of me, so delicately nudging my clit all the while, were too much to take. I was writhing, about to scream and embarrass myself.

Only he pulled me closer and kissed me again, muffling my moans and letting the orgasm wash over me. My heart pounded as I looked around, wondering if anyone had seen me in one of my most intimate moments. I'd be struggling to look any of Jonathan's employees straight in the eye for a while.

Not only that, but I still did not have the pictures I needed for my art project.

CHAPTER 42

Jonathan

I kissed Morticia again. She pushed me off, though she was breathing hard.

A few moments later, my assistant knocked on the door.

"You have a visitor," she told me. "It's your father."

"I better go," Morticia said in that raspy voice that made me want to bend her over my desk and fuck her until she screamed. "I'll take Cindy Lou back for you if you want."

I nodded absently and handed Morticia the cat and her bag. The assistant walked her out.

My heart pounded, and I tried to calm down. When I was a kid, my parents had rarely wanted anything to do with me. As the middle son, I had been lost in the shuffle. It didn't help that whenever they did want to pay attention to me, I would freak out under the pressure.

I am a billionaire. I run a successful alcohol company, I manage a hedge fund, and I'm about to have a major real estate development, I told myself. *I have a cat and a girlfriend, though she is fake, and that's probably going to blow up in my face.*

My father walked in moments later. He and I were the same height and had the same platinum hair and blue eyes. I had idolized him when I was a child.

He barely seemed to remember I existed.

Once you have a ten-figure net worth and Hamilton Yards up and running, everything will change, I reassured myself.

"Drink?" I offered.

He scowled at me. "For goodness sake, Jonathan, it's ten in the morning. No wonder you haven't managed to make anything of yourself if that's how you carry on."

I tried to pivot. "Just the perks of being in the alcohol business."

"So I hear," my father said, nose wrinkled as if he had smelled something disgusting.

"So how can I help you?" I asked, gesturing to the chair in front of my desk, the desk on which I had just gotten Morticia off.

"I didn't come to see you, obviously," my father replied.

I forced myself to keep my face a frozen mask of corporate pleasantness like all the good CEOs had.

"I came over here to see Belle," he continued.

"Belle?"

Jonathan and Owen claimed that our parents had decided that Belle was a disappointment and wanted nothing more to do with her. When we talked to Belle, the feeling was mutual.

"I thought you had disowned her," I said tentatively.

"No one said anything about that," my father huffed. "We were at a holiday party with the Richmonds. They had mentioned that Belle was dating one of the Svenssons."

I narrowed my eyes. "I don't believe that is the case anymore."

"Too bad," my father said. "For a minute there, I thought she might have redeemed herself. Of course she managed to ruin it. Like your mother said, someone that tall needs a tall man. And they don't grow on trees."

"Or she could find someone that makes her happy," I replied tersely.

My father barked out a laugh. "Don't be naïve. Belle needs to settle for what she can get." He scowled. "Too bad your brothers settled." Then his features rearranged back into their handsome mask. "But if they supply grandchildren, then I suppose that's all that matters."

Jack and Owen would kill me for real if I blabbed their business to Dad. But he had come to see me! Even if it was only for information about my siblings. Surely it wouldn't hurt to tell him just a few tidbits?

"Chloe and Holly run their own restaurants. They're very successful," I reminded him. "Chloe's bistro has a number of franchise locations. I'm hoping I can talk her or Holly into branching out here in my development."

"A development, you say?" my father asked, intrigued.

"Yes," I said. I launched into my spiel, describing the hotels, condos, and restaurants, all in an impeccably renovated industrial complex with historic brick buildings.

My father regarded me with interest for the first time in my life. "Maybe you'll make something of yourself after all. Of course, first, you'll need to get rid of that goth girl."

It took me a second to realize who he was talking about. "Morticia?"

"Surely the internet is incorrect and there isn't something going on between you two," he said, lip curling slightly. "I have high standards for my children."

"Of course not," I said in a rush. "There's nothing; it's just for TV."

CHAPTER 43

Morticia

"You slept with him again?" Emma demanded the next day.

I had not actually slept with Jonathan the night before, though I had spent the evening in his condo. I had been too busy editing that horror show footage of Dorothy and fielding questions from Jonathan on how best to make the Hamilton Yards development palatable to her.

"Shh! Keep your voice down!" I whispered to her as I sketched out my dessert idea. It was for the holiday-card baking challenge. I had only half listened when Anastasia had explained the rules. Keeley had seemed mad when I was in the bottom three but wasn't let go.

"I can't believe Keeley did better than you," Lilith said, glaring across the studio at our cousin.

"I think she's buying votes," I replied.

"Wish I had that kind of disposable income," she remarked as she took pictures of bottles of alcohol arranged at my station for Instagram teasers, though really the photo session was just an excuse to gossip.

"So you did sleep with him," Emma said giddily.

"Not exactly. He just got a bit…handsy in his office."

"In his office!" Emma said, shaking her head.

"Dirty, dirty girl." Lilith smirked.

"Sounds like Jonathan knows what he's doing!" Emma said.

I carefully separated eggs for the eggnog crème brûlée soufflés I was making.

"You don't want a guy who's got a pretty package, but you open it up and it's all coal," Lilith said.

"I cannot with the Christmas metaphors right now."

"I don't think he's got a fake Christmas tree in his living room," Emma said with a giggle.

"I think his Yule log is nice and thick and ready to be shoved in your mouth," Lilith piled on.

"Yum, all that cream filling!"

I shoved Lilith and Emma away from my baking station. "I'm trying to cook here!"

"Make me proud!" Lilith said, blowing me a kiss. "Also, you have to bake these for the rest of us later!"

There was no way I was making my dessert twice. I loved my sister and my friend, but soufflés were deceptively hard. The eggs had to be the proper age, the cream had to be the thickest and richest, and the oven had to be the perfect temperature.

Would be nice to get a picture of Jonathan's thick cream all over you…

I melted the butter in a saucepan then added the flour. Once the doughy taste was cooked off, I added the cream, stirring until it was blended. Then I grated in fresh nutmeg and added rum, sugar, and a pinch of salt, stirring until it boiled, smoothed, and then thickened.

Simultaneously, I started on the crème brûlée custard, combining cream, vanilla bean, and a pinch of salt. Then I grated nutmeg into the saucepan. I had had the crazy idea that I would make a small, thin crème brûlée, place it carefully on top of the soufflé, and then quickly caramelize a sugar crust on top. This would create the crackle of the burnt sugar, the custardiness of the crème brûlée filling, and the bite and airiness of the soufflé.

To keep my egg yolks from curdling when I added them to the warm cream, I blended them with a bit of the spiced liquid in another bowl and added that back to the double boiler, stirred until the mixture thickened, then set it aside to cool.

While it did so, I whipped the egg whites with cream of tartar. I had carefully selected fresh, free-range eggs. Fresh eggs were harder to whip, but the bubbles formed more closely together, creating a more structurally sound soufflé. Once I had stiff peaks—

Stiff, hee-hee!

—I carefully folded the egg whites into the soufflé mixture. I couldn't stir it, as that would deflate all the bubbles.

Once the crème brûlée was half-submerged in a water bath and cooking away merrily in the oven, I tried to figure out what cocktail to serve. It should be fruity, so I headed to the pantry for some oranges and grapefruit. Citrus was technically a winter fruit. People used to give each other expensive boxes of oranges, tangerines, and grapefruits for the holidays. I was trying to decide whether I wanted to make a tangerine-based cocktail or a grapefruit-based one when I heard commotion out in the studio.

I poked my head out of the pantry then cursed. Keeley was at my station, and she had the oven open!

"Don't you dare!" I yelled, racing toward her.

She screamed and slammed the oven door shut.

"You're trying to sabotage my dessert," I shouted, jabbing my finger at her.

"I was trying to save it. Look, your soufflé is all flat," she protested.

I wrenched open the door. The soufflé had deflated and imploded. It was a pancake now.

"*You* did that!" I yelled at her. "You ruined it when you slammed the oven door."

"Did not," Keeley insisted. "You just can't cook. That was your fault."

I checked at the clock. Crap! I did not have enough time to make another soufflé. I could serve crème brûlée and what, cocktails and fruit? That didn't seem impressive enough, especially since Keeley was making an intricate tart.

I ran back to the pantry and looked around in desperation. The reality was that I was not a chef. I baked as a hobby. Maybe a trained pastry chef could create something miraculous; however, I was only an artist.

An idea bloomed in my mind.

I checked my crème brûlées. At least they hadn't been ruined. Originally, I had been planning on simply pouring the sugar on and torching it, but what if I went above and beyond? In the past, I had done wood burning for various art projects, and I also knew how to weld. Surely making art with a crème brûlée torch couldn't be that difficult.

Using one of the Platinum Provisions high-end butane torches provided at our stations, I did a few test runs on sugar on a plate. It ran a bit, so I wasn't going to be able to do anything intricate. But I could create snowflakes, a tree, and reindeer.

I pulled the crème brûlées out of the oven and let them sit and rest. Then I made the bourbon-and-tangerine cocktail with orange bitters, simple syrup, a bit of fresh lemon juice, and a generous amount of fresh tangerine juice and garnished it with a tangerine peel.

Only ten minutes left. I poured the sugar onto the crème brûlée and went to work, first carefully melting the sugar and letting it set then turning the flame up to create the burnt umber char marks for the holiday designs.

"Spatulas down! Time to take your holiday-card pictures!" Anastasia called just as I finished the last sparkle of the snowflake. "Remember, your dessert should be as photogenic as you and Jonathan would be as Mr. and Mrs. Frost."

Lilith and Emma took each girl's picture with Jonathan. They all had made big, impressive desserts. I studied my ramekins and tried to compose a winning holiday card of Jonathan, broad shouldered and handsome in his suit, and me, covered in egg and tangerine zest and reeking of burned sugar.

Keeley pranced over with her tart. "Take my picture from this side," she ordered, striking a Betty Boop pose as she pretended to cut into the tart and serve it to Jonathan.

I hated to admit it, but it was a pretty good picture.

"You're next," Emma said, motioning me up.

I had pulled off my T-shirt, which left me in my black chemise. It was more photogenic than the stained T-shirt, though the studio was chilly.

"Are we going clothing optional now?" Jonathan asked with a quirk of his mouth. "Because I would have no complaints with that."

"It's a miracle you manage to get anything done," I retorted, "if the only thing you can think of is sex."

"How do you want your picture?" Emma asked me.

I studied the photo setup the bake-off was using. I had originally designed it way back in November when I was still riding the high of Halloween. It was a perfect backdrop for someone with a towering cake or, *ahem*, an elaborate soufflé. However, I had none of that now.

"Outside!" I told everyone.

It was snowing slightly. Jonathan stood against the backdrop of the gray winter sky. I checked the camera, making sure we had his profile perfect. "We need to be in the bottom third of the shot," I told Lilith, moving the tripod back and composing the shot.

"What in the world are you doing?" Belle asked me.

"A minimalist couple's portrait."

I had nixed the cocktail from the shot. It was orange. It would have gone great with the photo I had planned for the soufflé, but hey, it's art—you adjust. I stood facing Jonathan, my hand outstretched, balancing one of the small ramekins. Jonathan's hand came up to cup mine. The wind blew my hair around me as Lilith snapped the photos.

"You know," Jonathan said, "if these pictures don't turn out how you want them to, we can always do a parody of the video of Dorothy that's going viral."

CHAPTER 44

Jonathan

"You two are barely visible," Belle remarked as we all stared at the black-and-white photo on the tiny camera screen.

"No, this is exactly what I want," Morticia declared. "It has to be ten feet tall to appreciate the full effect."

"You are so extra," her sister Lilith said.

"I think the naked yoga pictures would be better," I told Morticia.

"You have no vision," she retorted. She took out her phone as we went inside for the judges to taste the desserts. "I can't believe people are watching Dorothy do naked yoga."

"You did a very tasteful job covering her. I especially liked the elf faces that were at the chest area," I said to Morticia.

"You joke, but I'm the one that had to edit that all together."

"When she signs off on Hamilton Yards," I promised Morticia, "I will take you anywhere in the world you want to go as a thank-you for your sacrifice."

The judges were lukewarm on Morticia's desserts. "It's a basic crème brûlée," Nick said. "It tastes fine; you can't go wrong with nutmeg and rum."

"I'm impressed with the design," Anu said. "I've never seen anyone make designs on the burned sugar the way you have."

"Those are a bit corporate," Nick said. "I could see this at a conference or like an upscale chain hotel restaurant. I give it a C."

"B for effort," Anu told Morticia. "I hope this dessert doesn't send you home."

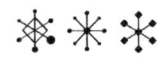

※ ※ ※

"We have to serve desserts like those crème brûlées at the hotel that will be at Hamilton Yards," I told Morticia.

We were in my condo. She was setting up for another photo shoot, while I was trying to subtly prompt her to help me with the development. "You think you could make one with a logo to show Dorothy?"

She shrugged. "Sure."

I kissed her. "I'm so close to her signing, I can taste it!" I kissed Morticia again, harder this time, reveling in the way she melted against me. "You're the best thing to happen to me. The Harringtons can suck it once I win Hamilton Yards."

Morticia seemed apprehensive.

"Don't worry," I assured her, "we will keep all the historic character, including art pieces. Shoot, we can build live-work studio spaces for artists. It will be amazing."

She was thoughtful. "Yes, I suppose that would be pretty cool."

I wrapped her in my arms. "I need you to help me," I told her. "You believe in this project. You wouldn't have talked to Dorothy the other day if you didn't." I leaned in and kissed her.

"I'm not really sure how I can help convince her. Shouldn't you have a marketing team on it?" she asked uncertainly.

"If you recall, I had a marketing team for the Hillrock West Distillery, and look where that got me. You're the real deal, Morticia. Dorothy recognizes a fellow artist. That's the edge we have over the Harringtons. You and me—we're the power couple."

Morticia snorted as she looked through the camera viewfinder.

"Like that picture you took. Do I understand it? No. But you had a vision. People respect that. They respect your conviction."

"And my conviction is telling me that we need more shirtless pictures of you on Instagram."

"You want to go do another minimalist photo shoot? I'm thinking black and white, really greased up."

Morticia rolled her eyes. "What I really need is some of you and your cat. You have to have a mix of thirst pictures and cute ones that make women go, 'Yes, I want to marry that one.'"

I laughed as I helped her move the couch. "I figured people would like the spicier ones," I said.

"We don't want them too spicy."

"Why?" I asked as she adjusted the lights. "I bet you look at them all the time. Shoot, I bet you get off looking at them and thinking about me."

She looked slightly guilty and swallowed.

I smirked. "I knew it! Don't worry," I said, kissing her. "I'm going to give you a hot set of pictures, then I'll watch you touch yourself until you come, looking at my face."

"You are a walking, talking ego," she said, batting my chest playfully. "Now go over there and let me take your picture."

Ignoring her, I took the camera out of her hand and pulled her back to me, snapping pictures as I kissed down her chest to her tits. She moaned, her head tipping back slightly.

"You know where we can take even better pictures?" I asked her. I kissed under her jaw, my hand creeping under her skirt and snapping more pictures. "The bedroom."

CHAPTER 45

Morticia

This is not a good idea.

I had talked a big game about taking raunchy photos of Jonathan and me in compromising positions. However, if I was being honest, I was too chickenshit to go through with it. In the end, I probably would have drawn the scenes I needed by hand. But now Jonathan was taking the pictures himself.

You should stop him. It wasn't right. He didn't know what I was using them for.

Think of the scholarship money. Besides, his face wouldn't be shown, and neither would mine. And X-rated body parts would be covered.

It still seemed wrong. I should push his hands away, push away the mouth that was pressing hot kisses along my skin. But I had a plan. I was going to execute that plan.

Maybe this is a bad plan.

Jonathan's hand pressed between my legs, making me moan.

Actually, no, this is a good plan. I needed him.

"Let's go enjoy the view, then, shall we?" I smiled.

"Yes. The view. And not what I explicitly mentioned."

I followed him down the hall and through the master bedroom door, all the while being heavily plagued with second thoughts.

The master bedroom was posh and masculine. I walked up to the window. It did, funnily enough, have a nice view out onto the Hamilton Yards property he was so insistent on developing.

"Maybe I should photograph you in front of this window," I told him.

"And maybe one day, I'll fuck you in front of that window," he replied. "But not tonight."

He leaned in and kissed me on the neck, and I turned my head to meet him. His mouth was soft, and he cupped the back of my head, kissing me deeply.

It was going to be more than just some fun in his office this time. The bulge in his pants against my ass just reaffirmed that thought. His arms wrapped around me, inching lower and lower on my body, making my flesh prickle.

He unbuttoned my blouse bit by bit, pulling it off of me, and I shrugged to help him along—all part of the plan. *Just remember that falling for him is not part of the plan.*

Feeling the roughness of his stubble against my shoulder, the anticipation built inside me. I turned to face him and see his smile.

"Fuck, I can't believe how beautiful you are, Morticia. And I would say that now is when you tell me how hot I am," he said with a half smile, "but I think we all know that."

He tossed me the camera, and I barely caught it. I swore at him. "That's expensive!"

"So am I." Jonathan unbuttoned his jacket. "So how do you think about me? I know you fantasize about me. Now's your chance to get a lifetime of material." His blazer hit the floor, and he was stripping himself out of his button-down shirt much faster than I could snap the photos. "Let me give you something better to remember me by," he said, deep voice reverberating around the room. "You'll study the pictures..."

Click.

"Remembering that these were the moments..."

Click.

"Right before I gave you the best, hardest fuck of your entire life."

Jonathan was hot, and I hated that I was so easily tempted by him. In the low light in the bedroom, the shadows played off his toned chest, the bulging pecs tapering down to washboard abs.

Click.

He led me toward his bed. I continued snapping pictures as he took my free hand, running it over his half-naked body and down into his pants. I snapped more as I undid his belt then cupped a hand against his groin, making him hiss.

He shrugged off the pants then kissed me as he undid my skirt. I let it fall and let him see my body in only underwear through the camera lens. His appreciation was still there and very, very strong.

The coolness of the air around me contrasted wonderfully with the warmth of his touch. I ached to feel more of his fingers against me.

He kissed me, his tongue slipping into my mouth, tangling with mine.

"I think you're definitely going to want pictures of this next part," he said.

He took the camera from me and snapped photos as he unhooked my bra to free my tits, my nipples hard in the cool air. He ran his fingers around the hard peaks, letting them perk up and point out playfully, his touch sending little shocks of electricity through my body. His hands trailed up and down my torso, stopping periodically at my breasts to take brief enjoyment of them.

Then he guided me down to the bed, kissing me again, his hand now going between my legs and feeling my pussy.

Click went the camera as he stroked me, making me moan in anticipation.

"Knew it. You're so fucking horny for me, aren't you? You can't stop thinking about me. And you haven't even had my cock. You're just a horny little elf."

"We have not," I said, "progressed to the part of our relationship where we are using Christmas foreplay."

"Then next time," Jonathan said, "I'm going to dress you up in a reindeer costume, skimpy this time, with straps so I can hold on while I take you from the back."

The horny part of me that had hijacked my brain and was begging for his cock thought that was a very good idea.

He stroked my pussy hard through my panties, making me cry out as he drove me crazy.

"You're so wet," he murmured, snapping more pictures. "You have to remember how wet you got for me."

"Why?" I gasped. "Isn't this the first and last time we'll do this? I know you are a one-and-done type of guy."

"Oh no," he purred. "This is just in case I get run over by a reindeer. I want to make sure that you're ruined for any other man."

"*Fuck*," I whimpered, "you're going to make me come."

"Not yet," he said cheerfully, taking his hand away and leaving me gasping on the bed.

He pulled down his silky boxer briefs; his erection jutted out, hard and thick. Jonathan pressed his cock to my pussy through my panties, rubbing it in the slick wetness, and took one last picture.

"A dick pic for the ages," he said then tossed the camera aside.

"You better not break that," I warned, grabbing for the camera as it almost fell off the bed.

"I'll buy you a new one for Christmas," he assured me as he wiggled my panties down my legs. "After I make you scream out a Christmas carol."

Then I was lying fully naked before him. He posed in front of me, and I snapped one last picture.

That's the view I want to wake up to every morning.

God, why did he have to be so fucking hot? It wasn't remotely fair.

He plucked the camera out of my hands, setting it aside gently this time. Then his entire body pressed down on me, his smile strong. His naked form atop mine was overwhelming and potent. His cock throbbed against my pussy, and he tickled my clit with the tip. I wanted him inside me. So damn bad.

He kissed me hard again. Then he left me briefly to open a nightstand drawer. He pulled out a condom, rolled it over his length, and tossed the trash elsewhere. Room cleanliness was a concern for another time. Right now, I was all that mattered to him.

His cock aimed right for my pussy, his eyes right on mine. I was his only fascination, the only thing in the world at that time, and he was absolutely set on making me his.

Planting one more kiss on my lips, he thrust himself in. The bliss hit me like the Polar Express. All of him surged within me, causing me to cry out with delight. He filled me to the very brim, his thick cock ramming into me to the hilt, as if he had been made perfectly just for me.

"You're a fucking vise. So damn good, Morticia."

I laughed, grinding onto his cock and coaxing him to do his part in making this a mind-blowing experience that neither of us would ever forget. As he set a steady pace, I continued grinding against him, grabbing him by the ass and holding him tighter so he could fuck me harder and faster and not worry about anything else.

Not one to be outdone, he squeezed his hand into the tightness between us, those deft fingers of his rubbing my clit with the rhythm of our tryst.

We clung to each other, our need for one another growing fervent and powerful, every thrust spiking the absolute bliss through me again and again. Every move was building on the last, every bit of it all.

"Come for me, Morticia. Come for me, harder than you've ever come before."

I bit my lip, feeling self-conscious.

"I need this. I need to hear you." He grunted. He trembled in his need for me, screaming toward his climax as quickly as I was. I was his weakness, just as he was mine.

One more stroke, one more thrust, one more everything, and I...

I came.

The overwhelming feeling of bliss pounded through my body, burned behind my eyes, and sent my legs trembling. I never wanted it to end.

Jonathan collapsed into a pile of sweat on top of me. I rolled him over and fumbled for the camera, taking one last picture of him—his slightly sweaty hair over his face, lips parted, one hand resting on my ass.

Click.

My heart squeezed like the camera shutter.

Click.

He smiled and looked up at me through those long silver eyelashes.

Click.

Fuck.

I think I'm in love.

No, it can't be; it's endorphins, pheromones, a lifetime of bad decisions!

"Morticia," he murmured, "you look like you've seen the Ghost of Christmas Past." Jonathan laughed softly and flipped us over so he was on top of me. "I want to make you come again," he whispered, pressing kisses along my collarbone.

The doorbell rang. Jonathan kissed me and rolled off.

"But not right now. I was a gentleman and had food delivered, because while I do enjoy your cooking above all else, you probably want a break. I was going to order Italian," he said conversationally as he dressed, "but then I figured you're Italian, which might be weird, so I ordered sushi. They have a special Christmas roll that's all arranged like a snowman."

He went into the hall.

I shook myself out of my stunned silence. Hastily pulling my clothes on, I padded to the living room. I needed to leave. I had my pictures. In fact, I had so many pictures that I could probably finish the art piece tonight and send it off.

Jonathan opened the door as I hunted for my shoes.

His voice was slightly muffled as he greeted whoever had arrived.

"Sarah?"

CHAPTER 46

Jonathan

Sarah was standing there in the doorway. Sarah. She was here! After years of not hearing from her, after she had just walked out of my life, taking a piece of my heart with her, there she was.

"Jonathan?" she said.

I tentatively reached out for her, hardly believing she was real. "Sarah?"

But Morticia was behind me. "Sarah, for fuck's sake, what are you doing here? Did Keeley send you over?" Morticia demanded. "Geez, Jonathan, I'm so sorry. My family is nuts. Honestly, Sarah," she scolded, "you can't just show up at people's apartment unannounced."

Sarah's face screwed up in fury. "You said you loved me!" she screamed at me. Then she burst into tears and ran to the stairs. The door slammed behind her.

"Do you know my cousin?" Morticia asked me in confusion.

"Sarah is your cousin?" I was caught between my need to show Morticia that I cared about her and my need for closure with Sarah. "I'll be right back," I stammered. "Just wait for me, okay? I'll explain."

I raced to the elevator, hoping to beat Sarah downstairs. She was just exiting the stairwell as the doors opened at the lobby.

"Sarah!" I yelled.

She was sobbing. "You said you were going to love me forever," she said accusingly.

"You left," I reminded her, trying to figure out where to put my hands.

Sarah was here. I had dreamed about this moment for years after she had left. I didn't think I had even gotten over her leaving. Periodically, when I had a magazine article or a big marketing push, I had wondered if she would see it and think of me.

But lately, I hadn't thought of her at all. Morticia had been the one on my mind.

"You were supposed to wait for me." Sarah sniffled, taking a few steps over to me and resting against my chest. "Why are you with her?"

"Morticia?"

"You cheated on me," Sarah yelled around the sobs.

I was speechless. "You left. It's been years. How is that cheating?"

"It's emotional cheating," she insisted.

Impossibly high platform heels clacked on the polished concrete floor behind me.

"I thought that was you," Keeley snapped. "When I saw you with your holier-than-thou attitude walking piously down the street, I knew you were up to something."

Sarah sobbing in my arms, Keeley yelling at her—it was too early in the morning for me to deal with hysterical women.

The elevator dinged. Morticia walked out, looked around, and slowly returned into the elevator.

"No, don't leave," I begged her, disentangling Sarah then running and hauling Morticia back into the lobby.

"You're sleeping with him?" Keeley screeched.

"She stole the love of my life. You had no right to sleep with my husband-to-be!" Sarah screamed at Morticia.

"Oh, this is rich," Keeley exclaimed gleefully. "You slept with Jonathan after all the shit you gave me about sleeping with Trevor. Morticia, you're a dirty fucking hypocrite."

"Sleeping with Jonathan is not the same as sleeping with Trevor," Morticia said, lip curling up to reveal sharp teeth. "I do have standards."

"Who the fuck is Trevor?" I yelled.

The women looked at me.

"Sarah's husband," Keeley said impatiently.

"That you slept with on her wedding night," Morticia shot back.

"That's not as bad as you! You're cheating on the bake-off contest!" Keeley yelled, launching herself at Morticia.

She took out a Taser and brandished it at her cousin.

"Sarah, you left me," I said slowly, "to marry some guy named Trevor?"

Sarah dabbed her eyes.

Keeley smirked. "Sarah, Sarah, you dirty little lying slut; you had everyone convinced you were a virgin!"

"I am a virgin," Sarah insisted.

"No, you're not," I retorted.

I was worried what Morticia would think of me now that she knew Sarah was the former love of my life. I chanced a glance at Morticia. She didn't seem as if she cared. I didn't know if I was hurt or relieved.

You were only with her to win that property.

Yes, but after last night...

It's for the best if she doesn't like you, I assured myself. *Especially if Sarah is her cousin. Morticia would probably also just run off in the middle of the night.*

"Jonathan says you two did it," Keeley exclaimed. "Though I'm sure it wasn't that good."

It hadn't been that great now that I thought back on it. I had been young, and Sarah had clearly had some mental hang-ups. Hindsight was probably making things a lot better than they actually had been.

"I'm a virgin now," Sarah insisted. "I performed a purity ceremony and took a vow."

"Did you sew your hymen back on?" Morticia asked, one black eyebrow raised.

"Why?" I asked Sarah. "Why did you leave?"

"Because," she spat, "you refused to do what I wanted you to do. You and I were supposed to go live in the woods on a homestead and have twenty children, and I told you that's what I wanted. You promised you would, but then you decided to start that hedge fund and go to all those parties."

I frowned. "I told you I had to attend those events for networking. I invited you. I bought you nice dresses."

"I didn't want to go!" She stamped her foot. "I wanted you to stay home with me. You never did what I wanted."

"I was trying to make money to support us!" I said incredulously. "One of us had to work."

"I didn't want you to work. I wanted you to start a homestead with me."

Morticia snorted. "Jonathan, with his five-thousand-dollar suits, on a homestead, raising goats and farming?"

I bit back a curse. "Sarah, I wanted to be a billionaire. You knew my aspirations. We were supposed to be happy together."

She blinked up at me. "I know," she said, lip trembling. "I saw a magazine article about how you were the newest Frost billionaire. I'm so proud of you. I miss you, and I screwed up. I never slept with Trevor, so I'm going to ask the priest for an annulment. Once I leave him, you and I will be together forever. We'll live in your high-rise, and we can raise our twenty kids there."

CHAPTER 47

Morticia

"Aaannnddd I'm out," I said, sliding past Jonathan. "You and your future football team factory clearly have a lot to catch up on."

"Morticia, wait," Jonathan pleaded helplessly.

I turned and walked to the front door. A part of me desperately wanted him to run after me, to tell me, "Screw Sarah. Screw your crazy family. You're the only one that I love."

It's the endorphins talking, I told myself. *Sex is addictive.* One step. Another.

Jonathan didn't run after me.

I forced myself to keep my back straight as I walked out into the cold night.

This is for the best. You have the pictures you need. You will win that internship. You will live in a house with three other people and work for peanuts in a windowless archive room.

Life is grand.

※ ※ ※

"What the fuck—Sarah just showed up?" Lilith demanded later that evening.

I had taken the train across town to Emma's apartment. Now we were all crammed inside the small studio. I was baking apple-caramel cinnamon rolls, because if there was ever a day I needed those, it was today.

"Yep," I said, "she just appeared. Told him she was sorry, and she loved him, and she was leaving Trevor and wanted him back."

"And you just let it happen?" Lilith asked incredulously.

"I thought you were gunning for him! You were going to have him wrapped up under the tree by Christmas," Emma cajoled, stealing a spoonful of caramel sauce before I could bat her hand away.

"I was never after him. It was all part of my evil master plan to take spicy pictures for my art piece."

"Still," Lilith said, "it's the principle of the thing. Sarah's married. She can't have both Jonathan and Trevor."

"Since they didn't consummate it," Emma said, making air quotes, "she could qualify for an annulment."

"It's just too much drama for me. I had the pictures I needed, so I vamoosed and let them sort it out."

"Wait, did you say you got the pictures?" Lilith was wide-eyed.

I nodded.

"Let me see!" Lilith cried, reaching for my bag.

I attacked my twin with a wooden spoon. She grabbed another off the counter, and we fenced. Emma snuck under us and grabbed the camera, flipping through my pictures of Jonathan.

"Oh. My. God! These are so hot." She gasped. "Girl. You are not letting Sarah just waltz in and take that."

"If that's what Jonathan wants," I said unhappily.

"What do *you* want?" Lilith asked me.

"I want…" I wanted sex, yes, but I also wanted to hang out with Jonathan and cook in his kitchen. I shrugged. "I guess I want to get to know him better. We haven't even had a cat playdate yet."

"You can't quit before you even start," Emma said.

"I don't know if he even likes me."

"He took you out on a date then took you back to his condo and fucked your brains out. Sounds like he likes you," my twin said.

"But he loves Sarah," I countered.

"Sarah is like the cheap dime-store plastic ornament on your Christmas tree that's made in China from toxic waste," Lilith said, wrinkling her nose. "No one wants celluloid ornaments on their Christmas tree. That stuff off-gasses and randomly bursts into flames, then boom! Your whole house is a fireball."

"You are the handcrafted porcelain ornament with sentimental value," Emma told me.

"No!" Lilith barked. "She's Artemis, goddess of the moon, goddess of the hunt, fighting for her prize! You do not back down!"

"I'm not fighting over a man," I said flatly, crossing my arms.

My twin placed her hands on my shoulders. "You can't just give up. Maybe this is your one shot in your entire lifetime at true love. Go ovaries to the wall. If you flame out in a nuclear bomb of glory, we will build a shrine in your honor."

"It's going to be just like Justin all over again," I groaned.

"No it won't, because Jonathan actually wants you," Lilith reminded me. "You're not a stalker. You're a new positive woman."

"I don't even know how to win this kind of fight."

"Food. Sex. Christmas," Emma said, holding up a copy of *Vanity Rag* magazine. "This article says it's the surefire way to win a man in time to take to a holiday dinner. May the force of Christmas be with you. Also," she added, "there's this whole new trend of naked yoga making the rounds. Have you seen this?" She pulled up a video.

"That's Dorothy." I face-palmed. "I sent her the video I made of her to approve. I was hoping she would come to her senses and be like, 'No, I do not want the gaping maw of my vagina all over the internet,' but she must have posted it herself."

"Her hashtag game is on point," Lilith said in admiration. "It's everywhere. There are people copying it. The Kardashians gave her a shout-out."

"She is hosting a retreat in a couple days," Emma told me. "She says all are welcome."

"I'm going to skip that."

"Jonathan might like some naked yoga!" Lilith waggled her eyebrows.

"Sex, food, and Christmas," Emma chanted. "You have to channel your inner sex goddess."

"Agreed," Lilith said. "I mean, come on. Sarah is your competition? Sarah who refused to sleep with her own husband for the last eight months? Give Jonathan super porn-starry sex; blow him and blow his mind. He'll be wrapped around your little finger."

"If you really give him a good show," Emma said in excitement, "Jonathan might even pay for your apartment in Los Angeles!"

CHAPTER 48

Jonathan

I was kicking myself for not running after Morticia. I had been in shock. Also, Sarah had sunk her nails into the thin fabric of my unbuttoned dress shirt.

"Please," she begged, "take me back. I'm in a loveless, sexless marriage, and I need you."

As soon as I disentangled myself from Sarah, Keeley latched onto me like a bedazzled octopus.

"Don't listen to her," she insisted. "You need to sample all of the DiRizzo cousins before you make your choice." She ran her fingers up my bare chest.

"Don't touch him!" Sarah shrieked, launching herself at Keeley. "He's mine."

She grabbed my shirt. Then Keeley grabbed another chunk of the fabric. They pulled, and it ripped off of me into pieces. I used the distraction to cut and run outside.

"Dude!"

"Carl." My relief was quickly replaced by stomach-churning anxiety when I noticed Greg was with him. He was not happy.

"Man," Carl said, "your life is awesome! You've got girls fighting all over you. And, dude, if I'm not mistaken, I'd say you just got laid!"

Greg's eyes narrowed and flicked to the glass doors, through which Sarah and Keeley were still arguing. "You were supposed to make Morticia love you and then win us that property," he said in a clipped tone. "Instead, you're manwhoring around."

"He better not be manwhoring around!" Dana Holbrook called out. She and my sister were walking toward us.

"We're going to dinner," Belle told me. "Do you want me to bring you anything?"

"Yes, I mean no. I mean, can I hide, I mean *stay* at your house?" I gave her a pleading look.

Belle looked over to the fighting young women inside my condo lobby.

"I guess it's a good thing your date canceled after all," Dana told Belle. "This looks like it could be a potential lawsuit."

"You had a date?" I blurted.

Carl glanced nervously at Greg, and we all braced for the explosion. But Greg was like the reindeer that had eaten the last sugar cube.

"Hmm," he said, "funny about that. Must be the holidays. I'm sure people double-book." He smirked at Belle.

My sister's nostrils flared.

"The fighting?" Dana prompted. "I need an extra pair of hands." She looked between me and the Svenssons.

"I'm not going back in there," I said incredulously.

Greg brushed an invisible spec of lint off his cuff. "I just received this suit back from the tailor," he said.

As soon as my sister and Dana were inside, I turned on Greg. "You can't go messing with my sister's life," I warned him.

Greg looked down his nose at me. "You and I," he said in a low growl, "are not equals. You have a half-baked hedge fund and no property under management. If you want to run with the real billionaires, then you need to step up. Clock is ticking."

"Yep!" Carl said. "I'm halfway through my Advent calendar!"

Greg looked up at the night sky then back at me. "Do not ruin this. You have one job."

He and Carl stalked off.

My sister and Dana came out, marching Keeley and Sarah between them.

"Your building's clear," Belle told me.

When I went back up to my condo, my cat was curled up in front of the Christmas tree, which twinkled in the light from the fireplace. I had taken down all the stockings Morticia had put up except hers.

How was I going to apologize to Morticia? It was a bad look. I started trying to compose a text. Should I do cute and flirty, sexy and enticing, or just plain groveling?

I went with the cute approach. I had a cat now, damnit. I was going to use it!

I found a little Santa hat and put it on Cindy Lou's head and took a picture, captioning it with *Merry Catmas!*

I sent it. No response.

Jonathan: *You need to bring Salem so they can play in the Christmas tree.*

I waited a beat. No response from Morticia. I paced.

Jonathan: *If you don't like the cute approach, I can send you a very tasteful dick pic.*

Jonathan: *I wasn't sure if I should go the cute route or the sexy route.*

Jonathan: *I can also take a picture of me naked with the cat.*

Morticia: *Please don't. I like your cock in one piece, thanks.*

Yes! She wanted me!

Jonathan: *So does this mean you're not going to tie me up and kidnap me and throw me off a mountain* How the Grinch Stole Christmas *style?*

Morticia: *I'm not throwing you anywhere, but I can't promise I won't tie you up.*

Morticia: *The one good thing about Christmas is that there is a lot of ribbon on that tree.*

The doorbell rang. When I opened it, Morticia was standing there in her black trench coat. She came inside, set down her bag, then untied her belt like a Christmas bow.

I was immediately hard. I unfastened my zipper, needing relief.

"Merry Catmas," she purred, opening the trench to reveal only the black, lacy fabric of lingerie. "Now put your face in my pussy."

I grabbed her, kissing her hard, then knelt down in front of her to lick her through the fabric. She moaned, her fingers tugging at my hair.

She pulled my head back. "I told you I was going to tie you up," she said, pulling me to my feet.

We kissed hard. I stepped out of my pants, needing to feel her. Then we stumbled into the living room, and she was quick to encourage me to fall back into an armchair.

She was down only to her bra and panties, me in my boxer briefs. She took one of the red ribbons from the tree. I was breathing hard as she tied my wrists together in a neat bow behind my head.

My cock throbbed for her as she trailed her fingers down my torso then straddled me, gyrating.

"Are you wet for me?" I asked.

One of her hands slipped down between her legs.

I hissed.

"So wet," she breathed. She undid her bra and kept her dance going. Then Morticia sat on my lap, pressing her breasts into my face. I strained to touch her, but she put a finger against my lips.

"Look. Don't touch."

Sure. At least for now.

"Oh, so you're giving me a challenge, huh?"

"Is it that hard to resist me?"

"I'm still so hot for you, babe, that bending you over something and railing you like a savage beast would be more than enough for me."

She just chuckled, still making that sexy noise and rubbing against me.

It was driving me crazy that I couldn't touch her.

She straddled me, her panties right over my bulge, rubbing me through it all as she continued to gyrate. Then she moved off of me, her hands trailing down my body. She grabbed the waistband of my underpants and pulled them down to let my cock spring out.

"Merry Christmas," I purred.

Morticia made an appreciative noise as her delicate hand stroked down and over my cock, making me throb and shudder from her touch.

"You know," she said, "you were right. I think I do need a little frosting on my cookies."

She leaned down and kissed the head of my cock before running her tongue up and down my length.

God, she was good. Damn good.

Tickling my balls, she was just giving me anything and everything to enjoy. My smile grew wider and wider. She looked up at me with a seductive smile and then took all of me in.

"Fuck!" I strained against her.

She released the head of my cock with a pop, her dark lipstick a calling card in the light of the fireplace. I needed her—and not her mouth. With a bulge of my biceps, I broke the loose tie of the ribbon on my wrists.

"I have to say I'm impressed with how personal your gift giving is," I growled. My now free hand sank down to tangle in her dark hair.

Morticia licked her lips and looked up at me with a raised eyebrow. I tugged her up and crushed our mouths together for a powerful kiss. God, I would never grow tired of her lips on mine. It just felt so right.

"Though I do like how you tie a bow, we're going with my plan instead," I whispered to her. I stood us up and guided her over to the couch. I spun her around and bent her right over the side of it and slapped her ass. "Maybe I should tie you up."

"You can try," she said over her shoulder.

Her blow job had gotten me hard, harder than I'd ever been. I needed her pussy. I pulled down her lacy black panties, and a condom fell out onto the floor.

"Someone came prepared," I growled. I opened it and swiftly slid it on.

I guided my cock into her hot, tight slit, hearing her moan loudly with the swift penetration. Fuck, she was so tight around me. Just about perfection. Seeing her back arch as I started to fuck her was even more wonderful. Everything about her was just some sort of magic.

Morticia was my kind of woman. My woman.

I threw my hands onto her hips and pushed her hotter, higher, wanting her to scream for me, for her to come like she never had before. Feeling her shudder around me just pushed me harder and more intensely to enjoy everything she was doing to me. I watched her hands curl, pulling on the couch cushion. Morticia was reveling in the pleasure.

Her back arched, and I wrapped my arms around her chest, my fingers around her breasts, feeling how wonderful and perky they were. Fuck, everything about her was perfect, even the things less enlightened men would call flaws. They were what made her intoxicating.

I fucked her harder. Faster. Brought her closer, rubbing her clit as I thrust into her. I wanted her to scream for me. I wanted her to absolutely realize that I was the one that was doing this to her, and that she should be mine forever more.

That was a weird thought coming to me so quickly, but damn if it didn't feel right.

I was inching toward my limit just as much as she was. One more thrust, one more massage of that little clit of hers, and she cried out as my cock slammed inside her, her entire body shuddering beneath me. Feeling her like that finished me off too. All of me rushed out, pumping everything I had into her.

She was bent over on the couch, spent.

I pressed kisses to her neck. "Next time, I want to hear you scream 'Merry Christmas.'"

CHAPTER 49

Morticia

I woke up extremely sore in Jonathan's empty bed the next morning. I was not a big exerciser. Running around in the studio during the bake-off was probably the most exercise I'd had all year—not including this marathon sex session.

I want to hear you scream "Merry Christmas"...

That had been the last coherent thing I'd remembered before passing out from exhaustion and exertion. Now it was...I peered at the fancy digital alarm clock on his nightstand...seven a.m., and I was not wide awake, but I was more awake than I would have been had I gone to bed at my usual time of five a.m.

I yawned then looked down. I had absolutely no clothes on. Panic set in. It was one thing to have sex in the dimly lit living room with only the Christmas lights and the fire for lighting. Now it was a bright, sunshiny morning, and I did not want to parade around naked in front of Jonathan. His body was perfect, and mine was…probably not what he was used to seeing.

He slept with Sarah.

And that was a problem. He hadn't just slept with her; he said he had loved her. Maybe he was still stuck on her. I wondered why she would leave him. Who left a man like Jonathan?

Probably the type of person who makes a crazy collage of half-naked pictures of him.

Cindy Lou Who pranced into the room.

"You've sure reacclimated to the life of luxury," I told the gray cat. "I was going to bring Salem over here for a kitty playdate, but he's uncouth and might damage your delicate sensibilities."

"She's definitely spoiled rotten," Jonathan said from the doorway.

I jerked, grasping for the covers and drawing them up over me.

Jonathan sauntered over. He was carrying a plate of the cinnamon buns I'd made the night before. He was wearing a Santa hat and gray sweatpants. He sat on the corner of the bed and pulled the sheets down, pressing soft kisses along my collarbone to my chest. "You can't possibly be shy after last night," he all but purred. "Besides, I plan on repeating the experience."

I wasn't sure if I was ready to do that right now. I grabbed one of the cinnamon buns and took a huge bite.

"Damn," I said around the soft dough with the caramel and apple filling. "That's good. Eat this."

I held out the rest of it to Jonathan, feeding him the sugary bite. His teeth nipped my fingers slightly, making me shiver. The way he looked at me, his gaze so hot it was cold, was a lot to take in. Especially since he had probably looked at Sarah the exact same way.

I cleared my throat. "You and Sarah, huh."

Jonathan made a face and flopped down on the bed. "Fucking disaster," he said, closing his eyes. Then he opened them, those blue eyes staring up at me. Jonathan reached for my hand. "You won't ever leave me, will you, Morticia?"

"No, of course not," I lied.

❄ ❄ ❄

Jonathan was clearly gearing up for another round of Secret Santa. I, however, was feeling guilty. And I didn't like it.

"He probably didn't mean it," I told myself as the wind whipped my hair. I was heading out to Dorothy's property across the street to do a few sketch overlays on my collage to give it that personal touch. I was also hoping to calm my mind.

Being with Jonathan had been hot. And addictive. I'd had sex before, but it had been mediocre to downright bad sex. I had always secretly turned my nose up at those Wiccan practitioners who insisted sex was a spiritual worship, but now all I wanted was to worship Jonathan's body and have him worship mine.

"What yonder I see such a bright star." Dorothy's voice pierced through the winter morning. "Doth I see someone who hath gotten laid?" The older woman was cheerful as I approached the clearing with the sculpture.

"Well if you must—" I stopped short and gaped.

There were scores of completely naked people in a downward dog position. Dorothy was in front, leading the class, and she peered at me between her legs.

"Don't be ashamed," she ordered. "This is natural, and from the way you're limping a bit, I would say that you need to do some yoga. Now strip."

"I really have to do some work," I told her, backing away slowly.

"The cold will be good for you!" she called after me. "It will bring down the inflammation!"

She switched to a dancer's pose with a fluidity that my aching thighs envied. Her back leg up behind her head, Dorothy swiveled to face me. "You better tell your boyfriend that if he wants me to sell to him, I'm going to need a dedicated space to keep teaching my classes. I'm really on to something here. I have a waiting list, and I'm charging eighty bucks a session!" Dorothy informed me. "Shoot, I might even need an investor for my new business."

"Oh, sure," I said, still trying to make my escape. "He'll totally be down with that."

"You tell him," she added, "that he gets free classes whenever he wants! No clothing allowed, of course."

I felt faint. "That's very generous."

"You just need a little more practice!" she called as I hurried (to be honest, it was more of a slow stagger) off. "You're not used to a man that size. Try keeping a sex toy in there for a few hours a day."

Or not, I decided. Jonathan had been enough. Now I wanted a hot bath. Too bad there were four other people in my apartment. I was weighing the option of going back to Jonathan's condo, letting him give me an encore to last night's performance, and then taking a long bath or going back to the contestants' apartment when Sarah rounded the corner.

"I thought I saw you scuttling around," she said, glaring at me.

"You're the only one where she doesn't belong," my twin sister drawled as she, Emma, and Salem appeared behind Sarah.

"You two were always so creepy." Sarah had a sour expression on her face.

"And we believed you were always such a mousy, good girl. Come to find out that you had a whole life that you didn't tell anyone about. You lied to everyone," Lilith shot back.

"And you broke Jonathan's heart," I added.

"Stop pretending you care about him," Sarah cried. "You don't care about anyone. Besides, he's never going to choose you. He loves me. I'm divorcing Trevor, and Jonathan and I will live happily ever after. He's pined for me all these years."

"Oh, please," my sister scoffed. "I bet the only reason you came back was because you saw Morticia with him all over the internet, and you were mad that she extinguished the flame he had always carried for you."

Sarah's face screwed up. "You're just jealous," she spat. "I'm a born-again virgin who will be a dutiful wife and mother, while Morticia is just some starving artist that is freaky both in bed and out of it." She glared at me. "Jonathan's going to realize what kind of girl you are, and he's going to dump you by the wayside just like he did all the others." She was smug. "I watched him over the years, you know. I wanted him to be good and sorry for not behaving how I wanted him to behave. He always loved me; that's why he never had a girlfriend since me."

"He has Morticia now," Emma said coldly, "so you better run along back to Trevor."

"I don't know if Jonathan and I are quite like that," I said cautiously.

"Nonsense!" Lilith insisted. "It's clear he's infatuated with you."

"No he's not!" Sarah stamped her feet. "You probably put something in his drink. As soon as he comes to his senses, he's running back to me."

"The holidays really do make people insane. You can't have two men," Lilith insisted. "What are you going to do, have some sort of reverse harem?"

"Maybe," she screeched.

Lilith barked out a laugh. "As if. I bet Jonathan's seen through your smoke screen. He's not going to want anything to do with your judgmental ass. You can't even cook. You made that nasty vegan lasagna at your wedding. It had those cardboard noodles in it."

"I'll show you," Sarah said. "I'll show you I can cook. He's going to come crawling back to me, and we will be married by Christmas."

CHAPTER 50

Jonathan

Though Morticia had said she wasn't going to leave me, she did just that after we ate.

"Don't forget," I reminded her as she shrugged on her trench coat. "We should schedule a playdate."

"For the cats," she added.

"Well, that too." I kissed her again. "Stay," I whispered. "I need you to stay."

"I have to do another shopping session for the bake-off," she said, pushing away from me.

I paced around the living room after she left.

You're acting paranoid and crazy. I needed her here though. I needed her with me forever.

"She's not going to leave," I tried to reassure myself. But if she found out about my scheme with the Svenssons to manipulate her into sweet-talking Dorothy, then she would be out of my life for good.

"She won't find out."

Morticia: *You still wanting Hamilton Yards?*
Jonathan: *Yes!*
Morticia: *Just spoke to Dorothy. She has a list of demands including space to put her naked yoga studio.*
Jonathan: *...*
Morticia: *Don't ask.*

I pumped my fist.

Jonathan: *This development is in the bag.*
Carl: *You made up with Morticia! You dog! I knew as soon as she had a taste of the full Frost holiday spectacular she was going to be on board.*
Greg: *We should schedule a meeting with her and Dorothy to make sure we're all on the same page.*
Jonathan: *Apparently there are demands, including a space for naked yoga.*
Greg: *We will promise whatever she wants. Even if she puts it in the contract, I'll have my lawyers craft it in such a way that we can basically do whatever we want.*

That was not going to work for me. I looked out the window at the industrial complex. I had seen the renderings in the Svensson Investment offices. They had changed the whole character of the property. The proposed towers dwarfed the eight- and ten-story brick factory buildings.

They even had one tower slamming right down in the middle of a former factory.

I wanted to be with Morticia for the rest of my life. But once she saw what was planned for the Hamilton Yards development, she was going to leave me.

※ ※ ※

Morticia texted me sporadically the rest of the day. No sexy pictures, though, which was too bad. She also didn't join me that evening. I had somehow already grown accustomed to sleeping next to her, and the bed felt empty without her. When I woke up the next morning, I promised myself that after that evening's bake-off was done, she was all mine.

While I ate a cinnamon roll, I checked the daily sales report then fastened Cindy Lou into her harness for a walk in the cold winter morning air. A man who looked my age but had a beer belly and sun-damaged skin jumped in front of me when I walked out of my building.

"Stay away from my wife," he said menacingly.

Trevor. I stared at the man who Sarah had left me for.

"You think you're going to steal her away from me with your billions and your lies?" he blustered. "Sarah told me how you treated her, how you thought she was just an object."

"What the fuck?" I demanded. "None of that is true."

"You calling my wife a liar?" he demanded.

"Maybe," I said. I was several inches taller than him and drew up to my full height.

Trevor shook his head. "She said you were self-absorbed and obsessed with money and that you ignored her and threatened her."

"I *never*."

"I don't believe you," he replied, nostrils flared. "You better stay the hell away from Sarah if you know what's good for you. I'm going to make sure that everyone knows what a piece of shit you are."

If everyone believed I was some sort of monster, not only would the distillery—and, subsequently, all my employees and suppliers—suffer, but I could bend over and kiss the Hamilton Yards development good-bye. I would not let Trevor ruin my reputation.

"You think you can try and slander me?" I said, hearing the cold fury in my voice. "I will destroy you."

Trevor glared at me. "This is war," he said before stomping off.

Shit. I clearly didn't know Sarah at all. Maybe it was just like with Belle. I had been blindsided when she had disappeared. I had no idea what had happened to make her leave. Of course, when Owen had laid it all out to me and my brothers, it made sense. It also blanketed me with a thick layer of guilt that I hadn't been a good brother and that it had in fact been my fault that she had left. Just like it was my fault my parents didn't like me as much as my brothers and why, apparently, it was also likely my fault that Sarah had up and left. I was the common denominator.

"Stop feeling sorry for yourself," I snarled at my reflection in the lobby window. "Man up." I needed to put my business first. This was about my reputation. I was going to come out on top. I would secure Hamilton Yards, my parents would be proud, I'd be able to offer Belle the world as an apology, and I would somehow convince Greg not to completely corporatize the development.

"You're a billionaire," I told myself, straightening my suit. "Act like it. Get the job done and end Trevor before he even has a chance to slander you."

To do that, however, I needed the Svenssons.

"Go talk to them as equals. You're a development partner," I pep talked myself as I ate another of Morticia's cinnamon rolls, which I had brought along for fortification. "You are ice; you are powerful."

Cindy Lou batted at my shoe.

"I know, Cindy Lou. I told you I was going to take you on a walk, but I have a big, important surprise meeting to keep us from having to move to a nonpenthouse unit."

Cindy Lou looked up at me and yowled reproachfully. I edged to the door. The cat howled like a banshee. I sighed.

"Fine," I told the cat, "you win. But this is not a reflection on my manhood. I am still a powerful billionaire."

❄ ❄ ❄

"Why the fuck are you in my office?" Greg asked in a clipped tone.

Cindy Lou chuffed reproachfully. Greg's head snapped up. He looked between me, the cat, and Carl.

Carl launched into a deflection. "I told him not to bring the cat," he said. "I told him you don't like animals."

"I had to bring her. I promised her I'd take her on a walk."

"You fucking walk your cat?"

I clapped my hands over Cindy Lou's ears. "Cindy Lou Who is a high-society lady, and she would appreciate it if you watched your language around her."

Greg was silent for a moment. "Get out of my office," he commanded, turning back to his paperwork.

"Look," I protested, "I need—"

"Carl," Greg barked.

"I need help!" I yelled. "I fucked up, and I need a lawyer or—wait, you have a brother who's ex-Special Forces, right? Crawford? Can you have him make someone disappear?"

Greg put down his pen. "This is going to cost you."

"Sure, anything," I said.

Greg listened as I gave the CliffsNotes version.

"And they're spreading lies about me," I said irately. "I loved Sarah. I carried a torch for her!"

"You did," Carl said. "Greg, you should have seen him; it was pathetic." Carl huffed a laugh. "Who in their right mind pines after some woman who humiliated him—yeah, dude, she treated you like shit—and left him then turns around and emasculates him?"

Greg's jaw was tense, the tendons on his neck prominent. I thought I heard a molar crack.

"I mean," Carl stammered, hastily backtracking. "I mean, you and Belle's situation isn't quite the same thing."

"I am not carrying a torch for Belle, as you so stupidly put it," Greg said, his flat gray gaze fixed on Carl.

"No, of course not," Carl said in a rush. "You're the boss. You're the cold-hearted investor."

"We'll be on the lookout for Trevor. If he says something, I'll send the lawyers after him. He won't see it coming. We'll ruin him." Greg turned to Carl. "Call Josh and Eric and give them a heads-up. And have Blade start tracking it."

"Should I get Garrett on it too?" Carl asked.

"No," Greg barked. "I cannot deal with Garrett. He's been on my case for the last week, constantly calling me about what presents all our little brothers are receiving. It's excessive. I don't see why each one needs a present from all of us. It's hundreds of presents. You should see the house in Harrogate on Christmas Day," he told me with a thousand-yard stare. "The wrapping paper…there's so much wrapping paper."

My phone buzzed.

"Is that Belle?" Greg asked, attention snapping to me.

"Actually…" I looked at my phone.

Belle: *Where the hell are you! We are about to start filming!*

❋ ❋ ❋

I raced into the studio just as they were sending one of the contestants home.

"It's because of her!" the bachelorette shouted at Keeley. "She sabotaged my macaroons by putting water in the food coloring! You need to arrest that bitch!"

I grimaced as the security guards led the brunette out.

"I would say that we had all the drama out of the way first thing," Anastasia announced to the remaining three contestants. "But we have an extra-special surprise: a wild-card contestant, a blast from the past, and our billionaire holiday bachelor's first love."

No.

"Sarah DiRizzo!"

CHAPTER 51

Morticia

No fucking way.

Sarah pranced out. She had really done herself up. Instead of her usual mousy good-girl vibe, she had her hair in bouncy ringlets, she was wearing tall platform high heels, and she had donned a polyester candy-striped short dress that barely covered her red underwear with the white snowflakes. How did I know this? Because her dress rode up when she walked.

"Would you like to tell us a little about yourself?" Anastasia asked Sarah as the camera guys zoomed in.

"I am a baker and an aspiring homemaker," Sarah began.

"Gold digger," Keeley fake sneezed.

"You're the gold digger!" Sarah yelled at her older sister. "You and Morticia."

"It seems as if we have a family baking feud in the house," Anastasia said. "We'll have to see which DiRizzo, if any of them, wins this round and Jonathan's heart. Today's challenge is the edible decorations challenge. Edible Christmas tree ornaments, gingerbread houses, and more. We want you to show us how to best bring in the holiday cheer with decorations so good you could eat them!"

"Just concentrate on baking," I told myself. "In a couple weeks, this will all be over with."

My collage was almost done. I was putting on the finishing touches to give it that extra bit of oomph that was going to win me a scholarship.

Sarah and Keeley could fight over Jonathan, and I would walk away, head held high. Except I didn't want to walk away. I wanted to tie my hair up and throw down. How dare Sarah come back after just ghosting Jonathan? The image of him lying on the bed next to me and asking me to promise I wouldn't leave him stabbed me in the heart.

Sarah didn't deserve him back, and it clearly went without saying that Keeley did not deserve him.

And you do?

Maybe. I'd be better than those two.

But you don't even like him.

Okay, so maybe I liked him a teensy little bit. Jonathan pushed all my buttons, and not just the one between my legs. I always did like an angsty, emo guy with a tragic backstory. Jonathan had the added bonus of being all wrapped up in a, dare I say, edible package.

Instead of obsessing about his Christmas package, I needed to concentrate on my Christmas dessert.

Sarah had already begun mixing a huge bowl of Rice Krispies Treats that she was going to form into shapes.

"She'll probably cover it in fondant," I muttered as I went to collect my ingredients. I needed to make sure I collected everything I needed before I started baking. There was no way I was taking my eyes off my station for a moment.

Ornaments were a must, and since I was good at art, I could decorate them nicely. For the dessert, I needed something more, though. A cake? I did love cake, but cake wasn't really a decoration. For a moment, I considered gingerbread, but that was too expected—and besides, Keeley had a bucket of powdered ginger at her station and was probably baking some gingerbread horror show.

I decided on miniature cake ornaments shaped like presents, tarts shaped like stars, and garland made out of sugared cranberries, gingersnap, and caramel popcorn. Of course, I really needed a tree to display my edible ornaments. Handing them to the judges on a plate wouldn't provide the full effect.

"Guess I'm making a Christmas tree cake," I said, grabbing a large bag of cake flour.

Sarah shot me a dirty look when I went back to my station and started on my ornaments. "I know what you're doing with Jonathan," she said. "You're trying to make him love you. It won't work."

"I'm just there for a good time," I told her. "Nothing serious. Which makes it even more pathetic that he doesn't want anything to do with you."

"He will," Sarah insisted. "As soon as he tastes my cooking, he'll come crawling back." She stomped off.

"How did she weasel her way in here?" I complained to Lilith as I chopped up the pecans for the shortbread ornaments I was baking.

"Apparently," Lilith drawled as she took pictures of the dough, "Belle had to bribe Sarah with being on the bake-off so that she would get out and stay out of Jonathan's building."

※ ※ ※

My tree wasn't going to be that big, so I didn't need to make large ornaments or a lot of them, which was good. As usual, I was extremely ambitious. I worked on my ornaments all afternoon. Before I slid them into the oven, I carefully used a straw to make a little hole in each that I could thread my candy ribbon through so I could hang it on the Christmas tree cake.

For the cake, I had a chocolate tier, a cranberry rose tier, a vanilla bean tier, and a red velvet tier in the oven. To prevent the cake from looking like a bright-green wedding cake, I was going to cut the layers and shape them a bit to feel more like a tree. I had just slid the pans of batter into the oven when I saw Jonathan standing off to the side and motioning me to him.

I looked around furtively. Keeley seemed engrossed in her gingerbread house, but I was concerned she would sabotage my dish. I could just ignore Jonathan, but I hadn't seen him in more than a day, and so help me, I missed him.

"Two minutes," I told myself, ducking around the cameras.

Jonathan grabbed me and pulled me around a corner.

"My cake!"

Jonathan wrapped me in his strong arms, crushing his mouth to mine. As I clung to him, I forgot all about cake, trying not to moan loudly as his tongue claimed my mouth.

"Funny that," he said in that deep voice that I was quickly becoming addicted to. "I was just thinking about your cupcakes earlier today and how much they needed some frosting."

I was definitely needing a little frosting on my Christmas cookies. He kissed me again. I wanted him right now, but I was also worried about my cake.

"I could fuck you right now," he offered.

"Right here?" I said breathlessly.

"You don't understand," he said, blue eyes intense. "I'm addicted to you. I want you wrapped up under my tree."

One of the production staff walked by, and I used the opportunity to duck under Jonathan's arm before I could be sweet-talked into a quickie. When I scurried back to my station, I did an inventory of my cookies.

They looked fine.

Except for the most important one, which is seriously lacking in frosting and Jonathan Frost!

I shoved my libido into the closet then peeked into the oven. My cakes were also okay. One looked like it was rising a little faster than the others, but it didn't seem like it was going to spill out.

While they baked, I worked on decorating the rest of my cookie ornaments. After I set my finished cakes out to cool, I made the crunchy caramel popcorn and the candied cranberries for the garland. Using the smaller cake, I formed the little cake presents, cutting out colored fondant and wrapping the cakes after smothering them in buttercream, cream cheese, and chocolate frosting.

I still had an hour and a half on the clock, which was more than enough time to make my cake Christmas tree. I had a pattern ready to go and carefully cut the large sheet cakes and progressively smaller cakes into tiers, spreading frosting and spiked custardy cream filling and cognac-infused fruit between the layers. I tasted the extra slices of the cake as I went just to make sure Keeley hadn't sabotaged it while I was gone. When I had the shape the way I wanted it, I draped the cake in fondant then carefully molded it and carved it to look like abstracted pine needles.

Finally, I draped the garland around the cake tree, hung the ornaments with fondant ribbon, and placed the little cake presents under the tree. I snapped a few pictures of the dessert. Though it was heavily Christmas themed, I thought it was still pretty cool.

I was first up to the judges' table. Jonathan was making bedroom eyes at me. I tried to ignore him as I presented my cake. "While the challenge," I began, "was edible decorations, I couldn't just bring you a basket of snacks."

"I'll always take a basket of your snacks," Jonathan said with shit-eating grin on his face.

I ignored him. "Some of us have standards, and we needed a nice way to display everything. Hence the cake Christmas tree. Everything you see here is edible."

Anu took one of the carefully decorated ornaments. "Exquisite workmanship," she said. "You could make a killing baking and decorating cookies."

Nick took one of the strands of garland, eating a few pieces of popcorn. "This is so freaking good. More restaurants are trending to rustic dessert because it's cheaper. And because while a sugary crème brûlée feels like cheating, caramel popcorn and a few gingersnaps feel like a light snack."

"He can have the popcorn," Jonathan said. "I want a taste of your cake."

He picked up the serving knife, cutting a huge wedge out of the side.

"What is that?" Anu asked as Jonathan started to wiggle the cake slice out.

"What?" I peered. There was a purple thing in the cake. *Is that a...Oh hell no!*

As Jonathan pulled the slice out, I shrieked, "Wait, wait!" But it was too late.

"Did you bake a dildo into your cake?" Anu asked, laughing and holding a napkin over her face.

"*Keeley.*"

I was on camera and could not completely go all evil witch on them, but god, I was going to ruin my cousin!

Jonathan took a bite of his cake. "If you wanted a dick in your cake," he told me, "you could have just called me. Or was this a subtle hint?"

"It's not," I said through gritted teeth, "a hint of any kind. We'll just cut that right off." I grabbed the knife.

"Ohh," Nick and Jonathan both said at the same time, wincing.

"Just put a napkin over it," Nick begged.

Jonathan reached out and poked the dildo with a fork. "It's not edible, is it?"

"No."

I slapped his hand away. The motion caused the dildo to wobble. There was a high-pitched whining noise, then liquid shot out of the top, spraying all over me, while the garbled sounds of Elvis Presley's "Santa Claus Is Back in Town" strained out of the cake.

"Hm," Jonathan said after a moment. "Yeah, my dick doesn't play music."

❋ ❋ ❋

I was mortified after the bake-off challenge. Keeley and Sarah were laughing when I stalked back into the greenroom. I reeked of the gingerbread-flavored cheap vodka that had been put in the dildo.

"Guess you're just as weird and awkward and inappropriate as ever," Keeley sneered.

"You put that there," I spat.

"No I didn't!" she said with feigned innocence. "You put that there as some sort of love letter to Jonathan. Honestly, I don't know what he sees in you."

"It's because he secretly wants to be with me," Sarah said smugly. "He's trying to find a poor substitute."

"Oh, shut up," Keeley spat. "You're such a little Goody Two-shoes hypocrite."

I left them to bicker and grabbed a bottle of the whiskey and some cake and headed outside through a back exit. One of the production assistants tried to stop me, but I snarled at him, and he jumped back.

Several hours later, it had turned dark, and a not-insignificant amount of the whiskey had disappeared.

A pair of expensive Italian leather shoes paused in front of me.

CHAPTER 52

Jonathan

I almost ran into my brother Owen as I raced out of the building. I had wanted to find Morticia; I was quickly becoming addicted to her. "The Svenssons didn't send you, did they?" I asked in apprehension.

Owen scowled at me. "I'm here for a meeting with Belle about the interface for the voting for the finale. But since you mentioned it, for the record, I did warn you about going into business with them. But of course, you are a terrible judge of character."

"No, I'm not!"

"You still carry the torch for Mom and Dad, and now you're getting back together with Sarah?" He held out his phone.

On the screen was an article about my relationship with Sarah. The pulled quotes mentioned how she was my great love and how she intended for us to get back together.

"You aren't seriously still in love with her, are you? Beck Svensson told me that now she and her husband are trying to ruin your reputation," Owen asked.

Was I still in love with her? I had been heartbroken when she had left. But now her husband was trying to ruin me. "I don't know if Sarah actually knows what Trevor's up to."

Owen sighed. "You have to stop making excuses for people. Do you not remember how miserable you were when you were with her? She fucked with your diet and went on that vegan kick where you had to come over to my condo and sneak hamburgers. Remember how she would hardly ever sleep with you, or how she always wanted to check your phone and would accuse you of being unfaithful?"

"It wasn't that bad," I said automatically. The reality was that though she and I had had good moments, the bad far outweighed them. At the end, I had been constantly walking on eggshells. The contrast with Sarah's behavior was even more stark when compared with the way Morticia treated me.

And I felt extra bad that I was lying to Morticia about the development.

I'm going to figure out a way to make it work.

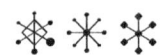

❇ ❇ ❇

"Did you know," Morticia asked me, "that you can buy dildos online? All kinds. There are ones that sing and ones that light up and ones that you can buy for bachelorette parties that shoot out Jell-O shots, and you can play games to try and squirt it in your friends' mouths."

"Yes," I said, biting back a laugh. "I'm told it's big business. I was wavering between investing my hedge fund in sex toys and porn or alcohol. We went with the alcohol because it's hard to advertise porn."

"You're such a businessman," she slurred, leaning back against the brick wall.

"Profit above all else," I quipped, "which is why Sarah claims she left me."

"Her loss," Morticia retorted, taking another swig from the bottle of whiskey.

"Aw, did Morticia actually say she liked me?"

"I did not."

"But you liked something else about me," I replied, dragging her to her feet and shoving her back against the wall.

She wrapped her arms around me. The whiskey bottle dropped with a *clunk* as I spread her legs, grinding my hand against her pussy.

"You drunk enough for hot and dirty sex?" I whispered.

"I've made worse decisions regarding you," she slurred, pressing hot kisses to my mouth and jaw.

My hands roamed down her body, going to her hips, lower, and under her skirt.

"You meant now?" she asked, a bit of accusation in her voice. "What if someone sees?"

"Isn't that the fun of it?"

She was frozen in apprehension, sobering up a bit, but she wasn't saying no. I felt her panties, which were already a bit wet from the mere idea of me fucking her against this brick wall.

I imagined that her mind was spinning, darting to the door and the path around the building. It was dark. The filming was done. I had waited for her then come out to search for her, hoping she hadn't left. She was probably afraid of getting caught.

I had no such fear. If they caught me, oh no! The whole world would know I was crazy about this woman. What a terrible fate. For her sake, though, I would be careful about it—as careful as I could be while fucking someone in public, anyway. My cock was throbbing at the thought as I turned her around and undid my slacks.

Morticia was still paranoid, but hey, most people didn't use that back greenroom door. "Maybe we should go to your condo."

"You really want to wait?" I whispered, rubbing her through her panties. "You're soaking wet. I know your pussy is hot and ready for my cock."

The thought of fucking her outside and the threat of getting caught were making me fucking hard. I pushed her skirt up higher and tugged down her panties. I wanted to take my time, but Morticia would kill me if we were caught.

She hissed as the chill of the air caressed her wet pussy. I teased her clit. Before I pulled her panties to the side and slid myself in, I fished a condom out of my pocket. Yes, I'd had something like this planned—if not here, well, just in case I couldn't control myself elsewhere.

I entered her and enjoyed the feeling of her clenching around me. She moaned, and I clapped a hand over her mouth, pressing kisses to her neck. Then I escalated the situation slowly, sliding in and out of her, hearing her moan and feeling her shudder around me.

She braced herself on the brick wall while my hand slipped between her legs to spice things up for her every so often. A little flick of the clit would get a rise out of her, and she would twitch her ass against me as I slid inside her. A moan from her was just as good as the sex itself for me.

"We...we should rethink this," she said, her breath hitching with pleasure.

"In for a penny, in for a pound, babe."

"You're going to make me scream, Jonathan."

I just laughed. She was getting close, the excitement of doing something so bad spiking, the anticipation of the moment ravaging her. Her pants and moans became more rapid and uncontrollable by the moment. I grabbed her ass, bringing her up higher, her toes barely brushing the ground as I fucked her hard. I rammed my cock into her as she bit her lip, trying not to scream.

She was about to be sent over the edge. Two more thrusts, then her body vibrated in my grasp until I couldn't hold her back anymore. I thrust into her again, and then I was done. I buried my face in her hair as I came.

I turned her around slowly to face me. She blinked up at me with her dark eyes. I kissed her, wrapping my arms around her. "I don't care if you put dildos in the food," I told her. "You're the only woman I want."

"I didn't put that there," she murmured, resting her head against my chest.

My heart squeezed, and I pressed kisses along her temple and forehead. "Stay with me, Morticia," I told her. "Stay with me forever." I picked her up and began carrying her back to my condo.

Maybe I'll do this on our wedding day.

Maybe you're moving too fast and forgetting that you're just using her.

But I was high on Christmas and the cold and the way she nestled easily in my arms.

I will fix everything, and she will be mine forever.

CHAPTER 53

Morticia

I woke up the next morning with a wretched headache. "Tea," I croaked. "I need tea." I patted around on the comforter, hoping my headache tea had miraculously appeared along with some leftover pizza.

The door opened. Jonathan appeared with a steaming mug and crackers. He was wearing only workout pants.

"I tried to make you toast," he said. He set the plate and tea on the nightstand. "But I burned it."

I grabbed the mug.

"It's Christmastime tea," he said happily as I inhaled the cinnamon-and-clove scent.

"I don't care, as long as it's hot." I sipped the tea.

"You're hot." Jonathan kissed me. "You taste like Christmas."

I wrinkled my nose. "I probably smell like it too." The tea had helped defog my brain, and I was starting to recall just what I had done after drinking all that whiskey.

"Last night was amazing," Jonathan murmured.

I swung my legs off the bed, and Jonathan followed me into the bathroom.

"I can't get over having you all to myself." He nuzzled my neck, kissing it slightly.

"We also have things to do today, and we just did it."

Jonathan ran his hands down my torso, caressing my tits. "I told you," he said, "you stay with me, and this is just one of many relationship perks."

"Is that what this is?"

"Yes," he said. "We have had sex in my living room, in my office, and outside a building I owned. And I'm about to fuck you in my bathroom. We are definitely in a sexual relationship."

"You're insatiable, you know that?"

"And you fucking love it."

I couldn't really disagree with him there. I just didn't say it, because the last thing this man needed was encouragement. His bulge was already pressing against my ass. He was completely ready for this. And honestly, so was I. It was almost scary how accustomed I was becoming to being with Jonathan. I loved the feel of his arms around me, the way his eyes lit up when he saw me, the way he was focused entirely on me.

Wait, who said anything about love? This is just sex, I assured myself.

I flashed him a simple smile, and that was all he needed to be off. His hands slid down my body and between my legs, rubbing my folds over the fabric. His touch was often more than enough to get the fire inside me properly burning. He pushed his fingers into my opening, fucking me a bit with them, getting me ready for the real thing.

Unlike the last time he had taken me for a quickie, though, he pulled my panties down my legs and helped me step out of them so he gained complete access to my pussy from under my skirt.

That I was fully clothed otherwise didn't matter to him. It only mattered that he had the ability to make me come for him, and he fully intended to use it. Taking advantage of the vulnerability he had created, he fussed briefly with a condom and then thrust himself into me, and it was as electric as it always was.

We were perfectly in tune, our souls united and unable to get enough of one another. He was good to me, and I was good to him as I fucked him right back, my ass clapping against his thighs and motivating him to give me more.

He was perfection—sheer, wonderful bliss that I simply couldn't get enough of.

"I want to hear you say it," Jonathan said as he thrust into me, bringing me close to the edge.

"What?" I gasped.

"You know." He paused slightly, and I moaned, needing release. "What's your favorite holiday?"

"Fuck you."

He moved slightly in me, making me whimper. I needed to come.

He swiped a finger over my clit. I whimpered.

"You're gonna say it, or I'm leaving you like this."

I nodded, biting my lip.

He grabbed my hips, pulled out, then jackhammered into me.

"Merry Christmas!" I shouted as the orgasm washed over me.

Jonathan shuddered with his own release a few moments later.

"I feel dirty," I complained as he nuzzled my hair.

"Yeah, Christmas cookie decorating is messy," he replied. "All that frosting all over you."

"I mean, it wasn't; you were wearing a condom. Next time, I guess you'll have to frost my tits."

❈ ❋ ❉

I kicked him out of the bathroom while I showered. I could not have any more distractions. Besides, I needed my head clear to finish that collage.

Jonathan waited outside the glass shower door, sipping the rest of my tea and shouting out his appreciation as I scrubbed myself off.

I was about to give in and have hot shower sex when his phone rang. He drew a heart in the steam on the glass as he answered it then ducked out to go to his study.

The deadline for the scholarship was fast approaching.

Come the new year, I would be in Los Angeles. I stepped out of the shower. As I was toweling off, I looked at the heart Jonathan had drawn on the glass. He seemed really attached to me.

"Nonsense," I assured myself. "He's just horny. This is a casual thing. No feelings." Still, he would probably be put out if he realized I was going.

I wondered if I should tell Jonathan I was leaving. But then, it wasn't really any of his business. Plus, I'd have to explain about the scholarship; it would be a whole thing. And If I didn't get the internship, I would feel dumb for making a big deal about it.

❈ ❋ ❉

Jonathan was off the phone and playing with Cindy Lou when I walked out. My clothes were still dirty from the night before and this morning, so I'd commandeered one of his shirts. It was crazy how much it smelled like him and how happy that made me.

"You must want me to fuck you again if you're walking out here wearing my clothes," he said, drawing me toward him.

It would be so easy to give in, forget the internship, and let him carry me away.

It's just the honeymoon period of early infatuation. Don't throw away your future for some guy!

"You're going to have to pay me back for this later," Jonathan murmured.

My phone beeped.

Lilith: *Your turn to babysit Salem. Emma and I are here to do more photo shoots.*

Emma: *Really, we are here for the free booze, but sure, marketing contract money, whoo!*

Morticia: *Need to finish the painting.*

Lilith: *S'fine just get the cat.*

My sister was waiting in the bar. She handed me Salem's leash. "Someone got laid!"

"Well," I said, thinking back to what Jonathan and I had done outside. "We weren't really lying down."

"Dirty girl!" Emma said with a laugh. "No wonder he's obsessed with you. I bet none of those bar bimbos he was always with let him hit it from the back outside!"

"It wasn't like that."

"I bet Sarah didn't let him do that either."

"She probably just starfished once a year," Lilith said. "Let's be honest: you're so much better than her. And I should know, because we are identical twins, and I am amazing. That makes you amazing. Now go finish that project and make me proud!"

"Keep it down!" I looked around furtively, hoping no one heard. Then I waved, picked up Salem, and left.

I was super close to finishing the piece. I went over the to-do list in my head as I climbed the stairs to the apartment, which felt a lot bigger now that many of the contestants were gone. Unfortunately, Keeley was still there. I found her in my room, poking around.

"Get out," I said flatly.

She turned to glare at me. "I know you're hiding something."

"After you ruined my cake," I said, baring my teeth, "you have some kind of a death wish." Salem added a hiss to punctuate my words.

Keeley took a small step back. Then her eyes flicked down. "Of course you're wearing his shirt!" she yelled. "I bet you're going to turn it into some sort of shrine to him. Just you wait. You think he wants someone like you? You're going to be booted to the curb. You're not even going to make it until Christmas Eve."

I tried to calm my panic as I changed clothes. Had Keeley found the collage? Surely not. Surely she would have thrown it in my face if she had.

I needed to smuggle it out of the apartment. I couldn't take it to Emma's apartment across town because I still needed to be able to work on it. But there was an artist in residence across the street…

Dorothy was signing autographs outside her studio space when I came by with the painting secure in a black portfolio case.

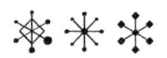

"And don't forget," Dorothy was telling the middle-aged women listening with rapt attention, "that the key to keeping a man wrapped around your little finger is to keep it spicy and surprising. That's why they stray; they get bored. Just go up to him one day and smash his cock between your tits, and it will be like you have a whole new husband."

The women thanked her profusely and hugged her.

"I'm branching into life advice," Dorothy said proudly. "I'm going to be a guru. I'm trying to convince Dana to give me my own show on Romance Creative. It will be called *The Spice of Life*, and I will help couples get their groove on."

She peered at me.

"Now, I know you don't think you need any help in that department, but let me tell you, Jonathan's a good man, but you have to put in the work too. Besides, sex is self-care. Ooh, I like that saying," she exclaimed, taking out a notepad and scribbling. "I'm going to put that on coffee mugs to sell. You have to help make more videos of me," she added, flipping the notebook closed. "I need to go viral again."

"I'm sure that won't be an issue," I replied, still slightly in shock. On my shoulder, Salem hissed at one of the Christmas geese that flapped its wings at him.

"Whatcha got there?" Dorothy asked, motioning to the portfolio case.

"I need studio space," I told her. "I would ask to rent, but I'm flat broke. How about a barter, since you need more viral content?"

"Deal," Dorothy said, shaking my hand. "Let's see how this is progressing." She opened the portfolio and set the canvas up on a nearby table. She wolf whistled as she inspected it. "Zarah is going to cream her pants when she sees this!" Dorothy said, gazing at the collage.

I had tried to abstract it as much as possible, but you could still tell the body parts and see that what they were doing was not engaging in wholesome holiday activities.

"Actually," she said, snapping her fingers, "this gives me a great idea for another retreat. Sex story painting with you and your partners. People would get a kick out of that. You think that would go viral?"

"Are you planning your quest for internet domination?" asked a male voice from the doorway.

"Jonathan!" I freaked out, scrambling to try and hide the painting.

He could not see it. I would be ruined!

CHAPTER 54

Jonathan

Though I wanted to stay in bed with Morticia all day, work was waiting for me.

Not that I had that much to do. After the big push a few months ago, now we were coasting. Lately, I'd been spending my morning worrying about securing the Hamilton Yards development and not about the alcohol sales. Every time I looked at the sales chart, it had shot up another order of magnitude. We were completely sold out of a number of our products and had long wait lists for many items. *The Great Christmas Bake-Off* had been a huge marketing win on my part.

The betting on who was going to win the bake-off and, subsequently, me was at a fever pitch online.

Each girl had a vicious camp of fans. Sarah, the dark horse, was being chewed out by everyone. Someone had dug up all her history, and social media was flooded with memes and polls calling for her to be removed from the contest. There also were exposés on Trevor, her husband. Many of them read as if someone's edgelord little brother had written them, and I wouldn't have put it past the Svenssons to have farmed the character assasination out to their *Fortnite*-obsessed tween brothers.

Dana Holbrook, of course, pretended she had had no idea that Sarah was married, and there were interviews in which she acted very shocked while promoting the show. Then there were TikTok video memes of people pouring flaming shots to flame out that cheater.

It was ugly and very profitable.

"I'm dreaming of a black Christmas!" I sang. "Got to make twenty billion more dollars." I wrote my goal on the whiteboard in my office.

"Then you better do more than sit around."

"Hey! My brothers! Did you all come here to visit me?"

"I'm trying to convince them to start a legitimate company and not a hedge fund," my oldest brother growled as he herded Matt and Oliver into my office.

"See?" Owen told them. "This is what happens when you don't run a technology-based company."

"Yeah," Matt said excitedly, "but Jonathan has a wet bar in his office."

"Also, Jonathan isn't making the *TechBiz* list this year," Jack drawled as he headed over to the bar.

"Yes, but I can drink at ten a.m., and I will make the list next year after I secure Hamilton Yards. You want to see the property?" I asked, pulling the plans out of my desk.

"Is that what you're putting there?" Jack asked. He frowned as he looked over the plans while we headed downstairs. "It seems very corporate."

"It's what Greg Svensson wants," I said with a slight grimace.

"Jonathan is a cautionary tale," Owen told Matt and Oliver. "If you putter around and waste time on hedge funds and don't found a tech start-up, then you have to let the Svenssons foist their bad ideas all over you."

"Don't be lazy like Jonathan. Got it," Oliver said.

"That's rich coming from you all," I said as we headed across the street. "I'm here working hard, while you all are clearly not at work."

"It's almost Christmas," Jack countered. "Most of my employees have traveled home."

"Same," Owen said. "I provide a very good work-life balance for my staff."

"I have free alcohol," I said mulishly. "My workers are still in the office and will be until the bitter end. There are sales bonuses attached to how much product we can move."

"That's very Ebenezer Scrooge of you," Jack teased. "I thought you were Mr. Pro-Christmas."

"I'm pro my net worth first," I retorted.

"Yeah," Matt huffed. "I heard from one of the Svensson brothers that you have some sort of scheme going to convince the old bat to sell."

Oliver laughed. "You have that crazy goth artist girl wrapped around your little finger."

I grabbed both of them by the collar. "*Shut up*," I hissed at them, looking around and hoping no one heard them. "Don't ruin this for me. I need Dorothy to sell to me. I almost have her ready to sign."

"Is that why you're letting Morticia treat you like a pampered dog?"

"I swear," I hissed as we rounded the corner. There was an old studio space there that Greg had said he was just going to burn down. The door was open, and lights were on. Morticia and the old woman were visible through the windows. Shit. Had they heard my brothers?

I mimed slitting my throat at them as I walked over, hoping to salvage the situation. They had surely seen us if not heard us.

Play it cool.

Morticia was fussing with some sort of art piece. I didn't get a good look at it, though, because I was too focused on Dorothy.

"How is the most beautiful woman this side of the Hudson River?" I asked in greeting.

"Now, I don't think your girlfriend is going to appreciate your flirting with me, young man," Dorothy said.

I winked at Morticia, who was flushed and wide-eyed. "I'm sure she won't mind sharing."

"I bet she does mind!" Dorothy said, cackling and pointing behind her to the new piece, which was now covered. "Have you seen—"

"The sketch I did of Hamilton Yards," Morticia butted in. "I was just talking to Dorothy about all our ideas for making this a cool, marketable place. Live, work, play," she chirped. "And make art!"

Morticia whipped out her sketchbook to show me a meticulous sketch of a bird's-eye view of the property. "We can turn this building across the way into artists' studios, and you can form a foundation to run it. We can also have the foundation host art-themed events like the Christmas market and also summer events that can be educational.

This building you can use as an event space, of course, since Dorothy wants to host art retreats there."

"Oh yes!" Dorothy exclaimed, "These are all amazing ideas. Morticia's so creative, though I'm sure you've seen her work, especially since—"

"Gardens!" Morticia said desperately. "Lots of gardens and topiaries and sculptures. We could host all sorts of art fairs. There's so much open space here."

"Do you have enough square footage here to support that?" Owen asked, studying the drawing with a frown. "You don't want to put a tower in here for a revenue base?"

"I don't know. What do you think, Morticia? You're the one with all the great ideas," Dorothy asked.

"Um," Morticia said.

I waited expectantly, hoping I was sending her thought waves communicating what I needed. Greg wanted a forest of towers. Not having towers was not an option.

"Maybe just one," Morticia said.

I made a subtle "increase" motion.

"Two, no, three?"

"Yes," Dorothy said. "We can have one super-tall one and then two shorter ones near it so that it looks like a cock and balls."

❈ ❈ ❈

"A cock-and-ball tower?" I asked Morticia when she showed up at my condo later that evening after work. She was smudged with paint. Salem was on a leash next to her. I kissed her nose.

"Dorothy seemed to like it," she said.

"I know!" I kissed her again. "And you've made more headway with her in a few weeks than I have in a year. It's nuts!"

"You have to speak her language," Morticia said.

"I've been bringing her alcohol."

"Yes, but she likes sex," Morticia replied. I helped her out of her black trench coat. She surveyed the Italian war zone that was my kitchen counter. "I'm scared to ask what you're doing," she said.

"I was making lasagna to surprise you!"

She inspected the dough I had started. "It's so cute that you tried," she said, picking it up and throwing it into the trash.

"I spent a lot of time on that!" I protested.

"It had the texture of a cheap dildo," she replied.

I wrapped her in my arms. "I didn't bring you here to cook for me," I whispered, "just to fuck you and eat you out whenever possible."

"I want lasagna, and I want to cook in a kitchen that doesn't have a million other women in it," she grumped. "Honestly, anyone who says girls are clean is clearly lying. There is nail polish glued to the ceiling of the apartment."

I laughed and kissed her.

She measured out ingredients for the dough. I hovered around her, pretending to help.

"You can stir the tomato sauce," she finally said in exasperation and handed me a spoon. "At least your meat is only partially burned." She inspected the ground beef and onions I had made.

"It's just a little char," I said.

Morticia snorted.

"Hey, Cindy Lou!" I called to the cat. "You want a snack?"

Cindy Lou Who, however, was ignoring me in favor of giving Salem the third degree. She did not appreciate having another cat in her domain.

"If I had known you were bringing Salem," I told Morticia, "I would have dressed Cindy Lou up. She's only wearing her Christmas collar."

Morticia peered at the cat. "Wait, is she wearing a Tiffany collar?"

"Yep!" I said proudly. "And it's Christmas themed." I picked up the cat. Her tail twitched as she glared at Salem. "See?" I said, unfastening the collar. "It has rubies and emeralds and diamonds for Christmas and little charms. I have a whole closet of clothes for her, too, but I don't think she likes them."

I went to the bedroom that I had converted to Cindy Lou's room and pulled out the Santa hat and sweater I'd bought for her. It took me a minute to wrestle her into the garments before returning to the kitchen. "Behold!" I announced. "My cat in her Christmas finery."

"You are so extra," Morticia said. She wiped her hands and took out her phone. "Look pretty," she ordered. "The entire world needs to witness this insanity."

When the photos were complete, I set Cindy Lou down then tossed a few of the cat toys out onto the floor. Both cats pounced. "I can't wait to have kids," I told Morticia. "I want to have a bunch of daughters and spoil them rotten."

"Define a bunch," she replied as she fed the dough through the pasta maker.

"Like, five, but I'm open to suggestions," I told her, waggling my eyebrows.

"That's a no from me, dog. The Christmas toy shop is going to close after two."

"You only want two kids?" I asked her.

"Kids are expensive."

"Money," I said magnanimously, waving the tomato sauce–covered spoon, "is no object."

"Fine. Three," she replied.

"You know what would be funny?" I asked, nudging her. "If we had kids, but they came out with half white hair and half black hair like Cruella de Vil and one blue eye and one…" I stared into her eyes. "You know, I thought your eyes were brown, but they're actually a very, very dark gray."

"They're brown," she said.

"They're beautiful," I told her, tipping her head back and kissing her brow.

We watched the cats play tag with the toys while we assembled the lasagna, which actually meant that Morticia meticulously directed the assembly, and I was allowed to carefully place the noodles.

"You're serious about your pasta," I remarked as I slid the pan into the oven.

"I'm Italian," she replied. "Pasta is life."

We sat on the couch, and I opened a bottle of expensive red wine. "It's French," I admitted, "but hopefully you can survive."

She laughed and curled up like a cat next to me on the couch.

Our cats had decided that they were actually friends and were now lying next to each other on the rug in front of the fireplace. It was cozy—the fire going, soft Christmas music playing in the background, the lights and ornaments twinkling on the tree, and the spell of cheese, garlic, and tomato sauce wafting from the oven.

"So what are your Christmas plans?" Morticia asked me. "I'm going to guess that your family goes all out. Is it one big, happy, festive occasion? Your parents are still married, right?"

I stared into the flames. "Yeah still married. Not a happy holiday though."

"Why? Didn't you grow up in Connecticut in a nice house?"

I raised an eyebrow.

"What?" she said. "I let you come all over me. Of course I'm going to internet stalk you a little bit."

I laughed bitterly. "I grew up in a beautiful house that was always impeccably decorated for Christmas. My parents would go all out, throw holiday parties, dress us in matching Christmas outfits, give lots of presents, the works."

"Sounds nice."

"Funny thing about appearances—they can be deceiving. My parents were actually very cold people, only concerned with how we made them look and not how they made us feel. They wanted a bunch of successful kids for the status symbols, but they were too busy to raise us. My mom didn't want people to think she was a bad mother, so instead of hiring a nanny or three, which was what she really needed for me and my brothers," I admitted, "she foisted us all on Belle. Which didn't end well. Now three of my siblings refuse to even talk to them. We haven't had a really happy Christmas in fifteen years, probably, if we ever really had one."

"You still talk to them?"

"Yeah. My siblings think I shouldn't, but…" I shrugged. "I just want us to have a happy Christmas, you know, all together again."

"Sometimes," Morticia said, "family is the people you choose, not who you're related to."

"I'm just not ready to give up," I said, tipping my head back, tangling my fingers in her hair. "And what about you? I can't believe you hate Christmas so much. No big happy Italian Christmases in your childhood?"

She huffed a laugh. "Except for the food, we're pretty bad Italians," she replied, staring out the window. "More the fighting-and-eating kind of Italians rather than eating-and-loving Italians." She drifted off, not seeming willing to tell me more.

I held her close to me. "You stick with me for the holidays. I'll make you fall in love with Christmas and give you a holiday season to remember."

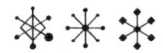

❄ ❄ ❄

Morticia was scarce the next few days, and I barely got so much as a one-word text back whenever I messaged her. I was worried. What if she had heard my brothers talking about how I was pulling a fast one to secure the property? I would be ruined.

I paced around my condo at night, working myself up, trying to decipher from her texts whether she had figured out what I was up to.

The reality was that all the ideas she kept spouting to me about the property were not going to happen. Greg would never allow it. He might allow a small event space but not enough for artists' retreats. He would want to rent it out for conventions and weddings and other big moneymakers.

Tacky little art retreats for naked yoga and nude painting were not going to generate revenue.

The whole idea of small studio spaces to rent out to artists was a nonstarter. Those types of uses never drew tourists, and the artists were so messy and territorial that they didn't want anyone in their studios anyway.

No, it wasn't going to happen.

When Morticia finds out, she's going to hate you.

CHAPTER 55

Morticia

Though it had originally begun as a ruse to keep Jonathan from discovering the painting, now that I was generating ideas for the development of the Hamilton Yards property, I was starting to become excited about it. A part of me was sad that I was going to be leaving for the Getty internship.

You may not even get the internship.

Was it weird that that didn't make me all that sad? I could stay in Manhattan and help make the development cool and artistic. Jonathan seemed to like my ideas, and Dorothy was very excited about them.

She was also excited about my project. "Oh yes!" she said as I added some red and green highlights then pasted on watercolor holly sprigs, gingerbread people fucking like rabbits, and hand-drawn baked goods.

"Oh, oh!" Dorothy said, pushing my shoulder lightly. She had been drinking all afternoon and watching me work. "Put a candy cane there, not a Santa hat."

I swapped out the strategically placed Christmas fig leaf on the deep V at the base of Jonathan's abs.

"Perfection!" Dorothy kissed her fingers like a chef then poured me a glass of cranberry flavored vodka. "Shots!" she called in celebration.

"That's more than a shot," I said. "That's like a fifth of the bottle."

She sloshed the clear bottle. "It's almost empty anyways. We might as well finish it off."

❄ ❋ ❅

I was pretty woozy as I stumbled outside to hand the package to the FedEx guy for the scheduled pickup.

"Don't worry," Dorothy told me confidently as we headed back inside the building. "I've been singing my praises of you to Zarah and the Getty folks. You're a shoo-in." Then she turned to me, suddenly serious, as if she hadn't been drinking for the last few hours. "What do you think of Jonathan?"

"He's hot." I was too drunk for this conversation.

"Yes, he is, and I bet you're going over there right after this to get some, what with staring at his naked body all day." She looked out over the property. "When I bought this in the sixties, it was a steal. I always wanted to make it into a big artists' retreat, but life happened. I never had the capital. You seem convinced that Jonathan is going to do good things with this property."

"He seems to want to build something unique and special. But I'm not going to stand here and convince you to sell.

Maybe just have a meeting?" I suggested, trying to sound competent and not stupid drunk. "See what he has to say officially, and of course have it in writing."

Dorothy tapped her forehead. "I will do that. But you need to be involved. I like your vision."

"Sure thing," I promised, waving as I left.

I was likely winning the scholarship. I was finally done with that project. I was almost done with the bake-off, god help me, and now I was going to celebrate.

Before I headed over, I sent Jonathan a photo that had not made it onto the collage. The picture was of me from behind with nothing on except a big red bow barely covering my ass.

Morticia: *I'm ready for some frosting on my cookies.*

❄ ❄ ❄

Jonathan opened the door naked, half-hard. I was half-wet.

"Damn, did you come over here just to let me come down your chimney?"

"No," I said. I took off my clothes and left them on the floor like breadcrumbs leading back to his bedroom. "I came over here to have you cover my Christmas cookies with frosting." I grinned. I was feeling insatiable.

"Show me," he said in that deep voice.

I turned to look over my shoulder at him and crooked my finger.

Jonathan stalked me into his bedroom and pushed me onto the bed. His cock jutted out tall and hard for me.

I wanted it in my mouth. I scooted over to him, turning the seductress act on. "Seems I've been neglecting you the past few days," I remarked, trailing my nails over his chest. "How about we get a little creative? I want to blow your mind."

I placed my hands on my chest and slid them down as I dropped to my knees. His cock throbbed against my chest, and I raised my boobs, squeezing it between them. A smile came across his face and gave me a clear indication of what I should be doing next.

Rolling his cock between my tits, I jerked him off, all the while leaning in and kissing his cock on the head. I watched his eyes roll back as I continued to worship him. Feeling him throb between my breasts was something I hadn't expected to enjoy.

Soon I started to lick his cock, trailing my tongue along the vein and enjoying the taste of him. I took him through my lips and pushed him deeper down my throat. I took all of him, and this time, he wasn't going to get away from me.

His groan was long and intense, his fingers going through my hair, stroking and petting me as I continued to bob up and down on him, massaging his cock between my breasts.

"Fuck, I knew Christmas was secretly your favorite holiday, Morticia. You're so horny for my Christmas package."

I shot him a glare. "Halloween will always be my number one."

"I mean..." Jonathan hissed as I licked the tip of his cock. "I'll happily eat your pumpkin pie and add a little whipped cream on there."

Another jolt must have hit him as his head fell back. The way his cock was throbbing, I was going to guess that he was close. "Fuck, I'm...I'm..."

There weren't many ways for him to end that line in that situation. Even so, I stood firm, sucking him, licking him, massaging him, yearning for that eruption.

His breathing became more rapid. He was there, and I gladly took him down my throat, pushing myself to the limits. Right before he came, I pulled off, letting the hot cum drip down my tits. He sucked in a breath. His nostrils flared, and he picked me up to toss me back on the bed. Somehow he was hard again.

"Never expected you to be such a cocksucker, Morticia," Jonathan said.

"Please," I said around his hot kisses. "I told you, Halloween is my holiday. I'm not the innocent Christmas girl. You're going to get down and dirty and slutty when you're with me."

"And the filthier and dirtier you show me you can be, the more I fall in love with you," he said roughly.

I was not going to acknowledge *that*.

It's just the hormones. I was still horny, though. I drew a snowflake pattern in the cum on my chest. Jonathan kissed me hard again.

"You're so fucking hot," he murmured while one of his hands snuck down between my legs to tease my clit.

I reached down between his legs and took his hard length in my hand. He was throbbing. "All natural," he said roughly, taking the tip of his cock and teasing my aching clit with it. "I know you're horny for me," Jonathan whispered. "But I'm tired of fucking your mouth." He pulled a condom out of the nightstand. "You must need a little bit of relief yourself after the cocksucking you just did."

I raised an eyebrow as he presented me with it.

"Show me how you do it. Ride me. Be the little cock-hungry Christmas slut you want to be," he said in that deep voice.

I took the condom and smiled craftily. I was high on life. It was finally turning a corner, and Jonathan's cock was my reward.

Unwrapping the condom, I rolled it down his cock, watching him again shudder blissfully under my touch. I climbed on top of him, his cock throbbing behind my ass, ready to take me. I grabbed him by the shaft and guided him right into me, my pussy aching with need for him.

The first moments of him entering me were always so damn good. A tide of bliss rose inside me, so powerful, so good—it really got my fires burning and made me yearn with anticipation of what was to come.

I rocked up and down on his cock, letting the bliss fill me, watching him shudder as my pussy squeezed him like a vise. He had told me to take command here, but he couldn't help himself from joining in and enjoying my body as much as I was enjoying his.

His hands glided up my sides, caressing my breasts despite them being stained with our previous act's mess. As he sucked on them, a little perk of bliss spiked. All the while, I slid up and down his cock, enjoying every bit of friction between us, every bit of ecstasy that came from our bodies meeting.

I was moaning for him soon enough, trying to hold onto his shoulders, trying to fuck him harder and faster. As I struggled to maintain my pace, he took over. With his large hands on my hips, he used his strength to make our fucking a faster, more sudden, stronger thing.

In the heights of my ecstasy, I tried to remind myself not to get too attached, that I was going to be leaving, but I wanted to be here with him forever. All that mattered was the incredible energy between us, Jonathan telling me hoarsely that he loved me, and the intensity of it all.

All of it was so goddamn perfect.

He must have been right there with me when my sensitive body couldn't take it anymore. The orgasm erupted through me, sending me screaming in delight. I felt him do the same, his hands clamping down on my hips, holding me tightly as he finished, the heat pulsing within me, even through the condom.

I collapsed on top of him, the wonderful aches of the moment pounding through me. Jonathan pressed kisses to my neck and face and lips. "I love you, Morticia," he whispered, cradling me tightly.

He doesn't mean it; it was just the orgasm.

But a part of me wished he did—and wanted to say it back.

CHAPTER 56

Jonathan

The next morning I woke up to Morticia's phone ringing. She didn't stir. It went to voicemail then started ringing again. I fished it out of one of the piles of clothes on the floor.

Belle.

"Hey," I said sleepily, answering it.

My sister huffed out an irritated breath on the other end of the line. "I thought we told you not to sleep with the contestants!"

I stretched. "I've had a stressful holiday season," I told her.

"Don't let anyone see you with her," my sister ordered.

"Uh-huh."

"Seriously. If someone other than Morticia wins the competition, you have to pretend to be in love for a few months. People want the holiday romance. I'm even thinking of doing a spin-off series of you and the winner's first few months together."

"Uh…" I looked back at Morticia. "That's not going to work for me."

"Guess what? A lot of things that have happened have not worked for me," Belle said sharply.

I cringed. I knew it; she was still mad at me.

"Okay," I said, "I'll do the spin-off." I did not want my sister to disappear again.

Morticia would understand. Hopefully.

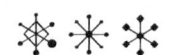

※ ※ ※

I walked into the studio a few hours later, preparing for a long but fairly generic holiday bake-off session. Sarah was making big eyes at me as she and the other three remaining contestants lined up.

"Ladies," Anastasia announced, "congratulations on making it this far. Unfortunately, one person has to go home. Sarah, you received the fewest fan votes."

"Probably because she's married!" Keeley said loudly.

"Yes, but I'm going to divorce him!" Sarah cried out.

"Anna," Anastasia said to the other contestant, "the judges gave you low marks on your edible merengue wreaths. Though you scored a bit higher on the fan voting, the fact that your merengue wasn't cooked all the way and collapsed meant you had the lowest scores from the judges."

Anna shot a death glare at Keeley then left the set.

"For our remaining ladies, the holidays are about family," Anastasia said. "But as we all know, family can be awkward, annoying, and sometimes downright terrifying—especially when you're about to meet the in-laws for the first time. For this challenge, you need to bake to impress. Put your best winter boot forward and make a dessert to impress not just any in-laws but your future in-laws. As special guests here today, we have Dr. Diane Frost and Dr. David Frost with us."

I inhaled my drink then hastily coughed and wiped my mouth as my parents sauntered into the studio. I wasn't ready for this; I didn't have conversation topics. I should have worn a different suit! I scuttled behind the cameras to Belle.

"What the fuck—" I started to say then stopped short. She was furious! It wafted off of her in frigid waves.

"I did not ask them to be here," she said icily.

Her gaze swiveled around. Dana shrugged. Gunnar had an *Oh shit!* look on his face.

I trailed Belle as she stalked him. Gunnar backed up until he was pressed against a wall.

"You," Belle hissed, jabbing at him with a sharp finger.

"I thought we were doing raw drama!" Gunnar babbled. "You brought on his ex!" He gestured to me. "I thought it would be cool to have his parents."

"*My* parents," Belle spat, "that I *hate*."

I cringed. My fantasy of a happy family Christmas might not happen after all if Belle flat-out hated Mom and Dad.

"You didn't even ask me."

"I own this production company," Gunnar whined.

"Wrong," Belle barked. "My investment firm owns it. You work for me."

"Do you want me to get rid of them?" Gunnar offered.

"No," Belle said. "It's too late. But we will discuss this later."

Gunnar shrank.

"Jonathan." Belle turned her cold gaze on me. "Go make chitchat with them. We need some B-roll that makes it look like you all have a loving relationship."

I set down my water and went over to my parents.

My father frowned when he saw me. "We came all the way out here and took time out of our day," he said sharply. "I thought Belle would at least acknowledge us."

"She's busy," I said. "But I can tell you all about the bake-off."

"I don't care about the bake-off," my mother said. She was reading through medical research papers, making notes with a red pen. She didn't even look up at me. "These women lead sad little lives. They just want to be bakers and homemakers. They need to get real jobs."

"They're accomplished," I countered. Then I thought about Sarah and Keeley. "Mostly. Morticia sure is. She's been doing an excellent job on the marketing for the distillery."

"And what are you going to do with your life after you finish with this hobby of yours?" my father asked.

I gritted my teeth.

"Hopefully start a tech firm like Jack or Owen. Though," my father said loftily, "that may be too much for you. You were always a bit of a disappointment, to be honest."

"That's why we had so many kids," my mother said, highlighting a passage in one of the papers. "Statistically, most of them were going to be failures. At least Jack and Owen turned out well."

"Belle needs to make them call us," my father said, scowling.

My mother finally looked up at me, blinking. "It's not too late for you to become a doctor. You could have a respectable profession."

"I have Hamilton Yards that I'm trying to get off the ground," I reminded them. "It's going to have artists' workspaces and residences and a foundation that hosts educational creative activities and retreats."

"Honestly, your development idea isn't even that interesting. You should build a hospital or a research center. Who wants to travel to a place that just does arts and crafts?" My mother made a face.

I was annoyed. I tried to be understanding—they were both busy and held important jobs—but it was as if they didn't even care. "Actually," I said irritably, "before I develop Hamilton Yards, I am going to be doing a Kardashian-style reality TV show with my pretend wife, whichever of the three wins the competition."

"Good god, why?" David Frost's lip curled back in disgust.

"What will the neighbors say?" my mother hissed. "Don't you dare do that show!"

"Too late. I already agreed," I told them.

"Don't be so flippant about it," my mother said. "You're going to ruin our reputation."

"You're already on thin ice as it is," my father said coldly.

"None of those women up there are worth any of this, especially that emo girl," my mother said, angling her head toward Morticia.

My blood ran cold. "Funny you should say that," I said, "because she's actually the smartest of the bunch. She doesn't take shit from people, and she certainly wouldn't from you."

"Watch your tone," my father demanded.

"Uh-huh," I said. Then I stood up and buttoned my suit jacket before I could say something I was going to regret. "I need to go talk to the producers."

"Starting to see the light?" Belle asked when I went back over to her. She was standing half in shadow with her arms crossed.

"They're just out of their element," I said, grasping for any excuse. All my excuses were flimsy, though, and deep down, I knew that. I just didn't want to believe it yet.

"You always make excuses for them," Belle told me, eyes narrowed.

"There's the man I wanted to see!" Dorothy piped up behind me. "And the lady. When are the cocktails coming out?" she asked Belle.

"Not til the judging."

"That's all right," Dorothy said, taking a liquor bottle out of her purse. "I brought my own. Shot?" She offered the bottle to me.

I declined. "I need to stay sharp to be around my parents."

"You better be drinking when you bring all your good-looking billionaire friends by tomorrow. I want to talk business," the old woman declared.

"Of course," I said, trying to seem cool and professional and not like a little kid on Christmas. "We will be there tomorrow, whenever is convenient for you."

"Anytime works for me," she replied. "But Morticia isn't a morning person, so she'd probably appreciate the afternoon."

"Morticia?" I asked uncertainly.

"She has to be there to communicate my vision," Dorothy insisted.

"Right, right."

In my head, I was screaming, *Oh shit*. Greg did not know about any of these promises. He thought Morticia was a tool not a power player at the table.

"Now why are they not serving drinks?" Dorothy asked me.

CHAPTER 57

Morticia

Jonathan's parents were impressive. Both were tall. His mother was a brunette dressed in fashionable yet understated clothes. Jonathan had inherited his good looks from his father: platinum hair, strong jaw, broad shoulders, and ice-blue eyes. If that was what he was going to look like in twenty years, I had no complaints.

You seriously think you're going to be with him twenty years from now? I scolded myself. I took another look at his parents. They were surveying the room, thinly veiled disgust on their faces.

Jonathan had been talking to them earlier. From our conversation the previous night, he seemed to respect their opinion. I needed to bake a dessert that they would appreciate. I didn't have it in me to throw the competition and let Keeley—or heaven forbid, Sarah—win.

Since this was the meet-the-in-laws challenge, I decided to make a dish that represented who my family was—not the lying, cheating, sabotaging part but the Italian part that loved to eat.

I was going to make a Struffoli. A rustic Italian dish, the southern cousin to the French croquembouche. This Neapolitan dessert was made by frying sweet, spiced dough pieces then glazing them with honey and sprinkling them with nuts and Christmas sprinkles and arranging them in a wreath. It was a homey and tasty dessert and was not super sweet because it used honey. Besides, I couldn't go wrong with fried dough. Unfortunately, it wasn't an elegant dessert, and from the looks of Jonathan's mother, she would want a fashionable dish that she could put on Instagram. I needed to refine the Struffoli.

I took out the stand mixer and added eggs, egg yolks, and sugar to the bowl and then beat them with the wire whisk attachment until they were frothy. The dough needed to be light and fluffy so that the little glazed puffs would melt in one's mouth. I added softened butter then orange zest and anise liqueur for a slight hint of bitterness and depth. I let the dough rest on the counter while I contemplated my options.

Since the Struffoli was typically formed into a wreath, it made sense to run with that option. I started making the dough for various traditional Italian cookies like dense, buttery, nutty Italian wedding cookies, fruity cuccidati fig cookies, hazelnut-and-chocolate baci di dama cookies, and fruity horn cookies filled with bright-red cherry jam. I also made the dough for thumbprint cookies to add some more color to the wreath.

The Struffoli was best served warm. I would be using the cookies as decoration on the wreath, so I baked them first. I rolled out the dough and cut out the cookies then put them in the oven. I had way overbaked, as usual, which was good, because the production assistants and my sister kept coming by to steal some.

"Don't take my nice ones," I warned Lilith as she snagged a thumbprint filled with green apple filling. "You can have one of those over there. They're a little wonky."

"They're so tasty though," my twin said around the crumbs. "Just like Mimi used to make."

I was sad for a moment. My grandmother had loved to bake and eat sweets. We would make thousands of cookies over the holidays that she would gift away to neighbors in personalized boxes that I decorated.

The cookies went into the fridge to cool. They were not going to be intricately decorated, just drizzled with frosting. I didn't want to stray too far from the rustic nature of the dessert. Besides, I had to start on the Struffoli. Though I wanted it to be warm, I didn't want it to be too hot while I assembled it, or the puffs would be crushed.

I rolled out the dough, cutting it into squares then rolling them lightly to be the size of marbles. I had a pretty impressive pile by the time I was ready to start frying. I checked the temperature of the oil then carefully dropped in the first handful of dough balls, monitoring them to make sure they were cooking correctly. That was why I didn't notice Keeley was coming my way with a big vat of icing until she was right beside me.

"Whoops!" she shrieked. She tripped over literally nothing and then dumped the vat of pink icing all over my stove and into the hot oil.

The oil roiled, and then a fireball shot up to the ceiling, catching some of the dangling Christmas décor on fire. The lights popped, and the power flickered. I grabbed the fire extinguisher under my table and sprayed it all over the stove and the ceiling. The white fluff landed all over my food and Keeley's.

Keeley's mouth made a huge O. Then she cried, "You ruined my dish!"

I was furious. I picked up a handful of the ruined doughballs and hurled them at her. They spattered against her outfit.

"You threw frosting all over me!" I yelled back. "And set the studio on fire."

"Morticia's trying to sabotage me," Keeley complained to Anastasia.

"Girls," Dana barked. "Are you trying to ruin us? Fuck." She looked around. The production assistants were scurrying to clean up. "Just go to new stations," Dana said in disgust.

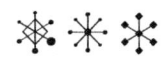

❉ ❊ ❉

It was late by the time I had remade all my dough.

My cookies at least had been cooling in the fridge during the fireball icing incident, and I retrieved them and started frosting and decorating them while I heated up my oil. Then I remade the fried doughballs.

Jonathan's parents were irritated by the whole ordeal. They kept checking their phones and watches. Jonathan also seemed antsy. He would periodically go talk to his parents, a strained expression on his face, but they barely engaged except to rebuff him.

I winced as I glazed the dough puffs. I felt sorry for him. I knew how it felt to have your parents not want to be around you. My mother had always acted as if Lilith and I had ruined her life. As soon as she could pawn my twin and me off on her sister, she had found an Italian lover and split.

"Ten minutes!" Anastasia called.

I hurried to assemble my wreath. With the cookies and the glistening fried balls of dough, it looked very rustic and natural.

"Time!" Anastasia called as I was adding the last few dustings of sprinkles to the wreath.

The judges applauded. Jonathan's parents looked completely over the whole event.

"Since this is the meet-the-in-laws challenge, Jonathan isn't the only one subjecting you all to his parents. He's going to meet your families as well," Anastasia announced.

"How?" Keeley asked snottily. "Morticia's parents don't even want her."

"Sarah and Keeley have the same parents," Anastasia said as my aunt and uncle, waving awkwardly for the camera, were hustled into the studio. "Morticia's twin and her good friend Dorothy are going to stand in for her parents to give us some variety."

My aunt and uncle were dressed in their New Jersey best. My uncle was wearing a black tracksuit, while my aunt had stuffed herself into a leopard-print dress and wobbly high heels. Jonathan's mom looked as if she was going to have an aneurism.

"First up," Anastasia said, "is Sarah to present her dish. The rest of you can go to the greenroom."

"No," Dr. Diane Frost said loudly.

"Uh, no?" Anastasia repeated.

"You've wasted quite enough of our time already. Go on, Jonathan, tell them how busy we are. We simply cannot sit through three rounds of dessert. We'll do them all at once or not at all."

"Okay, uh—"

Anastasia shot Dana Holbrook a questioning look. Dana waved her hand, and a larger round table was procured. Jonathan's dad pulled out the chair for his wife. We all set our desserts on at the table and took our seats.

"What an interesting confection," Anu remarked as Sarah's cake was placed in the center of the table. She had made strawberry cheesecake, which, to me, didn't say Christmas.

"This is my grandmother's recipe," Sarah began, handing out strawberry cocktails.

"No it's not," Lilith piped up. "I saw how much cream cheese you put in there—or didn't put in. Mimi liked to go overboard on her desserts."

"Did she?" Diane said, turning up her nose.

"You know," Jonathan's dad said, "as a world-renowned surgeon, I always tell my patients not to eat sugary foods. All of this"—he gestured at the spread—"will kill you."

"Then that's exactly how I want to die!" Dorothy declared loudly, slicing off a giant piece of cheesecake. She took a bite then spat it out.

Nick barked out a laugh.

"Yeah, that's no good. What is that? It tastes like boiled milk," Dorothy said, wiping her mouth.

"It's heart healthy," Sarah retorted, snatching the piece away from Dorothy.

"Heart healthy my ass! It's Christmas!" Dorothy insisted and took a swig of her drink. "If I want to eat my weight in cheesecake, goddamn it, I'm gonna do it! Besides," she continued, "I run a naked yoga retreat. If you're out there exercising in the cold, you would be shocked at how many calories you burn off. You need some cheesecake after all that."

"Morticia, you allow this behavior from your...I'm sorry, what is the relationship between you two?" Diane asked, lip curled, as she pointed between me and Dorothy.

"I'm her sex guru," Dorothy said matter-of-factly before I could answer.

Jonathan snickered.

"It's not funny," his father admonished. "Honestly, why can't you just grow up? You're in your twenties. By the time I was your age, I already had my MD and my own surgical practice. Yet here you are, wasting your life on cooking shows."

Jonathan's mouth was a thin line. He looked unhappy. If I had been a well-bred, well-behaved young lady, I would have fretted about walking the line between not offending his parents and saying something nice about Jonathan to pump up his ego a bit. But luckily, I was not a well-behaved woman.

The production assistants plunked my wreath down on the table. I reached out and grabbed a hunk of ooey, gooey fried dough and took a noisy bite. Jonathan's mom winced.

"Yep," I drawled. "Jonathan's totally wasting his life away. What with all the billions and the alcohol and the soaking-wet panties women are throwing at him." I took a bite of the thumbprint cookie. *Damn, I made a good cookie!* "I bet you're super jealous of him, huh?"

"Hardly," his father spat. "He gets paid to do nothing. He's not doing anything of value."

Jonathan seemed nervous. But men like his father didn't scare me.

"I bet you work a lot harder than him. But it takes skill to turn a small business into a billion-dollar enterprise in a couple of years. He might make it look easy because he's young and hot as fuck."

Dorothy cheered around her own handful of fried dough.

"To any outsider, it's clear that you're putting your son down because you wish you had his life."

"I don't want his life," his father snarled, slamming his hands down on the table. "I want him to act according to my standards."

"Good thing for him he's not," I said, grabbing another handful of doughballs. "Because from where I'm sitting, if you want him to act anything like you, the world can do without it."

CHAPTER 58

Jonathan

My father glared at Morticia. I was tense, thinking he'd better not go after her. Instead he grabbed his coat. My mom stood up.

"You need to shape up if you want to continue to be a part of the Frost family," he warned me.

"Boo-hoo," Morticia said.

My dad glared at her.

Morticia was unafraid. "Frost my cookies!" She made a V with two fingers and licked between them with a vulgar gesture.

"Oh my goodness!" my mother exclaimed, clasping a hand to her chest and literally clutching her pearls.

Dorothy, who had been sneaking drinks all evening, cackled and almost fell out of her chair.

"I don't care which of these bimbos you pick," my father snarled, "but it better not be her."

"She's feral," my mother hissed at me.

Morticia was unfazed after my parents stormed out. She took another noisy bite of her dessert.

Anu also tried a piece of the wreath. "Can't go wrong with fried dough," she quipped.

"And cookies!" Nick added.

Keeley slammed her fists on the table. "They didn't even try my dessert!"

"They didn't try anyone's dessert," Morticia reminded her.

"Because you ruined it," her cousin insisted.

Keeley ran and grabbed the strawberry shortcake she had made. She tried to force-feed me a spoonful of the berry-filled, crumbly scone and whipped cream.

"Eat it!" she insisted. "You need to eat this now."

Splat!

"Ow!" Keeley yelled as one of the doughballs hit her in the face.

"Get away from him," Morticia warned.

"You can't have him all to yourself." Keeley started sobbing. "This isn't fair. I demand a recount!"

Dorothy took a bite of one of the strawberry shortcakes. "It's fine," she said with a shrug. "It's pretty basic though."

❄ ❄ ❄

I was reeling after the bake-off had ended. My parents had been so dismissive and rude!

I couldn't even be all that elated that Morticia had stood up for me, because she had done it to my father. He was never going to let me live that down. He hated being wrong, he hated when people called him out, and he hated any perception that he was not in control of a situation. And Morticia had been in complete control.

I wondered if she still wanted to even be with me. I stared out my office window. I was supposed to be prepping for the next day's meeting. I needed to break it to Greg that we were not going to slam twenty towers into the ground. He was not going to be pleased.

I wondered if Morticia thought less of me now that she had seen the way my parents acted. Was she worried I was going to turn out like my father?

There was knocking on the glass door. Morticia was there with a stack of boxes. "Busy?" she asked in that raspy voice. "I brought you something to eat."

"That was nice of you."

She huffed a laugh. "I had an ulterior motive. I wanted an excuse to use your kitchen and play with your cat and not have to be stuck in that tiny apartment with Keeley."

I cocked my head. "How did you even get inside?"

She pulled my key card out of her pocket. "Filched it off of you."

I patted my pockets and took out my wallet. Sure enough, the card was missing.

"I should give you your own," I told her as I opened the first box.

"Oh, are we at that point yet?" she teased.

I breathed in as the smell of rich, salty spaghetti carbonara wafted up. "If you're going to make me food like this," I remarked, "then yeah, you can have a key card."

That earned me a small smile.

"Besides," I said as I took a big bite of the pasta, the fatty bits of prosciutto bursting on my tongue. "Whoever wins the bake-off—and I'm pretty sure at this point that it's going to be you—is supposed to do a reality TV show with me to document our blossoming relationship."

"Somehow I doubt your sister used that word," Morticia said dryly.

"So that's a little of my own flair. But the point is you're going to be stuck here for another few months at least," I said cheerfully. "It will be great! You can work at my company if you want or do whatever artist stuff you do. We always need marketing." I twirled another bite of pasta around my fork then looked up at her and smiled. "I love having you in my life, Morticia."

"Right," she said faintly. She cleared her throat. "I have desserts in that other box—cookies, Struffoli. Have to run."

What was her deal? I was suddenly anxious. She wasn't going to leave, was she? I thought she wanted to be with me.

Maybe she's just tired. She made you all this food, after all, and took care of your cat, I told myself. *Concentrate on Hamilton Yards.*

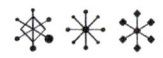

❋ ❋ ❋

As I had anticipated, Greg was not pleased when I showed him my revisions to his plan the next morning in my office.

"What the fuck is this?" he demanded as he and Carl reviewed the spreadsheets and site plan I had edited based on Morticia's sketch. "Where the fuck are my towers?"

I pulled up the Pinterest board Morticia had made. "Instead of eighty-story towers, we can have a renovated industrial building to be used for artists' studios."

"No," Greg growled.

"Just consider it," I begged. "This is the only way Dorothy will sign off on the land deal."

"We can promise all of this to her," Greg warned me, "but so help me god, I will not be privy to a development that includes…" he read off one of the line items "… a plaza for naked yoga."

"Dorothy is very insistent that there be space for her classes," I told him as we headed downstairs. "She wants to sell to someone that has the vision of an artistic, unique space."

"You were supposed to fuck Morticia and then convince her to sway Dorothy to our side not fuck her, fall in love with her, and then inherit all of her crazy ideas. You need to shape up, or I'm finding another development partner," Greg snarled.

I blew out a breath, the fog hovering in front of me as we made our way through the abandoned industrial property to Dorothy's tiny art studio. She and Morticia were outside when we arrived. Morticia was brewing something in a cauldron.

"There are my hot billionaires!" Dorothy said, arms spread wide. "You boys want some grog?"

"It's ten thirty in the morning," Greg said, incredulous.

"Of course," I said loudly, "we'd all love some, thank you."

Dorothy had tree stumps arranged around the fire. Greg gingerly sat on one. One of the geese came close, honking, and attacked Greg's shoes. Morticia came by with a cracked tray and handed him a steaming mug of grog. He sipped it then coughed furiously.

"That will warm you up," Dorothy told him as Carl thwapped his brother on the back. "Now," she said, settling on her own tree stump, the geese gathering around her, "tell me all about your plans for Hamilton Yards. I've heard about it from Jonathan, and I've been liking what I'm hearing, but I need more specifics."

"What has he told you?" Greg asked apprehensively.

"On the list," Dorothy said, ticking off her fingers, "is free artist studio space, a big event space where I can hold my creative spiritual retreats, and lots of open space for festivals and nude yoga. Oh, and of course, we're having three towers arranged like a cock and balls."

Greg was stunned.

"We can work on the configuration," I said hastily as his gray gaze swiveled over to me.

"No," Dorothy insisted. "I want it written in the contract that it's going to be a cock-and-ball tower." She whipped out a sketch she had done. "In fact, I think you should put little round hats on the ball towers to make them look more like testicles."

Greg opened his mouth then closed it.

"We can't promise that Hamilton Yards will be built exactly like this," Carl began.

"You can't?" Morticia interjected. "Because I was asking around, and apparently there are developments where there are deed restrictions placed on the property ahead of time, and the site is rezoned for a specific site plan. We could do the same here just to ensure that we are all on the same page."

She smiled. It was all teeth.

Dorothy beamed. "Isn't she smart as a whip?"

CHAPTER 59

Morticia

"I'm concerned," I told Dorothy after the Svenssons and Jonathan had left the meeting. "They seem like they're trying to pull a fast one."

"I don't think Jonathan would do that," she said, puttering around the fire.

"I think he means well, but I don't trust those Svenssons," I told her. "They basically bought up all of Harrogate and are turning it into their own little fiefdom."

"But they're so good-looking." She sighed.

"We should be cautious," I warned her.

"It's Christmas," Dorothy told me, pouring me more grog. "Live a little! You need to go shopping for the party tonight anyway."

"What party?"

"Jonathan's company party. I got an invite," she told me. "I'm wearing my feather dress. It's nothing but mesh, sequins, and feathers. I look stunning in it."

"I'm sure you do."

※ ※ ※

I wondered why Jonathan hadn't invited me to his party as I headed back to his condo. The meeting had made me nervous for Dorothy. The three men had seemed as if they were hiding something.

Jonathan was in his study when I returned. I needed to talk to him. I didn't care about parties. I did like him, but if he decided that we weren't like that, it was no skin off my back. I'd only been with him a few weeks, true, and even though it felt easy and perfect and right to be with him, I had survived worse things than losing Jonathan. But I was not going to let him screw over my friends.

"That meeting went pretty well," he said brightly when he saw me. He stood up as I stalked up to him. He reached out to kiss me, but I pushed him down in the chair. "Are we getting kinky tonight?" he purred.

"No," I said, "we are having a serious discussion. What are you and the Svenssons playing at with Dorothy?"

"What? We aren't—nothing!" he sputtered.

"They seemed perturbed at the suggestions we made for Hamilton Yards," I countered.

"They're just super-conservative developer types," he assured me. He pulled out sheets of paper. "Look," he said. "I have it all worked out—the pro forma works."

I didn't know a lot about real estate finance. But there were a lot of black numbers on the spreadsheet, and the site plan *seemed* reasonable to my untrained eye.

"I promise," Jonathan said, gaze sincere. "You know me, Morticia. You know that I'm all about unique and creative things. I own a whole craft distillery, bringing hyperlocal liquor to a global market, and I'm a judge in *The Great Christmas Bake-Off*. I'm all about artistic expression."

His voice was soothing. I wanted to believe him.

He wrapped his arms around me. "Besides," he added with a sigh, resting his head on the top of mine. "I've been doing some thinking about my father."

"He's wrong about you," I said, voice slightly muffled against his chest. "You're not a failure."

"I guess."

"Seriously."

He leaned down and kissed me, then his blue eyes grew dark.

"I've decided I don't want to be anything like him. If my dad went into real estate, he would be just like Greg, wanting to maximize profits and throw a tower everywhere to show people how great he was. All my life, I wanted to be like him, but I don't think I ever will. I'm totally on board with making Hamilton Yards unique and artistic," he promised, smiling down at me.

"My parents will have aneurisms," he continued, dancing me around, "but so what? I'll have you. We'll develop Hamilton Yards together. It will be amazing, especially since we're right across the street. I'll have everything I love within a few hundred feet of me at all times."

Oof.

Someone was lying in this room, and it wasn't Jonathan. He was clearly on board with Dorothy's and my vision. However, I was still planning on taking the Getty internship.

That would put me across the country and far away from the man who was looking at me with adoration.

Just don't take the internship, insisted the starry-eyed romantic, who I usually kept locked in a box in the cellar.

Not take the internship? That went against everything I believed in, everything I had worked for. One didn't just turn down a Getty internship.

Relax, I chided myself. *You haven't even won it. They may not give it to you, and this issue would just disappear.*

But I should at least give Jonathan a heads-up, right? That would be the adult thing to do.

I took a deep breath. "I need to tell you something…"

"Wait, wait!" Jonathan said in excitement. "I have a surprise first!" He put his hands over my eyes and guided me down the hall to the bedroom.

"We could just have sex in your study," I told him.

"This is better—well, not better than sex," he amended, "but I'm pretty excited. Ta-da!" he announced when I opened my eyes.

There in front of me was a rack holding several beautiful, gauzy, gothic dresses that were just my style.

"The Hillrock West Distillery company party is tonight," he said. "I was hoping to convince you to go with me. To sweeten the deal, you may have your choice of gown, m'Christmas baking lady."

I thumbed through the dresses then froze. "These are Kate Spencer dresses." My eyes bugged out. She was known for gothic, Victorian-style dresses. They were hand sewn, they cost a fortune, and there was a waiting list to buy them. Yet Jonathan had five of them right here!

"I figured you would like them." He was pleased with himself.

"They're beautiful," I purred.

There was an all-black dress with a trumpet flare. I earmarked that one for a big Halloween ball that I was going to convince Jonathan to host in the fall, because hello, black lace! The next dress was a skeleton-bride ball gown with artfully ripped lace and satin skirt, complete with a veil.

Might be my wedding dress. The third though…

"I thought this one was a little bit Christmas, a little bit Halloween," he said as I pulled it off the rack and held it up.

It was a white dress—not pure, virginal white but that gothic New Orleans creamy white lace. Instead of flowers, the lace pattern was snowflakes. I slid it on. The dress stopped at knee length then had a layer of gauzy tendrils that fluttered as I walked.

"Gorgeous," I said, salivating.

"I must admit, I did bring you in here for something else," Jonathan whispered. He pressed his bulge against me. After the evening I had had, stress relief in the form of sex sounded like a very good idea.

I scrambled to take the dress off before Jonathan ripped it. I tugged off my tights as he shrugged off his suit. He grabbed my ass, pulling me toward him as he sat on the edge of the bed. He pressed his face to my hot pussy, teasing me with his tongue.

I thrust back against him as his tongue circled around my clit and down to my opening. He went back to teasing my clit while he slipped one finger, two fingers into me and curled them. I moaned loudly, and Jonathan gave a muffled laugh.

I heard a condom packet rip. Then he grabbed my hips, angling me toward his cock. He brought himself toward my tight, hot pussy, ready to take me. His hands on my hips, he began to penetrate me slowly.

It was so damn intense. Every hard, thick inch of him spread me apart. I sank down on his cock, taking all of him. Large hands digging into my hips, he easily lifted me up then back down onto his cock at a better angle.

It was like a damn tsunami with his cock sliding out and pushing into me. My entire body was shuddering from the immense friction inside me, the whole act hitting some deep nerve, making this all too blissful. Was this what people meant when they said the G-spot?

Something about what Jonathan was doing was hitting me just right, and I was soon moaning and cooing in enjoyment.

I heard the smile as he said in that deep voice, "I love how you spread your legs for me, your pussy begging for my cock."

He lifted me up again and then pulled me back on his cock, harder this time, making me cry out from the pleasure of the friction.

"Yes," I moaned. "Take me harder. Take me faster. Make me come."

Jonathan didn't need that much encouragement to go all the way, to give me anything and everything that I wanted. He started to fuck me hard and fast, his cock slamming up into me.

The pressure inside me was growing into an even more incredible wad of ecstasy. I didn't have anything to grab, so I let my hands roam over my body and pinch my tits.

"Damn," Jonathan purred. "I need to fuck you like this in front of a mirror next time."

I couldn't answer, because all of it was coming at me, too much, too fast. But I was holding on, ready to ride it out, ready to savor the feeling. When it hit, *goddamn* did it hit me—all the intensity of the moment tore through me, every bit of my being igniting.

Jonathan thrust up into me once more, then his cock throbbed within me.

After it was over, he dragged us back onto the bed. I lay panting in his arms as he pressed kisses to my forehead.

I wish I could stay with him forever.

CHAPTER 60

Jonathan

I dozed next to Morticia on the bed. If this was going to be our life forever, I had no complaints. "So," I asked her, "are you going to take the job offer?"

"What?" she murmured.

"My job offer to work with me on Hamilton Yards or marketing or whatever you want?"

"Uh—"

"Come on," I begged, "say yes! All I want is to spend every minute with my girlfriend."

"Every minute?"

"Okay, so sometimes we're going to be working, but at least a good chunk of every day." I pressed kisses along her neck.

"I'll think about it," she said with a sigh.

"Strongly think about it," I cajoled. "You don't have anything else planned, do you? Of course, if you have art projects planned, then you can totally do those. But I need you here with me."

"I'm not going to leave you," she said, stroking my face.

I kissed her hard, feeling elated.

She pushed me off. "Your holiday party is soon," she reminded me, tapping the watch on my wrist.

"We could skip it."

She raised one black eyebrow. "You can't skip your own company holiday party."

She didn't even let me shower with her as she scrubbed down then washed her hair. Afterward, she combed it out, parted it, and put it up in an updo. Then she shimmied into the dress.

I ran my hands up along the sides. "I want to fuck you in this dress."

"Don't you dare ruin this dress," Morticia warned me, tapping me on the nose.

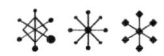

※ ※ ※

The party was hopping when we walked across the street to the distillery offices a few minutes later.

"How are you late to your own party?" Carl asked loudly, clapping me on the back when he saw me.

"Har har. You want a drink?" I asked Morticia. On offer was a variety of Christmas-themed cocktails made with my company's product. On a large screen was a graph of our sales chart. People cheered and took shots every time the numbers jumped.

I handed Morticia a dark-red cocktail with a candy cane stirrer. "Merry Christmas," I toasted.

She stretched up on her toes and kissed me hard.

"Holy shit. I thought you didn't want me to rip you out of your dress," I said, reeling slightly.

She pointed upward. "Mistletoe means you kiss. Fun fact," she continued, "if you make tea out of the berries, you can die a terrible death."

"There goes my idea for a mistletoe-infused alcohol," I said, taking a sip of my drink.

I followed Morticia to the snack table, where Belle and Dana were selecting from the variety of savory pastries, mini quiches, and other appetizers.

"You ready for the bake-off to be over?" Morticia asked them.

"I was ready for it to be over a month ago," Dana replied.

"Our ratings are through the roof," Belle remarked. "We're getting a lot of interest in sponsorship deals for next year."

"You can't just toss another of your little brothers into the fire?" Dana joked.

"I'll have you know I participated of my own free will," I said. "We're even thinking about making a cookbook based on the various alcohols that were used in the dishes on the bake-off. You know," I said to Morticia, wrapping an arm around her, "that may be the perfect project for you when you come work for me."

"She's working for you?" Greg asked as he approached.

Belle narrowed her eyes at him.

Greg grabbed my arm to haul me away. "We're going to discuss business," he told her.

"Well then," Belle drawled, "I guess we should let the men discuss business."

"Did you convince Morticia to get on board with our vision?" Greg asked in a low voice once we were safely across the room.

"I'm working on it," I lied.

"I will not spend money turning a chunk of that real estate venture into free studios for artists," he reminded me. "You better read her the riot act, or this deal is not happening."

"Are we talking about the Hamilton Yards development?" Dorothy piped up from under my elbow. Another older woman stood next to her wearing a colorful kaftan and a turban. "I was just telling Zarah about the development and the artist retreats we're going to have on my property," she said. "Zarah's big into art—very involved with the Getty Museum in Los Angeles. She even has a scholarship that she gives out to interns every year."

Greg gave me a pointed look. "We do look forward to working with you to create a successful development, Dorothy," he said smoothly. "Excuse me. I need to talk to Owen."

Dorothy watched Greg head across the room to talk to my older brother. "He needs to get with the program," she said.

"I'm sure once he sees all the pictures of the pretty naked yoga girls," Zarah drawled, "he'll be throwing money at this project."

Dorothy snapped her fingers. "This lady is super smart. Greg!" Dorothy called, power walking through the crowd and waving her phone. "Oh, Greg!"

Zarah turned her gaze to me. "And Morticia, the artist, will be involved in Hamilton Yards as well?" the older woman asked.

"Definitely," I said. "Very heavily involved. She's going to be working for me doing marketing and then, obviously, locking down this development."

"Hm." Zarah furrowed her brow. "That will be a lot on her plate then. She applied for a prestigious internship at the Getty Museum. It starts at the beginning of January. We had a meeting to pick the finalist just yesterday. Morticia was everyone's top choice, especially for the art piece she submitted for the scholarship. If she's going to be traveling back and forth, then she may not get as much out of it as someone else."

White noise rushed in my ears. Morticia was leaving? To Los Angeles? For an internship? I felt sick.

"No. No way," I said emphatically. "You must be misinformed. Morticia told me she was staying; she said she wasn't leaving. *She promised*. There is a mistake. If Morticia had any intention of taking the internship, she would have told me. I didn't even know she had applied! She must have just done it on a whim."

"It was too grueling an application process to do on a whim," Zarah replied.

"Morticia has no intention of taking an internship in Los Angeles." I barked out a laugh. "That's on the other side of the country from me. There's no way we're doing the long-distance thing. There is no way she's accepting the offer. You should give it to someone else."

"I see," Zarah said finally. "Thank you for informing me. I will tell the panel."

I felt guilty. I should tell Zarah that maybe she should ignore what I had said. But then Morticia smiled at me from across the room. I couldn't lose her. I had to keep her with me. She wouldn't find out. She would be happy with me.

CHAPTER 61

Morticia

Jonathan gazed at me adoringly. It almost hurt my heart that I was going to have to leave him in January.

"So you really think they are giving me the internship?" I whispered to Dorothy.

"Oh, definitely," she said. "I heard through the grapevine that you were at the top of everyone's list! Now, I know you're going to be off living your best artist's life in Los Angeles, but you have to come back while I hash out the Hamilton Yards development. Those Svenssons are trying to railroad me, I just know it."

"If it isn't the two most beautiful women at the party," Jonathan said, sauntering up to us.

"You charmer!" Dorothy giggled.

I smiled up at him. Jonathan was funny and sweet and, of course, hot.

And you're just going to leave him.

Not leave...the internship is for a year. People have long-distance relationships.

The live band started playing "What's This?" from *The Nightmare Before Christmas*.

"They're playing our song!" Jonathan said and grabbed me around the waist.

"How is this our song?" I asked with a laugh as he twirled me on the dance floor.

"It's Christmas music and Halloween music," he said as the band rocked out to its own cover version of the song.

I was laughing and happy after it was over. *Maybe I should reject the internship.*

No. I decided Jonathan would be understanding. Besides, there were airplanes and video chats.

I did want to do something nice for him, though, to cut back some of my guilt. I tugged him away from the party and upstairs to his darkened office.

His smile was dangerous as he softly shut the door behind us. "If anyone asks, I have work that can't wait for tomorrow."

"Is this another pained metaphor for fucking me?"

"Would you prefer it not be?"

I smirked. "No, no, let's have me stand here in this fancy dress, watching you...I don't know, crunch numbers in Excel or whatever it is you do."

He grunted. "Hey, maybe that's exactly what I intend to do."

I reached behind me and found the zipper of my dress, pulling it down enough to loosen it and reveal the bra and panties beneath it. I sauntered over to his big, fancy executive chair, spun it around, and sat down on it, nice and wide legged for him.

"Now," I said, "you could crunch a bunch of numbers and do some meaningless math."

"That does sound utterly enthralling, yes."

"Or you could have this." I waved my hand down my body.

"You are making a very compelling argument, Morticia. I can't deny that." He licked his lips as he looked at me, and it was then that I knew that after a long moment of thinking and soul searching, he had made his decision.

"Why don't you use that tongue on my lips instead of your own?"

He smiled and moved to do as I asked, but I raised a finger between us. "I didn't mean those lips."

His smile grew wider. "I like the way you think."

Jonathan dropped to one knee then the other. His fingers trailed down my body, and my flesh perked up from his touch as it continued down my form, over my abdomen, and toward my pussy. My skin prickled as he went between my legs, making everything come alive when he reached my clit.

The bliss spiked through me as he delicately touched me there, his lips feathering down my abdomen and following the same path as his fingers. The heat of his breath against me was so damn potent that the anticipation of it all made me yearn for that lip-to-lip kiss I had asked for.

He was in no rush to give me that but in plenty of rush to keep the teasing flowing. A little lick here, there, anything to keep the blood flowing through me and inch me toward something even better.

Soon, though, his licks squeezed past my panties, thrusting toward my folds. God, he was so damn good at this. From the first time he had introduced his tongue to my pussy, I had been falling more and more in love with him.

He wasted little time in setting the speed, his licks running along my slit, slicking from one side to another. He was fervent in his attention to detail, pressing me hotter and higher, making me cry out for him as he pushed me up the chair with anything and everything he did.

Soon, I was arching up in the chair, crying out his name as the heat and pressure thudded through me. Hearing me whimper with need only inspired him more, and his tongue lashes became more intense. He sensed me getting close and increased his rhythm, sending me careening off the edge of pleasure.

If there hadn't been a party going on downstairs, I would have been worried about being overheard.

As I descended from my Jonathan-induced high, he stood tall and stripped down, showing me that delectable chest of his, dropping his pants, and generally making me disbelieve that such a fine man could be so infatuated with me.

But he was. He was hard and more than ready to give me everything.

He wanted to change it up a little though. "I've done things your way. Now it's my turn to decide how we have some fun."

Jonathan proceeded to slap all the stuff off the desk, not caring about the mess and clatter it made on the floor nearby. When he slid off his boxer briefs, his cock sprang to life. He opened a drawer and pulled out a condom.

"Always prepared," he said in answer to my raised eyebrow. "I just knew I'd be ramming my thick, hard cock into your pussy one of these days." He handed me the condom. "Ride me. Show me how much you appreciate my cock and tongue."

I narrowed my eyes. If he'd liked the way I thought, I had to say that the feeling was more than mutual.

In anticipation, my pussy ready for him again, I slid my panties off and hopped onto the desk with him. I shared a brief kiss, leaning in, our bodies meeting, the brief contact building in anticipation of what was to come.

I straddled him and rolled the condom onto him, more than ready to plunge him into me after so much prelude.

Feeling him slide into me…god, I would never ever get tired of it.

I needed this. He hadn't quenched the fire he'd started with his tongue; he only seemed to stoke it. Since I was in control, I was quick to hit my stride, bucking up and down on his cock. His hands wrapped around my hips as we increased the pace. Every thrust shot the bliss all the way through my body, my heart racing as we hit our apex faster.

His hands slid up my sides, squeezing my breasts, completely appreciating all of me that was in front of him. He always looked at me as if I were a goddess and always treated me like one too.

We were fully in concert at this point, knowing one another so well. Our fucking was symphonic, both of us enjoying a continuous parade of new and higher highs as time passed. I yearned for more of him as much as he yearned for more of me.

Faster. Harder. Hotter. We were fully into one another, enjoying the absolute bliss of the moment. The heat flooded through my body as we inched closer and closer to absolute heaven.

We were so in sync with one another that we hit our climaxes at the exact same moment. The bliss marvelously tore through me as it always did, my body going briefly rigid, before I had no choice but to collapse into a pile of orgasmic goo on top of him, his arms wrapping around me as I fell.

I think I'm addicted to this man.

"I can't wait for when you're working for me," he said roughly. "We're going to do this every day."

Fuck. I really needed to tell him. But what if he hated me?

CHAPTER 62

Jonathan

L ife was good. It was just a few more days until Christmas, Morticia was going to stay with me forever, and I was going to have my development. I just had to survive one more round of *The Great Christmas Bake-Off*.

Morticia stood in front of the camera with her cousins.

"Welcome to the finale of *The Great Christmas Bake-Off*," Anastasia announced. "Today is the day the final two contestants make their most impressive and most personal dessert that perfectly encapsulates their time with Jonathan. But first, we must send someone home."

Please don't send Morticia.

"Sarah, you were our wild card contestant. Unfortunately, the judges said the texture of your cheesecake was too wet."

"And the fans said you were crazy," Keeley piped up.

Sarah turned on her cousin. "I will have Jonathan. Just you wait." She stomped off the set.

Or not, I chuckled to myself. That problem was easy to solve. Now I just needed Morticia to win. Then I would take her back to my condo, and we would have a very merry Christmas.

"Unlike other challenges," Anastasia said, "for the finale, we will have a three-hour voting window then announce the results live. To our audience watching at home, thank you for tuning in, and I hope you have your cocktails ready. Ladies, start your baking. Your time begins now."

Morticia and Keeley exchanged angry looks, and then they went to gather ingredients. I wondered what Morticia was going to bake.

She has to win, right? I didn't know what I was going to do if I had to be subjected to Keeley for the next ninety days before the deadline had passed for us to have a quiet, fake breakup.

While they worked, I grabbed my laptop bag to head across the street to my office for a meeting with Weston and Blade from ThinkX.

"Be back on time," Belle told me, pausing her conversation with one of the producers.

"Can you text me to remind me?" I asked.

"Sure," she said then regarded me suspiciously. "What are you pulling with the Hamilton Yards development?"

I shifted my weight. "Greg said I wasn't supposed to tell you," I whined.

Belle raised her arm; I flinched. She smirked and smoothed back her hair. I laughed nervously.

"The perks of being a big sister," she said smugly.

She was my big sister, and I was pretty sure she would help me, her favorite little brother. Also, she had an intimate knowledge of Greg and could potentially help solve my problem on the Hamilton Yards development. I looked around furtively and gestured her into the hallway.

"I might have sort of made promises to Dorothy that Greg is not going to want to keep," I said in a low voice. "Does he have any Achilles' heels or weaknesses that I could use to prod him into going along with the vision that Dorothy has bought into?"

"Is this the mass nude yoga session I keep hearing about?" Belle asked, eyebrow raised.

"Among other things." I grimaced. "Weirdly enough, I think that's the part he has the least issue with."

Belle hissed a breath out from between her teeth. "Of course he does."

"No, not like that!" I said, waving my arms. "Morticia promised Dorothy all this free artist space. And there's only three towers instead of the whole grove of them that Greg wants."

"So to summarize," Belle said dryly, "you've been making terrible decisions and lying about them to people, including a powerful man who gets off on grinding others into the dust and is in a constant state of war with his own family members. And who I have on good authority is a sociopath."

I winced. "So no weaknesses?"

"Don't try and screw him over," she warned.

I sagged.

Then she added, "That is, not unless you're one hundred percent sure you're going to win."

"And then he respects my chutzpah and we skip happily ever after into the sunset of capitalist profit?" I asked hopefully.

"No," Belle said with a snort. "Then you sleep with a gun under your pillow for the rest of your life, waiting for him to get even."

Oof.

She patted me on the head. "Good luck, little brother. Hopefully Greg murders you for screwing him over before New Year's and not after, because we'll get a better deal on inheritance taxes."

I groaned. Then I trudged across the street to my office building.

Blade and Weston were waiting in my office when I arrived and set down my bags. "How bad a person is Greg, really?" I asked them.

"Our brother Greg?" Blade asked. "The man who, when Weston lost his watch in the Hudson River, forced everyone to swim out in the cold and the ice chunks to retrieve it?"

"The man who, when a famous restaurateur seated one of the Holbrooks before him, even though he was there first, mailed him a single used shoe every week for the next year?" Weston added. "The restaurateur was posting about it online because he couldn't figure out what the hell was going on."

"That doesn't sound too bad," I said.

Blade snorted. "Those are just the times people annoyed him. Are you going to aggravate him or try and ruin him? Because there was this one time this guy tried to cut him out of a real estate deal. Greg had me dig up some dirt on this guy and turned him over to the feds. He's been in jail for years," Blade said flatly.

"But if I don't have dirt—I mean if a *hypothetical* person didn't have dirt, then nothing would happen? Hypothetically?" I asked.

"Everyone has dirt," Blade stated. "And if they don't, you can gather enough dust and dead skin cells to make it look like they have dirt."

"Fuck."

"But it's not like you're going to do anything crazy, *right*?" Weston asked me. "I mean, come on, man, you should see the numbers on this company! Your valuation is through the roof. Your net worth is officially out of the danger zone. You're halfway to eleven figures. *TechBiz* magazine had us run the latest numbers for their January issue of the list of billionaires to watch out for in the New Year."

"It's five billion?" I perked up as Blade pulled up the charts on the screen.

"It's five point eight," Blade told me. "You're running with, well, not the big dogs, but you're in the top two hundred. With the Hamilton Yards development next year, I bet you're in the top one hundred fifty, maybe even top hundred."

"Top one hundred list, here I come!" I crowed.

I also realized that I needed to find some other way of dealing with the Hamilton Yards development. I could not get on Greg's bad side. I would have to work something out with Morticia. Maybe if I came clean? What if I bribed her? I couldn't lose her, but I also couldn't lose that development.

CHAPTER 63

Morticia

You cannot lose, I told myself.

It would be bad enough to not be with Jonathan while I was in California completing my internship. But to have him living with Keeley, sharing a house with her, even if it was supposed to be fake? I knew how Keeley was. She had slept with Sarah's fiancé on the night before their wedding. If Keeley had her way, she would sink her claws into Jonathan and never let go.

More to the point, what if Jonathan broke up with me? What if he was angry that I had lied to him and said he didn't want anything to do with me? I chewed on my lip as I sketched out my idea for a cake.

His declaration that a song from *The Nightmare Before Christmas* was ours gave me the inspiration for the cake. I was going to make a towering Tim Burton Christmas cake. The confection was going to feel a little surreal and off-balance, and the top of the cake would have the Tim Burton signature curl.

I set about making the layers of the cake. The largest bottom layer would be mocha chocolate cake with chocolate rum cream filling. Then came a triple-layer white cake with orange curd filling, a cinnamon sponge cake with mascarpone filling, and mixed berry filling. The top layer was going to be more chocolate cake with salted caramel chocolate ganache and heavy whipped cream as filling between the layers.

Sketch done, I began mixing the cakes. We had a fair amount of time. Mixing the cake batter was usually meditative, but I was fretting about coming clean to Jonathan about the internship. I also hadn't yet received a message from the Getty Museum confirming the internship, though today was supposed to be the day they notified the winners.

Maybe you weren't chosen after all.

But Dorothy had promised I would be. Though I was excited about the internship, I was sad that I was going to have to leave Jonathan.

I needed to concentrate. Keeley occupied the station next to mine. I knew she had a sabotage planned, so I needed to be on my guard. She was making some sort of layered icebox cake. She had a domed bowl out, and I heard her tell Anastasia when she came over to ask if she was making a Christmas-themed baked Alaska.

My cake was going to be much better than hers. I was sure of it. I watched her like a hawk while I carefully poured my various cake mixtures into pans lined with parchment paper and slid them into one of the two ovens I was using.

While they baked, I worked on the frosting and fillings. It was like prepping a painting palette. All the colorful fruity and custardy fillings, not to mention the chocolate ganache and the caramel, made a tasty array of colors and smells.

"I so have this in the bag." I took a celebratory shot of rum as I pulled the last double boiler off of the heat and took the first of my cakes out of the oven. I placed the chocolate cakes in the blast freezer. I liked my chocolate cake to be ooey and gooey. There was nothing worse than dry chocolate cake.

While the cakes cooled enough for me to be able to cut them and assemble all the layers, I started on the decorations and the structure for the cake. Using PVC pipe and dowels, I rigged up a structure that was going to make the cakes look like they were teetering in that quintessential Tim Burton aesthetic.

To avoid going too kitschy, instead of festooning the cake with generic characters from *The Nightmare Before Christmas*, I was highlighting the natural surroundings in the cake decorations. On one layer, I had the woods surrounding the town and the gate. A curved path of icing led up to the next cake tier with the whimsical Halloween Town, which was decorated with mini Christmas decorations and white frosting snow. The path continued to the next tier with Jack's mansion, then to the next with the snow-covered graveyard with little miniature singing zombies in Christmas hats. At the very top, I would have miniatures of Jack Skellington and Sally.

I was super proud of this cake, and I hummed the *Nightmare Before Christmas* soundtrack as I carefully made all the decorations, carving them out of fondant and drizzling shapes in royal icing.

When I went to the fridge to check my cakes, they were cool. I carefully carried them back to my station then evened up the tops and assembled all the layers.

I had the first cake frosted and covered in fondant and was carefully setting the next layer in place when Keeley let out a scream.

"She sabotaged me!" she yelled. "Morticia tried to ruin me." My cousin came storming over to me, holding several bowls of melty, soupy cake and ice cream.

"You couldn't handle that I was going to win and be Mrs. Frost and that Jonathan was going to fall in love with me," Keeley sobbed, "so you ruined my dessert!"

"I didn't touch your dessert," I retorted.

"Yes you did," she cried, tears rolling down her face. "Look at it."

The melted ice cream in the bowl sloshed. I cursed as I tried to keep it from landing on my cake.

"Now I won't have a dessert," Keeley blubbered dramatically.

"I bet you just forgot about it," I said brusquely.

"You don't even care!" Keeley cried. "That's how I know you ruined it."

"Just look at the footage," I countered. "You'll see that I didn't touch it."

Anastasia hurried over with Dana. "We actually don't have any footage of that area," Dana admitted, tablet in hand. "The fire the other day ruined the camera feed to that area. We see Morticia go over to the blast freezer," she narrated as the video played.

"Yes," I said tersely. "I was going to fetch my cakes."

"You were going to sabotage me!" my cousin interjected.

"Keeley," Dana pleaded, "can you just redo the dessert?"

"I'll try," she said. "But it's not going to be right."

She sniffled, and I turned back to my cake.

"I bet she did that herself," Lilith muttered, ducking next to my station.

"Did you see her do it?" I whispered.

"No," she admitted. "I was too busy moderating comments on the *Bake-Off* Instagram account. For some reason, there are a ton of trolls out. Dana begged me and Emma to help them comb through comments. It's nasty."

"What are they saying?"

My twin looked cagey. "Oh, you know, the usual…"

"It's not about me, is it?"

"They just feel like you're not a good match for Jonathan, that you're too thorny and opinionated, and he deserves better," she admitted.

"Geez." My heart sank.

"You can't listen to what people write on the internet," my twin insisted. "They're all just jealous. You still have a small but vocal fan base that is arguing with them."

I blew out a breath. Lilith rubbed my shoulders.

"Eyes on the prize. You're going to win the guy, the bake-off, the internship, and the scholarship," she said, pep talking me. "After this, we're going out for drinks, and who knows! We might even splurge and head to New Jersey for an all-you-can-eat buffet!"

"Yes, because nothing says celebration like an all-you-can-eat buffet," I said with a snort as I started on the next cake layer.

Lilith stole a scrap of the chocolate cake I had cut off to even it out. "Yum! You have this in the bag, sister."

I hoped so. When my cake was finally finished, I placed the figures of Jack and Sally on the tip-top, right where the frosting made that signature Tim Burton curl.

"Time!" Anastasia called.

Keeley burst into tears. "My cake isn't great, and it's all her fault."

"Oh, for crying out loud!" I said, rolling my eyes. "It's all your fault, Keeley. Instead of actually trying to do a good job, you decided to concoct this elaborate sabotage plan."

Keeley cried louder. "Why are you so mean to me?"

"Oh, for the love of—can we just get on with the judging?" I demanded.

"It's Christmas," Keeley bawled. "Why can't you be nicer to me? I'm your family."

Because a few Christmases ago, you got me locked up in a psych ward! I wanted to scream. But that was not going to look good on camera.

I hissed out a breath. "And people wonder why I hate Christmas."

Anastasia's eyes widened slightly.

"Well," she said, "Keeley, since your dessert is in a precarious position, why don't you go first?"

My cousin sniffled and wheeled her cake over to the judges' table.

"I made a baked Alaska peppermint bark cake," she said. "This was the cake I always dreamed of as a little girl. I wanted a white Christmas wedding with the winter prince of my dreams." She sliced into it, and half-melted ice cream oozed out.

Keeley started crying again.

Anu took a piece of the cake, scooping it with a spoon. "The flavors are really nice," she told Keeley gently.

"You know," Nick said, "sometimes things don't work out as you planned them, but you have to roll with it."

"Just like in a relationship," Anu said and winked.

Keeley sniffled and nodded.

Jonathan looked slightly perturbed and poked at the soupy mixture. "You can't get so hysterical. This is baking, after all," he remarked. "It's not like lives are on the line."

"But there is money and love on the line," Anastasia piped up. "Let's see our next contestant. Morticia, could you show us your dessert?"

"This is a beautiful cake," Anu said when I wheeled it over.

Jonathan had a soft smile on his face.

"I don't know," Nick said, frowning as he sliced off a piece. "I never did like cartoon characters on cakes. It feels a little childish."

"There's nothing childish about Christmas," I quipped. "Adults can enjoy a Christmas movie."

"But if you look back on previous *Bake-Offs* with Holly and Chloe," Nick said, "they had elegant, sophisticated desserts, and you have Disney."

"It's Tim Burton!"

Nick shrugged. "I mean, the cake itself is nice. It's just not restaurant quality. Compared to some of your earlier dishes, this just isn't doing it for me."

"I like it," Jonathan stated. "I would serve this at a holiday party."

❄ ❄ ❄

I paced around in the lobby, refreshing Instagram and reading through the comments while we waited for all the votes to come in. People were being pretty mean online. The camps were split on whether I had sabotaged Keeley.

There was also a knockdown, drag-out fight in progress about whether cartoons and especially Disney were only for kids. I was happy to see the Tim Burton fans come out in full force. Someone had posted the snippets of video on the Disney superfan forums, and people were responding in droves.

"Belle said she's about ready to nuke the whole Instagram account," Lilith joked as she and Emma came into the lobby after they had finished taking pictures of the desserts. "It's all over the gossip sites now. There's betting. It's a fever pitch—everyone is trying to get their votes in."

"Are they worried the system is going to crash?"

"Apparently ThinkX and Quantum Cyber have it under control," Lilith said. "Owen Frost and two of the Svenssons are overseeing the voting. They have a whole war room set up like it's a military operation."

I looked down at my phone to see a particularly nasty insult pop up on the Facebook feed.

"Baking and Christmas are serious business, apparently."

"Your comment on not liking Christmas didn't help matters," Lilith reminded me.

"More like gasoline on a Victorian candle-lit Christmas tree," Emma joked.

"How are my chances?"

"The bookies say Keeley is the favorite to win."

"Crap."

"Hey, at least you're nabbing the internship," Lilith said.

At that moment, my phone rang, displaying a number with a California area code.

My heart pounded.

"Morticia speaking," I answered, trying to stay cool.

"Ah, Morticia, this is Zarah with the Getty Museum."

"Hi," I said. "I'm so glad you called."

"I wanted to personally give you the news," Zarah began.

Lilith and Emma were silently jumping up and down with joy.

"We are not offering you the scholarship or the internship. I wanted to have a woman-to-woman talk about that," she said forcefully.

"Wait, what, why? Why are you not offering it?" I begged, feeling like I was going to pass out.

"You were on the top of our list," Zarah said. "Your art piece was powerful, evocative, and rule breaking, and we loved it. And your resumé, especially with your involvement in the Art Zurich Biennial Expo in Harrogate, was also a huge selling point."

"Right," I said weakly. "Then why…"

"However," Zarah said, "when we heard that you weren't planning on accepting, obviously we went with the next candidate."

"Wait!" I cried. "That's not—"

"You cannot rearrange your life because of a man," Zarah lectured. "Jonathan may be rich, hot, and good in bed, but you can't throw away your ambitions just because he wants you to sacrifice your career so you can support him in his shady endeavors."

"I was going to accept," I said hoarsely. "I wanted this opportunity. Why would you think I wasn't going to accept?"

"Interesting," Zarah said. "When I talked to your boyfriend at the Christmas party the other night, he was very emphatic that he had a job for you and that there was absolutely no way you were accepting that internship. He said you were staying with him."

"I—" I couldn't breathe, let alone talk.

"I hope you make better choices in the future," Zarah said in a clipped tone. "Once you come to your senses, you're free to apply next year."

"Oh my god," I said, sinking to the floor. "That bastard! That fucking prick!"

Lilith wrapped her arms around me.

"I can't fucking believe this," I choked out. "He ruined my life; he ruined my dream."

"It's okay to cry," Emma said, rubbing my back.

"I'm not going to cry," I hissed through gritted teeth.

That fucker.

CHAPTER 64

Jonathan

Morticia and Keeley stood in front of the judges' table a few hours later. Morticia looked unhappy. I smiled at her, but she turned away from me.

"Bake-off fans, we have the votes tallied. Thanks to everyone for a wonderful season and to all our contestants for participating," Anastasia said to the cameras. "Just to remind everyone, on the line are bragging rights, a cash bonus, and Jonathan, who is the real prize."

As Anastasia opened the envelope, I held my breath. It had to be Morticia. I wanted the perfect Christmas with the woman I loved.

"The winner is Keeley! Congratulations!" Anastasia said.

Keeley jumped up and down, screaming. "Oh my god!" she squealed. "I won! I won!" She grabbed the microphone from Anastasia. "I just want to thank all my fans and everyone who voted for me. You made it possible for me to meet the love of my life."

Morticia's expression didn't changed. What was she thinking?

"Baby!" Keeley yelled, tottering over to me in her high heels. "We're going to have such a merry Christmas."

I couldn't look at her; I could only look at Morticia. Was she heartbroken? She didn't seem to be. Her face was a porcelain mask.

"Morticia, do you have anything you want to say to the fans?" Anastasia offered.

Morticia looked straight at the camera. "Jonathan and Keeley deserve each other and this bullshit holiday." Then she turned and stalked out.

I wanted to run after her, but Keeley had me in a vise grip. When I finally disentangled myself, I ran into the hallway, looking wildly for Morticia. She was tightening the belt on her black trench coat.

"Morticia!" I called. I knew she had heard me, because she flinched but then pushed through the double doors and headed outside.

"Morticia, wait!" I called, running to catch up to her. I grabbed her by the upper arms. "I know you're disappointed, but I don't have to do the spin-off show with Keeley," I assured her. "You and I can just keep a low profile until the three months are up, and I break up with her."

"You better not do that," Morticia replied mildly.

I was confused. "Why? I don't understand."

Morticia blinked at me. "I'm certainly not hanging around you and being your girlfriend."

"Look," I said reassuringly, "the thing with Keeley—it's just a show; it's not real. I don't even like her. I love you."

"No you don't," she spat.

"I do, honestly. I'd do anything for you," I pleaded.

She pushed me off. "Fuck you. You wouldn't do anything for me. In fact, you actively sought to sabotage my life."

"No, I—"

"And now you're fucking lying about it!" She ran a hand through her hair. "Oh my god, I can't believe I ever trusted you!"

"Oh shit, you found out." My mind raced, trying to find a way to spin the lie.

"Of course I found out," she screeched. "Did you honestly think you were going to get away with it?"

"Let me explain," I said in a rush. "It was Greg's idea; he wanted me to make you fall in love with me to convince you to convince Dorothy to sell us the property. I told him it was a dumb idea. I had no intention of actually using you like that. I had already been attracted to you. And then, after spending time with you, I fell in love with you! I just had to get him off my case. Of course I'm not going to try and pull a fast one over on Dorothy. But maybe," I pleaded, "you could help us negotiate with her to agree to a few more towers. Then I think Greg would be on board."

Morticia's mouth hung open, and her eyes were wide. "You fucking piece of lying shit. You did what?"

"Er...I thought you found out?"

"I found out," she hissed, "about how you told the Getty Museum that I had no intention of taking the position or the scholarship and torpedoed my chances of moving up in the art world."

"Oh, that!" I laughed nervously.

Morticia advanced on me.

I took a step back. "I thought we agreed that you were going to stay here and work at my company and work on the Hamilton Yards development," I said in a rush.

"Right," she said, teeth bared. "The Hamilton Yards development. The development that you were going to screw my friend Dorothy on. That development. Well, guess what. I'm going to make sure that development never happens. I'm going to screw you over like you screwed me."

"I didn't mean to. I love you," I said hoarsely.

"Don't you dare claim to love me when you would ruin the Getty Museum opportunity for me!"

"I couldn't lose you," I begged, taking her hand and falling to my knees in front of her. "You don't understand. Everyone always leaves me—Sarah, my sisters, my own mother. I couldn't lose you. I just couldn't!"

Morticia snatched her hand back. "Did you ever consider," she said, her tone bitter, "that you're the reason they all leave."

I stared up at Morticia. With her dark hair and clothes, she was silhouetted against the winter sky. "Sometimes," I said in a quiet voice.

But there would be no mercy. She turned slowly then looked over her shoulder. "You deserve to be alone."

CHAPTER 65

Morticia

It was like a scene out of one of those angsty anime shows—Jonathan left alone, kneeling on the cold concrete, snow falling around him, and me striding away in my black trench coat.

"I could have been packing for sunny California right now," I seethed as I stalked off. Now I had nothing.

Footsteps crunched behind me in the snow.

"Oh my god," Emma said as she and Lilith ran up to me with Salem hanging onto Lilith's purse strap.

"You really told him off," Lilith said. "And now you're hitting him where it hurts: in his wallet."

"Come," Emma commanded. "You need a drink—not a distillery drink, because I'm sure, after that little display, Jonathan has cut off our expense account."

"I have to do something first," I told them. I headed across the street to enter the industrial property that Dorothy owned.

The older woman was in her converted container studio, happily painting what looked like a flower morphing into a vagina.

"There's the girl I wanted to see! Did they call you about the Getty Internship yet?" she asked, setting down her paintbrush.

I immediately started crying. Dorothy hustled to pour me a drink and shoved me down on the couch while I explained the depths of my stupidity.

"You haven't signed anything yet, have you?" I asked.

"Oh no, of course not," Dorothy assured me.

"I can't believe he was using me this whole time." I blew my nose. "I never should have vouched for him to begin with," I said dejectedly. "You trusted me, and I let you down."

Dorothy wrapped me in a hug. "The pretty ones are always dangerous," she said kindly. "Nothing's been signed, so no harm done. Well, not to me, anyway. You look like you've been through the wringer."

"At least he has to be subjected to Keeley," I said grimly. "That seems like suitable punishment, though I could have used the prize money."

"That hussy beat you out?" Dorothy demanded. She lifted her glasses and peered at a wall clock that looked as if it had been made from a junkyard in *Alice and Wonderland*. "Shoot, I can never read that dang thing, and I missed the winner's announcement."

"They gave it to Keeley after she served everyone melted ice cream," I explained.

"They deserve each other," Dorothy assured me, handing me a whiskey.

"I'm sure she's going to make him miserable," I said. Then I started crying again.

My phone buzzed as Dorothy was pouring me another drink.

Dana: *You need to come by and pick up your final payment.*

I was half-tempted to tell her to keep it, but apparently now I did need the money, as I was internshipless and jobless.

I trudged back up to the studio. Workers were already dismantling the set. It was going to be as if the bake-off had never happened.

Dana was waiting in the production office with Gunnar. *Guess Belle couldn't face me herself.*

Not that I wanted anything to do with any of the Frosts or the Svenssons for that matter.

"Here's your check," Gunnar said, handing it over to me. "If you could wait to cash it until the New Year, that would be much appreciated for the tax benefits."

"Your brothers have already tried to screw me over; don't start with me," I warned him. "I'm cashing this check this evening, and if it bounces, I'm taking it out of your flesh."

Gunnar gulped.

Dana laughed. "Don't come between a girl and her money!" she said. "And I believe I did promise you a sculpture in the Holbrook Enterprises tower," she added. "Or are you leaving? I thought Lilith mentioned you won an internship in Los Angeles."

"No," I seethed. "I didn't get it."

"Don't feel too bad," she assured me. "These internships are all scams. They overwork you and take credit for everything you do. Building this sculpture is going to be much more beneficial to your career as an artist."

"I guess," I mumbled.

"Besides," Dana added. "We're going to be doing a wedding-themed show in the spring, and it's good that I know you'll be in town, because we will want your and Lilith's help. The social media game on this was on point this year, and it was all thanks to you! Have a Merry Christmas!" Dana waved me out of her office.

Workers pushed past me with boxes, rushing to pack. Christmas Eve was the day after tomorrow. I was sure they wanted to go home to their families.

I, unfortunately, had nowhere to go. I stood outside the studio, looking up at the softly falling snow. I had told Penny and Garrett they could renovate the carriage house in Harrogate because I had been so sure I would be going to Los Angeles for that internship. I didn't want to stay in the main house with them and be subjected to their in-love-ness.

Strains of holiday music floated along the cool breeze. Someone somewhere was baking cookies.

"I hate Christmas!" I yelled up into the sky.

I never should have become involved with Jonathan.

My phone beeped with an incoming email message. It was from the Getty Museum! My heart soared. Maybe they were rethinking their decision. I could go to California and forget all about Jonathan.

But when I opened the email, all it said was that they were shipping my project back to me. I sagged.

"There you are," Lilith said as she and Emma came out of the studio, lugging boxes of equipment. "We need to take all our stuff back to Emma's," she said. "And look!" She held up a plastic Tupperware container. "I have leftover cake."

"We'll buy all the junk food on the way. Pizza, pasta, and those buttery garlic knots. Oh, and Chinese!" Emma said. I took one of the boxes from her, and we walked through the snow to the subway. "And pretzels."

※ ※ ※

"Tell us," Emma asked as we stuffed ourselves, "what sculpture are you going to put in the Holbrooks' lobby?"

I lay back on her twin bed, which doubled as the couch and the dining table. "I'm going to build a tree house so I have somewhere to live," I said.

"Aw, you can stay here," Emma assured me as she unwrapped a chili cheese dog.

"You should build a giant dildo," Lilith suggested, swiping fries in cheese sauce.

"Holbrook Enterprises is a conservative company. The sculpture will probably end up being something boring and generic."

"Hey, if they pay, they can have whatever they want!"

Emma opened a carton of sesame noodles. "So not a peep from Jonathan?"

"Nope." I sighed. And then my phone went off.

"Speak of the ghost of Christmas sexy times," Lilith said. She grabbed my phone and handed it to me.

The food was lead in my stomach as I read the message.

Jonathan: *You're such a fucking hypocrite.*

There on the screen was a picture of my art piece.

CHAPTER 66

Jonathan

I was still sitting outside in the blowing snow after Morticia left. I had moved to a bench after almost getting run over by a production assistant who was backing a truck up for loading.

Now I was sitting on a bench. It was like when I was a kid and my mom was supposed to pick me up from a hockey game. She had promised she was coming, but I had sat outside long after the other kids had gone home, trying to make up excuses for why my mom had forgotten. Eventually, Belle had shown up and taken me home.

You deserve to be alone.

Morticia's words bounced around my head. She was right—I did deserve to be alone. I had lied to her, ruined her career, and used her for my own financial gain. That wasn't how you treated someone you loved. In fact, that was how my parents had treated me and my siblings.

They were shitty. I was shitty. The whole holiday season was shitty. I lay on the bench, and the snow pressed against my cheek, numbing it.

Someone shook my shoulder.

"You're ruining your suit," Belle said. "Come inside."

"I should just freeze to death out here."

"You owe Romance Creative money," she quipped. "So you can't die until you pay that off. Besides, you have more interviews to do. We have to sell the 'happy couple' narrative."

I groaned as I followed my older sister dejectedly into the studio.

She sighed. "I heard."

"I'm a terrible person."

"No argument here," Belle replied as she blotted my suit with a towel. "Seriously, this is a nice wool and you rolled around in the snow with it on," she said, unbuttoning my jacket.

"I'm a grown man," I complained. "I can clean myself."

She ignored me and ran a comb through my hair. "You're covered in leaves and snowflakes."

"What am I going to do?"

"You screwed up, so you need to fix it," she replied.

"I lost the development." I moaned, "When the Svenssons find out, they're going to ruin me."

"You just leave Greg to me," she replied tartly. "We're family. No one gets away with hurting my little brother. Unless you deserve it, of course." Belle rapped me lightly with the comb.

"How am I going to convince Morticia to forgive me?" I asked my sister.

"You can't," she said, "but you can at least make right what you did wrong."

"How?"

"You're a billionaire. I'm sure the Getty Museum will give her an internship if you make a sizeable enough donation. Money can be exchanged for goods and services," Belle quipped.

However, money could not be used to bribe such a renowned institution as the Getty Museum, as Zarah informed me forcefully over the phone. "I will not have you make a mockery of this institution."

"Surely," I said smoothly, "there is a precedent for this. I just want to pay you to have an internship position. Everyone wins."

"Except for our reputation. You may make a donation, but that will in no way influence an internship for Morticia. This year's interns have been selected already. However, we will happily take your money."

I blew out a breath when I hung up. "Now what? That didn't work."

"Now you have to pretend you can't wait to start the rest of your life with Keeley," my sister informed me.

I wanted to go home and stare at my Christmas tree and hope Morticia would appear and forgive me.

Instead, Belle led me over to two stools against a window that overlooked the courtyard behind the studio.

Morticia and I had sex over there.

"How do you feel about winning the bake-off?" Anastasia asked Keeley once the cameras were rolling. "And earning the chance to be Mrs. Jonathan Frost?"

Keeley was practically jumping up and down. "I can't wait! We're going to have a big holiday party with his family. I'll cook for everyone."

"Hopefully not ice cream soup," I muttered.

Keeley hit me playfully. "Oh, stop it! You're such a teaser. Isn't he such a flirt!" She giggled and mugged for the camera.

"And I believe you two are going to be moving in together in the next few days. There is a spin-off season of Jonathan and Keeley coming out for all you bake-off fans," Anastasia said, plugging the show.

"If you want to see the train wreck in real time, tune in," I added dryly.

"Such a kidder!" Keeley repeated. Her eye was twitching slightly.

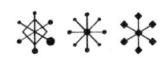

❋ ❋ ❋

"Dude," Carl said to me later that evening.

I had been instructed to take Keeley out on the town and get photographed by the paparazzi. Keeley had wanted to go to a restaurant, but I didn't have it in me to sit and pretend to be her boyfriend through a three-hour tasting menu. Instead, I took her to a club that the Svensson brothers had rented out for the night. Scores of them were in town, psyching themselves up to go to Harrogate for Christmas and New Year's.

"Greg is *pissed*. What the fuck happened, man?" Carl asked.

The lights from the club reflected in his eyes with the pulse of the music. His brothers had invited a number of hot models and dancers. The girls were drinking and flirting with the handsome, blond, rich Svenssons. Keeley had joined them on the dance floor once she realized I wasn't going to come dance with her.

All I wanted was Morticia. She would have hated it here, however.

In fact, even I didn't like it. It was strange, because usually this was totally my scene. But now, all I wanted was to be sitting by the fire in my condo with Morticia and our cats, talking and having a drink, with dinner in the oven. A Christmas movie we'd seen a hundred times before would be on, and we would be chatting over it while periodically making sardonic comments.

Carl snapped his fingers in front of my face. "Dude," he said, "do you not understand? Greg is going to go ballistic. He thinks you spilled the beans on purpose. Now he's got Weston and Blade chasing conspiracy theories. He thinks you're in league with the Holbrooks."

I shook my head. "Morticia found out."

"But how? I thought you had it in the bag," Carl asked.

"I fucked up," I admitted.

Carl blew out a breath. "Dorothy called a meeting for tomorrow. I'm hoping that we can sweet-talk her into continuing the deal. You need to be on your A game," he warned me.

"I'll be there tomorrow," I said, rubbing two fingers on my temple. "Maybe we'll work something out."

My heart wasn't in it. I didn't think I could even stay in the same condo now that Morticia wasn't going to be there.

"I loved her so much," I said.

"Her?" Carl wrinkled his nose. "I thought you were over her."

"Morticia? No! It's only been a few hours!" I exclaimed.

"Oh," Carl said, "I thought you were talking about *her*." He jerked his chin. Coming in our direction was Sarah.

"Jonathan," she cooed, running to me.

I stepped away from her. "I'm not getting back together with you, Sarah."

"Oh, so you're going to pine over Morticia but not me?" She pouted.

"You left me," I snarled, "and didn't even tell me what had happened. I didn't know what I had done. Then it just turned out you got what, bored? Tired?"

"I made a mistake!" she cried. "I was young and stupid! But I love you!"

I shrugged. "It's too late."

Sarah breathed heavily. "It doesn't matter. You'll come crawling back to me soon enough once you face the reality of the situation."

"Carl," I said to my friend, "can you have security throw her out?"

Sarah opened the large black folder she was carrying. "You can throw me out," she said, "but not before you see these."

She handed me several large prints on photo paper. I peered at them in the darkness. Carl turned on his phone flashlight and shined it on the papers.

"Holy shit! Who is that? Are those people doing it? And why are there baked goods and cupcakes and shit all over their faces? Still," he added, "it is pretty hot."

"Did you make this?" I growled at Sarah.

"That's not me," she said, "though it is two people we all know."

I peered at the pictures.

Carl said, "Uh, Jonathan, isn't that the tattoo you got that St. Patrick's Day when we drank that rancid Sheridan's and were basically hallucinating?"

I felt sick.

Sarah smirked. "I didn't make these—these are recent photos." She tapped the female figure that was present in a few of the areas of the collage. "It seems Morticia didn't actually want you for your sparkling personality. It looks to me like she was using you."

"Why?" I asked desperately.

"Oh, I don't know," Sarah drawled. "I heard her talking about some scholarship she needed to win."

Carl was alarmed. "Morticia didn't publish this or sell the rights, did she? This painting cannot go up online. People will think you're crazy. This is, like, weird sex shit. Why did you let her take all these pictures?"

"I didn't think she was going to make a fucking shrine out of this! What the fuck?" I shouted furiously. She was going to ruin my reputation!

"A little something you don't know about Morticia," Sarah said. "She has a pattern of creepy obsessions. When we were in high school, she stalked this kid named Justin and tried to poison him. She claimed it was a love potion. They hauled her off to the loony bin."

"What the fuck? She didn't tell me any of this. Holy shit." I turned on my heel, not even bothering to look for my suit jacket. "That fucking bitch." If this collage hit the internet, it would ruin all the progress I had made with the Hillrock West Distillery brand. And for her to be all high and mighty that I had deceived her... "That fucking bitch."

I texted her angrily on the car ride over to her friend's apartment. I had Emma's address on file from the accounting department. When I arrived, all it took was a smile to a tipsy group of girls coming out of the building, and I was in, pounding up the stairs to the apartment.

"Jonathan!" Morticia said in shock when she opened the door. "Let me explain…"

"Explain!" I exploded. I threw the pictures at her. "You are a lunatic," I spat. "You made some sort of demented art project about me."

"It wasn't about that," she pleaded.

"Don't try and lie. Your cousin Sarah told me all about your stalker issues, which you also never told me about. So who was really using who, huh?"

"I—" She shrugged helplessly. "I needed to win the scholarship."

I barked out a laugh. "And to think I was feeling bad that I cost you the position. I can't believe I even missed you. To be honest, it's good you're out of my life."

"Fuck you!" she forced out, her hands clenched into fists. "I don't have a bunch of rich family members propping up my terrible business dealings. I have to hustle."

"You think I didn't work hard for my money?" I demanded.

"No!" she said. Tears leaked from her eyes, smearing her black eyeliner and mascara. "I don't think that you work hard. You just bounce around the world like an idiot man-child, and people give you chance after chance and bend over backward for you to be successful. For fuck's sake, until I came along, you were struggling to sell alcohol. Alcohol! In America!"

"You're just upset because someone finally called you out on your shit," I snarled. "You like to pretend that you're so above everything, that you're too cool for Christmas, and you're some independent woman. And yet you stalked some poor boy in high school and freaked him out so much they hauled you off to a mental institution."

"That is not what happened," she cried. "Keeley mixed up a poisonous concoction, gave it to Justin, then lied and told everyone I did it. Of course they didn't believe me, because who's going to believe the poor parentless girl with the black makeup when they could believe Keeley with her bouncing blond curls and stable home life?" She wiped her face, smearing the dark makeup further. "You know why I hate Christmas? Because that December, I had to spend Christmas in a horrific psych ward through no fault of my own. You think Christmas is about family and giving, but it's not. It's about money and power and people who lord that over the people they claim to care about most."

She pinched her nose and took a few breaths. Then she looked up at me. Her expression wasn't angry anymore, just sad. "I am sorry, Jonathan, that I made that collage. They're shipping it back to me, and when it arrives, I'll burn it. Just do yourself a favor and stay away from Keeley. She'll ruin your business and your life."

She shut the door quietly in my face. I wished she would have slammed it.

I believed Morticia. I believed every word. Keeley had always rubbed me the wrong way. Who could set up their own family member like that? Spending Christmas in a psych ward—it sounded horrible.

Do not feel sorry for her, I told myself. *She could have ruined your business.*

But no harm no foul, right?

I stared at the closed door. I wanted to knock on it and beg her to talk, but there was too much between us. I needed some holiday magic to mend the chasm, but there wasn't any. There was only the cold wind of winter.

CHAPTER 67

Morticia

My friends stared at me in shock after I shut the door in Jonathan's face.

"Holy shit," Lilith said after a moment.

"I think I need to find somewhere else to live." I rubbed my arm and looked down at the floor. "There's an artist's retreat in the winter in Florida."

"There are snakes and aggressive iguanas there," Emma told me. "You don't want to move to Florida."

I slumped down on the floor beside the bed. "I shouldn't have made that collage," I groaned.

"Fair is fair. Jonathan cost you the scholarship."

"That I won because I made art of him without his consent. Maybe I do belong in a psych ward." I tipped my head back and stared at the cracks in the plaster ceiling.

"Men can make anyone criminally insane," Lilith assured me. She cut off a slightly smushed piece of the cake

I had made for the bake-off and handed it to me. "You need chocolate and sugar."

"And alcohol!" Emma added. "We're going to stick to wine, though, since that is not produced by you-know-who's company."

❄ ❄ ❄

The next morning, I still didn't have any clarity.

I didn't know where I was going to live. I didn't know where I was going to work. And it was the day before Christmas Eve. The city, normally bustling, had emptied out. Snow flurries erupted every so often, belching big, fat flakes that slid down the back of my neck as Lilith and I trudged across town to meet with our friend Holly. Emma had a meeting for her investment group with Dana and Belle.

The gray sky and empty streets were depressing. Everyone who was out was clearly doing last-minute Christmas shopping or taking their kids for one more visit to Santa Claus. I, however, was filled with existential dread at having to spend Christmas alone, unable to even go to a restaurant. Instead, I would be forced to contemplate the terrible reality of my life.

The lobby of the Quantum Cyber building was empty when Lilith, Salem, and I walked in. Holly, Owen Frost's fiancée, was sitting on a barstool behind the glass case, reading *War and Peace*.

"That's heavy for the holidays," Lilith remarked.

Holly laughed and peeled back the cover of the book to reveal the actual title.

"*His Curvy Alien Holiday Abduction*," I read.

"Don't judge me!" Holly said. "I needed something to pass the time. Owen's employees all left at the beginning of this week. There are some people in the hotel upstairs, so I'm a little busier in the evening, before the hotel restaurant opens, but it's been boring."

She pulled out two sandwiches from the glass case and stuck them in the panini maker. "On the house," Holly said. Then she leaned on the counter and looked at me. "I'm still shocked that you, of all people, were in *The Great Christmas Bake-Off*."

"And I wish I had never done it," I complained. "It was such a disaster."

"At least you got paid for it," Lilith reminded me.

Holly sighed. "I wish it had worked out with Jonathan. I was looking forward to being your sister-in-law."

"Whoa, whoa, we weren't like that," I insisted. "We were barely even dating." But a part of me had wanted a happily ever after with him.

"Really?" Lilith asked incredulously. "Because you were obsessed with him."

I cringed.

"And not just sexually," my twin added. "You were constantly over at his place, making him food, taking care of his cat, and watching Christmas movies. You were really happy when he texted you."

"The way Owen recounted his brother talking about you," Holly added, "Jonathan already had your whole lives together planned out."

"He did?" I shook my head. "It doesn't matter. He lied. I lied. The whole relationship has been nuked from orbit."

"Maybe you can give him another chance," Holly suggested. "The holidays make everything heightened emotionally. You could try again in the New Year."

"But he ruined my scholarship opportunity," I protested. "He went behind my back."

Lilith looked away. The panini maker sounded, and Holly scooped out the sandwiches, cut them into triangles, and set them on the little metal café table.

I picked up one of the ham-and-Swiss triangles, the cheese pulling as I took a bite.

"Can I be real?" Lilith said.

"Yeah."

"I'm glad you aren't going to California," my twin said bluntly.

I sucked in an angry breath. "You—"

"Wait!" She held up a hand. "You're my twin sister. We do everything together. I know that you will eventually have your own life, but I want you to have it, you know, very close to me. Like, live on the same street. I was worried that if you went to California, you would maybe meet someone or just decide to stay there. And then I might never see you again."

"It's not like I was going to the New World," I said softly, "where we're a three-month boat ride apart."

"I know," Lilith said, "but California is on the other side of the country."

"It was my dream job."

"Was it?" Holly wrinkled her nose. "Wouldn't you have to sit in a windowless room, looking at old paintings and trying to restore them for basically no money?"

"It's prestigious," I argued. "It's the Getty Museum."

"I thought your dream was always to own your own art studio and have people pay you a ton of money to do sculptures and humongous paintings," Holly countered.

"Sometimes you have to change your dreams," I said.

"Or sometimes you just have to go for it!" Holly exclaimed.

"I've been going for it for years," I complained.

"You had tons of great pieces at the Art Biennial," Holly reminded me. "That's momentum."

"And," Lilith add, "you're doing a big sculpture for the Holbrooks."

Holly nodded. "I told Owen we should do a big sculpture in here! Something interactive."

In spite of myself, I was excited about the large sculpture. I hadn't been looking forward to actually doing the Getty internship, just to having done it so it would look good on my resumé.

"Arguably," Lilith went on, "you were more excited about Jonathan and Dorothy's crackpot development scheme than you were about spending a year chained to a restoration table."

I fumed. "I can't believe he was using me to score Hamilton Yards."

"Yeah, I have no excuses for that behavior," Holly said, eating the last of the panini triangles. "But," she continued, "if you loved him, maybe you should at least let him grovel and apologize."

I thought about Jonathan and about how concerned he had been that I was going to leave him, how shitty his parents had acted, and how he had gone out of his way to find dresses I liked. I remembered how easy it was to be around him and how I didn't feel on edge with him, as if I constantly had to pretend to be something I wasn't. I remembered how he had walked into his apartment, found a cat, and immediately decided she was his baby. He was primary colors with beautiful, big, strong emotions.

Was I ready to walk away from that?

My phone dinged with an incoming text. It was a picture of Cindy Lou Who looking sad.

> **Jonathan:** *I suck, and I'm sorry. Here's a cat showing how sad I am.*

Salem nudged my hand. He probably recognized Cindy Lou.

Holly read over my shoulder. "Is that the cat you found?"

"Yeah. Jonathan kept her."

Holly peered at the picture. "Is she wearing a sapphire collar and a fur-trimmed hat?"

"Jonathan spoils her rotten," I said with a soft smile. "She has her own room in his house, with a closet and everything."

Get it together, I ordered myself, though my heart wasn't really in it.

"Are you going to go at least hear him out?" Lilith asked.

"No." The rational part of me was back in control.

"Really? You might be able to swing a condo out of it," Lilith wheedled. "We wouldn't have to live in Emma's apartment."

"I'm not forgiving him," the rational part of me decided, though the hopeless romantic in me was shrieking in protest.

But before I could compose the nasty message, heels clicked on the marble floor of the large atrium.

"And look at all the losers gathered here. Especially the biggest of them all," Sarah taunted. "I told you Jonathan was mine." My cousin smirked. "I ruined Keeley, and I kicked you to the curb. Victory smells so good. He and I are spending Christmas together, of course."

"Doubtful," I said.

"You better believe it," she replied. "I was just on a talk show with him." She looked me up and down. "Of course, he wasn't going to want you for real. You're just a garbage girl with no parents and stalker tendencies. I'm the one he loves and has always loved. I've been pulling the strings this whole time! You were never going to be with him. He's vulnerable and heartbroken right now due to Keeley's and your betrayal," she bragged. "Now's my time to move in and remind him how much he loved me." She laughed. "I'm ovulating right now. I just have to convince him to sleep with me, and I'll get pregnant. Then Jonathan is mine forever!"

I stood up, eyes narrowed. As angry as I was at Jonathan, I would not allow him to be tied to my insane cousin for the rest of his life.

"Just try me."

CHAPTER 68

Jonathan

I spent all night moping about Morticia.

Had I been too harsh with her? If I had just come at it a different way, said that I saw the collage and that I was fine with it, and could we please get back together, then maybe all would have been forgiven, and I could have had the merry Christmas I dreamed of. Instead, I had blown it. I'd had the perfect chance to win her back and salvage the real estate deal.

Now it was morning. I had had no sleep. I was hungover. And I had a meeting with the Svenssons and Dorothy.

Cindy Lou Who sat outside the shower as I stood under the freezing water, trying to clear my head. Unfortunately, the cold couldn't clear my broken heart.

Greg and Carl Svensson were waiting in the lobby of my office building when I headed in.

"Your receptionist said that Dorothy is already upstairs," Carl told me as we headed to the elevators.

"I don't know why you're late," Greg spat without even greeting me. "Considering that Carl said you left early last night."

I yawned.

"Do you even care about this deal?" Greg demanded.

Turning to him, I replied, "Honestly, no. I just lost the love of my life because I was stupid."

"And you're about to lose the deal of a lifetime if you don't shape up," Greg warned. "The old lady seems to like you. Don't screw this up for me."

Dorothy was pouring whiskey into her coffee when we walked in. "You boys are up early!"

"Got enough of that to share?" I asked her.

She slid the mug over to me and patted my hand.

Greg started in. "First, I just wanted to thank you for meeting with us on such short notice," he said smoothly. "We understand that Jonathan has not been conducting himself in a manner befitting the type of individual Svensson Investment does business with. We would be more than happy to continue pursuing the Hamilton Yards development without Mr. Frost on the team."

I stared at Greg. "You're throwing me under the bus!" I said in shock.

"Jonathan," Greg said irritably, "you lied to Dorothy and manipulated Morticia."

"It was your idea," I snarled at him.

"Don't be preposterous!" Greg thundered. "Ms. Dorothy, don't believe a word Jonathan says. He's a liar. I can assure you that he won't be doing business in Manhattan again."

I started to protest, but she cut me off.

"Honestly, Greg," Dorothy remarked. She took a sip of her whiskey and coffee. "I just called this meeting as a courtesy to you all. I know you put a lot of work into this development proposal. However, I have decided to go with another development company. It's not personal; they just offered me a better deal."

"Who is it?" Greg demanded. "Is it the Harringtons? Or is it the Holbrooks?"

"I'm not going to divulge anyone's trade secrets, and nothing's been officially signed—still have to have the lawyers look over everything—but I'm sure you'll hear soon enough." She pushed her chair back and downed the rest of the coffee.

"Merry Christmas, boys. I hope Santa brings you something nice."

❄ ❋ ❆

There was going to be nothing nice for me for Christmas.

Christmas Eve was in less than twelve hours. I had told my brothers I was going to host a Christmas Eve party. However, I hadn't even shopped for it. I didn't have the energy to even try and pretend I knew how to put a menu together. I had been banking on Morticia and my mom being there. In my head, I had had the perfect holiday constructed. Now none of it was coming to pass.

I ran a hand through my hair as I prepared for my *TechBiz Evening Business Report* TV appearance.

There had been rumors circulating about my big development deal. The host was surely going to ask for information. I needed to come up with some answers about why it had fallen through. Honestly, though, I didn't care about the real estate deal. I didn't care that I was on the *TechBiz* show to talk about my unusual and creative path to being a young billionaire. I just wanted Morticia. I missed her.

I forced myself to relax and be charming as the TV host introduced me.

"And with us today is our newest billionaire wunderkind, Jonathan Frost, who has become a billionaire not through cryptocurrency or a social media app but through something very analogue, a physical product—probably one of the oldest in human history: alcohol."

The host smiled up at me as I offered a perfunctory air kiss to her cheek.

"Can you tell us a little bit about your vision for the Hillrock West Distillery?" the host asked me, annoyingly chipper.

"Well," I said, trying to act as if I was paying attention and engaged, "I had started my hedge fund, and we didn't want to invest in the standard tech and energy stocks. We wanted to differentiate ourselves. There was a need to distribute craft liquor nationally, and we jumped in to fill it. And our results speak for themselves."

"They sure do!" the host said. "And so do your Instagram ads. Wowza!"

A picture of me with very little clothing on popped up on the screen behind us.

"I'm sure all the other hedge funds that aren't headed by an investor with model good looks wish they had you as their secret weapon!" the host said with a giggle.

"The credit goes to the marketing team," I said, inwardly wincing. I remembered when Morticia had taken that picture.

"Because it's Christmas," the host continued, "we're doing a fun segment for the holidays. We asked viewers to submit questions for you once we announced your scheduled appearance on the show."

Here we go. What was I going to say about the Hamilton Yards development?

"The number-one question that came up over and over again," she said, "was 'How can I turn my kid into a billionaire?' Now, we know you can't really answer that effectively, so we have some special guests to help you out. Dr. and Dr. Frost, welcome!"

I tried to keep my fake professional smile on as my parents strutted out.

"Dr. David Frost and Dr. Diane Frost," the host gushed, "thank you for joining us. We know you all are very busy. But please tell us how you managed to raise such a successful son."

My mother had her hostess smile on, the one that would fool guests at her Christmas parties into believing she was mother of the year and that we were all one big, happy family. "We raised our kids with a good work ethic and to be very independent and goal driven. And," she added with a fake laugh, "it doesn't hurt to have a great role model in my husband, Dr. Frost."

"That's right," my father boasted. "We receive a number of comments from friends and acquaintances about all our sons, but lately, they all want to know about Jonathan. It seems that he's really found a niche that other people who aren't creative thinkers have overlooked."

I couldn't believe it! This was what I had always wanted—my parents praising me and telling the world how proud they were of me. But it felt hollow. A part of me knew they didn't actually mean it and were just playing a part for their own gain.

"And you're okay with his participation in *The Great Christmas Bake-Off*?" the TV show host asked. "Romance Creative was recently sold to your daughter Belle's investment firm. We just received the numbers, and *The Great Christmas Bake-Off* was the highest-ranking show for weeks this month, so congrats on that."

My father worked his jaw then said, "I'm sure it's all in good fun."

"Do you expect Keeley to be your future daughter-in-law?"

"No!" A woman wearing a red Mrs. Claus outfit sprinted into the production studio, security guards and production assistants chasing her.

"I will not be silenced!" Sarah declared as she turned around and sprayed whipped cream in one of the guard's faces. "Jonathan will not be marrying Keeley!" Sarah declared, holding a tablet aloft. "Keeley has been cheating on him. She is in violation of the rules of *The Great Christmas Bake-Off*."

Sarah tapped the tablet, and on the screen played a very graphic home porno movie of someone who was obviously Keeley and a man who looked like one of the many blond Svensson brothers getting it on.

"See?" she declared triumphantly. "Keeley is done, and Morticia is down." She turned to me. "Jonathan, this means that you have to marry me."

"You're already married!" I said in horror. "Where is Trevor?"

"You've been carrying on with a married woman?" my father asked with a frown.

"Oh, don't even," I told my father with a sneer. "You come on here and act like you were father of the year, as if the last time we talked, you and Mom hadn't just insulted me and told me what a disappointment I was. I got to where I was in spite of you. And to be honest, I didn't do it by myself, either. I had the help of my family—my *real* family, namely Belle, who was more of a parent than either of you ever were."

"You take that back!" my father roared as my mom glared at me.

"It seems," I said, giving the hostess a toothy smile, "that I will be spending Christmas single this year. Seeing as how the sanctity of *The Great Christmas Bake-Off* was defiled."

Sarah threw her arms around me. "Jonathan, what we had was true love. We need to be together. I'll spend Christmas with you."

I took off the microphone and handed it to the host. "I have another meeting," I told her. I fumbled Sarah off of me then dodged as one of the security guards, whipped cream dripping down his shirt, grabbed her.

CHAPTER 69

Morticia

"Like you're going to stop me," Sarah mocked. "Jonathan doesn't even want to see you." She turned and ran outside.

I chased her.

Trevor was waiting in front of the building in an SUV. "Take me to the Hillrock West distillery," my cousin ordered.

I looked at Trevor incredulously. "You know she's going over there to declare her undying love for Jonathan, right?"

"No she's not," Trevor said stubbornly as Sarah jumped into the passenger's side of the car. "She's going over there to tell him off and get closure. Then we're going back to the nice hotel room I rented."

"Oy vey," Holly declared as they drove off.

"Are you just going to let them go?" Lilith asked me.

Salem howled his displeasure at being outside in the snow, which was wet!

"Hell no!" I called Jonathan to try and give him a heads-up, but he didn't answer.

Morticia: *Call me back!!! And don't talk to Sarah!*

No response.

I turned to Holly. "Can I borrow one of Owen's cars?"

She chewed her lip. "I don't know if I have the keys; let me text him."

"No, I meant 'borrow.'" I made air quotes.

Holly was horrified. "You're going to steal his car?"

"Not steal, borrow," I corrected, pulling out a screwdriver and a knife. "I'm sure Owen will forgive us once we save his little brother from an astronomical child-support payment."

Holly huffed after me as I ran back into the building.

"Since when do you know how to hot-wire a car?" my friend demanded.

"Please." I snorted. "This is just me going through life."

My friends and I raced out of the elevator to the fastest-looking black sports car. I stuck a flat piece of metal down between the glass and the window, wiggled it, popped the lock, then sat in the seat and stuck a screwdriver in the ignition.

"Oh my god, Morticia, don't ruin the car! Owen loves his cars!" Holly fretted.

I grabbed the wires in the steering wheel, cutting the plastic away then tapping them together until the engine roared to life.

"Lord help me, I need some cake and some wine," Holly moaned.

I revved the engine. "Let's go!"

"Oh no, I'm driving," Holly insisted. "It's a two-seater, and I've been stress eating all holiday season. I won't be able to fit in the seat with one of you." She shoved me over. Lilith and I crammed together in the passenger's seat.

"Drive fast," I told her as she adjusted the seat.

Holly turned on the radio. Weezer's "O Holy Night" blasted out, the electric guitar making the car vibrate.

"Whoo!" Holly yelled. She put the car in gear and slammed on the gas, and we careened around the parking deck to the exit.

"I think I'm going to hurl," Lilith grumbled as Holly peeled into traffic. In her lap, Salem made pukey *hork hork* noises.

"Hurry!" we yelled to Holly, who zipped around a semitruck.

On the way to Jonathan's office I tried texting and calling him. He didn't respond. Had Sarah already sunk her claws into him?

Holly took a sharp turn, and Lilith and I held on for dear life. "And you were worried about me ruining the car?" I shouted to Holly over the blaring music.

"We're on a mission to save Christmas!" she yelled back as we turned onto Jonathan's street.

It was snowing hard. Through the flurries, I could make out a man with no coat, clearly unconcerned about the snow, looking picturesque.

My heart jumped then jumped again as the car skidded a bit on the wet pavement when Holly screeched to a stop in front of Jonathan's condo.

Lilith flung open the door, and I climbed over her to stagger out.

"Morticia!" Jonathan exclaimed in shock.

CHAPTER 70

Jonathan

A Charlie Brown Christmas was playing on the TV when I returned to my condo. I had kept it on for Cindy Lou Who. The little gray cat pranced over, purring when she saw me.

"Christmas is coming, but I'm not happy. I don't feel the way I'm supposed to feel," Charlie Brown said on the TV.

"My life is a disaster," I told the cat as the Peanuts gang wandered around town in their winter gear. Outside it was snowing again: big, fat, wet flakes.

> **Jack:** *Owen told me what happened. I know you said you wanted to host a Christmas Eve party, but we can have it at Owen's place.*
> **Owen:** *Why are you volunteering me?*
> **Jonathan:** *No, I'll do it.*
> **Jack:** *Have you bought any food?*

No, I hadn't. I needed to, but I didn't have the energy. I wished Morticia were here.

Cindy Lou headbutted me and looked up at me with big eyes. I snapped a few pictures then sent the best, saddest-looking one to Morticia.

She didn't respond.

"What should I make for dinner, Cindy Lou?" I asked her, scratching behind her ears.

I was not a cook. I was better than Owen, who had once tried to make chicken, which had turned out burned on the outside and frozen on the inside. My skills weren't all that much better, though my food wasn't going to be raw.

I had had grand visions of a holiday party with ham and turkey and lots of Christmas-themed desserts.

I checked my fridge. "We could serve cheese," I suggested to Cindy Lou, poking at the hard block of cheddar. I checked the freezer. "And frozen peas."

The door to my condo beeped, and Cindy Lou raced to the front door. My heart clenched. Was it Morticia? I hadn't gotten the key back from her.

"Oh, hey, Belle." I sagged when I saw my sister.

"'Hey, Belle'?" my sister repeated with a quirk of her mouth.

I took a deep breath. "I owe you an apology."

"What for?" she asked, setting her bag on the counter.

I looked at the floor.

"You did everything for me when we were growing up. You were there when Mom and Dad weren't. I should have cut them off long ago and been more appreciative of you."

"Aww," Belle cooed, wrapping me in a hug. I sank against her. "You're my baby brother. I love you so much."

"I love you, too," I mumbled against her shoulder.

"I'm always going to be here for you. I'll always have your back, and I'll always help you in any way that I can." She brushed the hair off of my forehead. "Now what's wrong? You need your big sis to beat anyone up?"

I looked out the window. "I think all my problems are of my own making, but I appreciate the sentiment. Though," I added, "if you can keep Greg from ruining me, that would be awesome."

She laughed. "You know…" she began, opening up her bag and taking out several folders heavy with contract documents. "The key to dealing with men like Greg is to always be on the offensive. Which is why, little brother, my investment firm is going to be developing Hamilton Yards across the street." She opened the folder. It contained a contract tabbed with yellow notes that read SIGN HERE. "Your hedge fund will be a cash backer, of course. Not a partner, because Dorothy doesn't trust you like that yet," she cautioned.

My mouth fell open. "Are you serious? Greg is going to flip out!"

"Just an added bonus!" Belle singsonged. She handed me a pen.

I scanned through the documents.

"Don't you dare complain about the terms," Belle warned. "Dorothy was wary of having you on board. I told her you were just a good-looking ATM. But," she added, "assuming this development does as well as I project, you could be looking at being in the big leagues in the next few years."

I did my own mental math. She was getting a much bigger percentage than I was. "So could you," I said.

She smirked. "Nothing like being a girl boss."

I signed all the papers. As Belle placed them back in the folder, I shifted my weight restlessly.

"Need something else?" she asked. A knowing smile played on her face as if she knew what I wanted.

"What am I going to do about Morticia?"

Belle was thoughtful. "I'm going to be offering her some consulting work on the Hamilton Yards project in the New Year. Hopefully you will at least make a very sincere apology, since I assume we will all be working together in some capacity."

"I need ideas," I begged, trailing her out the door.

"I'm sure you'll think of something," she replied.

Fuck.

I paced around the condo. The clock was ticking. What could I do to tell Morticia I was sorry? I needed to assure her that I knew what I had done was wrong. I flipped through my phone to look at the pictures I had of her. I stopped on the last one we had taken of the two of us out in the snow. She had called it the minimalist portrait. I missed her.

I wanted to tell her I loved her—to write it out in the snow and take her up in a helicopter to look down on the words. However, she would probably see any declarations as being devious and underhanded.

Could I buy her a condo? Send her to Paris for Christmas? Whether she would even want to hear from me was the bigger question.

I checked my phone. She had not responded to my text. "She probably blocked you," I told myself.

That meant whatever my grand gesture was, it had better be good. I needed to think.

I strapped Cindy Lou into her harness and took her outside. The cat was batting at snowflakes as they drifted down out of the sky. It was going to be a white Christmas. But I didn't feel the holiday spirit.

What did Morticia want? She liked art. She was mad about the development. I had an idea bouncing in my head. I needed to refine it, though, and consult with Dorothy. Once I had my idea finalized, I would write a heartfelt note and have it delivered to Morticia on nice paper. Except my handwriting wasn't pretty.

"Can you pay people to write calligraphy?" I took out my phone to check and saw that Morticia had written to me.

While I was trying to decipher the text, a car roared in the distance. It sounded like one of Owen's fancy sports cars. But when the silver McLaren pulled up at the sidewalk, Morticia staggered out.

CHAPTER 71

Morticia

"Hold on," I told Jonathan, "I think I might puke."

The driver's-side window rolled down. "I'm not a bad driver!" Holly yelled out.

"You're a terrible driver!" Lilith shot back.

I let them argue as I turned my attention to Jonathan. He was blinking at me in the snow.

"Did you get my messages?" I asked.

He nodded. He seemed dumbfounded. "I'm sorry, Morticia," he said in a rush. "I was planning on having a whole presentation ready and making a grand gesture."

"Do you need me to come back later?" I asked tentatively.

He shook his head.

"For what it's worth," I told him, "I'm sorry too. I should not have taken those pictures of you and used them in that art piece."

We stared at each other with the falling snow a curtain between us.

Jonathan looked sad and smiled ruefully. "I know you still probably aren't the type to forgive and forget. You'll probably carry a grudge to your grave. But," he said before I could protest, "I did have more than an apology to offer you. Since I ruined your internship at—oh shit!"

He tackled me into a snowbank. Cindy Lou jumped out of the drift, mewing furiously and shaking the snow off of the Christmas coat Jonathan had dressed her in.

The SUV that had almost run us over was stopped on the sidewalk, steam billowing out from under the hood. The passenger door opened, and Sarah jumped out.

"Jonathan!" she yelled, rushing into his arms.

"Wait now, wait a minute!" Trevor demanded over the hissing of the car. "That's my wife!"

"Jonathan, you're taking me back, right?" Sarah pleaded.

"No he's not," I said forcefully.

"Don't tell me you want *her*," Sarah said derisively. "She's like the Ghost of Christmas Future, all spooky and a killjoy."

"Then you're the Ghost of Christmas Past!" my cousin Keeley screamed as she joined the fray. "You're a has-been, and Jonathan doesn't want spoiled leftovers that have been in the fridge since last Christmas!"

There were leaves in her hair, and she was wearing the same fur-lined dress she had been wearing at the bake-off.

"I'm the Ghost of Christmas Present," Keeley said, tugging on Jonathan's arm. "I'm all fun and joy, and I'll suck your dick." She knelt down.

Jonathan jumped back with a curse.

"Leave him alone," Sarah hollered, kicking her sister.

"Screw you!" Keeley screeched. "Mom and Dad always liked you more! You pretended to be a Goody Two-shoes, but you're over here cheating on your husband."

"You slept with him first," Sarah howled back.

"You said you were coming here for closure," Trevor bellowed. "I knew I should have left you sooner!"

"Well, you can leave me now, because I'm getting an annulment," Sarah hissed.

"You've been married for eight months," Keeley complained. "The priest won't allow it."

"He will because they haven't had sex."

"Stop telling everyone my private business," Sarah snapped at me.

"It is my business now if you're over here trying to manipulate my boyfriend," I shot back.

"Wait, I'm your boyfriend again?" Jonathan asked hopefully.

"You clearly need me. Your cat is out here in a red Santa outfit with a fur-lined hood and a diamond belt buckle, while you don't even have on a coat," I told him flatly. "You're a mess."

"But I didn't get to make my grand gesture," he said.

"It's shocking and shameful," I said above all the noise, "how much more appealing a man seems when other women are fighting over him. There's some sort of economic theory." I made a disgusted sound but then shrugged. "But yeah, I guess we're back together. So sue me; I like to win. And I'm petty."

"It's the scarcity theory," Jonathan's sister said, appearing out of the snow in a sleeveless black dress and flats.

I shivered just looking at her. Next to her was Dorothy in her multicolored patchwork-quilt coat.

"It makes low-value items seem like high-value items when there is high demand."

"I'm not a low-value item," Jonathan protested.

Yet another high-end sports car pulled up alongside the SUV, which had started to belch black smoke.

The door swung up like one on the Batmobile, and a blond Svensson jumped out, clearly pleased with himself.

"See, Greg!" he said, gesturing grandly.

Greg Svensson unfolded himself from the car, looked around at the bedlam, and cursed. "Wilder, what the hell is wrong with you? I can't believe you wasted my time."

"No," Wilder said happily, "I ruined the spin-off Belle was planning. I banged Keeley last night, and now it's all over the news. We sullied the sanctity of *The Great Christmas Bake-Off*."

Greg pinched the bridge of his nose.

"That was you who slept with my cousin?" I asked. "You better check him for STDs."

"I plan to," Greg said.

"But it was a great revenge plan," Wilder insisted. "This was my Christmas present to you, Greg, to cheer you up after Belle stole another development from you."

"You own Hamilton Yards now?" I asked her, flabbergasted.

Dorothy beamed. "Girl power! Belle's got vision, and she's not a Scammy McScammerson."

"I need a drink," Greg muttered.

"I have whiskey in my purse," Dorothy offered, pulling a mostly empty bottle from the humongous bag. "You can have it."

Wilder jogged over to take it from her. He opened it and sniffed it. "Is this yours, Jonathan?"

"Yep," my boyfriend replied. *Yes, that's right, boyfriend. Suck it, Sarah!*

"Nicely done!" Wilder flashed Jonathan a thumbs-up.

Greg grabbed the bottle from him, annoyed.

"No hard feelings?" Belle purred to Greg. "It wasn't personal. Just business."

He shook his head slowly. "And on Christmas, Belle? Have you no shame?"

"You're still invited to the Christmas party," she said, grinning.

Greg's eyes narrowed. "Is Jonathan cooking?"

Another silver sports car pulled up; this one was almost dead silent.

The window was down, and Owen Frost peered out at us. "Of course he's not cooking. In fact, I bet he only serves alcohol and potato chips."

"I'm ordering Waffle House," Jonathan said defensively. "They're open on Christmas Eve. They have hash browns and gravy. Speaking of, I'm not sure if they deliver, so I need to borrow your truck, Owen."

"No. Buy your own damn car. I don't need another car ruined this holiday season."

"Why do all of you have such nice cars?" I demanded.

"It's like all the reindeer showed up—you know, like in those cheesy Christmas car commercials," Jonathan said, nudging me.

"I'm here because my car was reported stolen," Owen interjected. "I was going to call the police, but imagine my surprise when I watched the security feed and saw my own fiancée stealing the car."

Holly was chagrined. "We were in a rush."

"We were trying to save your baby brother from a lifetime of being shackled to crazy," Lilith added.

Owen looked around.

"Now that everyone is here," Jonathan said, "can I please make my grand gesture and apology statement?"

"I don't need a grand gesture," I told him. "So long as we don't eat Waffle House for Christmas."

"Nothing wrong with Waffle House!" Holly piped up. "I was a waitress at Waffle House. I looked damn fine in my uniform too!"

"My grand gesture," Jonathan cut in.

"Owen, move your car so I can leave," Greg ordered. "The holidays are bad enough without all these hysterics."

Owen crossed his arms. "No. If I have to hear it, so do you."

"Get on with it!" Dorothy called out. "I have to make my famous Christmas punch. I'm contributing that to your party!"

Jonathan jumped onto the hood of the car we had borrowed from Owen and shushed him when he complained. "Morticia," he began, "you are everything I always wanted for Christmas. When I dreamed of finding the love of my life, I dreamed of it happening during the perfect Christmas with food, family, and laughter. Now I've found you, and that makes this the best Christmas ever. Well, that and the fact that it's a white Christmas," he said.

I smiled and crossed my arms.

"Since I ruined your plans to work for the Getty Museum, I'm offering you a substitute. I am starting a foundation to run events and manage the resident artists at the new Hamilton Yards development. You can be in charge if you want. I know it's not as great as the Getty, but you'll have a multimillion-dollar annual budget and a nice office that will let you bring pets to work."

Salem, who was licking the snow off of Cindy Lou's face, meowed.

I thought about it. "Sounds like a lot of work," I said finally.

"You can hire interns," Jonathan added.

Interns. I could boss them around, make them fetch my tea, mold them into my own vision for what a true artist should be.

"Then I accept," I told him.

Jonathan smiled with relief.

"This is insane," Greg stated.

"Did you bring the key fob?" Holly asked Owen. "Because I turned off the car without thinking, and if you didn't, Morticia will have to hot-wire it again."

❄ ❄ ❄

It took a minute to sort out the car situation. Owen didn't want Holly driving it with all the wires hanging out, so she commandeered his other car, much to his chagrin.

Lilith left with Belle to talk about job opportunities.

Keeley tried to throw herself at Wilder, who seemed ready and willing to have another go before Greg snapped at him and stuffed him back into their car.

Trevor would have left Sarah and ridden off into the Bud Light sunset, but his radiator was busted. They started arguing about who was going to keep the china in the divorce.

Jonathan and I picked up our respective cats then slowly walked back into his condo building.

"I think we're just going to have to let natural selection take its course on that one," I said as we rode the elevator upstairs.

He kissed me outside the condo then twirled me around inside.

He grinned. "At least I have Christmas china!" He pushed me against the long reclaimed-wood table, which was set for Christmas dinner.

I ran my fingers through his hair as his hands went up my skirt, making me moan. I had missed this!

"You're an insatiable asshole," I told him.

He smirked. "And you can't get enough of me, so it all works out, really."

He encouraged me to bend myself over the table, and I didn't need much prodding to go along with him. We had built a strong enough rapport that we knew how to please one another completely without even saying words anymore.

I needed him now. When the craving hit me, it hit me super hard.

He pulled my panties down, dropped his slacks just enough to reveal his cock, and rolled the condom over it. Then, with nothing else left to do, he impaled me right then and there.

Lightning tore through me, and I cried out. He filled me completely. The surge of ecstasy spread through me again and again as he started to fuck me. I was already murmuring and trying to keep myself together.

His hands wrapped around my body, feeling me up through my dress. My nipples perked up, yearning for his touch. His roaming hands pulled me back, urging me hotter, higher, and making me cry for more. My panting and moaning spilled out as the pleasure filled me. I arched against him as he fucked me, not even bending over the table anymore.

Even in this web of clothes and lust, he was still finding more ways to please me and make me his. His finger on my clit added a whole new spike of bliss with every sinful stroke of his cock inside me.

I heaved, nibbling on my lip to endure this a little longer, desperately afraid of screaming out for him and having the whole street listen in and hear what was going on.

As I approached the edge, Jonathan grabbed my chin, turned me to face him, and looked into my eyes as if I was the most beautiful thing in the world. He kissed me, hard and strong, as if I was the last woman he was ever going to enjoy, the last woman that would ever be his.

And Jonathan would be the last man to ever be mine.

Love made me feel the strangest things.

I loved it.

I loved him.

The orgasm seared through me and shook me as my screams of bliss were muffled by his kiss. His ecstatic groan followed my own, proof that he was completely loving this every bit as much as I was.

Warmth flushed through my body. My heart was racing but steadily slowing as our kiss broke.

We shared another long, knowing gaze in the intense afterglow, grinning broadly at each other.

Jonathan kissed me.

"I would go again," he said, "but I need to figure out the best way to order Waffle House delivery."

I glared at him. "We're not serving Waffle House on Christmas."

CHAPTER 72

Jonathan

"It's almost Christmas!" I said happily.

Morticia smiled up at me in bemusement as I parked at the high-end grocery store.

"How many people are coming to your holiday party?"

"Not that many," I said as I grabbed a cart. "Just my family and then all the Svenssons that are in town."

"So that's like fifty of them."

"Yeah, that sounds right."

"Are they going to come after your sister stole their business?" she asked me.

"She stole *Greg's* business," I corrected. "And a lot of them find Greg aggravating, so I'm sure even some of the Harrogate Svenssons will come in for the party just to see the fireworks."

"Lordy," Morticia said.

I followed her around the store, detailing my party plans. "And then," I said, "I think we should play Christmas movie trivia. Or name that Christmas carol. I'm not sure which."

"Aren't you going to have a bunch of drunk Svensson brothers in attendance?" she commented.

"You're right. We'd better do a drinking game so they participate."

I watched her in confusion as she loaded cans of Italian tomatoes into the cart. "Uh…"

"What?" Morticia challenged. "I'm Italian. We're having Italian food at Christmas."

"Lasagna?" I asked hopefully.

"And ravioli," she added, reaching for a huge bag of flour. I beat her to it and put it in the cart. She looked at it for a moment. "Better grab another one."

I ran to fetch a second cart then met her back at the fish counter.

"Fried baccalà or salted white cod," she said as the fish monger handed her a huge wrapped package. "Battered and fried. It doesn't get more Italian than that."

Then the fishmonger handed her another armful of wrapped packages.

"Since it is Christmas Eve," she explained, "traditionally, you're supposed to eat fish. But with the way everyone in our friend circle drinks, we should serve some red meat too. But I'm still making spaghetti with clams and swordfish with a creamy anchovy sauce."

My mouth was watering.

"Oh!" She snapped her fingers. "Octopus. I need to make an octopus salad."

I grinned at her. "For someone who claims not to like Christmas, you sure are going all out."

"My grandmother loved Christmas," she said. "Though it was more of an open-house friend affair that lasted Christmas Eve, Christmas Day, and Santo Stefano or Boxing Day."

We headed to the next aisle.

"Mimi, my sister, and I baked enough cookies to bury you alive, and we wrapped them up in little boxes to give out as gifts for people who came by."

"That's a nice dessert idea."

She gave me a look. "The cookie boxes were not dessert; that's what people take home. Dessert is tiramisu, of course, so we need ladyfingers. Plus I'm making cakes. Which reminds me, I need more chocolate."

I fetched a packet and returned to join her at the meat counter.

She looked and frowned. "No. A lot more."

❈ ❈ ❈

All the food barely fit in my car. Then Morticia made us take a detour to an Italian specialty store to buy fresh mozzarella, burrata, and other cheeses and cured meats. "They make them in-house," she said.

When we returned, waiting in the foyer outside my condo was a large, rectangular package wrapped in butcher paper, which the doorman had brought up.

"It's for you," I said to Morticia, reading the tag. "From the Getty Museum."

She stared at it for a moment, then horrified recognition crossed her features. "We should just burn this," Morticia insisted, dragging the package back out into the hallway.

"Oh, hell no!" I exclaimed. "That's the famous painting, isn't it! This is going in a place of honor." I unwrapped it with a flourish.

Morticia shuddered. "It's even cringier than I remembered."

"Please," I snorted. "This is art!"

I dug out a hammer, nails, and picture hooks to hang it on the wall above the fireplace while Morticia sorted ingredients. To add an extra oomph, I pinned some garland above it. Then I stepped back to inspect the piece. The pictures Sarah had shown me really hadn't done it justice. I could see why the Getty had wanted Morticia to work for them. The painting was well-balanced, interesting, and layered.

"You can't hang that there!" Morticia said in horror.

"It's here or in the bedroom," I told her. "Here, at least it seems less creepy. Like, oh, you have a problem with my overly sexualized painting? Well, it's art, and you clearly do not have a refined enough palate."

"I should have added some more Christmas fig leaves," she said, staring up at it.

"Please," I said smugly, "you love staring at my naked body."

The doorbell rang then rang again. The cats bounded over.

"You invited guests?" Morticia asked.

"Reinforcements," I replied as my brothers, sister, Chloe, Holly, Lilith, and Emma piled in.

"Are you making fried baccalà?" Emma asked hopefully.

"It's for the party tomorrow," Morticia said. "We're doing prep work."

"But you have to feed us," Matt complained to me.

"Like you're actually going to do any work," I told him. "Only people who work get to eat."

"I'll work more than you," my brother shot back.

Owen and Jack's huskies bounded into the living room. I ran in to make sure they didn't bother our cats. But the animals were happily playing with one of the many toys I had bought for Cindy Lou.

"You are so extra!" Chloe, Jack's girlfriend, commented as she set down bags full of ingredients. "Is your cat wearing a diamond collar?"

"Forget the collar; get a load of this painting!" Jack said, following her into the living room.

"You need to cover that," Morticia complained, rushing in.

"No way!" I said. "This is exactly what I need to show everyone that I am a legit billionaire. Nothing screams 'new money' like partially nude portraits of yourself."

CHAPTER 73

Morticia

"Can you take the lasagna out?" I asked Jonathan the next afternoon.

It was Christmas Eve, and his condo was packed for the party. Jazzy Christmas music played over the sound system. I had freshened up the garlands and fluffed out the ribbons on the tree a bit. The fire was burning along merrily.

"I should have brought up some of those creepy dolls Mimi used to collect and put them in Christmas outfits. Then it would feel like old times!" Lilith told me. She set a basket of cheesy garlic bread on the long dining room table with a bowl of marinara sauce beside it for dipping.

"We're having a classy, high-end Christmas party," I reminded my twin.

"Is that why you have that naked painting up?" she asked me, pointing.

"There aren't any kids coming," Jonathan said, walking by with the large pan of lasagna. "So everyone can experience Morticia's artistic prowess."

He was wearing a red smoking jacket and a Santa hat, and he looked smoking hot.

"I think I may need to open my present early tonight," I told him, smoothing his lapels.

Jonathan grinned. "Glad to see you getting into the Christmas spirit."

"You're not bringing your little brothers?" Owen asked Greg with a grin.

The elder Svensson scowled. "I'm going to be stuck with them in Harrogate for the next ten days," he grumbled. "That's too much family and Christmas time."

"Family is important, Greg," Carl said as he cut out a giant slice of lasagna.

"Did you get all your Christmas shopping done?" Jonathan asked.

"I have a hundred brothers. I'm not giving them all presents."

"Yeah," Carl joked, "he had his secretary do it instead."

"You should have just done the shopping yourself," Belle said, scooping up fried calamari and fried puffy white cod. "Considering that you don't have a development taking up all of your time."

Greg bared his teeth.

I stifled a laugh as Belle took a bite of the fried squid.

"You know," Dorothy told him, "if Belle hadn't come to me with her proposal, I was going to make you a counteroffer."

"You were?" Greg asked.

"Yep. A holiday evening to remember in exchange for the Hamilton Yards property."

Greg blanched.

Belle laughed. "That would probably make him the most expensive lay ever, though I'm not going to say he isn't worth it." She winked at Greg.

I thought I heard a molar crack over the Christmas music as his jaw clenched.

"The sexual tension is strong with this one," Holly whispered to me.

I picked up the empty calamari basket and headed out onto the porch, where Oliver and Matt were frying more calamari and white cod under Lilith's strict supervision while joking with several of the Svensson brothers and drinking cranberry old fashioneds.

"Got any more in the queue?" I asked.

"Barely," Oliver grumbled. "People keep eating them."

I laughed and grabbed what they did have and went back into the main room. The front door was propped open so people could stream in and out.

"Merry Christmas!" my friend Penny yelled. She was trailed by Garrett Svensson. "Wow!" She looked around then snapped her fingers in front of my face. "Who are you and what have you done with Morticia? Did you put up all these decorations by yourself?"

"I was under duress," I assured her.

"You were being paid," Dana Holbrook called out over Penny's head as she unwound her scarf.

"Did you bring your cousins?" Garrett asked her.

Dana rolled her eyes. "Of course not."

"Too bad," Garrett said. "It would have provided the entertainment."

Several more Svenssons packed into Jonathan's condo. I was gripped with icy fear as I surveyed the crowd. "I don't think I have enough food," I said, slightly panicked.

Chloe laughed and waved to Jack, who was wheeling in a cart bearing steaming containers. "I have extra from the restaurant," she said. "Hope you don't mind. I feel bad, because everyone ate like a third of what you had bought yesterday."

"You don't understand," I moaned. "I'm Italian. I can't run out of food. This is a travesty."

Chloe snorted. "Honestly, you have a ton of food. I'm just here to use all these strapping, good-looking men as garbage disposals!"

The timer dinged, and I went into the kitchen to pull another lasagna out of the oven and put the next one in.

"I'm sorry," Jonathan said, coming up behind me after I had slid the lasagna into the oven. "Did you say you were worried about not having enough food? The fridge is packed, and it's like a sauna in here with the oven and the stove and the fire hazard of portable burners and the hot plates all over the table."

"I have to have enough food so people can have seconds and thirds and take a to-go box home," I said stubbornly.

He kissed me. "I love you."

"I love you too," I told him. "But we need to talk about your kitchen."

"It's huge!" he protested.

"I don't have enough burners," I told him flatly. "If I'm going to spend any amount of time here, I need another fridge and freezer and a third oven."

Jonathan laughed. "If you ask nicely, maybe Santa will give you the house of your dreams for Christmas."

"I was going to save my Christmas wishes for things like world peace," I said. "I figured a new kitchen might also miraculously appear under the tree if I let you come down my chimney!"

The End

FROSTING HER Cake Pop

A SHORT ROMANTIC COMEDY

CHAPTER 1

Morticia

"You can't tell me you're also one of those people that goes all out for Valentine's Day," I remarked to Jonathan as we walked down the street. It was February and freezing cold. Jonathan wasn't even wearing a jacket, though Cindy Lou Who was decked out in a hot-pink coat and little cat-sized booties. Salem was roughing it in a Halloween-themed sweater.

"You can't judge me," he retorted. "It's nine months until Halloween, and you're already preparing."

"Yes," I said, "nine months, so it's practically here already. Besides, it is a major, legitimate holiday, unlike Valentine's Day, which is basically Amazon Prime Day masquerading as a real holiday."

"Please," Jonathan said. "I'm going to wine and dine you. Rose petals, an opera serenade, chocolates shaped like sex organs, the works!"

I made a face. "That's not romantic."

"For someone who says she doesn't like Valentine's Day, you seem like you're already setting expectations."

"How is not wanting a life-sized solid-chocolate dildo setting unreasonable expectations?" I countered.

"Are you kidding me?" Jonathan said. "That's a hot item." He checked his watch. "We better head back. Don't want to be late for naked yoga."

※ ※ ※

Yes, naked yoga. Thirty minutes later, I stood out in the cleared courtyard of one of the industrial buildings. Dorothy had insisted that as one of my first duties as the head of the Hamilton Yards Art Foundation, I make the naked yoga sessions more official.

I had replied that part of that meant that people had to be at least modestly clothed.

She had told me that I needed to be out there, then, to inspect.

And that was why I was outside in February, shivering in a two-piece swimsuit on a yoga mat that had already frozen to the ground.

Dorothy waltzed to the front of the class. She was wearing pasties on her boobs and a skimpy thong bottom. Everything else proudly hung free.

"Breathe in," she instructed the crowd. "Let the cold air fill your lungs—we're trying to stave off inflammation, and we were all out drinking last night—and exhale."

I winced as my back popped.

"Valentine's Day is coming up, ladies, and I know you all want to impress your men! Let's firm up those thighs and those vaginal cavities. Also, don't forget, thanks to our sponsor today, Bath and Body Twerks, they have provided a free Valentine's Day gift for everyone. Don't forget to take yours! Now, everyone give me a garland pose!"

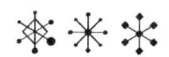

※ ※ ※

My thighs were burning after the lesson. I staggered across the property to my office. I had set up temporary shop in another converted shipping container.

My intern was waiting there for me. "Hi!" Arlo Svensson chirped. "I have your tea, Supreme Mistress of the World." The tween carefully set the steaming cup down on my desk.

Apparently shit had gone down over Christmas at the Svensson estate, and it had ended with Hunter shipping a kid to Manhattan every couple of weeks to live with—that is, annoy—Greg and work at his firm. Greg had told me he would write me a big, fat check if I took the kids in. They made tea and answered my phone while I cosplayed Miranda Priestly.

"Madam," Arlo said seriously, "your significant other has requested your presence at a Valentine's Day event tomorrow evening. I have penciled it in on your calendar."

"Ugh, Valentine's Day." I leaned back in my chair.

"Shall I send out a sardonic tweet for you?"

I smirked. I had been training my interns well. Now that I was on the fourth iteration, I had it down pat.

"Not today," I said loftily.

As much as I did not like standing out in the freezing cold, I did feel invigorated after the half-naked yoga sessions.

I worked on my strategic plan for art-themed events in the complex through the afternoon. It still got dark around four thirty, and as the shadows lengthened, I started thinking about packing up.

At five, the door opened, sending the wind howling in to scatter my papers. Arlo raced to pick them up.

"I need a vestibule," I complained.

Jonathan bounded in, scooping me up and kissing me.

"Ew!" Arlo gagged, covering his face.

Carl followed Jonathan, "Ew!" Carl mimicked Arlo. "It's a child." He rushed at his little brother, and the two tussled. "Same time tomorrow?" Carl asked me.

"You may go," I told Arlo with a wave of my hand.

Jonathan smirked. "You're really enjoying your interns."

"I am the queen of my own fiefdom."

Jonathan was thoughtful. "You're surprisingly good with kids."

I felt self-conscious. We hadn't really had a serious talk about THE FUTURE. I hadn't even officially moved into Jonathan's condo. I stayed over a lot, but it still felt like his space. Officially, I was living at Emma's tiny apartment, sleeping on my yoga mat on the floor. But Jonathan's bed was much more comfortable.

He was looking at me softly.

"I guess I should go back to Emma's," I said, feeling awkward.

"Did you all have plans?" he asked.

"Er, no," I said, "but I should do laundry." I waved a hand vaguely.

"You can do laundry at my place," Jonathan offered. "In fact," he continued, "don't you think it's time to just go ahead and move in?"

"I don't know. That seems like a lot," I said. "It's such a big step. We should, you know, really talk about it."

"Sure," he said lightly. "No worries. I just don't want you sleeping in your office like a Hobbit!"

CHAPTER 2

Jonathan

Morticia had been really weirded out by my suggestion that she move in with me. I didn't see what the big deal was. She practically lived there already. It felt so right and relaxing to be around her, like we were meant to be. But maybe she didn't feel the same way.

First, she hadn't seemed excited about my Valentine's Day plans. Then she didn't want to move in with me. And that was going to be a real problem, because I had just found the perfect house. I had a whole reveal planned. Was my big Valentine's Day plan about to implode?

Morticia didn't seem to be picking up on my internal turmoil as we walked into my condo. I needed to know if I should table the surprise or not. Maybe I should save the house for her birthday and just do something quiet for Valentine's Day.

She unpacked her bag, taking out a bright-pink gift sack.

I glared at it. "Who sent that to you?"

"Jealous?" she teased. "Maybe I have a secret admirer."

"You better not," I growled playfully, wrapping my arms around her. "I'm the only man for you."

"Oh, I don't know," Morticia purred. "I think this gift bag might contain something that can give you a run for your money."

I relaxed slightly when I saw the Bath and Body Twerks logo on the bag when she turned it around. Then I tensed for a different reason as she pulled out a vibrator and slowly untied the bow. She turned it on, and it buzzed.

"Oh, and look at that; it's already charged."

"Give me that." I swiped at it.

"Uh-uh," she said. "You were jealous and aggressive and hurt its feelings." She laughed and swept over to the couch while I tried not to combust.

She was eyeballing me the whole time as she sexily reclined on the couch. Her gaze was enough to get me hard, but I wasn't budging. I wanted to see what she was planning.

Morticia didn't seem to be deterred. She put on a little striptease for me, shimmying out of her shirt and jeans until she was in nothing but her underwear.

The temptation to join her was growing very strong, but I crossed my arms, ready to stand my ground.

She ran that vibrating dildo down her body, tickling the outside of her panties, flashing me a slightly orgasmic glare. She shivered a bit as she glided the toy up and down her body before rolling it up to her chest. She let it tickle her nipples before she unhooked her bra and unveiled her breasts.

The vibration of the toy against her tits made her nipples pebble hard. It was enough to make a man fantasize about suckling on them. And I knew I could do better than a plastic dick powered by a pair of double As.

She kept those big dark eyes pointed at me as if she was yearning for me to give her what she really wanted. But she had started the teasing game. I smirked as I watched the show.

The toy led the way toward her panties, buzzing around the outside again, poking at her pussy, teasing me with the knowledge that it could have been me touching her instead. Her fingers slid into her panties to rub herself. Morticia moaned playfully, and likely overly theatrically, to tempt me.

I hated that it was somehow working.

She danced her panties off, now fully naked and flaunting her curves in front of me. The vibrator caught my eyes, and they followed it down as she poked at herself. She slid one finger inside herself, then two fingers...then three. She stopped there, as any more might get too kinky for what was meant to be a huge game of temptation.

The dildo rubbed against her pussy, teasing her clit. She exhaled at the contact, teasing her clit a bit more before going down to her slit. She mocked being about to penetrate herself with it, running it around her folds but never truly entering herself.

"It's going to be my cock in you," I growled.

She laughed.

My dumbass had been had. In a hasty rush that hadn't consumed me since I was an awkward teenager, I threw off my T-shirt, kicked off my pants, and scrambled for the condom in my pocket. Morticia was more than happy to wait for me to get my act together.

Then I was on her. She reached down and ran a hand along my thick cock.

I didn't care. I needed her. She was my temptress, my weakness, and I needed to enjoy her to the absolute fullest. My cock throbbed for her, and I threw that vibrator against the wall. She didn't need it. She had me.

I slid into her, feeling her perfect pussy squeeze all around me, everything so damned wonderful at that moment. She cried out as I took her, my thick, hard cock filling her. I increased the pace, rocking in and out of her. Her legs closed around me, my arms around her, as I took her again and again, feeling all of her bare body against mine, the anticipation growing.

I loved everything about her—the feeling of her body beneath my hands, the way she looked at me, her cunning and brilliance, just fucking everything. All those things came to a head when I was inside her, when it was all this close.

She was mine.

I needed to claim her. Take her. Enjoy her.

Her fingernails clawed down my back as she cried out and moaned for me—she was close, and that pushed me to the edge.

Almost simultaneously, we hit our heights together, our grips on one another tightening, our bliss soaring.

Fuck.

I loved her. More than anything in the world.

I couldn't lose her.

CHAPTER 3

Morticia

Even though the sex had been amazing, Jonathan didn't cuddle around me that night as we slept like he normally did.

You blew it, my mind taunted. *Blew it, because of course someone like you can't just act like a normal, decent person and keep a man. You have to run everyone off with your bad attitude.*

He's probably already decided he's going to break up with you. Watch him do it after Valentine's Day.

After not being able to sleep, I finally got up and went into the kitchen to make Jonathan a surprise Valentine's Day breakfast complete with heart-shaped waffles. I had it all ready to go when he got out of the shower.

"Oh!" He seemed shocked when he saw the breakfast. "Morticia, I have an early meeting," he said. "I didn't realize…"

"No, it's okay," I chirped, feeling crushed inside. "I should have asked. I can make you a to-go box."

"I'm running late," he said, giving me a quick kiss. "Meeting with the Svenssons—you know how they are."

Fuck.

※ ※ ※

"Where's your intern?" Emma asked me the next afternoon. She and Lilith had come over to my office to eat the mound of breakfast food I had made.

"He went back to Harrogate," I said. "They're having a big Valentine's Day festival."

"You two aren't going to the Valentine's Day festival?" Emma asked.

"October is my month," I said.

"The Valentine's Day festival consists of people standing around in the cold, eating frozen chocolate hearts," Lilith said with a grimace. "Besides, you must have something big planned with Jonathan."

I made a face. I had been feeling bad all day about it. "He did; he was really excited, then I shot him down," I admitted.

"Ouch."

"You have to start going with the flow more," Emma said gently. "You know, loosen up."

"I tried to make it up to him, you know," I said defensively.

Emma and Lilith made loud porno sounds.

"Okay, okay, yes, we all know what that means," I said irritably.

"You should have just let him treat you and pamper you," Emma told me. "You knew he was going to be really into Valentine's Day."

"I know, and he looked like a kicked puppy," I said. "I felt like a bitch. Then he asked me to move in with him, and I said no, and then I felt like a bigger bitch."

Emma made a face.

"Ugh, I should have said yes!" I said, slapping myself on the forehead. "I can't keep living in your apartment, can I?"

"I mean, it's just like having a sleepover," Emma said slowly.

"I've been there for months," I told her. "I'm sorry. I've been taking advantage of you."

"No, no, take your time."

"Wait, you're still living with Emma?" Lilith said to me, incredulous. "I thought you lived with Jonathan."

"She's over there enough that it doesn't matter," Emma said in my defense.

"Bitch," Lilith declared, "you have a nice place to live. You need to get your shit and get out of Emma's house."

"I will, I will. But what if I blew my chance?" I fretted.

"Just put your best self forward," Emma told me.

"No," Lilith insisted. "You need to throw a big Valentine's Day after-party. Show him that you're all in on Valentine's Day. Surprise him! Balloons, cake, alcohol, family, cats in cute outfits. The works!"

I chewed on my lip and looked at the clock. "I don't know if I can. The day's almost over."

"You have to," Lilith said sagely. "Nothing says 'I love you' like a surprise party."

CHAPTER 4

Jonathan

Carl was waiting in the conference room when I skidded in.

"Did we get it?" I asked him.

"Good morning," Carl said in an exaggerated tone. "So nice to see you, Carl. Here, Carl, I brought you some of the delicious-looking Valentine's Day breakfast that my girlfriend made. Oh wait, you didn't."

"I didn't get any either," I said irritably. "Because I was coming to see you."

"Bidding has started." He pointed to the Sotheby's auction on the computer. He tapped a button, and it displayed on the large presentation screen at the front of the conference room.

"Why aren't you bidding?" I asked as I studied the screen. The numbers kept ticking up. "This is the perfect house," I reminded Carl. "It's a historic Victorian house from the 1870s. It has the original wood trim, and it comes with a lot of original furniture."

"It's also a money pit," Carl warned. "That's why the bids aren't that high. I'm waiting until the last minute to jump in with our bid."

I sat on pins and needles, watching the price go up and up. What if I didn't win the bidding?

Maybe that would be for the best.

"I don't think Morticia wants to move in with me."

"*What?*" Carl said in shock. "Then why are we trying to buy this house?"

I shrugged unhappily. "Maybe we should table it."

"Shit!" Carl said as the computer dinged. "The algorithm I set up already placed our bid. Maybe someone else will put in a higher bid."

The timer ticked. Our bid stayed there.

"Dude," Carl said, "this is a lot of house. If Morticia is about to dump you, this is going to end badly for you. I was doing some research, and the house needed an estimated eight million dollars' worth of restoration. This is on top of the five million the previous owner spent redoing the gas lighting."

"Oh shit."

The timer kept running down, and still, no one else bid.

"Fuck, this is the worst Valentine's Day ever," I groaned, resting my head in my hands.

Carl frowned. "Didn't you say that one Valentine's Day, you tried to give your teacher a snake that you had found in the yard?"

"Oh yeah, that did not go over well either."

The timer buzzed.

"Congrats, and my condolences," Carl said as the screen flashed information about taking payment and the fraud charges that would result if I did not send payment. "You are now the proud homeowner of a large Victorian row house with a haunted attic and a garden infested with poisonous weeds."

"Great." I slumped over and thunked my head against the table. "Should I go for it or call the whole Valentine's Day surprise off?"

"If I'm not mistaken, you already booked the caterers, so to cancel, you'd be out the money, and they still wouldn't give you the food. At least now if Morticia doesn't show up, you and I have a nice meal."

❊ ❊ ❊

The caterers and the decorator met me at the Victorian house later after the money had been transferred, papers signed, and keys delivered. Both seemed apprehensive as I unlocked the heavy wooden door with a creak.

"I'm not sure if the oven works," I warned.

"I have my own heating equipment," the caterer said grimly, glaring at the very old kitchen.

The decorator rallied and began making notes as a cleaning crew showed up to start wiping up the dust.

"I'm having them concentrate on the foyer," the decorator told me.

"And the kitchen!" the caterer yelled.

I tried to plan my big speech to Morticia to convince her that we did, in fact, need to not only move in together but plan the rest of our lives together.

"This is my moonshot," I pep talked myself. I paced, trying to stay out of the way of the people setting up moody lighting, sheer drapes, and a table set for two.

It was dark by the time everything was finished. The smell of the food wafted through the house. Everything looked perfect. The gaslighting in the house still worked, and the lamps burned cheerfully.

Now I just had to bring Morticia to the house. I wrote and rewrote the text so that it was worded in a way that would bring her to me immediately.

Jonathan: *Can you come see me? I need to talk to you about something.*

I sent her a pin of my location. Then I waited.

CHAPTER 5

Morticia

I had no idea what Jonathan wanted to talk to me about. The text sounded serious. I spun scenarios in my head as I finished crafting the invitation text for the Valentine's Day after-party.

"Do you think anyone's going to show up last minute?"

"Those of us who are single will happily be there," Emma assured me.

I attached a location pin to the invitation. We would meet at the bar adjacent to the distillery. I figured that way, people could get whatever drinks they wanted.

"I better go see what Jonathan wants," I said.

"If he does break up with you," Emma told me, "then the party can be a pity party for you."

"Also," Lilith added, "I bet one of the Svensson brothers would be the perfect rebound!"

❄︎ ❄︎ ❄︎

My stomach churned as I showed up at the location of the pin Jonathan had sent me. It was a beautiful old Victorian house. I almost came apart when I noticed that the lights framing the doorway were real gaslights!

"Morticia!" Jonathan said, throwing open the front door. "You came!"

"Wow!" I gushed, taking off my coat as I stepped into the grand foyer. "What is this place? Oh my god, look! All the gaslights! This is amazing! Do you know how unique this is?"

"Yeah, and expensive," he said under his breath.

"What?"

"Nothing. You hungry?"

"Starving." I hadn't been able to eat much of the breakfast I had made because I had been so stressed. "But first, what did you need to talk to me about that's so important?"

Jonathan threw open the double French doors that let into an ornate dining room. The table was set for two. There were tasteful Valentine's Day decorations around.

"This is amazing!" I told him, trying not to freak out. I had a party planned! People were going to be showing up in an hour. Jonathan was supposed to be there.

"I thought I would surprise you," he said as he held out the seat for me.

I'll just get through dinner; then we can go to the party. Maybe no one will show up.

But my phone was already blowing up with confirmations. Half the Svensson clan was going to be there.

The chef brought out the first course.

"I wanted to have an intimate Valentine's Day with you, Morticia," Jonathan said. "To tell you how much I loved you and appreciated having you in my life."

My phone kept going off. I was starting to sweat. All those gaslights.

Sure is warm in here...

Jonathan looked sad. "Do you not want to be here?"

"No. I mean yes! Of course I want to be here!" I said desperately. I took a bite of the fried cheese appetizer that was soaked in spicy honey. "This is amazing!"

I itched to grab my phone.

"You can answer it," Jonathan said, face unreadable.

"It's not that!" I said in a rush. "I felt so bad for not being into Valentine's Day that I planned a surprise Valentine's Day party for you! But I think that we're not going to make it." I held up the menu. "This looks intense."

Jonathan visibly relaxed and then burst out laughing.

"And here I was worried I had overdone it on Valentine's Day."

"I mean, I didn't have a lot of décor planned," I said. "Just food and booze."

The phone went off. I grabbed it to silence it but clapped a hand over my mouth in shock when I saw the picture. "Never mind. I think some of the Svenssons are bringing their own, *ahem*, creative decorations."

Jonathan grinned.

"Oh no," I said, scrolling through the group text. "Now Dorothy is on board too. Geez. Your Valentine's Day plan is way more wholesome than my plan."

Jonathan grabbed my hand. "I love you," he said sincerely.

"I love you, too," I told him, turning off my phone. I would deal with that shit show later. It honestly sounded like they weren't going to miss us anyway. "And I do want to move in with you."

"You do?" Jonathan was ecstatic. He stood up and ran around the table in excitement then waltzed us through the house and into the foyer. "This house is going to be amazing," he said. "You're going to love it here."

"Here?" I squawked.

"Yep!" he said. "I bought this! We are proud homeowners."

"Geez, this must have cost a fortune."

"Actually," Jonathan said, "they were practically giving it away. The place just eats money."

"But it's so historic!"

"Yep. It's a special snowflake."

The chef coughed delicately from the doorway to the dining room. "The oysters are out on the table."

I laughed. "Guess we better eat up. I've been told oysters are an aphrodisiac."

A gong sounded.

"What was that?"

We looked to the front door. Through the window, we saw a number of faces, including Dorothy, Emma, Lilith, and several Svensson brothers. I opened the door, and they piled in.

"We came early to help set up!" Dorothy said, waving in the Svenssons, who were carrying several crates. "We bought out your booze supply at the bar," she continued as the Svenssons marveled at the gaslights—*my* gaslights.

"I don't understand," I said. "How did you even know I was here? Why did you move the party?"

"This is the pin you sent out!" Lilith said in exasperation. "I tried to tell Dorothy that it was a mistake, but she insisted that you knew your own mind, so here we are."

"Oh!" one of the Svenssons exclaimed. "You have oysters!"

"That's my romantic Valentine's Day dinner," I informed them as they grabbed several.

"Oh shit," Wilder said. Jonathan laughed.

"Ugh, sorry I ruined your plans," I apologized.

"You didn't," he said happily. "My only plan was to spend Valentine's Day with you."

He kissed me hard as the doorbell rang again with more partiers.

"Now," he announced. "Who wants to toast Morticia's and my new house?" He bent down and whispered in my ear, "FYI, it's haunted."

"You really do know me well!" I kissed him happily. "I can't wait to move in with you!"

The End

Thick and Chewy Gingerbread Cookies

✺ ✷ ✵

This recipe comes from Cook's Illustrated Magazine, not any family members, haha! It makes about 18 large or 30 small gingerbread cookies. The frosting is all mine!

For the Cookies:
3 cups unbleached all-purpose flour
¾ cup firmly packed dark brown sugar
¾ teaspoon baking soda
2 teaspoons ground cinnamon 2 teaspoons ground ginger
½ teaspoon ground cloves (totally optional – I leave it out as I hate cloves)
½ teaspoon salt
12 tablespoons unsalted butter, softened but still cool
¾ cup fancy (not cooking) molasses 2 tablespoons milk

Directions:
1. In a food processor, process the flour, brown sugar, baking soda, cinnamon, ginger, cloves and salt until combined, about 10 seconds. Scatter the butter pieces over the flour mixture and process until the mixture is sandy and resembles very fine meal, about 15 seconds.
2. With the machine running, gradually add the molasses and milk. Process until the dough is evenly moistened and forms a soft mass, about 10 seconds.

3. Scrape dough out onto a work surface and divide it half. Working with one piece at a time, roll the dough, ¼ inch thick, between 2 sheets of parchment paper. Leaving the dough sandwiched between the parchment layers, stack on a baking sheet and freeze until firm, 15-20 minutes.
4. Adjust the oven racks to the upper and lower middle positions and heat the oven to 350 degrees F. Line 2 baking sheets with parchment paper.
5. Remove 1 dough sheet from the freezer; place on work surface. Peel off top parchment sheet and gently lay it back in place. Flip the dough over; peel off and discard second parchment layer.
6. Cut the dough using cookie cutters of your choice. Transfer shapes to prepared baking sheets, using a wide metal spatula, spacing them ¾ inches apart. Set scraps aside. Repeat with remaining dough until baking sheets are full.
7. Bake the cookies for 8 – 11 minutes, until they are set in the centers and the dough barely retains an imprint when touched very gently with a fingertip. The baking sheets should be rotated from front to back and switching positions top to bottom, halfway through the baking time. Do not overbake. Cool cookies on the sheets for 2 minutes, then remove the cookies with a wide metal spatula to a wire rack to cool completely.
8. Gather the scraps; repeat rolling, cutting and baking.

For the Royal Icing:
3 ¾ cups confectioners' sugar
3 large egg whites
½ teaspoon cream of tartar
Pinch kosher salt

Using an electric mixer, combine the ingredients. Whip until stiff and glossy.

Acknowledgements

❄ ❄ ❄

A big thank you to Red Adept Editing for editing and proofreading.

And finally a big thank you to all the readers! I had a great time writing this book, and I hope it put you in the Christmas spirit!

About the Author

If you like steamy romance novels with a creative streak, then I'm your girl!

Architect by day, writer by night, I love matcha green tea, chocolate, and books! So many books...

Sign up for my mailing list to get special bonus content, free books, giveaways, and more!

http://alinajacobs.com/mailinglist.html

Printed in Great Britain
by Amazon